Playlist

Bruises by Lewis Capaldi
Sweater Weather by The Neighborhood
Kiss It Better by Rhianna
Slow Motion by Trey Song
Pretty poison by Nessa Barrett
You Put a Spell on Me by Austin Giorgio
Such a Whore by JVLA
The Only Exception by Paramore
Season Of The Witch by Lana Del Rey
Looking at Me by Sabrina Carpenter
MONTERO by Lil Nas X
All I See Is Him by Jude York

Trigger Warning

Please proceed with caution! This book is filled with triggers and your mental health is always a priority! The following content includes but is not limited to:
Breath play, knife play, blood play, unaliving, ritualistic cannibalism double penetration, double vaginal penetration, ass play, pegging, violence, gore, ritualistic practices, witchcraft, attempted SA not from main character, graphic torture and more.

Demise

Book 3 in the Gallows Hill Series

KATELYN TAYLOR

Copyright © 2025 by Katelyn Taylor

All rights reserved.

No part of this book may be reproduced in any form or by any electronic or mechanical means, including information storage and retrieval systems, without written permission from the author, except for the use of brief quotations in a book review.

Dedication

To all the spooky witches, your time is here. And there is a ton of cock in this book, so win, win.

Prologue

To become a member of the Brethren, you must have a desire to protect our heritage, to honor our history. You must have a thirst for vengeance, ready to battle anyone who threatens this society or our carefully built world.

To become an Elder is another task entirely. The induction is meant to test you, push you. It is different for each to prove your loyalty, to show how far you're willing to go for your fellow brothers. Only the elite are gifted with the opportunity to become an Elder. Waste that gift, and you will find yourself on the wrong end of this holy ground.

Keep your brothers by your side, and your eyes open wide. Evil lurks around every corner, attempting to creep in at every turn. You must stay strong, stay true and remain ever faithful to us. If not, may the witches of the past, present, and future unleash their wrath on you. An unfaithful man that would make you an unworthy one to save.

Join us, or perish, these are your two choices. Tread carefully now, your chances are limited to one.

Chapter One

Skyla

My head is reeling, and I'm rendered absolutely speechless.

"Wh-here are you taking me?" I stutter.

"Somewhere safe," he assures me before turning back to face the road.

"Why? Why are you doing this?" I ask.

The car slows for a moment as he turns his head to look at me once more. That familiar face, a face I never would have guessed, never would have suspected.

"Professor Corwin, what's going on?"

"I told you I'd come for you, my love. It took a little longer than I would have liked, and I'm sorry for that. Those boys were circling you like sharks," he says with a sneer and a shake of his head as he glances back to the road.

"I don't understand. You're my stalker? How? Why?"

"Stalker?" he asks with furrowed brows before he lets out a deep chuckle. "Is that what they told you? You can't listen to them, Giselle. They will say anything to turn you against me."

"Skyla," I say shakily.

1

"Hm?"

"My name. You called me Giselle, but I'm Skyla. Giselle was my mother."

"Oh yes, that's what I meant. The resemblance is uncanny, though. You're like Giselle reincarnated," he says, his eyes running over me as slow as molasses, leaving behind a thick, sticky feeling in their wake.

I hear his blinker before he veers the car to the right, turning into a parking lot of a warehouse. I frown at our surroundings, looking around as much as I can before coming to the realization that we are in the middle of absolutely nowhere.

Shutting off the car, he pockets the keys before grabbing a duffle bag from the front seat. He gets out of the car and opens the back passenger door, scooping his hands beneath my arms and lifting me up and out of the car.

My balance wavers as I stand on my feet before he lifts me up and into his arms. I can't hold back the terrified whimper that escapes me when he rests his nose against my neck, inhaling deeply.

An angry noise reverberates through his chest as he growls.

"You smell like them. It's disgusting. Make no mistake, there will be consequences for letting them touch what is mine," he says as he starts walking us towards the warehouse.

I tremble in his arms as the cold night pricks at my skin, sending chills running up and down my body. Then again, that could be the paralyzing fear.

When the door to the warehouse opens, I'm surprised, no, stunned. On the outside, it looks like a storage facility, maybe some kind of factory. On the inside, though? It's a house. Like a fully blown decorated and furnished home. The layout is open, where you can see nearly every room and hallway from one spot. The furniture is a soft cream color with deep brown hardwood floors throughout. The kitchen is large, with a four-stooled island and a commercial-grade oven.

"It's amazing, right?" Professor Corwin boasts proudly. "It cost me a quarter million dollars to get it ready. I'm sorry for the delay," he says, pressing a wet, slimy kiss to my forehead that makes my skin crawl.

My mind races with what to do, how to act, how to get the hell out of here. The best thing I can think of is to play along, engage enough to where he lowers his guard, and I'm able to break free. Or try to wait it out long enough for the guys to track me down and rescue me.

If they are even alive. For all I know, he murdered them all while I was out cold.

Fuck, I can't think like that.

"Thank you," I say quickly. "My love-e."

I cringe at the stiffness in my tone, knowing I have to do better than that.

"It's too much trouble. I wish you didn't have to go through it all for me," I say as I stare up at him.

I hadn't noticed him all that much before. Sure, I saw him in class every day, but from a distance. Not so close that I can count every single smile line. Not so close that I can see the practically colorless brown that fills his eyes, accompanied by his extremely receding salt and pepper hair.

He smiles down at me sweetly, or at least I think it's supposed to be sweet. Instead, it makes my stomach roil.

"It was no trouble at all, nothing but the best for you."

I do my best to muster an adoring smile as I nod.

"I appreciate it more than you know. How...how did we get here, so quickly, that is?" I ask, fishing for any and every bit of information I can gather.

"It wasn't all that quick. I may have overestimated the dosage for the packet of apple cider," he says with a frown.

"Apple cider?" I ask, my mind trying to follow the last memory I had.

The drink Wesley gave me in the kitchen, right before everything went black.

"You drugged the cider packet?" I ask.

"Well, my options were quite limited, and I know what a weakness you have for the stuff," he smiles, like it's an endearing thing. "Don't be mad, my love. I did it for us, for your safety."

"I-I know," I say, giving him a shaky smile. "Thank you for coming for me. Did you...take care of the guys?"

In a split second, his demeanor shifts. His posture becomes rigid, his hold on me practically punishing.

"No, not yet. My first priority was getting you out of there and home where you belong. I'll take care of them soon, though. Don't worry."

Fear pangs inside me as I give him a watery smile.

"T-thank you."

He nods and presses another slobbery kiss to my face before walking us deeper through the 'house.'

"You're probably still tired, aren't you?"

"Very. Would you mind if I rested for a little?" I ask.

"Not at all, my love," he says as he walks into a bedroom, kicking the door shut behind him.

He sets me on the edge of the bed before placing down the duffle bag that was also in his arms. My legs and hands are still bound, and he bends down and begins untying them. Relief fills me, a perfect opportunity practically being laid at my feet once I feel the rope loosen. Though as quick as that hope came, it fades when his hands reach for the waistline of my leggings as he begins dragging the material down my legs.

I pinch my thighs together, attempting to scoot away from him.

Demise

"What are you doing?"

His eyes flick up to me in irritation; the former adoring look long forgotten.

"You reek of them. You need a bath."

I pull away from his grasp, doing my best to keep my tone even.

"If you just undo my hands, I can get undressed. I'm kind of shy," I say with a weak smile.

A short laugh escapes him as he shakes his head.

"My love, I've watched you get spit-roasted over a dozen times. You're a slut."

His hand cracks on my bare thigh as he rips the material down my legs before tossing them behind him. I feel his hand raise, pinching my face, squeezing my cheeks together punishingly, forcing my lips to pout as he speaks.

"But you're my slut," he says before crushing his lips to mine.

Nausea rises inside me as I do everything I can to fight against him. My legs thrash, and my tied hands pound against him, but nothing works. He's stronger than he looks, a lot stronger. Bile begins to pool at the back of my throat, but instead of trying to push it down, I let it go.

Vomit spews out of my mouth and all over him as I heave. He shouts, shoving me to the ground, wiping the puke from his face before grabbing the rope and quickly tying my legs up as I begin to crawl away. My nails dig into the long carpet, and for a moment, I think I have a good hold. Until one sharp yank from him has my bare legs dragging across the carpet and beneath him.

"Stop fucking moving!" he snarls. "Ugh, disgusting!"

When he finishes the knot, I do the only thing I can think of, I kick. Granted, with my legs tied together, it isn't all that effective, but I do land a kick to his knee that seems to take his breath away. Until rage turns his eyes black, and he draws his leg back, delivering a kick to my gut. Then another, and another. By the fourth kick, I'm vomiting all over again. I don't know if it's from the drugs, the fear, or the pain. It doesn't matter either way.

On the last kick, I hear a sharp crack that steals all the air from my lungs and forces me to lay on my back. I howl and scream in pain, and it seems to shake Professor Corwin from his anger fueled haze. He stares down at me for a moment, what looks like remorse across his face, as he turns his back and stomps off towards the shower, shutting the bathroom door behind himself.

There I lie, half-naked, covered in vomit, hurting, and absolutely terrified of what's to come.

Chapter Two

Wesley

I'm sitting at the kitchen island, filtering through security footage from the school, desperate for a clue, any clue. I'm amazing at what I do, always have been. There has never been a mission or task that I've been given that I haven't completed with exemplary performance, hence why this entire situation is so goddamn infuriating.

Whoever it is, they are smart. They never make a mistake. They always have their footsteps covered and are apparently fantastic at leading us on a wild goose chase. At first glance, Andrew Hutchinson was a perfect suspect. He had the motive and the means, but him allowing me to triangulate his location while facetiming me busted that theory. Clark Lewis was a close second, he was her mother's age, had resources to pull off most, if not all, of the stalker's moves, and he had several motives. That, again, was a bust.

Fuck, at this point, I'm looking into Skyla's best friend, Maggie, again. Ronan had already looked into her, and I did the same. The most I could dig up through her phone records was that she used to fuck her stepsister. Interesting, but not what I was looking for. Who knows, though, maybe she's more clever than she's letting on. The motive is definitely there. Fuck, I don't know. At this point, I'm just pissed off.

Things could be worse, I suppose. How mad can a man be when he finally got the girl?

Okay, maybe that's a stretch. I don't know if I exactly got the girl so much as got to eat her delectable cunt while one of her boyfriends watched and jacked off to it.

Fuck, that was hot.

I've wanted Skyla from the first moment I laid eyes on her. With every day that passed, my desire for her only grew until I could hardly see straight unless I was with her. That seven-mile drive to and from the university was the highlight of my day, every day. Sometimes, I'd take alternate routes, complaining of traffic when really, all I wanted was a few extra minutes with her. A few more minutes where it was just her and I before her horde of men came rolling in, all quickly and efficiently showing me the way out.

I can't blame them, if she was mine, truly mine, I wouldn't want to share her with anyone that I didn't have to. To be honest, I don't think I've crossed that line in her mind that she 'has to have me' but I will. Soon. Even if I have to win over every single one of the guys to do it, or beat the fucking shit out of them until they agree. I foresee that being the only plausible route when going through Griggs.

For now, though, I'm calling her mine. She got really drowsy earlier, no doubt the exhaustion from all the stress finally catching up to her. I carried her to her room and laid her down before I came back down here to work. Kinda tempted to crawl into bed beside her. Maybe she's already awake. I'd be more than interested for round two with her; even Liam could join again.

Conveniently, Liam gets up from his bed in the living

room, limping his way over to the kitchen to grab a drink and snagging my attention. Has he been awake this whole time? His stupid comedy movie from the nineties ended over two hours ago. I thought he was passed out. I don't miss the way he's watching me, and I don't attempt to hide the way I'm watching him.

Skyla is absolutely the goal, but a time or two with one of her guys wouldn't be the worst way to spend an afternoon. It may sound stereotypical, but in the military on missions where we couldn't leave our position for days at a time, needs arose, and we all found ways of...release. Then, when we would return back home or to base...well, let's just say I'm not a fan of labels. Love is love, and pleasure is pleasure; nothing more to it.

Ronan told me he caught Liam and Asher together with Skyla. He seemed completely shocked but not judgmental. I, on the other hand, wasn't surprised at all. I'd noticed a shift in their dynamic over the last few weeks. I guess that's the beauty of being the man on the outside. I had a perfect view of everything.

Liam fills up a glass with water, turning around to face me as he drinks it. His light green eyes stay on mine as his Adam's apple begins working the liquid, pushing it down until the glass is empty. His tongue runs along his lips before lifting the hem of his shirt up, dabbing at his chin where I know there is no water. It does give the opportunity to show off his toned abs.

This kid doesn't know what kind of fire he's playing with. It seems like it's a game to him, like he's trying to goad me. He's gonna be shocked when he realizes that I don't bluff.

"What are you doing?" I ask him.

"Nothing." He smirks, dropping his shirt and sauntering as best as he can towards me.

Broken leg and the guy is still trying to swagger.

His forearms rest against the counter, and he leans onto them, placing his face only a few inches from my own.

"I was parched. You didn't offer me the drink I wanted earlier, so I had to make do."

I raise an eyebrow to him and stare. That teasing smile doesn't leave his face until I lift my hand to the back of his neck, moving up before my fingers grab a hold of his hair and yank.

His smile drops, and a short gasp escapes him as I lean over him. I purposely let my lips trail over his as I speak.

"If you want to suck my cock, all you have to do is ask nicely."

Liam's pupils are blown as he stares at me, his tongue darting out to trace over his lip as I yank on his hair once more. Another gasp escapes him, this one sounding a hell of a lot more like a moan.

"You want to be my good boy and drink my cum?" I ask.

He goes to speak when a voice shouts in the otherwise quiet house.

"What the fuck is going on here?" Asher snaps.

Liam jolts but I don't release my hold on him, keeping him in place as I stare at Asher.

"Your boyfriend was just telling me how badly he wants to suck my cock."

An offended scoff escapes Asher as he shakes his head.

"Boyfriend? You're out of your goddamn mind."

I don't miss the hurt that flashes across Liam's face when Asher says that and honestly, it pisses me off. So, I help the kid out.

"Oh? Was I mistaken? Perfect, more for me," I say before I drag Liam's mouth to mine.

To my surprise, he doesn't react immediately. But one nip of my teeth against his lip, he opens up for me. His hands come to my face, and I drag him closer, my tongue tangling

Demise

with his just as he's ripped away from me and hauled into Asher's side.

I smirk, wiping my mouth with the side of my hand as Asher's hand flexes around Liam's hip, keeping him plastered to him. A dazed-looking Liam stares at me until Asher wraps his hand around his throat, pulling his lips to him. He kisses Liam savagely, hungrily, and I can tell that it's mainly to show me up. I'll be honest though, the only real winner in this scenario is Liam, and when Asher rips away from him, the idiot is grinning like he just won the goddamn lottery.

My work here is done.

"What the fuck did we just walk in on?" Griggs grouches, his eyes moving from me to Liam and Asher, Ronan behind him with a stoic look.

"Just call me Cupid, happy to lend my services to either of you gentlemen," I say as I raise my brows suggestively.

Griggs scowls, and Ronan rolls his eyes before scanning the room.

"Where's Skyla?"

"Asleep," I answer. "She was tired, so I carried her to her room for a nap."

"You carried her?" Griggs asks sharply.

My gaze darts to Liam, who's now the one with the shit-eating grin.

"Yeah, did we forget to mention Skyla added a new boyfriend?"

"What?" Asher and Griggs ask simultaneously.

"About time; I was getting sick of your lovesick bullshit," Ronan says as he turns to head up the stairs, always the first to seek Skyla out.

I chuckle at him and shake my head.

"You touched her?" Griggs asks, stepping up to me.

Letting out a low sigh, I stand up, eye to eye with him, as I tip my head to the side. He may be a crazy bastard who is highly skilled, but so am I. He doesn't scare me.

"I did. She wanted it, I wanted it. It happened. That gonna be a problem, Griggs?" I challenge.

His jaw is clenched tight, and his pulse is thundering in his neck.

"If she brings in one more goddamn guy, I'm gutting him like a pig, onsite," Griggs grumbles.

"Good luck telling her that." Liam laughs.

"Skyla? Skyla?" Ronan suddenly calls out from the top floor. "What the FUCK!"

His tone sets us all on edge. We take off upstairs, Liam being easily left in the dust as we race to the top. Griggs is the first, followed by me, and then Asher. We push into Skyla's room to find the bed empty and a frazzled looking Ronan standing on the balcony.

"Where is she?" he asks with crazed eyes.

My head swivels around the room like she's probably just hiding somewhere before looking back at him.

"I-I don't know. I just put her down here."

"How long ago?" Griggs asks.

"I don't know, three hours ago? Maybe four?"

"Maybe four?" Asher snarls, wrapping his fists in my shirt. "Where the FUCK is my wife?"

"I've been here!" I defend. "So has Liam! No one got in. No alarms went off, no sounds, nothing."

"Then where the fuck is she, Wes?" Ronan snaps.

I run a hand through my hair, pulling my phone from my pocket as I pull up the surveillance footage. I run through the last four hours of video from the front of the house at triple speed, not seeing a thing. It takes several minutes to work through this much footage before I switch to the back of the house. I run through the film for another five minutes when Griggs leans over, pausing the footage.

"There!" he says.

I squint, trying to see what he's talking about. A quick black flash can be seen from the corner before the footage blips, and it's gone.

No.

Pulling up my next app, I begin running security checks, hoping to fucking God that I'm wrong.

"Come on, come on, come on," I mutter to myself before my heart sinks.

"Well?" Asher asks as my eyes raise from the screen.

"Someone hacked into the main line, made a duplicate footage to camouflage themselves," I say.

"Meaning?" Ronan hedges, understanding and fear already written all over his face.

My eyes come to Vincent's just as I hear an out of breath Liam crest the stairs.

"He's got her," I whisper.

Chapter Three

Vincent

Wesley's words ring through my head for several seconds before my mind is actually able to process them.

He's *got* her. He *has* Skyla. He *took* her. And it's all this dumb motherfucker's fault. I can't even blink before my body moves of its own accord. My hands are wrapped around Wesley's throat, and I'm squeezing like I never have before. I snapped plenty of throats in my life, crushed plenty of tracheas. I have no doubt this one will be the most satisfying of all.

Wesley's eyes bulge out of his head, but he doesn't fight me. Just frantically grabs at my hands to release him. Yeah, fucking right.

I feel several pairs of hands on me, attempting to pry me from him. There is no point, though. I won't let go of him, not for anything. Not until he pays for what he's done.

"Vincent, c'mon. You're gonna kill him!" Ronan barks.

"Good," I grit through clenched teeth, my body shaking as I hold Wesley down with everything I have.

"No, not good. We need to focus our energy on finding Skyla, not tearing each other apart."

I don't care if he has a point. I'm fucking tired of these pieces of shits being so goddamn reckless with my siren's life. It's happened too many times, and some fucking consequences are more than due.

"What will she think when she finds out you killed him? She cares about him. It'll hurt her," Ronan says. "Please!" he begs as his arms strain, yanking on me violently while Wesley's face turns a pale blue.

"Come on, Vincent. We have to find her, we need you. She needs you," Ronan says.

My head turns to look at him, fury vibrating through me as my body shakes. He nods his head quickly.

"Skyla needs you."

Turning back to Wesley, I lower my face to his as I snarl.

"She will never forgive you, and I'll never forget this."

Tossing him to the ground, he lands on the floor in a heap, coughing and gasping for breath as Ronan kneels beside him. He's checking on him like a good little bitch while I actually do something important. Swiping Wesley's phone, I begin flicking through the apps that are open, fast-forwarding the footage of the back of the house. The man carrying an unconscious Skyla disappears into the woods, and I pull up a separate screen to look at a map of the area.

There is a parking lot for a liquor store on the other side of those woods. Pulling up Wesley's app once more, I'm able to tap into the city's street cameras, accessing the one that points directly to that parking lot. Sure enough, the guy is parked close enough for me to make out who has her as he loads her into the back seat of his piece of shit car.

"Motherfucker," I growl under my breath.

"Who?" Asher asks as he and Liam lean over my shoulder.

"What the fuck? Professor Corwin?" Liam balks. "He's the stalker? How?"

"He saw a pretty girl and got obsessed," I gnash at his stupidity before moving my eyes back to the camera, not missing a second as he climbs behind the wheel and takes a right out of the parking lot.

It takes me a moment to figure out how to work this system, but once I get the hang of it, I begin following them through the street cameras. I glance at Asher before continuing my search.

"Look up his assets. Properties, family. Wherever he could be taking her."

Asher already has his phone out and is frantically tapping his fingers against the screen. Apparently, Ronan was doing the same thing because he steps beside me, showing me a screen.

Two properties belong to Nicholas Corwin. One apartment just off campus, and then a warehouse out in Vermont that was purchased a little over three months ago.

When the cameras show him heading for the freeway going northbound, I know we have our answer. Motherfucker is taking her to Vermont.

Tossing Wesley's phone at Ronan's chest, I stomp through the house, running down the stairs towards my keys and helmet.

"Keep tracking them just in case. They have to be heading for that warehouse."

"Where are you going?" Ronan shouts.

"I'm going to get my girl!" I snarl as I rip the door open and sprint for my bike.

I fire it up before running into the garage, grabbing two five-gallon jugs of gas that I've had on hand for instances like this. I also grab a blanket and a first aid kit, just in case, before tossing it all into the back of Wesley's car.

In the time it takes me to do all that, the fuck wads have

finally managed to make it outside. Asher is locking the place up behind them as Wesley jumps into the driver's seat, and Ronan is carrying Liam's broken ass to the car.

Meanwhile, I plug in the coordinates of the address into my GPS, throwing my leg over my bike as I slam on my helmet. I'm not waiting for them in their fucking car. I'll get there faster on my bike, or at least I'll try. Every second counts, and I won't count on anyone but myself to get my girl. Once I have her in my arms again, all bets are off. Everyone is going to burn from the ground fucking up, starting with Nicholas fucking Corwin.

I'm coming, Siren. I'm coming. Be strong for me. I'm coming.

Chapter Four

Skyla

I don't know how long I lay on the bedroom floor. My ribs are screaming in pain, my stomach coiled tight with nothing left to empty, and my legs ache where the thick rope is now cutting into my bare skin.

Eventually, the bathroom door opens, and Professor Corwin steps out with a towel wrapped around his waist. His chest hair is a mixture of black and grey, spreading everywhere on his torso. The beer belly straining against the towel has me cringing as I look away in an attempt to mask my disgust.

His footsteps move across the room before pausing before me. I feel my body begin to shake in fear as his arms slip beneath me, lifting me into the air as he turns around and walks into the bathroom.

Setting me down into the tub, he plugs the drain before turning on the water. I flinch at the feeling before my eyes hesitantly meet his. He's watching me with a pinched look as he scoops some of the filling water in his hands, pouring it over my hair.

"You're a mess, my love."

I don't say anything, I just watch him quietly. He lets out a ragged sigh as he shakes his head.

"It wasn't supposed to be like this. It should have been easy from the start, you know?"

"What should have?" I ask carefully.

He grabs a loofa, covering it with soap before beginning to wash my shirt and legs. I'm a little confused why he's doing it, but I'll take this over him stripping me naked.

"Everything. You know, I met your mom in the same class that I met you."

"My mom?" I echo.

His murky brown eyes come to me as he nods, mindlessly wiping the vomit off me as he continues.

"She was so beautiful, like sunlight walking into a room," he smiles. "I sat by her on the first day. The way she looked at me, I knew it was always going to be us, forever."

I swallow roughly, waiting for him to continue. When he doesn't, though, I push for more.

"And then you saw me, and you thought I looked like her?"

He looks at me and shakes his head. "You don't just look like her. You're a spitting image, her doppelganger. I couldn't believe it when I laid my eyes on you. I watched you for weeks, waiting for an opening to show you all we could be."

The wistfulness in his eyes slowly fades, a darkness taking over.

"Do you know what it was like to sit back and watch you with them? Watch them touch you, watch them hold you. Do you have any clue how many times I wanted to slit Walcott's throat in the middle of class just for breathing in your direction?!" he snarls.

I stay quiet, fear gripping me tightly as I try to gently steer the conversation away from the boys.

"So, you and my mom dated?"

He hesitates for a moment before that soft, dreamy look re-enters his eyes. Oh, my God, he's a fucking lunatic.

"We did, for several months, and we were really happy. Until that piece of shit Parris came along," he spits. "She hated him, couldn't stand the guy. He had just graduated, and his father chose *my* Giselle as his bride."

His movements become jerkier and more harsh as he soaks the loofa into the rising water and begins scrubbing at my bound legs.

"Then fucking Putnam came into the picture, just like they always do. He thought he was owed Giselle, that she...she was some kind of property! And being the pig that Henry was, he shared her like a common whore!" he snaps, his eyes practically popping out of their sockets.

He closes his eyes, blowing out a heavy breath before looking at me.

"And then she died; she was taken from the world, from me. I have no doubt in my mind that Putnam and Parris were behind it. They are behind everything bad in this goddamn world."

My body freezes, his words slowing in my mind as I try to process them.

"Wait, you think my father killed my mother?" I ask.

There is no way, right? No. This man is clearly unhinged. He's completely delusional, bouncing in and out of reality at the drop of a hat. He's confused and enraged over something that happened over twenty years ago.

"Of course, everyone knows it. The way her death was swept under the rug. You were sent away. Putnam went MIA for months. It's obvious!" he snarls, his hands shaking as he drops the loofa.

He falls to the ground, holding his head in his shaky hands as he begins to sob.

"Giselle! My sweet, sweet Giselle."

I don't move a muscle, tracking his movements carefully, when all of a sudden, his tears have dried, sobs have ceased, and he looks at me with a blank face that chills me to the bone.

"It's okay, though. Things are okay now. We can start our lives now, together."

Knowing this is probably the wrong move, I say something stupid, hoping maybe it will shake him out of whatever delusion he's living in.

"We can't, though. I'm Skyla, not Giselle. You don't love me; you love my mom, Professor Corwin."

"You're GISELLE!" he shouts, peeling my soaked shirt up and over my head. He's clearly not the sharpest tool in the shed since my shirt can't come off with my hands being tied. In his anger, he grabs the thin material, ripping it in two and exposing my breasts. Only my panties remain, but apparently I don't get to keep those either.

Corwin rips those off as well, cupping more and more water over me. He abandons the loofa, covering his hands in shampoo as he begins scrubbing my hair. He yanks and pulls my hair, and I wince before he shoves me underwater. I hold my breath as one hand pins me to the tub, and the other aggressively rinses my hair before yanking me from the water.

I gasp for air, heaving and coughing as he grabs a bottle of conditioner.

"I bought the products you love. I want you to smell the same way you always have," he says as he lathers my hair with a coconut scented shampoo. One that's definitely not one of mine. I guess we are back to thinking I'm my mother.

He gives me the same treatment as before, shoving my head underwater as he washes away the conditioner, scrubbing my head aggressively as he yanks me out once more.

"Much better," he says as I choke and gasp for air.

He pushes to his feet before bending down, scooping me out of the water, and carrying me into the bedroom. Water pours from my naked body, and I cringe as I feel his hands on my bare skin before he lays me on the bed.

"Now that you're clean, let's get you into some fresh clothes. I still have some of your old ones," he says as he begins rifling through that duffel bag he brought.

A white blouse and skirt in hand, he turns and sets the clothes beside me as his eyes roam over my body. I attempt to cover myself, but it doesn't work. Moving to the dresser, he rifles through one of the drawers before pulling out a knife. My eyes watch him carefully as he steps beside me, slicing the rope free between my hands and legs.

Instinctively, I stretch my limbs, the skin worn and raw from the rope. Corwin's eyes trace over my breasts, falling down to my legs before forcing them apart. He stares at me with pure lust, and fear clenches inside me. When his hand comes up, presumably to touch me, I fight.

Kicking him in the side of the head, I attempt to scramble off the bed, ignoring my screaming ribs as I scoot to the edge. I don't make it far before he recovers, smacking me across the face. Again and again, slap after slap sends my head spinning before he crawls on top of me, his towel falling away as his limp shriveled cock flops onto my thigh. It's fucking revolting, but I don't have time to focus on it before his hands wrap around my throat.

He's choking me hard, shaking me as he speaks through clenched teeth.

"Stop fucking fighting me, Giselle! Just fucking stop!"

I gag and choke as I attempt to breathe, and he squeezes harder. My fingers dig into his hand, attempting to claw myself free when he winds back his hand for a slap so hard it forces me

Demise

to see stars. Blinking hard, I shake my head as Corwin releases my throat, cupping my face tenderly.

"My love, are you okay?" he asks. "I'm so sorry. You just... you can't run. It's not safe, okay?"

I look at him in revulsion, but don't say anything as he nods to himself, like my silence is compliance. What a mistake that will be for him.

"Come on, lay down," he says as he lays on top of me, pinning me into place. My ribs scream as I attempt to shift beneath him, but he only bears more weight down on top of me.

"What about my clothes?" I wheeze.

"We don't need clothes between us. Rest, my love," he says as he nuzzles into me, the sound of his heavy sleeping breaths coming faster than I'd anticipated.

I try to move slowly, but I can't budge an inch. The pain inside me is so overwhelming, I'm ready to vomit all over again. My body begins to shake in fear, and Corwin seems to subconsciously press more weight down on me in response.

I don't know how many hours I lay there. Too many to know for sure. Each attempt at moving him off me is met with defeat, and I can't help but sob. I feel my eyes grow heavy despite my best efforts to stay alert. I know the drugs are still in my system, though. I know that it's partially out of my control, and before I can stop myself, my body shuts down, and I fall asleep.

Movement shakes me from my sleep. It's slight, but the motion jars my ribs, forcing a whimper out of me.

"Oh yeah," Corwin moans. "Wiggle on me, Giselle."

My eyes fly open to find Corwin grinding his semi-hard cock against my bare thigh.

"Stop it!" I snap, shoving my hands at his shoulder.

God, he's an overweight piece of shit.

An evil smile transforms his face as he looks at me.

"Oh, you want to play? Let's play."

His hand lifts up, cupping my breast before he pinches my nipple hard. I scream out in pain, and he pinches even harder. I swear I'm about to bleed. My screams echo through the house, and Corwin groans in pleasure.

"Good girl. Scream for me like a little slut. I know you like it rough. I've watched you get fucked by them nice and hard. You want it hard? I'll give it to you," he says as he uses his other hand to slip between my thighs.

My legs thrash, and I power through the pain radiating across my body as I use everything at my disposal. I buck and smack and kick and bite, but he thinks it's a game. He's getting off on it.

"Oh God, you're a wild one," he says as he attempts to subdue me.

I get a punch in, straight to the nose that sends his pleasured smile fading, anger replacing it as he punches me back. I see stars, and I feel blood begin to drip down my face as his fists drive into the side of my head and my stomach. It's nothing but hot flashes of pain over and over again.

I'm in a daze, trying to get my bearings, when I feel his fingers shove inside me. His nails are long and jagged, cutting into me as he painfully shoves his fingers in and out of me.

"STOP! NO!" I scream, picking up my efforts.

I feel tears pouring down my face as I fight against him. He shushes my screaming, flattening his tongue as he licks at the trail of tears down my face.

Demise

"Your tears taste so fucking good," he moans. "Not as good as the rest of you, though," he says, pulling his fingers from me, sucking on them as he moans.

I take the opportunity to knee him in the dick. He gasps in pain, rolling onto his back, and I tuck and roll, falling to my face as I land on the ground with a hard thud. The wind is knocked out of me as another sharp crack echoes inside my body. There goes another rib.

Army crawling the best I can without putting too much pressure on my stomach, I make my way around the front of the bed. The door is so close I can almost taste it, but a hand buries into my hair, yanking me backward.

"No, no, no!" I scream as my nails dig into the carpet, like that will be my saving grace. His arm wraps beneath my battered torso, forcing me onto my knees before I feel the head of his tiny cock line up against me.

His other hand is still in my hair before moving to my neck, forcing my face into the ground as he pushes his knees onto the back of my legs, effectively pinning me in place.

"Hold that cunt still," he grits through clenched teeth.

Another tear rolls down my face, this one solidifying my fate. I close my eyes as I begin to visualize a place, any place. Somewhere that I can go disassociate until this nightmare is over. Or I'm dead. I'd prefer either at this point.

A thunderous boom rattles the walls of the room as I force my eyes to look towards the doorway.

Vincent.

His gaze takes in the room before him, fully assessing the situation before his eyes go pitch black. What a sight it is, I'm sure. Me, naked and pinned to the carpet, my professor turned stalker also naked, ready to destroy me the way only the most depraved human could.

"Vincent," I whisper raggedly.

He doesn't hear me, though, or he doesn't react. Instead, he practically jumps across the room, tackling Corwin off me as he pins him to the ground and begins pummeling him into the ground.

In the next moment, Ronan and Wesley are rushing into the room, followed by Asher and then Liam hobbling as fast as he can with his boot.

"Baby!" Ronan yells as he drops to my side, eyes scanning over me as Wesley does the same on my other side. A wave of relief rushes over me when I look at them. If I wasn't in such a state of shock, I could fucking cry.

Wesley's dark blue eyes are filled with so much panic, so much pain it's like I can feel it inside my chest.

"I'm so sorry, little one. I—"

"Not now," Ronan snaps as he wraps me into his arms.

I want to tell him how much pain I'm in, but at the same time, I never want him to let me go. I didn't realize until now that I'm shaking, uncontrollably so. My eyes peer behind us to see Vincent still on top of Corwin, his face practically raw hamburger meat at this point. That doesn't stop Asher from joining in. His steel-toed boots deliver kick after kick to his stomach, forcing screams and groans to escape him. Blood and teeth spray and scatter across the beige carpet, but neither of them look close to stopping.

Liam's eyes frantically scan the room before landing on me. They zone in on my face. With all the blows to my cheeks and nose, I'm sure I look like I've been through hell.

"Did he touch you?" Ronan asks, pulling me away from him so he can look at me.

My stomach curls at the reminder of his hands on me. Vincent and Asher pause in their assault for a moment, all eyes on me when I give a shaky nod. Fury ignites in all their eyes, but it's Liam that makes the first move.

Demise

He reaches for the lamp on the side table, yanking it straight out of the wall before holding it above his head.

"Burn in hell," he grumbles before bringing it down with such force Corwin's head makes a sickening splat sound.

I cringe at that, looking away from the gore as Ronan tucks me into his chest again.

"It's okay, we've got you, baby. I've got you," he says as he goes to stand, attempting to pick me up with him.

I wheeze as my body tenses in pain, and he freezes, setting me back down.

"What's wrong?" Ronan asks.

"Where are you hurt?" Wesley asks before Vincent steps in, shoving Wesley back several feet.

"Get the fuck away from her! Where are you hurt, Siren?"

I look into his eyes, the blood lust and rage slowly receding, leaving only concern in their wake.

"M-my ribs," I stutter. "I th-think they're broken."

His jaw tenses, and he blows out a harsh breath through his nose before nodding once. Vincent pushes Ronan away, forcing him to release his hold on me, which, surprisingly, he does.

Slowly, Vincent wraps his arms around the back of my legs and my upper back, being careful not to jostle me too much as he lifts me up and moves me out of the room. My eyes land on the bed, my mother's clothes still there, and I panic.

"Wait! The clothes, the clothes! I need them!" I rush.

Asher moves over to the bed, scooping them up as I point to the duffle bag.

"Th-he bag, too!"

He grabs the bag as well, closing the distance between us before resting his forehead against mine. He doesn't say anything, but he doesn't need to. Everything that could be said is felt in this moment. Liam steps beside me, his fingers gently touching my hand. I startle at the contact, my head whipping around frantically; why, I'm not sure.

"Hey, hey. It's okay. It's just me. You're safe," Liam croons softly.

I inhale a shaky breath before I blow one out. My eyes go from Liam to Asher to Vincent and Ronan, then finally Wesley. All wearing broken-hearted expressions that vary between them all.

"Take me home, please?" I ask the room.

"We've got you, Siren. We've got you."

Chapter Five

Ronan

Vincent carries her carefully through the fucked up home/warehouse. Wesley jogs in front, opening the front door for him as he blows past without a single look. Liam is limping beside me, Asher on his left as his eyes move through the place, disgust written all over his face.

Wesley hits the key to his car, unlocking it before holding the back seat door open for Vincent. Asher pushes ahead, rounding the car and opening the other side before he slides in.

"Rest her head on my lap, keep her straight," Asher says.

Vincent nods as he climbs inside the SUV with Skyla in his arms, gently resting her head onto his lap before laying her the rest of the way down. He slips out of the car at the same time Liam climbs inside, carefully lifting her legs to rest on his lap as he takes his seat.

I look down at my beautiful, broken girl, anger, pain, and sadness thrumming in my veins. Part of me wishes Liam hadn't killed the son of a bitch. I think I speak for everyone here when I say I wish we could have made him suffer. For days, weeks, months. Hell, maybe even years. He would have deserved it, and more.

Out of all of us, I'm shocked that Liam was the one to deliver the kill, and so brutally. It looks like there is hope for him; he just needs the right motivation. One look at Skyla's face, her naked, exposed body, and the pain and fear in her eyes was all it took for him. At least Vincent and Asher got some good hits on him before he died. I hope it was excruciating.

Wesley grabs a blanket from the back of the car, covering Skyla with it. For shock or modesty, but probably both. She wraps herself in it gratefully, her body still shaking like a leaf.

I can't fucking believe that Nicholas Corwin was Skyla's stalker...all this time. It still doesn't make sense to me, to any of us. I would have suspected my own brother or even Henry Parris before the quiet history professor. Looking back, though, I suppose there were a few indicators, no matter how hidden they may have been.

He's the right age, and if what Lewis said was accurate, then he was no doubt one of the many men in love with Skyla's mom. He had access to Skyla easily on campus and in class, and as a faculty member, he was privy to things like her schedule, maybe even a key to her room. I'll definitely be having a chat with the headmaster when we get back. There is no way he was operating under everyone's radar, and if I find someone who knew, they'll get the torture that should have been saved for Corwin.

He clearly drugged her. We just haven't figured out how yet. I wonder if he told Skyla, not like now is the time or place to talk about it.

We're currently in central Vermont. It was a three hour drive just to get here, and with Corwin having over a four hour jump on us, I was terrified we'd be too late. We all were. Once

Demise

we figured out who it was, it didn't answer the question of what he was going to do with her. I'd hoped his plan wasn't just to kill her; he seemed too infatuated. Then again, according to his later letters, he was infuriated with her as well.

Skyla's eyes meet mine, and a barely there smile touches her mouth as she looks at me. I do my best to return it, but I know it doesn't show.

She said he touched her. Confirmed it. I want nothing more than to know every single detail she can recount to us, but at the same time, I never want to hear or think about it, ever.

Vincent steps away from his bike, moving to the trunk of Wesley's SUV before he pops it. He grabs the two five-gallon jugs of gas that he threw in there before we left the house. No one questioned him in the moment, and I sure as shit don't now.

He walks towards the building, moving inside as he begins dousing the floor with gas. I share a look with Wesley, or at least I try to. His eyes are solely focused on Skyla, like a kicked puppy watching her with a forlorn look. He blames himself, and honestly, so do I. So does Vincent. Fuck, he almost killed him back at the house, and based on the lack of help Asher and Liam were providing, I'd wager they wouldn't have been heartbroken if Vincent had succeeded. Wesley was tasked with watching her and keeping her safe, but he failed. Liam is semi-excusable. He can hardly walk at a reasonable pace. Wesley was the one physically and mentally able, and he fucking failed.

In the next moment, Vincent appears through the doorway, emptying the second jug of gas at the front step before tossing both cans inside. Then, with one flick of a match, he drops it. A trail of fire rips through the front of the building, growing larger and larger as Vincent jogs away.

Wesley runs to the driver's seat, and I slam the back door shut before jumping into the passenger seat. The car peels out as Wesley drives us onto the road, Vincent right behind on his bike. Three seconds later, an explosive boom comes from behind us, and I look in the car mirror to see a plume of smoke rising into the sky.

The cops will be here soon, as well as the fire department. This is a lot messier than the Brethren usually handle matters. In theory, Vincent probably could have cleaned up the place and made Corwin's body disappear, no problem. Clearly, he didn't have the patience for all that, and Skyla's injuries are priority.

"We need a doctor at my house; we will be there in less than three hours. Possible broken ribs...bring anything necessary to treat a victim of assault," Asher says quietly before hanging up the phone.

The car goes deathly silent, all eyes coming to Skyla. She looks up at Asher as if she wants to speak, but she doesn't. She stays silent, staring up at him in a way that unnerves me.

After a few seconds, she blinks before turning her head to the side, staring at the back of the seat blankly. I share a concerned look with Wesley and see Liam and Asher doing the same in the rearview mirror.

Pulling out my own phone, I tap out a message that I wish I didn't have to, but know I have no choice.

Me: There is an incident in Vermont. Nicholas Corwin has been stalking and threatening your daughter in law. He kidnapped her from their home and took her to a warehouse where he assaulted her. Your son blew the fucking place up.

. . .

I tell him that Asher is the one to blow the place up for obvious reasons. If Christopher finds out Vincent is the one that did it, he'll ask questions. Like why Asher has been spending so much time with a guy he's hated since birth. Why Griggs is committing careless acts of violence in the name of his son's wife. The best thing to do is to play it off like it was a hot headed moment of rage on Asher's part.

My brother's response comes surprisingly quick.

Christopher: Corwin? What reasoning did he have? This girl is proving to be more trouble than she's worth.

I bite my tongue at that last part as I type out my reply.

Me: He was in love with Giselle, clearly. Trying to re-create what he thought he could have had with her? I'm not sure.

Christopher: That worm wasn't even fit enough to breathe the same air as Giselle, let alone love her.

I'm surprised by the defensive nature of his text and go to respond when another comes in.

. . .

Christopher: Get back to Salem. I'll handle things in Vermont.

Me: On our way.

Chapter Six

Skyla

When we get back to Salem, the sun is just starting to rise. I never thought I'd be so grateful to see this small, secret filled, fucked up little town.

The car ride was silent the entire way. I'm not sure if that's what the guys thought I needed, or maybe it's what they needed. I don't really care either way. Every breath I take is like knives being sunk into me, and I have a pounding migraine. The thick barred gate of our house is a welcome sight as Wesley slowly drives through them, parking as close as possible to the front door.

Just as he puts it in park, Liam's door is opened, and Vincent's leather-clad arms are reaching for me. I go to him easily, a sense of comfort rolling over me as he cradles me gently, carrying me towards the door. The others follow behind us while Asher jogs ahead to unlock the door.

"Where is that fucking doctor?" Asher fumes under his breath.

My head turns to him as I shake it softly.

"I don't need a doctor right this second. I'm fine," I say, my words being cut short with a wince as Vincent begins moving up the staircase.

Asher smacks the back of Vincent's head.

"Be careful, asshole! You just hurt her."

Vincent's crazed eyes come to Asher, giving him a look drenched in murder. Asher ignores it, though, turning his gaze back to me.

"You need a doctor, princess. I'll go make a quick call," he says, pressing a featherlight kiss to my cheek before heading out the door.

I can hear Asher's shouts despite Vincent walking us all the way to the top of the stairs. He keeps going until we're at Asher's room before Ronan steps up from behind us, pushing the door open.

Vincent carefully lays me down on the bed before his fingers trace my face. I cringe when they brush where Professor Corwin hit me, and Vincent flinches, forcing himself to take a step back like he's afraid to hurt me.

"What do you need, Siren?" Vincent asks.

I shake my head in response, and he clenches his jaw as Liam steps into the room, moving past Vincent and Ronan as he rounds the bed. Slowly, he lowers himself down to lay beside me, a soft smile touching his face as his fingers begin playing with my hair.

"Hi, babygirl."

"Hi." I smile weakly.

I feel a body sit beside me, and I look over to see Vincent there, hesitantly laying down on my other side. I reach for his hand, interlacing our fingers together before he squeezes them once and brings them to his mouth. His lips press a soft kiss against them before resting back at our sides.

"Doctor will be here in less than five," Asher says as he

Demise

steps into the room, coming to take a seat at my feet beside Liam.

Ronan takes the last available seat at my feet as I look around at my guys.

"Thank you. Thank you for...coming for me," I say slowly, doing my best to find the right words.

"As if there would ever be a reality that I wouldn't come for you," Vincent says, pressing a gentle kiss to my lips.

When he pulls away, Liam's mouth is on mine.

"Same, babygirl."

I smile at him as Asher leans over, stealing a kiss of his own.

"I'll always come for you, princess."

Ronan nods, pressing his lips to mine for several seconds longer than the other guys before resting his forehead against my own.

"I love you so much, baby. I'll never let you go."

Emotion tightens my throat, and I glance to see Wesley hanging back awkwardly in the hall. I give him a small smile that he doesn't return, forcing me to frown. Those deep ocean blue eyes are practically burning two holes into me, his face emotionless and stoic.

Asher pushes to his feet, snarling.

"Stay the fuck away from her!" he snaps before slamming the door in Wesley's face.

I flinch at the sound of the slam, sadness blooming inside me that he isn't with us right now. That Asher is so angry with him; they all seem to be.

"Why did you do that?" I ask.

Asher spins to face me, outrage splashed across his face before he composes himself.

"This was all his fault! Corwin never should have been able to touch you, let alone take you."

I frown at that. "Didn't he come to save me too?"

"Yeah, after he fucked everything up," Vincent grumbles.

My eyes come to him for a moment before I shake my head.

"Tonight was no one's fault besides Professor Corwin's. Let him in. *Now*," I say, putting extra emphasis when Asher doesn't move.

His jaw is clenched, as sharp as granite, before he reaches for the doorknob, ripping it open as he shouts down the hall.

"Preston! Get in here!"

It takes a few seconds before Wesley carefully peeks his head inside, his eyes scanning the room before landing on me.

"Do you need something?"

I swallow for a moment, remembering the last memory I have with him. All the feelings I'd been trying to bury, the attraction, the...

"Thank you," I say softly. "For saving me."

Wesley opens his mouth but pauses, like he's rethinking his words, before he closes his mouth and nods. The doorbell rings through the house, and Wesley slips out of the room, making his way down the stairs to answer it.

He comes back upstairs with the doctor, who does a quick exam before determining that my ribs are cracked, not broken.

Yay.

She cleared me of a concussion and wrote me a prescription for pain meds while my ribs heal. She asked me as quietly as she could if there was any reason she should perform a rape kit. The silence was so immediate you would have heard a pin drop in the room. I gave her a quick head shake, relief easing through all of the guys' shoulders and faces.

Once she left, the guys began fussing over me, asking if I needed more blankets or food or a shower. In reality, all I wanted was sleep, and thankfully, none of them left. They all stayed, surrounding me, even Wesley from the corner as I closed my eyes and sank into a deep sleep.

Chapter Seven

Skyla

Rough fingers pinch my skin, that wet, slimy tongue running across my body.

No. No. NO!

"NOOOO!" I wake up screaming, a pair of hands shaking me gently.

"Skyla, wake up! Little one, come on. Wake up!" Wesley says hurriedly.

My eyes blink open to see the room dark and Wesley's panic-stricken face before me. It takes me a moment for my heart to stop racing and my breathing to normalize before I shake my head.

"Bad dream," I mutter.

Wesley opens his mouth to speak when the door is thrown open, Vincent, Asher, and Ronan spilling into the room, followed by Liam's cursing from down the hall.

"Stupid goddamn stairs! Can't wait to fucking get this walking boot off."

"What's wrong?" Ronan asks.

"What did he do?" Asher accuses.

"I'll fucking kill you," Vincent snaps at Wesley.

Wesley throws his hands up, taking a step away from me.

"She was having a nightmare. I heard her screaming and found her thrashing in bed."

Narrowed eyes watch him as Liam comes through the door, frustrated and out of breath.

"What happened?" he asks.

"Bad dream. I'm sorry I scared you guys."

"It's fine, baby. Do you need anything?"

I shake my head, and he nods.

"We will leave you be," he says as he pushes the others out.

Wesley begins to head out with them when I call out to him.

"Wait. Wesley, can we talk?"

Venomous looks are shot at him from all directions, but he doesn't even acknowledge them, nodding his head as he takes a step toward me.

Ronan watches us for several seconds before speaking.

"Alright, we will be just outside the door."

"Right outside the door," Asher tacks on, narrowing his eyes at Wesley.

I nod at them before turning my focus to Wesley as the door shuts. For a moment, we sit in silence, just staring at each other until he speaks.

"I'm so sorry, little one. I...I can't believe I fucked up this bad. I just...can't believe it," he says with a shake of his head.

I reach my hand out to cover his as I attempt to meet his eyes.

"Hey, I mean it. It wasn't anyone's fault but Corwin's. You did everything you could to protect me."

Wesley shakes his head. "That's not true, and we both know it. I just...I don't get how I missed it. I didn't hear a thing upstairs. He didn't wake you at all, and I can't figure out how."

Demise

I look down at our joined hands as I speak.

"I know how."

Pausing for a moment, my eyes slowly lift to his.

"He did something to the apple cider packets. He knew I was bound to have one soon, and then when I was out—"

"He grabbed you," he finishes with a head shake and a hollow laugh. "Still going to try to convince me that this isn't my fault? I'm the one who made you the goddamn cider!"

Wesley begins pacing the room, his fingers digging into that blond hair as he shakes his head.

"You have to know I'd never let anyone hurt you. Not if I could help it. I...I don't know. My guard was down. I was so fucking over the moon that you had given me a chance, me! I mean...men like me don't get women like you."

"What does that mean?"

His eyes swing to me. "It means I'm not a good man, not by a long shot. I've killed people, I break the law more times than I follow it, and I have a past that is not all sunshine and rainbows."

I nod. "How does that make you different from any of my other boyfriends?"

He doesn't say anything as I continue.

"You are not a bad man, Wesley, not by a long shot. I don't care what has happened in your past or what you've done. You're good, more than, and you aren't the lucky one in this relationship, I am."

He licks his lips, staying silent for several seconds before he looks at me.

"We're in a relationship?"

"Oh, well. Uh, I guess I shouldn't have assumed. Just because we messed around doesn't mean you want to actually be with me, I guess. And the whole me already having four boyfriends probably makes this—"

Wesley's finger comes to my lips, silencing me immediately as he speaks softly.

"I already told you. I want you, little one. I just didn't know if you wanted me too after...everything."

At this point, it feels futile to argue any further. He's going to take the blame that isn't his to take, and I suppose that is something he will have to deal with on his own.

"I want you, Wesley. You...fit, you know? Right here," I say, resting a hand over my chest.

Corny as that might be, it's true. He feels like a missing piece to a puzzle. Like a piece I didn't realize was missing until it was shown to me in the right light, and now I'm wondering what I've done without it all this time.

His hand moves to cover my own, curling his fingers around mine as he looks at me seriously.

"I'll be right here, as long as you want me, little one."

I smile softly as I lean into him, lifting my head as he places his lips on mine. Just like before, it's like fireworks and coming home all at the same time. His other hand lifts to cradle my face so gently, as if I were a porcelain doll about to shatter apart in his hands.

When we pull away, he gives me one of his breathtaking smiles and looks ready to say something when a loud voice shakes the house.

"No! Get the FUCK away from me! Where is Skyla? What happened!?" a familiar voice screams.

I frown at that, and Wesley tenses.

"Steph?" I question as I throw the blankets off me and attempt to stand up.

"You need to rest," Wesley says as he attempts to keep me in bed.

I shake my head and attempt to stand when Wesley scoops me into his arms and walks towards the door. When he opens it, Liam is there, watching us with a small smile. He doesn't say anything before he gestures for Wesley to walk first.

As he moves down the stairs, the foyer comes into sight and a furious looking Steph is standing by the door, talking to Ronan, Vincent, and Asher. Her eyes snap to me before the rest of the guys follow suit.

I watch as her gaze hones in on where Wesley is holding me before her mouth drops open.

"Sky, another one?!"

I look up at Wesley, who is wearing an impassive mask, before looking back to her.

"What are you doing here?"

"What am I doing?" Steph guffaws. "I get a concerning voicemail from my niece about my dead sister, and then she doesn't answer my calls for over fourteen hours. What do you think I'm doing here?"

Fuck. The voicemail. I forgot about that. Was that really only fourteen hours ago? How is that possible when so much has happened since I made that call?

"Where is my phone?" I ask the guys, who all just shake their heads and shrug their shoulders.

"Probably in the woods somewhere. No way he would have brought it to Vermont," Vincent says.

"Vermont? What's in Vermont? Who is he?" Steph intervenes.

I swallow roughly, exchanging a look with all the guys. We have to talk about everything, and as much as I would have liked to hold off on this conversation, it looks like I don't have a say in the matter.

"We need to talk," I say to the room.

We all moved to the living room and are scattered between the couch, Liam's bed, and the floor of the living room. I'm sitting up as much as I can handle on Liam's bed with Asher and Liam on either side of me.

"Why are you wincing? What's wrong?" Steph asks.

"I have a few cracked ribs," I say.

Her brows pinch before an outraged look flies to the guys. I sigh and roll my eyes at her.

"Seriously? Of course, it wasn't one of them."

"Well, what am I supposed to think?" she asks, tossing her hands out by her side.

Taking a moment to gather my thoughts, I decide to just dive right in.

"I've had a stalker."

"A stalker?" Steph echoes. "Since when?"

"Since...the first day of school."

Her mouth drops open, and I quickly continue.

"I didn't say anything because I didn't want to worry you! At first, I thought it was just Asher being an ass," I say as I glance to see him shrug. "Then I thought maybe Vincent. He was always lurking around every corner."

Vincent nods in agreement but stays silent as my eyes come back to my aunt.

"Then things became clear that it was someone else, someone obsessed with mom."

Steph frowns at that. "Why do you say that?"

"Because he was leaving her letters addressed to Giselle," Ronan supplies.

"What did they say?" she asks.

"They started out nice, loving. And then they turned... violent, enraged. He knew about the guys, and he was talking about how he'd take care of them. How disgusted he was to see me with them," I explain.

"I'm guessing it reminded him of when he saw Giselle with my father and Henry," Asher says.

Steph goes as still as a statue at that. She swallows roughly before turning to face me fully.

"What do you know about that?"

"I think the question we should be asking is what do *you* know about that?"

She hesitates for a moment before she speaks.

"Finish the story, then I'll share what I know."

Uneasy looks are cast around the room before I blow out a breath.

"I was kidnapped."

"WHAT!" she shrieks.

"Last night," I continue. "He drugged me and drove me to a warehouse in Vermont that he had renovated to look like a house. He wanted us to live there, to start over."

"Who?" Steph asks.

"Nicholas Corwin," Wesley says from the corner of the room.

Steph's nose wrinkles at that.

"That little dweeb? Are you sure it was really him? He was always afraid of his own shadow. I can't picture him being an aggressive stalker."

"Trust me, it was him. He told me how him and mom used to date before she got engaged to my—"

"Yeah, fucking right," Steph mocks. "He wishes. He used to follow your mom around like a sad puppy. He'd always leave her love notes, roses. It drove her crazy."

45

We all share curious looks with one another as Steph continues.

"Did he hurt you?"

"He was trying to touch me, and I fought back. Obviously, he didn't like that. He kicked me in the stomach and ribs and slapped me. If the guys would have gotten there five minutes later, I wouldn't be able to say that's all he did," I say as my eyes come to Vincent, remembering the wave of relief and safety that washed over me when he stormed into the room.

"Where is the son of a bitch now?" Steph asks, facing the guys.

"Burnt to a crisp in that creepy as fuck warehouse," Liam says, a cold tone to his voice.

Her jaw tightens as she nods her head. "Good."

I nod, something else that I haven't brought up chewing away at me.

"He said something else. He said that my dad was the one who killed my mom. Or Asher's dad. He said that's what everyone says happened...but mom's death was an accident, right?" I ask.

Steph goes pale and her body freezes as she looks at me. I blink at her before bowing my head slightly.

"Right?" My eyes move to the guys, noticing how all of them refuse to meet my eyes. "Did you all know?"

"Babygirl, it's just a rumor. There was never any proof. Just shit that dumb people made up." Liam shrugs.

"Steph?" I ask. She doesn't say anything, just continues staring at me.

I smack my hand down on the bed.

"Answer me!" I shout.

She startles before shaking her head.

"I think so. Like he said, there was never any proof, but I know without a doubt if anyone killed my sister, it was Henry."

Demise

Hurt stabs inside me as I shake my head.

"How? How could you not tell me? How could you let me come here, not knowing a thing?"

"I didn't have a choice, Sky! If he is a psycho murderer or not, if he wants his daughter with him, then you have to be by his side. Don't you understand by now? What the elders want, they get! This is literally life or death. I've only put your well-being first. I just...I've tried so hard to keep you as safe as I could. My...my baby," she cries, tears beginning to flow down her cheeks.

I feel a few tears of my own escape as I attempt to sniff them away and reach a hand out for her. She stands up, closing the distance between us as she leans over Liam to hold me. Her arms wrap me up like a hug as she cries into my neck.

"I'm so sorry, Sky. So sorry. I should have told you. I should have warned you. This place...it's why I never came back. It's hell on earth, and women...they don't last long. I can't believe you were gone...and I didn't even know. We almost lost you," she says as she pulls away, her eyes wet as she looks at me.

"Will you stay? For a little? I...I need you," I say brokenly.

I see the hesitancy on her face, but it only lasts a minute or two before she nods.

"Of course I will."

Chapter Eight

Asher

Stephanie and Skyla head up to her room after a little. Ronan brought them snacks for the movie day they are having in bed, while Vincent took a phone call before stepping out of the house. I'm sure Liam is downstairs eating, and Wesley is probably doing something on his laptop, per usual.

I decided to jump in the shower since the last twenty-four hours rendered me a little indisposed. Between learning the history of my father, Henry and Giselle, my wife being kidnapped, and learning that Wesley made a move on her... and Liam. Not fucking happy about that part.

Lathering my hair, I lean back into the warm water, rinsing out the shampoo when a knock comes from the bathroom door.

"Hey, man. I'm ordering lunch for everyone. What sounds good?" Liam asks.

I turn to look at him through the glass wall, and I watch as his carefree smile disappears, a look of hunger taking its place. His eyes rake over me from top to bottom, and for some reason, I don't feel the instinct to turn away, not in the slightest.

What the fuck is happening to me?

My pulse begins hammering in my neck, and I do my best to clear my throat as I keep my eyes on his.

"Whatever the princess wants, I'm good with."

Liam doesn't respond, though, because he's currently in a staring match with my cock. The way it involuntarily jerks at his attention says more than I'd ever admit out loud.

Slowly, his eyes lift to mine, those soft green eyes drowning in lust. His tongue peeks out, wetting his bottom lip before he grabs the back of his shirt with one hand, pulling it up and over his head. It hits the ground, revealing Liam's rippled abs. He always prides himself on staying in shape; he hits the gym several days a week in between classes, and it clearly shows.

Wait, fuck. Am I checking him out?

His sweats are the next to go, pushing them down with one hand until they stop on his walking boot. He wasn't wearing any boxers, and my eyes can't help but drop at the newly exposed skin. Goddamn, I'll never get over how many piercings he has. It's insane.

And kinda hot.

Fuck. What the hell is going on with me?

Liam prowls towards me, never taking his eyes off my own as he crosses the bathroom and rounds the glass wall to the shower. In an instant, he's in the shower with me, the spray just barely splattering against his skin as he closes the difference between us.

I don't move from my position, and I don't think he minds. He does all the work, submerging himself in the water as his hand goes to the back of my head, and he pulls me in for a kiss.

Freezing at the contact, I don't move a muscle as Liam's lips move against mine. They are so soft, so demanding, and I fucking hate the way my cock throbs the moment his skin touches mine.

He pulls away, resting his forehead against mine as he shakes his head.

"C'mon, Ash. Don't ice me out. Don't do this to me, to us," he begs.

"Us?" I question with half a scoff.

Liam's eyes come to mine, fucking pleading with me as his head pulls back even further to look at me.

"Yeah, us. I know you're scared. I am, too, if I'm being honest, but you feel something for me, and we both know it."

Excuses die on my tongue, none of them seeming strong enough. I open my mouth to deny his words, but I come up empty. My silence, however, is enough to push him away.

He lets out a humorless huff as he releases his hold on me and takes a step away.

"Fine. Fuck it, I'm done trying with you. I want you, but not bad enough to be some toy that you bring out of the closet every time you're in the mood to test the boundaries of your sexuality. I'm not a plaything you can turn off and on, Asher, and I'm tired of the hot and cold."

Liam stands stock still, waiting for me to say something. What is there to say, though? I don't know what's going on with me. I don't like men, never have. Liam is just...Liam, and that's not a good enough answer. So, I stay silent.

He shakes his head in disappointment, turning to step out of the shower when he looks over his shoulder at me.

"I'll see what Wesley is up to; I'm sure he'd love a midafternoon blowjob."

Anger flashes across my eyes, and before I know what I'm doing, I'm closing the distance between us. My hand wraps around his throat as I pin him to the tile wall. He doesn't fight me as he stares at me, his jaw hardened in hurt, his eyes begging me to do something, to say something.

The motherfucker just can't help but poke buttons, any

time, any place. Liam loves to goad the fuck out of people. And, fuck me, clearly, it's working.

"Say that again," I grit between clenched teeth.

"Why?" Liam rasps slightly, as my hold on him tightens. "Don't like the idea of me sucking someone else's cock? My mouth wrapped around them, and my tongue—"

He doesn't get a chance to finish that sentence. Not when my lips are crushed against his. Our tongues tangle around one another instantly, Liam's hands coming to rest on my hips as I hold him in place.

The kiss is savage, punishing, brutal, and fuck me, I love every goddamn second of it.

Forcing us apart, my hand on his throat pushes him away before forcing him down.

"You want to suck someone's cock? Get on your knees and choke on mine. It will be the only goddamn cock you'll feel down your throat."

Liam's eyes are on me, and he drops to his knees all too willingly. I release my hold on his throat, resting my hand behind his head as he sucks my raging hard cock into his mouth. Ecstasy washes over me as his tongue swirls around the tip. My mouth drops open on a silent moan as he pushes me deeper and deeper. My fingers curl around his wavy hair as I wind it around my fist, forcing him to take me deeper and faster with each bob of his head.

He moans around me, his eyes fluttering open as he looks up at me. I can literally feel a bead of pre-cum drip onto his tongue from that look alone. Goddamnit. He has no right to be this fucking pretty. I don't know how I never really saw it before, but Liam is so fucking pretty. And, no, that's not me just saying it because he easily has the most talented mouth I've experienced. Ever.

Sorry, princess.

I feel the building of my orgasm, and I'm torn between drawing it out to make it last as long as possible or coming right here and now. Unfortunately for me, my body seems to have made its own decision.

The pleasure increases more and more as I begin snapping my hips violently. Liam gags once, and a groan leaves me at that.

"Open that throat. Let me in," I grit through clenched teeth.

After a moment or two, he does as I say, and I force myself deeper than before. That's all it takes. I see double, literally losing my vision for a moment as I come. My cock throbs as it shoots cum down Liam's throat and he drinks it happily. His throat works overtime, his audible gulps echoing in the shower so fucking hot before he releases me with a wet 'pop'.

Slowly, he pushes to his feet, his right hand languidly stroking his cock as he looks at me. My eyes move down to his hand, watching in fascination as he twists his hand around his piercings, his forearm flexing with each stroke.

Hesitantly, I reach my hand out, taking his place as I wrap my hand around his cock the way I would my own. A groan falls from his lips as I come up to the head before pushing my hand back down again. His hand quickly falls away as he leans his back against the tiled wall and lets me take control.

I don't know what is coming over me. Jealousy. Lust. Curiosity. Whatever the driving factor is, it doesn't matter. When we are here, in moments like this, none of it matters. It's just about me and him.

My eyes don't leave his cock, that soft shade of pink practically mesmerizing beside all the silver. I don't realize that I'm staring until Liam says something.

"Stop looking at me like that. It's torture," Liam groans with a pitying laugh.

Demise

Our eyes meet, and his smile slips away, a seriousness taking over his face as I lower to my knees. I've never sucked cock before, obviously. I know what feels good, but I'd be lying if I said I wasn't intimidated as fuck right now.

My hand is still wrapped around him, stroking slowly as I look up to my best friend from my knees.

"I don't know what to do," I admit roughly.

Liam smiles, not a condescending or smug smile. A sweet one, one that looks like fucking sunlight and has my chest tightening the way it does when Skyla looks at me.

"I'll teach you, baby."

Before I can respond, he's pushing his cock up to my lips and I press a quick kiss to the tip, feeling cringey as fuck for it. What the hell, this is such a mistake.

Liam moans, though, catching me by surprise as his hand goes to rest on the back of my head.

"Again, please, Ash," he says breathily.

Something in me responds to his lust drunk tone. The way he says my nickname. Fuck, it's got me hard as a rock already. I do it again, another soft peck followed by another and another. I finally build the courage and stick out my tongue, swirling it around Liam's head before closing my mouth around him.

His mouth makes an O shape as he looks down at me while I look up. I breathe through my nose as I slowly begin pushing Liam deeper and deeper down my throat.

The feeling of his piercings is unlike anything I've ever experienced, each of them bumping against my tongue as I push my head down and back up again. Then again, I've never sucked cock until now, so I guess today is full of firsts.

"Fuck, yes," Liam praises. "Just like that, nice and slow."

I do as he says, letting his hand behind my head control the pace. I occasionally twirl my tongue around his cock, licking the sides of it as I bob my head. It's not as bad as I thought it would be, in fact, it's kind of fun.

Increasing my speed a little, I begin pushing Liam deeper, a thrill running through me when he moans from it. Like a junkie chasing their next fix, I'm chasing Liam's next sound. Each one is sweeter than the last, and I'm fucking desperate for them all.

My hand comes up to his balls, cupping them the way I love as I push him down my throat.

"Yeah, Ash. Touch my balls. Fuck!" Liam groans.

I play with his balls for a moment before I pull away, my hand lifting up to Liam's mouth before I rest my finger on his lips.

"Open," I say.

Curiosity sparks in those pretty pale eyes, but he does as I say, sucking on my finger the way I am on his cock. I begin mirroring the movements, our tongues moving in sync before I pull my finger out of his mouth.

He stares down at me with intrigue as I slip my hand between his legs, pushing into him slowly. His pupils blow at that, and he spreads his legs apart for easier access.

"Oh fuck," he says, anticipation forcing him to nearly tremble before me as my finger slips all the way into his ass.

He clenches around me for a moment as his cock throbs, and I curl my finger up, easily finding his prostate. I've never fingered a guy before, but it's not rocket science, and I know what I like, so I decide to just do that.

"Shit," he exhales roughly.

My head bobs in a steady rhythm before I release him for a moment, continuing to pump my finger in and out of him.

"You like that?" I ask.

"I never want you to stop." Liam sighs as he shakes his head and rests the back of it against the shower.

Demise

"I'm never gonna stop. This asshole is mine, you hear me? I'll lick it, finger it, or fuck it anytime I goddamn please."

His eyes spring open at that, head whipping down to me.

"Where do I sign up?" He laughs, pulling a chuckle out of me as well.

"Just be my good boy. Can you do that for me?" I ask.

His cock jerks, and he nods his head quickly as I smirk, sucking him back into my mouth as I increase the pace of my finger.

I focus on his prostate, working it as hard as I work Skyla's g-spot as I pull back enough to speak.

"You're mine, alright? Mine and Skyla's. I won't share you with anyone, so you can fucking forget it."

Liam moans incoherently as I work him over faster, pushing his cock to the back of my throat as I swirl my tongue around his head one more time. One more press against him is all he needs to let go.

His cum hits my tongue, warm and slightly salty. I'm not sure what to think of it at first, but I swallow it down all the same. More cum hits my tongue, and I don't mind it as much. I kind of like it, actually. Or at least I like the face that Liam makes when I swallow it.

When his orgasm has passed, I slowly pull my finger out before releasing his cock and standing up. We stare at each other for a moment before I move backwards, stepping back into the spray of the now tepid water as I turn around and finish showering.

Liam doesn't move for several seconds before he comes up behind me, wrapping his arms around my waist as he rests his cheek against my back. His lips move slowly as he speaks, his hold on me loose like he's giving me the choice to push him away.

"Did you mean that?"

"Mean what?" I rasp.

"That I'm yours. That you'll never stop. That you...want me too."

I roll my lips together as I stare up at the ceiling. I don't know what to say. Yes? Maybe? I don't know. It's complicated. I mean, we're already sharing my wife. Now I'm supposed to go to my wife and ask if it's okay that I fuck her boyfriend? Then again, I already know what her answer will be. This whole mess started at her insistence in the first place.

I feel Liam's hands begin to unwind from me, and I panic, spinning around to face him as I stop him. I force his arms to stay around me, and a look of confusion passes across his face. Leaning forward, I press my lips to his, lifting my hands to cradle his face. It's not a kiss of passion and wild abandon. It's not a carnal craving where I'm savagely dominating him. It's tender, soft, and I hope to God it conveys everything my words can't.

When we pull apart, I keep my hold on his face as I look into his eyes and speak.

"Yes."

Chapter Nine

Skyla

Stephanie and I spent the entire day in bed. Talking, laughing, crying. We vegged out and watched way too many episodes of any and every trash TV show we could get our hands on. The next morning, we woke up, Ronan made us breakfast, and Steph told us she would be staying somewhere the next town over for a little while.

I was relieved that she was staying in the States, partially because I missed her, but also because it feels like there was more to Mom's death than she's letting on. Or at least more suspicions that she has that she isn't saying. I tried broaching the topic several ways yesterday, and each attempt was met with a not-so-subtle deflection.

I'm helping clean up the kitchen when I notice Asher and Liam whispering in the hallway. My brows knit together as I lean past Ronan to watch them. Liam is talking to Asher about something, and Asher is shaking his head when I catch his eye. They both tense and I give a small smile and a wave because, honestly, I don't know what else to do.

Asher blows out a breath before walking into the kitchen, Liam following closely behind him. They both have serious looks on their faces, and I turn to face Ronan.

"Could you give us a second?" I ask.

He looks at them before turning back to me with a sweet smile.

"No problem," he says as he bends down, pressing a kiss against my cheek before he nods at the guys and grabs his keys.

Once the thunk of the front door sounds throughout the house, the silence is deafening. I wait for someone to talk but when neither does, I speak.

"Is everything okay?"

"Yeah, no. I don't know," Asher says as he runs his fingers through his hair.

I frown at that and Liam shakes his head.

"What he meant to say was, we've realized that we have feelings for each other."

I do my best to hold back the smile that spreads across my face. Smashing my lips together I nod my head.

"Okay."

"And we were wondering, I guess, hoping, that you'd be okay with that," Liam says as his hand laces with Asher's.

I'm surprised at how easily his fingers twine around Liam, and I'm even more surprised when I see them trade a soft smile. It literally makes me all gooey inside, and I don't even attempt to hold back my smile this time.

"Of course it is. I want you both happy."

"And we want you happy, princess," Asher says. "We love you so much. We don't want to mess anything up."

I shake my head as I stand between them, looking at both of them as I speak.

"You can't mess anything up. I love you both, so much. As

long as being together doesn't mean that you'll toss me to the side, I'm so happy for you guys."

Asher scoffs as Liam says, "Yeah, like that could ever be a thing."

I smile as my eyes come to Asher, curious on how my sweet and uneasy boy is doing. To my delight, he looks happy, at peace, and it warms me from my head to my toes.

"One request, though," I say.

"Anything," Asher says.

"Can we still all have group time? I don't want to miss out on...all of this," I say as I gesture between the two of them.

Matching grins spread across their faces.

"Babygirl, you're the filling to our sandwich. You aren't allowed to miss out."

Asher and I wrinkle our noses up as we look at Liam.

"Filling in your what?" I laugh.

"What?" Liam asks as he looks between us. "Our sandwich, you know, like a Skyla sandwich and we're the bread."

Asher lets out a disappointed sigh and Liam rolls his eyes before he presses a quick kiss to his cheek. The stoic look doesn't leave Asher's face, but it does soften.

Awwww.

Ronan came over a few hours ago with a brand new phone for me. Since we have no idea what Corwin did with mine, he bought me a new one, which I'm incredibly grateful for. We are officially on winter break, and I decide to rummage through the kitchen to take inventory. Steph and I used to always do holiday baking, and I'm in the mood for a little joy, as much as I can get my hands on really.

I've managed to scrounge up all the basics for sugar cookies and look up a recipe online when my phone buzzes.

Maggie: Hey babe! I miss you, I feel like we haven't talked in a while. Everything okay over there?

I grimace at the message. Yes? Kind of? No, not really. How did things escalate so fast with no warning, then like a passing storm at sea, the waters have calmed again like nothing ever happened? Honestly, it's not all that comforting. Instead, I find myself on edge more than ever.

Me: I know, I'm sorry. Want to come over tomorrow? Catch up?

Her response comes in almost immediately.

Maggie: Sure! I have to go to dinner with my parents tonight...wish me luck.

Ugh, she's told me enough about them to know that luck is the bare minimum of what she needs. Like most families in the Brethren, they are cold, distant, and expect their child to submit, being stripped of all individuality and personality. Clearly that's just the way things are done around here. Doesn't make it right, though.

Setting my phone down, I get back to mixing the dough together when a pair of arms wrap around me. It takes me a moment to recognize them, a new scent hitting my nose that I'm not overly used to.

"Hi, Wes," I smile.

He drops his head into the crook of my neck, placing a soft kiss against my skin as he speaks.

"Hi, little one. Whatcha doing?"

"Making some sugar cookies. Want to help?" I offer as I turn to look at him.

He gives me a dubious look but still begins rolling up the sleeves of his black dress shirt. My eyes can't help but be transfixed as I watch his corded forearms flex at the motion. Why are forearms so hot? Please, someone, explain it to me, because I don't understand it myself. They just are, though.

Wesley begins washing his hands as I finish mixing the ingredients and grab the rolling pin. I start rolling it out when he comes up behind me again, putting his hands on the very end of the pin as we roll it out together. Well, I'm trying to roll it; he's making jerky movements and pushing us from side to side before I laugh and look up at him.

Those blue eyes are practically sparkling as he winks at me before pinching off a piece of the dough and popping it into his mouth. My mouth drops in outrage.

"You can't eat the dough!"

"Why not?" he counters before popping another piece into his mouth.

I swat his hand away when he goes in for a third piece, but that doesn't deter him from grabbing it with his other hand and grinning at me. Looking around for the closest thing I can, I pinch some flour between my fingers before tossing it at his chest.

Now, it's his turn to look outraged. His mouth drops open, and he looks down at his shirt before back up to me. It was right then and there that I realized how royally I had fucked up. Calmly, Wesley reaches behind me, grabbing a fistful of flour before sprinkling it over my head.

I screech and swat him away, but he holds both of my hands with one hand while coating my head with the other. Then, it's on. We both reach for handfuls of flour, tossing it at each other before I grab two fistfuls and run to hide behind the kitchen island for cover. The air is thick with white powder, clouding the kitchen as we participate in all out baking warfare.

When we run out of flour, Wesley scoops up the remaining powder on the island, scooping it together into his hands before ninja rolling across the floor. Sometimes, I forget that he was in the military, a Navy Seal, no less.

His eyes land on mine and he ends his roll in a crouched position. Fear clenches my stomach before he pounces. I squeal again as he throws one more handful of flour to my face before landing on top of me. We both laugh as he begins wiping my eyes clean. When I can see again, I look up to notice that while I may not have won this battle, I got him good all the same.

Wesley's blond hair looks like it's been given some frosted tips, his pristine black shirt now a dusty grey, and that smile... okay, nothing is wrong with his smile; it's fucking perfect. He hesitates only for a second before leaning down and pressing his lips to mine. I kiss him back happily, chalky flour and all.

My tongue peeks out, swiping against Wesley's as he lifts his hand to cup my face. I sigh happily into his mouth as his other hand rests on my hip. His hand lingers briefly before it's trailing up under my shirt and into my bra. He rolls my nipple between his thumb and forefinger, and I can't help but moan when he does.

I feel his hips move between my legs, forcing them apart as he rolls them forward once. Our tongues are tangled as his teeth sink into my bottom lip, pulling it playfully as he rolls his hips again.

"Wes," I moan when footsteps sound down the hallway.

"What the fuck is going on? I heard Skyla screaming and—"

Ronan's words are cut short when he rounds the corner. I'm sure it's quite a sight. The usually pristine kitchen is coated with enriched flour while I'm dry humping his bond brother on the floor. Then again, with how soaked my panties currently are, there is nothing dry about this humping.

Wesley pulls away from me, a teasing smirk that seems to mirror something that Liam would wear on his face as he looks up at Ronan.

"Hey, Ro. You're just in time for the show."

"The show?" Ronan echoes, an unimpressed eyebrow raised as he speaks, though there is no denying his voice has taken on a deeper husk.

"Mhmm, unless, of course, you want to participate," he challenges with a waggle of his eyebrows.

Ronan doesn't say yes, but then again, he doesn't turn him down either. Instead, he watches us carefully for several seconds before his feet slowly move towards us. Excitement flashes in Wesley's eyes as he looks down at me, pressing a quick kiss to my mouth before standing up. I start to ask him what he's doing, but he lifts me up and over his shoulder before I can say anything.

Wordlessly, Wesley begins carrying me through the dining room, taking extra care with my ribs before heading to the staircase. He takes the steps two at a time, Ronan right on his heels before they push into my bedroom.

Wesley drops me onto the bed with a cautious bounce before he's kicking his shoes off and crawling on top of me. Ronan slips into the room, shutting the door before locking it.

I raise an eyebrow at him.

"What? No one else is allowed to join?" I tease.

"No," Ronan grits out huskily. "Right now, you're ours."

I feel my pussy pulse at the way he says ours, and my eyes swing back to see Wesley nodding in agreement before pressing his lips to mine once more. His hands move to my jeans, undoing the button with one hand while the other begins peeling the material down my legs before he discards them to the corner of the room. My panties quickly follow, as well as my shirt and bra, until I'm laying completely naked before these gorgeous men.

I can practically feel their eyes rake over me, taking in every inch of my body before Wesley drops to his knees off the side of the bed and yanks me to the edge. Before I can even right myself, he's diving in face first. My thighs wrap around his head as he runs his tongue through me, forcing a shudder to rip through my body as he does it again and again, his teeth nipping at my clit as he does.

Wesley and I haven't slept together yet, but he has gone down on me, and holy shit, I think this time is even better. As Wesley continues devouring me whole, I hear the jingle of Ronan's belt before he pushes down his pants, pulling out his hard cock. He closes the space between us, crawling onto the bed, his knees beside my head as he pushes the tip of his cock into my mouth.

"Open up, baby."

I do as he says, and he wastes no time sinking himself fully into my mouth and down my throat. Once he's fully seated, he grabs hold of my head, forcing himself a little deeper and causing me to gag.

"Fuck," he groans. "Just like that. Gag on my cock, baby."

I gag again and again, doing my best to take deep breaths through my nose. Though, there is only so much air you can breathe when you have a fat cock blocking your airway. I want the record to show that this isn't complaining; that's just factual.

Wesley's movements have slowed, and my eyes open to look down and see him watching us intently, his blue eyes lust drunk and hazy. He seems almost transfixed as he watches Ronan's cock slide in and out of my mouth.

"Stop staring at my cock like you want to be the one sucking it," Ronan growls as he fucks my throat harder.

Demise

Wesley pulls away from me, his mouth glistening as he speaks.

"Maybe I do."

Ronan grunts. "I know you do."

"So, let me. We know Sky loves it when her men play together, right, little one?" Wesley asks as he looks up at me.

I nod, surprised Ronan is somewhat entertaining this conversation. I never would have expected this from him. Literally, almost anyone in the world but him. Ask me if I'm mad about it.

"Come on, Ro," Wesley coaxes softly. "Do it for your girl. She's fucking dripping for it," Wesley says as he stands up, pulling his cock out and running the tip through me.

I gasp at the feeling, so close yet so far from where I need him.

Ronan casts a hesitant glance at me before looking back to Wesley.

"Fuck her," he demands.

A smile spreads across Wesley's face, but I don't miss the disappointment in his eyes as he shrugs.

"Not exactly a hardship," he says as he pushes inside me.

My mouth drops at the intrusion. His head feels bigger than the others, and it's hitting me in all the ways that fucking count. My god.

"Shit, little one. You feel like fucking heaven," Wesley groans.

"You too," I gasp. "So good."

"You like him filling you up?" Ronan asks as he pushes his cock down my throat.

I nod, a muffled whimper leaving my mouth as Wesley begins playing with my clit.

"Good," Ronan grits out. "I want you two to come, and then I want you both on your knees for me."

65

Wesley meets my eyes; surprise splashed across both of our faces. His pace picks up to a near rampant speed, and I wince for a moment as the shaking motion sends a pain ripping through my ribs. He gives me a look like he's checking in, and I give him a quick nod to continue. He nods as his hand begins rubbing my clit so fast it just looks like a blur and feels divine. I feel his cock push against my g-spot, and my pussy pulses at the feeling.

Ronan pulls his cock out of my mouth before rubbing the tip along the outline of my lips as he pushes back in.

"You guys like that? Like that I want you on your knees for me, ready and willing to suck daddy's cock?"

"Daddy, huh?" Wesley smirks.

"Her daddy," Ronan says.

Wesley's eyebrows raise as he shoots Ronan a wink.

"I don't know. Kinda like the sound of you being my daddy, too. What do you think, little one? Up for sharing?"

I smile around Ronan's cock as I nod, pulling a chuckle out of Ronan's chest. He reaches down, covering Wesley's hand with his as he begins playing with my clit as well. They work together in perfect unison, bringing a new feeling I have yet to experience and one that pushes me straight over the edge.

"Oh my God, oh my God, oh my God," I shout around Ronan's cock as I'm coming.

My pussy pulses, my body shakes, and it seems to be all Wesley needs to fall apart as well. I feel his cock swell inside of me, his moans filling the room as he gasps and grunts before his thrusts stop, and he blows out a shaky breath.

Ronan pulls out of my mouth as he moves off the bed to stand.

"Both of you, on your knees, now," Ronan barks in an authoritative tone that does something entirely too delicious to me.

Demise

Wesley and I scramble to the floor, resting on our knees as we both look up at Ronan. He stares down at us, stroking his cock as he reaches for Wesley first. His hand grips Wesley's cheeks, his eyes drilling into him as he speaks.

"Open."

His mouth falls open, ready and waiting for Ronan. He doesn't make Wesley wait long because, in the next second, he is pushing inside his mouth. A tremble runs through Ronan's body as Wesley pushes Ronan's cock down his throat before pulling almost all the way out and back again.

Wesley's hands come to Ronan's hips, steadying himself as he falls into a rhythm that seems to be heavenly if Ronan's face was anything to go off.

"Goddamnit. Forgot how good this mouth is," Ronan growls before he begins thrusting.

"You guys have done this before?" I ask, part in shock and partly turned all the way the fuck on.

Wesley smirks, pulling away from Ronan as he looks at me.

"It took years for me to wear him down. One drunken blowjob and he couldn't get enough."

"Shut up and choke on my cock," Ronan snaps as he shoves himself back into Wesley's mouth, taking him by surprise and making him gag. "There we go," Ronan encourages.

I watch them with rapt attention. There is a definite familiarity there. The way Wesley rests his hands easily, bobbing his head smoothly, occasionally looking up at Ronan. And Ronan is watching Wesley openly, not an ounce of embarrassment or shame on his face. Something else I find lacking is want. They don't look at each other the way Liam and Asher do. This feels more primal, sexual. It seems to be less about a deeper connection, and more of a carnal release.

Regardless of the foundation or direction this takes us all, the puddle between my legs is on board for the ride.

In the next moment, Ronan pulls away from Wesley, pushing his cock into my mouth. His cock is warm and wet, and it turns me on so much more to know that his best friend was the one keeping his cock warm just a second ago.

Pushing and pulling my head down on Ronan's cock, I feel another mouth come beside me. Wesley is to my left, his mouth latching onto the side of Ronan's cock before he steals it from me, pushing it back down his throat again. I take a page out of his playbook and steal it right back. Back and forth, both of us licking, sucking and swallowing around Ronan.

"Fuck. You both are being so good for me. So good for daddy."

Wesley shoots me a wink before he reaches up, slipping his hand to cup Ronan's balls and forcing his hips to jerk.

"I'm gonna come, fuck, I'm gonna come," Ronan moans urgently.

I continue sucking him as Wesley rubs his balls before Ronan speaks.

"Open your mouths, tongues out."

Wesley and I do as he says, watching Ronan stroke his cock before releasing his cum all over our tongues. He starts with me before moving to Wesley and then back to me. I feel Ronan's warm cum dripping down my chin, and when I look to see Wesley in the same state, I can't help but fucking love it.

Ronan releases his cock, shaking his head as he blows out a breath. He looks at me first, pinching my cheeks much like he did Wesley's earlier as he bends down and presses a kiss to my cum covered mouth. When he pulls away, Wesley looks up at him challengingly.

"Where's my kiss?"

Ronan scoffs, rolling his eyes as he strolls to the bathroom.

"You've got your girlfriend right next to you, kiss her."

Wesley releases an exaggerated sigh of disappointment.

Demise

"Oh darn, what a chore," he laughs before pressing a kiss to my lips.

The kiss is sticky and salty, and for all the reasons that it shouldn't be hot...not a single one is found because I've never been more satisfied and turned on all at once.

Chapter Ten

Vincent

We are sitting on the couch, my siren on my lap, exactly where she should be when the doorbell rings. I'm already pulling out my phone to check the security footage when Skyla shakes her head and laughs.

"It's just Maggie."

I frown at her. "You never know. What does she want?"

"Uh, to see me?" She laughs.

I snort. "Join the fucking club."

I'm starting to get more than a little pissed off that I haven't gotten more one on one time with my siren. It was bad enough when she had two boyfriends and a fiancé she couldn't stand. Now she has three boyfriends, a husband that she supposedly loves, and Wesley. Of course, I don't count Wesley as a fourth boyfriend because I don't trust him. Not with Skyla, not with anything.

It's his fault she was taken, his fault she endured hell, his fault we almost lost her. Him showing up out of the blue after all these years is suspicious, to say the least, and the way he magically fell for Skyla in the same moment...I don't trust him one fucking bit.

If I voiced my gut feeling, I'm sure I'd be dismissed as being pissed off that I have to share her with yet another person. Which, albeit is a bullet point on the list, but it's not my main reason.

It's also a reason that I don't like Bartlett. She makes far too many sexual comments about Skyla for my liking, and the fact that she was fucking Skyla's tormentor all summer doesn't bode well for her in my book. Sure, none of them had met Skyla back then, but that's not the point. Brenton has publicly attacked Skyla twice since she and Maggie met, and guess whose dorm room I watched Bartlett leave at three in the morning two days ago? You guessed it, Bridgette motherfucking Brenton.

My siren is so sweet, but she invites entirely too many untrustworthy snakes into her life. I'd be happy to make them all disappear if I knew she wouldn't hate me forever when I did.

Asher answers the door, and Bartlett blows past him as she moves through the house. Skyla jumps out of my lap, which pisses me the fuck off, before jumping into Bartlett's arms for a hug. I can feel myself glaring at her, but I don't give a fuck. Bitch needs to let go of the love of my life and now.

Lucky for her, she does, but Skyla loops her arm through Bartlett's and begins dragging her upstairs.

"Where are you going?" I call out.

"To catch up!" Skyla smiles, oblivious to my souring mood.

"And fuck!" Bartlett teases with a smile that has my eyes narrowing.

Asher shakes his head as he walks into the living room, Liam following behind him before jumping onto his bed. He lifts his walking boot onto the mattress, and I raise an eyebrow at him.

"When are you getting that fucking thing off? I'm sick of a bed in the middle of the goddamn living room."

"Tomorrow," Liam says.

"And it's my goddamn living room," Asher snaps. "It'll stay here for as long as it needs to be."

"Oh, my apologies, didn't mean to offend your boyfriend," I taunt.

Asher's jaw tenses as he takes a step towards me before Liam grabs his hand, stopping him with a head shake.

"Aw, look at that. You guys can even communicate with no words."

"What the fuck is your problem, Griggs?" Liam huffs.

"Probably hasn't gotten laid in a while," Wesley says with a bored tone as he and Ronan stride into the living room. "Where is Skyla at?"

A door shuts, followed by the sound of the girls giggling, and I mumble under my breath.

"Probably getting her pussy eaten by her bestie."

"Hot, I want to watch," Wesley says as he grabs a bag of chips and pops one into his mouth.

"Get in line, man. I was trying to encourage that shit in class the other day, I swear to God, Sky almost went for it," Liam says.

I look over to see Ronan typing on his phone, a pinched look to his face.

"What's wrong?"

His head snaps up to me as he pockets his phone and shakes his head.

"Nothing."

I look at him blankly but don't say a word as his eyes move to where Asher is now sitting on the edge of the bed beside Liam. He looks around the room before coming back to Asher.

Demise

"Asher's birthday is coming up. Christopher and I are making arrangements for the ceremony."

Ah, yes. The induction ceremony. Up until now, legacies have been doing the Brethren's bidding while still being a living, breathing human. After that ceremony, their souls are practically sold to the devil. Ironic, since the Brethren was founded by extremist Puritan Protestants.

I don't actually know what the ceremony entails since I haven't been inducted either. Though my birthday isn't for a while, it's only a matter of time. Then again, I lost my soul a long fucking time ago, so what's the point?

"Happy birthday to me," Asher drawls sarcastically. "What about Skyla and my wedding? Has he said anything about that?"

"Why? You want to rub it in our faces?" I sneer.

Asher turns to look at me. "Only a lot."

"Jesus, you guys fucking hate each other. How do you make it work?" Wesley mutters.

We all stay silent for several seconds before Liam speaks.

"Skyla is like a force. I'm pretty sure she could cure world hunger if she put her mind to it."

Surprisingly, everyone in the room lets out some variation of a laugh as we nod in agreement.

"No, Asher," Ronan says, redirecting the conversation. "He hasn't said anything about the wedding. Honestly, I don't think he's worried about it right now."

"Why not?" Asher asks.

Ronan pauses for a moment before he shakes his head. "I don't know."

Well, that doesn't sound good. Though, when is there anything ever good about a fucking Putnam. My eyes burn into the side of Asher's head, flashes of that night flickering on repeat in my head. The night Asher killed Nate is a night that I'll never escape, no matter how hard I try. The fucked up part is that I bet anything Asher doesn't even realize he's responsible, doesn't even understand how much blood is on his hands. Or maybe he does and doesn't care.

My blood begins to boil, hatred gnawing at every fiber of my body. It would be all too easy to reach inside my boot, grab my knife and stab the piece of fucking shit in the neck. I know I can't, though, and the reason I can't is the beautiful siren upstairs.

Goddamnit. Fuck this.

I jump to my feet, storming up the stairs without a care as to how loud my boots sound through the house against the echoing floor. When I reach the bedroom door, I practically kick it down. Maggie is laying sideways at the foot of the bed while Skyla is sitting crisscrossed. They are speaking earnestly about something when I storm in.

"Vincent, is everything oka—"

"Bartlett, you have exactly five seconds to get out of here," I say.

"Why, are you guys gonna fuck? I'm staying if you are. Just because I prefer women doesn't mean I don't want to watch a hot straight couple fuck."

"Five," I say through clenched teeth.

"Four." She raises a challenging eyebrow that has my building anger practically blinding, and Skyla must sense it.

"Give us a minute," she says softly.

Maggie huffs out an exaggerated sigh but pushes off the bed, stepping out of the room as I shrug off my leather jacket.

"What's going on?" Skyla asks gently, that soft lilt already doing something to me.

It's not enough. I'm fucking furious, and only one thing will settle me down.

Demise

"I need you, now," I say quickly as I pull my cock out of my pants.

She blinks once before she's pulling down her leggings. I push into her without a second's hesitation, a feral growl leaving me as I do.

"Shit," she hisses as I roll my hips hard, picking up a punishing pace in the next moment.

"What's going on?" she groans.

"Nothing," I say, blinking hard in an attempt to clear the rage that is currently clouding my vision.

"You're so mad, babe. You're shaking," she says gently.

"I hate him," I snarl. "I put up with him for you, only for you, but fuck, I hate him!"

"Who?" she asks as I snap my hips, my eyes dropping to hers as understanding crosses her face. "Asher?"

Just hearing his name on her lips has my anger ratcheting, and I recognize that I haven't felt this out of control in a long time. I do my best to fuck her hard, trying to chase the demons away, push the nightmares away. Nothing works, though.

"What do you need? Tell me?" Skyla begs.

"Blood. His fucking blood rolling down my knife," I gnash.

Her voice is quiet as she speaks.

"Use me."

"What?" I snap.

"Use me, like you did in the cabin. Use me."

The idea is intoxicating, but I don't enjoy hurting her, marking her. Though I won't deny, out of all the women I've been with, all the ones who I've played with using a knife, not a single one of them made it feel like pure ecstasy.

Despite my hesitation, I lift my boot, reaching inside and grabbing the knife. I flick the blade open, and I hear Skyla's breath intake, a nervous look passing across her face as she looks at me. My hand is digging into her fleshy thigh, and I press the silver blade against her skin, slowly dragging a line along it as a trail of blood follows in its wake. I do another and another and another until blood is covering my hand, smearing across her entire upper thigh. She whimpers softly but doesn't ask me to stop. My cuts are shallow, so shallow they won't even scar, but the bloodthirsty demons inside me crave more.

I move to her other leg as I draw more and more lines. More and more blood. It feels so empowering, so spiritual. Skyla Parris is my goddamn religion. From now until the end of my days, I'll happily kneel at her altar, worship her feet and taste her blood.

Pulling out of her, I bend down, dragging my tongue along her bloody thigh. She winces at it, but I mimic the move on her other thigh, that familiar copper taste springing across my tongue as I shove my cock back into her.

My eyes practically roll into the back of my head as I fuck her faster than before, my fingers playing with her bloody thighs, a sense of calm rolling over me with it. Yes, I'm fucked up, no, there is no hope for me.

I look down into those big, beautiful eyes, and between them, her soft whimpers, her pretty blood, and her sweet, sweet cunt, I come fucking hard. My cock pulses, throbbing and jerking inside her as I push it deeper and deeper, forcing her body to take every single drop I have to give. Her pussy pulses, and her screams echo through the house as she follows right behind me.

When her orgasm has passed, my body collapses on top of her, my head tucked into the crook of her neck; the only sound to be heard is our ragged breathing. I feel her hand lift to my head, her fingers running through my black hair soothingly. I close my eyes on instinct, enjoying this moment, savoring it.

"What did Asher do, baby?" she asks softly.

My eyes spring open, but all I see is her beautiful blonde

hair. The words are stuck in my throat, my own demons keeping them locked in a chokehold as I grapple with how to respond. I don't want to respond. I don't want to talk about it, but I know she won't accept that. Truthfully, she deserves to hear it. Deserves to know what a monster her 'husband' is.

"Asher killed Nathaniel."

The silence that follows my words is deafening, like I can hear Skyla rationalizing it in her head already. Making up every excuse in the book for him.

"What do you mean?" she asks carefully.

I can hear the doubt in her voice. Why would she take my word on this when she has Putnam whispering into her ear? The hurt consumes me, but I bury it quickly, pushing up and out of her before I stand.

I get dressed in a flash and turn to head out the door as Skyla sits up.

"Vincent, stop. Talk to me. Vincent!" she shouts as I step out of the door and slam it shut. The sound echoes through the house, and I tear down the stairs as fast as I can, heading for my bike. I need to get the fuck away from Salem for a while.

Maybe forever.

Chapter Eleven

Skyla

I wanted to go after Vincent, but by the time I even stood up, I heard the sound of his bike firing up and taking off. Maybe I reacted poorly to what he said, but who wouldn't ask questions? One of my boyfriends just accused my other boyfriend, husband technically, of murder.

I'd like to think I know Asher fairly well, and I'm not saying he isn't capable of murder, as fucked up as that might sound, but killing Vincent's bond brother? I just...wanted more information, I guess.

After I cleaned myself up, I slipped into some baggy clothes, my legs far too sensitive from the cuts. They don't bother me, though. In the moment, I can see what a release it is for him, an escape, a solace. I love that I can give that to him, that I can be that for him.

When I come down the stairs, I find Maggie sitting on the bed with Liam, playing a video game, and she's absolutely destroying him.

"Hey! You can't shoot me!" Liam whines.

Demise

"The fuck I can't. Keep up, Walcott. There is no place for losers on my team," she says as she makes her character run.

Liam grumbles as Asher shakes his head and scrolls on his phone. Obviously, Vincent left, but I'm not sure where Wesley and Ronan are. Asher looks up from his phone at me, smiling softly as he pockets it and pats the couch he's sitting on.

I hesitate for a moment before I make my way over to him, sinking into the cushions as his arm wraps around me. I can't get Vincent's words out of my head, though. Like word vomit, it slips out before I can help it.

"Did you guys know Nathaniel Ingersoll?"

Like all of the sounds in the world have been ripped away, the room goes deathly quiet. I'm not sure anyone even breathes before Maggie pauses the game, three sets of eyes on me. After a moment, Liam nods.

"Yeah, we did."

Okay, well I was hoping for a little more than that.

"What happened to him?" I ask.

Liam and Maggie glance at each other before looking back at me.

"He died," Maggie says.

"Yeah, I know," I huff out before taking a deep breath and turning to look at Asher, who is currently staring at the bottom of the bed frame.

"Ash?" I ask softly.

His eyes slowly come up to me, a blankness to his face.

"What happened to Nathaniel Ingersoll?"

He shrugs. "Same shit that happens to anyone who is caught breaking the rules, they're eliminated."

"Eliminated?" I echo. "Like what Vincent does?"

"There are more eliminators in the Brethren than just Griggs, princess," Asher answers.

"Well, Vincent just told me that you were the one to kill Nathaniel...any idea why he thinks that?"

Asher screws up his face at that as he shakes his head.

"I did not. I was only nineteen back then, about to be twenty. I hadn't even killed anyone until—"

His words break off as he glances at Maggie before those brown eyes come back to me.

"I didn't kill him, princess. I don't know why Griggs told you that, but he's a fucking liar."

There is a deep sincerity to his voice. It's a little comforting, I suppose, that my husband isn't a murderer...well, at least not the murderer of one of my boyfriends' best friends. Then again, it has me wondering why Vincent feels this way, why he's shifted the blame onto Asher. Maybe Vincent feels guilty for something? Maybe he had a hand in Nathaniel's death, whether he wants to admit it to himself or not, and he's deflecting? I don't really know, but without Vincent here, there is no more digging to be done on the matter, and based on the way he left, it's probably best to let it lie for a bit.

Maggie seems to take the lead in changing topics, and I'm grateful for it.

"I'm bored? Want to watch a Christmas movie and stuff our faces? I saw someone baked sugar cookies," Maggie says as she points to the large platter of cookies on the stove.

I smile over at them. After the great flour battle of Salem, and the even greater threesome that followed, Ronan and Wesley came downstairs and helped me clean up and make a bigger batch of cookies. Their argument was because we have so many people in and out of the house. Really, I think it was because we all know how snacky Wesley can be.

Nodding, I rise to my feet.

"I'll make some popcorn too."

"I'll lend you a hand," Maggie says as she tosses a remote to Liam. "Don't pick something stupid, Walcott."

Liam scoffs like he's offended as he picks up the remote and begins flicking through shows.

I walk into the pantry to grab a few bags of popcorn as Maggie grabs the milk, pouring several mugs full before reaching to put it away. When she does, the sleeve of her t-shirt rises, and something catches my eye.

What the fuck.

I reach out for her arm, stopping in her tracks as I push the sleeve up.

"Maggie, what happened?" I ask, my eyes taking on several round burn marks scattered under her upper arm. Just high enough to be concealed with the sleeve of a t-shirt.

She jerks at my touch, quickly yanking it down before she shakes her head.

"It's nothing."

"That's not nothing, Maggie," I argue.

"Drop it!" she snaps, a fierceness to her tone that I haven't heard from her before.

She blows out a breath, all the panic and anxiety from her face washing away as she shakes her head and gives me a pleading look. "Please?"

Slowly, I nod, and she closes the fridge before grabbing the cups of milk, walking into the living room, and setting them down before coming back for the cookies.

I share a look with Liam, but when I look to Asher, he's already back to doing something on his phone.

Once the popcorn is done, I pour the bags into a giant bowl and move into the living room. Asher and Liam are sitting together against the headboard of the bed. Maggie is laying on her stomach on the far left side and I crawl in between her and Asher before laying on my stomach too. Her eyes don't leave the screen, watching with rapt attention Santa Claus go down the chimney when I lean against her.

Slowly, her red hair shifts, and those green eyes come to me.

"I'm sorry," I mouth.

She shakes her head like she's telling me to forget it when I cover my hand with hers.

"No, I am," I whisper. "I love you; if you don't want to talk about it, we won't."

She gives me a weak smile, squeezing my hand as she nods.

"I love you too."

I smile at her, turning back to focus on the movie when Asher reaches down and begins massaging my leg. I give him a sweet smile over my shoulder, and he shoots me a wink. His arm is around Liam's shoulder, and it doesn't take long for Liam to slump down. He rests his head against Asher's chest, his leg intertwined with Asher's.

They are so cute it makes me want to puke and melt all at the same time.

Chapter Twelve

Liam

The day I've been looking forward to is finally here. I've finally got the all fucking clear. No cast, no walking boot. I'm like a brand new man.

Skyla squeezes my hand as she looks down at me. I smile up at her before I turn to see Asher listening to the doctor's instructions with rapt attention. He's really adopted the Mr. Responsible role lately. At least when daddy Ronan isn't around to do it for all of us.

The doctor asks if we have any questions, to which we all shake our heads before he leaves. I slide off the examination bed, surprised at how weak my leg is when I try to put my full weight on it. Fuck, it's been a while since I've been able to do a full gym routine, and it shows. I'm practically itching to get back to it. Upper body is not enough for me.

"You okay?" Skyla asks in that sweet voice that makes my heart melt, and my cock twitch all at the same time.

I grin up at her before planting a slobbery kiss on her cheek.

"Couldn't be better. Now I can finally fuck you standing up."

Intrigue enters her eyes, and I wink at her before Asher grabs the door.

"No, dumbass. The doctor said that you need to take it easy," he scolds.

I pout as I look back at him.

"Don't be jealous, I'll fuck you standing up too."

He lifts a bored eyebrow before leaning his head down to speak into my ear.

"If you think that you'll be the one to fuck me, you've got another thing coming."

My cock isn't just twitching; it's turned into a steel fucking pipe. Asher's melted chocolate eyes bore into me, nothing but promise and filthy fucking thoughts in them. I want to ask him to name a time and place, to beg on my fucking knees for that, but the moment has passed, and he slips by me to wrap his arm around Skyla.

Fuck, seeing them all cozied up together doesn't help my issue going on in my pants. I do my best to adjust as I walk, but between the sway of...well, both their hips, it's pretty fucking hard.

Skyla turns back to look at me, concern on her face.

"You okay? You're limping."

Asher turns to glance at me before he smirks.

"He's not limping, princess. He's trying to wrangle the boner I just gave him."

She tries to hold back a laugh as we pass through the waiting area of the doctor's office before moving out to the parking lot.

"Not just you," I defend. "My babygirl too," I say proudly.

We make our way out to Asher's Range Rover, and he opens the back door for me.

"Such a gentleman," I tease as I slide in.

He huffs as Skyla follows after me before he shuts the door

Demise

and heads for the driver's seat. Asher has barely even pulled out of the parking lot before I'm undoing both my seatbelt and Skyla's, dragging her up and over to my lap. Her legs part, forced to straddle me when Asher curses.

"What the fuck are you doing? Both of you buckle up, now."

"Calm down, Dad. Just having a little fun," I smirk as Skyla giggles.

"Fun? Aren't you the one who just got cleared from the last car accident?"

I wave him off. "That doesn't count. A psycho stalker cut my brake lines. Do you have brakes?"

Asher narrows his eyes in the rearview mirror, and I nod.

"Exactly. Now shut up. I'm trying to make out with my girlfriend."

"You mean my wife," Asher snaps.

"Tomato, potato," I say as I press my lips to Skyla's.

She comes to me easily, winding her arms around my neck. I feel her hips begin to grind against me, and I moan into her mouth. My balls are already so fucking blue they feel ready to fall off.

My hands slip beneath her shirt, pulling it up and over her head before I toss it to the side. The bra she is wearing is one of those front clasp ones, perfectly convenient in a time like this. I pinch the clasp between my fingers, her breasts springing free in my face.

Fucking heaven.

I cup one of her breasts in my hand, closing my mouth around her nipple as she lets out a moan and drops her head backwards. My tongue swirls around her nipple, my teeth nipping at it as Asher curses from the front seat.

I release Skyla's nipple with a pop before I tap the side of her ass.

"Turn around, babygirl. Slide those pants down and face Ash."

She does as I say quickly, kicking off her shoes before sliding her leggings off and to the side of the car. I pull my cock out, grabbing her silk thong and yanking it to the side before I rub the head of my cock through her. She takes in a sharp inhale through her teeth, and I look over her shoulder to see Asher staring more often in the rearview mirror than the road.

"Eyes on the road, big boy," I laugh as I sink myself into her.

We both let out simultaneous moans that has Asher whipping the car over to the shoulder. Horns honk and brakes screech across the road before the car is thrown into park, and Asher is spinning around in his seat. Skyla begins bouncing up and down on me, my hands cupping her tits as she does. My thumbs play with her nipples, rubbing and pulling on them when Asher steals the right one from me, pulling it into his mouth.

"Oh, my God," Skyla moans.

"Yeah, suck on her titty, Ash. Help me make our girl feel good," I encourage.

He moans around her, his hand reaching inside his pants to free his own cock. I watch with rapt attention as he begins stroking himself, his eyes closed as he licks and sucks Skyla. Goddamnit, they are so fucking hot. How did I get this lucky? To have Skyla is already a blessing from above, but to have them both? Luckiest bastard to ever live.

Just looking at Ash's cock again has my mouth watering, remembering how good he tasted, how amazing it felt to be taken by him. For him to have a moment that was just for us. He couldn't deny me then, just like he can't now. He wants me, and I've wanted him for longer than I realized.

I really never thought I'd see the day. The lines were always so clear in my head. I was never interested in men romantically; then again, I wasn't really interested in women romantically, either. Ash is different, though. He's just...Asher. I love the guy, of course, we've been best friends since birth, but it's more than that. I care about him. I want to see him happy, taken care of, pleasured. I want him in every shade under the sun and moon, just like I want Skyla. Once I figured that out, that's when I knew I was well and truly fucked for my best friend.

Skyla's pussy contracts around me, and it has my head dropping back to the headrest.

"Goddamn, babygirl. Your pretty little pussy hugs me so good. Such a tight little thing."

"Uh huh," she groans, one hand wrapping around my neck while the other cups the back of Asher's head. Smashed together between us, properly worshipped the way she deserves to be. See? A Skyla sandwich.

Asher releases her nipple, his eyes drunk with lust as he jerks his cock, his eyes on the both of us before they drop. He watches my cock slide in and out of Skyla before he does something I never see coming.

Pushing himself further through the opening between the front seat and the back, he buries his head in between Skyla and my legs and begins devouring...well, both of us. His tongue starts at the base of my cock before it draws a line up to Skyla, ending on her clit. A sharp moan rips through Skyla as he begins eating her pussy while I fuck her.

His head shakes back and forth, his tongue rubbing against her clit before he goes down again. I may or may not purposefully lift her up higher than necessary. So high for a moment, she comes off my cock. Just like I hope he would, Asher takes the opportunity to suck my cock down his throat. He pushes it all the way down, bobbing up and down several times. One of my hands comes to his cheek, attempting to push him off so I can keep fucking Skyla, but he only sinks down further, groaning as his hand jerking himself off picks up in speed.

"Holy fucking shit!" Skyla gasps as she watches him, lust and shock on her face. "Do you like that, Ash?"

His eyes flick up to her, his mouth stuffed full of my cock as he nods slowly.

"How does it taste? My pussy all over Liam's cock?" Skyla asks, forcing my cock to twitch in Asher's mouth before he slowly pulls up to speak.

"Like my two favorite flavors combined in one," he says before crushing his lips to Skyla.

I take the opportunity to pull her back to me, forcing her to sink fully onto me. She whimpers into Asher's mouth as I feel my balls begin to draw up. Asher tears his mouth away from hers before coming for me. His tongue tastes like Skyla, and it only makes my cock throb harder and harder. When his tongue wraps around mine and sucks, I'm a goner.

I thrust up, once, hard, forcing my piercings to do their job and send Skyla falling over the edge. In the next moment, Asher rips away from me, grabbing the back of Skyla's neck as he pushes his cock towards her and comes on her tongue. She sticks it out for him, allowing him to paint it nice and pretty before she pulls it back into her mouth and swallows.

I collapse into the seat, Skyla following right with me as Asher falls forward, practically smothering us as we sit there like the out of breath, sticky mess we are. And I love every fucking second of it.

Chapter Thirteen

Asher

When we get back to the house, we order some takeout for lunch when my phone rings. I grimace when I see who is calling, but I know I have no choice but to answer.

"Hello, Father."

"Son, you and your wife will be coming over to my home for dinner this evening."

My eyes move to Skyla, flashes of the last time he had us both come to the house still fresh in my mind. Like the sharp burn of each lash, it's practically imprinted in my head forever.

"We would love to, but we already have dinner plans—"

"Cancel them," he cuts in. "Be here at six PM, sharp. Oh, and I heard little Stephanie Thompson was back in the States. Bring her as well."

With that, he hangs up the phone.

Fuck.

My eyes swing to Skyla, a foreboding feeling settling in. I don't like her around him. I don't like the way he looks at her, the way he talks to her, and I don't like that I never have any idea what he's up to. It's like playing chess with only half a board. How are you supposed to play the game if you can't see the moves your opponent is making?

"What's wrong?" Skyla asks as she looks over to me.

"My dad called. We're going to dinner, and he wants us to bring Stephanie."

She frowns at that. "Stephanie won't agree. You're kidding, right? She's terrified of him."

Stephanie isn't the only one who is terrified of him. I see the fear in Skyla's eyes, the memories of the last time she was in his house, in his presence. I won't let him hurt her, though. Not again.

I nod. "It's not like we have a choice, princess."

She opens her mouth before closing it.

"I know."

The drive to pick up Stephanie is quiet. Skyla called her and asked if she wanted to go to dinner with us. She wasn't overly excited about me coming, but she agreed, nonetheless. We did leave out the location and extra company that would be there, but that's only because we knew she wouldn't come if we did. I also knew it wouldn't be good for either of us if we showed up without her.

Skyla is texting on her phone, wearing a pinched look of concern as she taps on the screen.

"What's wrong?" I ask.

She jerks like she forgot I was here for a moment before she looks up at me.

"Vincent. I haven't been able to get a hold of him since he left yesterday. I'm worried. He was really upset with me."

"Why?" I ask.

Her teeth chew on the inside of her lip for a moment before she releases it.

"Because he was vulnerable with me, he told me that you killed Nathaniel and I...didn't believe him."

Warmth fills my chest at that. I know that for Skyla's sake, I should at least tolerate Griggs, but it feels good to know that if it came down to the two of us, she'd take my side.

"It's not that I didn't believe him, I do, or I could, I guess," she continues, diminishing my happiness by the second. "I just didn't respond the right way, and he was so angry. He doesn't open up, ever, not even with me...I blew it."

I reach over and rest my hand on her knee, squeezing it gently.

"You didn't blow anything. That guy doesn't just love you; he lives you. You're the air in his lungs, the earth beneath him. You're not just his whole world; you're all of the worlds. You're his entire universe, princess. One disagreement will not tear you two apart. Trust me, if that's all it took, I would have instigated something between you two months ago."

She doesn't laugh like I hoped she would. Then again, tension breaking humor is more Liam's specialty than mine.

"I just hate that I hurt him. I want to apologize."

"Don't worry about it, really. I'm sure he's following us like the fucking creeper he is just to keep an eye on you. He's not far."

She looks out the window longingly, and it actually hurts something inside me. Not because she's longing for another, but because she's unhappy because he isn't here. I'm tempted to hunt the motherfucker down and drag him by his toes all the way to our house just so I can throw him at her feet like some sort of offering.

We pull up to Stephanie's place, a new flash of guilt passing across Skyla's face as she slides in the car.

"Hi, sweetheart," she smiles at Skyla. "Asher," she greets me curtly.

"Stephanie," I respond.

"Frigid in here," Skyla drawls sarcastically.

That forces a smirk to spread across Stephanie's face.

"Sorry, I'll get used to the little shit. One day."

"Looking forward to it," I scoff as I begin driving.

"As you should," she sasses.

I see where Skyla gets some of her fire from.

Skyla and Stephanie talk about her job and her boyfriend back in London. She tells Skyla how she needs to get back home soon, and as much as Skyla's disappointed, she understands. It's not until we make it through the other side of town and are less than a quarter mile from Putnam Manor that Stephanie begins to put it together.

"Wait, where are we going to dinner again?" she asks, her body language suddenly rigid, her tone brisk.

Skyla winces slightly before turning around to face her. She doesn't speak, but apparently, she doesn't need to. Stephanie takes one look at her face and panics. Leaping for the door, she tries the handle, but I've already engaged the child locks miles ago.

"No, no, no, no! How could you? Sky! Why are you doing this to me? I can't see him! I can't be in a room with him... them...any of them!" she screams in outrage.

"I'm sorry, Steph. We don't have a choice—"

"The fuck you don't! Let me out of this fucking car right now!" she screams.

"We don't!" I snap, not liking the tone she's taking with Skyla.

I make our final turn as the gate to the Manor opens, and

we begin moving down the driveway. I stare at Stephanie through the rearview mirror, doing my best to keep my temper in check.

"My father requested you, by name. He knew you were in town and said we had to bring you. The last time Skyla and I were here, we both earned so many lashes we could hardly walk. What do you think would have happened to us, to her, if we showed up without you?"

I can see Stephanie's pulse racing in her neck from here, her face white as a ghost as we pull up to the roundabout driveway and park. She swallows roughly, closing her eyes before a mask of composure falls over her. It's actually quite remarkable to witness.

She looks between us with a steady gaze as she speaks.

"I'm very upset with you both, but you're right, and now isn't the time or place. Let's just pray to fucking God we can make it out of here in one piece."

With that, she pushes her door open and slides out of the car. Skyla shares a nervous look with me, and I bring her hand up to my mouth, pressing a kiss to it before I nod.

"I won't let him hurt you, I promise."

Normally, I don't make promises. There is always a risk of breaking them. This one I can be absolutely sure of, though. Mainly because if he even lifts a finger towards her, I'm grabbing the 9mm I have hidden on me and emptying the clip between his eyes.

Chapter Fourteen

Skyla

As we walk up the stairs, my arm looped through Asher's and Steph's, I can see her shaking beside me. You wouldn't be able to tell though by looking at her. Her head is held high, eyes focused and hardened. She looks like a picturesque vision of poise. Yet I can feel the deep seated fear radiating from her. Hopefully, I'm the only one that will.

Per usual, the front door opens just as we reach the top, one of Christopher's butlers bowing as we enter. My steps slow for a moment when we enter the foyer, flashes of what it looked like last time. My eyes move to the crown molding against the floor. I remember staring at it. Fixating on it as I held onto Asher with everything I had. It was that white crown molding that held me through each lash.

"Stephanie Thompson," Christopher booms with a smile so fake it would make a car salesman cringe. "It's been years. You certainly have grown up," he says as he leans in, pressing a kiss to either cheek.

She returns the gesture, though hers hold a significant amount of disdain to them.

"You're looking as fabulous as ever, Christopher. If only Giselle could see you now."

His smile drops at my mother's name, and his eyes flash for a moment. It's a dangerous look, one filled with warning. There was a glimmer of something else in them, though. Sadness? Sorrow?

"Already bringing up the sister you'll never be?" my father says, stepping into the room beside Christopher.

"Just keeping the memory alive of the wife you never loved," she spars back to him.

Asher and I trade unnerved looks. I've never heard anyone speak to my father this way, or Asher's father, for that matter. With how terrified she was, you'd think she would cower, play dead, something.

My father doesn't react like Christopher did. Instead, he gives her a bored glance before turning to face me.

"Skyla," he says with a head dip.

"Father," I say in return.

He reaches his hand out for Asher, and he takes it, shaking my father's hand tightly before releasing it.

"A pleasure as always, Henry."

My father nods but doesn't say a word as he looks back to Stephanie.

"Why did you come?"

"I invited her, Henry. Don't scare off my dinner guest just yet."

I hear my father grumble something under his breath as he turns and moves to the dining room. Christopher's eyes move from Stephanie to me, that plastic smile back in place.

"And how is my favorite daughter-in-law doing?"

"I'm good, thank you for the invitation," I smile politely.

"I'd guess less than good. Being kidnapped by a deranged psychopath has to be less than pleasing."

My lips part in surprise. "How did you know?"

Christopher laughs like I told a joke before shaking his head.

"Sweetheart, you really think a member of my society can kidnap my daughter-in-law, burn down a property, and I wouldn't know about it?"

"I burned the place down," Asher interjects before Christopher stops him.

"No, you didn't. It was Corwin, understand?"

Asher stares at him for a moment before nodding. Christopher nods as well as he claps his hands together.

"Good, let's eat."

We all move into the dining room and take our seats, me in between Asher and Steph while Christopher takes his place at the head of the table, and my father takes his place across from Asher. I feel Asher's hand come to my knee, squeezing it softly in comfort as Christopher speaks.

"Though I will say, I'm pleased to know my son's affections have grown for you. We've come far from screwing whores and calling out Skyla's name, haven't we son?"

Asher freezes at that, and my brows knit together.

Christopher makes a face of mock surprise as our plates are set in front of us by the waitstaff.

"Oh, did you not know? I'd have thought you'd heard. If the Elders were hearing about my son's little tryst with the Lewis girl, I'd assumed you knew."

"When was this?" I ask before I can help myself, hoping to God it was so long ago that it doesn't matter.

Asher is staring at his food before his eyes come to me, his words clear but soft.

"Shortly after our ceremony...before we...made up," he says cryptically.

Hurt stabs through me. Lewis? Mercy Lewis? He fucked

her? Before or after the whole fork incident with Bridgette? Come to think of it, it had to have been before. Mercy was glaring at me with straight up contempt that day. No wonder she did. Asher was inside of her, calling out my name. Maybe that should give me some kind of peace, and to be fair, we weren't together...still, though. I can't believe he didn't tell me.

Reaching down to my knee, I push Asher's hand away and he looks up at me, hurt passing over his face before he lowers his head and nods.

"I made a mistake, an embarrassing one."

"That's all you ever do is make mistakes," Christopher tuts. "Let's hope that it will be the end of them, hmm?" he asks, none of us missing the threat in his tone.

Asher nods jerkily, which seems to satisfy Christopher because he turns his sights on Steph.

"Stephanie, now that you're back in the States, we must get you matched. Trenton Richards is newly available. His poor wife lost her life a few months ago, pregnant with their son as well. I believe you were in the same year as him?"

"Yeah," Stephanie answers. "He still knocking women around? What was his wife's cause of death exactly?"

Christopher gives a forced smile, the façade cracking by the moment.

"I'll be honest, I think all that time abroad has soiled your couth. It's a good thing you're home now and won't be returning," he says, his smile vanishing by the end of his sentence.

Steph gulps roughly but doesn't speak as Christopher yet again switches targets. Lucky me, I think I'm next.

"So, Skyla. If it's not too traumatic for you, I'd like to talk about what happened with Corwin."

"I don't think that's nec—" Asher starts but is silenced with a bang of Christopher's fist against the table.

"I don't believe I addressed you, *boy*," he spits.

Asher's nostrils flare as he lowers his head. Unwanted images flash through my head, and I grimace before facing Christopher and nodding.

"What do you want to know?"

"What was his reasoning?" my father asks sharply.

"For taking me?" I ask.

He nods.

I shrug. "He said that I looked just like Mom. That they used to date—"

Christopher scoffs. "He wished."

"And that me coming back was like a second chance," I continue. "He told me that she started dating my father and then...you."

My mouth opens to mention the whole 'him saying my father is the one that killed her' thing, but for some reason, I don't. Call it nerves or preservation. I mean, who in their right mind would accuse someone of murder right in front of them with no evidence? Someone looking to disappear, that's who.

"Anything else?" Christopher asks.

I scramble in my head, trying to come up with more to tell him.

"He was about to rape me," I say, the words coming out sharp as a knife, an awkward hush falling over the room. "He was stripping me naked and was going to rape me and then dress me in my mother's clothes when...Asher came in," I say, altering the story. Based on how Christopher and Asher spoke, they made it sound like Asher was the one to find me, alone. Not Vincent or Liam or Wesley or even Ronan.

Christopher watches me closely, like he's searching my face to sniff out the lies before he speaks.

"Well, I'm very sorry you had to endure that, and I'm glad that the son of a bitch is burning in hell."

I nod but don't say anything, my throat feeling suddenly

hot and tight. I attempt to clear it but when that doesn't work, I reach for some water, taking a small sip.

"Your mother and I were together. We shared her, together. Most bond brothers do, as you know," he says, setting me on edge.

Asher looks to me, nodding.

"He knows about Liam."

Liam. Just Liam.

I force my shoulders to relax as I nod.

"Yes, please relax, sweetheart. There is nothing to be afraid or ashamed of. Walcott is not promised to anyone, nor is he married. Even then, permitting Asher gives his blessing, it wouldn't be uncommon for you two to spend time together. A bond between brothers is...it's special, holy. Trivial things like right and wrong could never sever the tie."

I'm confused by his speech and by his acceptance. The way everyone made it seem, Christopher should be furious, disgusted. He should want to kill us all. Unless this is for show.

"Your mother was a very special woman," Christopher says as he begins cutting into his steak. "I think I can speak for everyone in that room that night when I say, I don't blame Walcott for wanting to spend time with you as well. You are... exquisite," he says as he stares at me with a longing in his eyes, picking up his bloody steak piece with his fork before resting it on his tongue.

It makes me squirm in my seat, and I do my best not to look away. He doesn't break our eye contact as he chews, a sinister smile playing at his mouth before he turns to my father and begins talking about business. Asher reaches for my knee again, but I scoot out of his reach. I don't know what to think, or how to feel right now. I need space, to process, to think, and most of all, I just want this dinner done and over with.

Chapter Fifteen

Vincent

I had to let off some steam, get some space. Even if I have to step foot under the same house as Asher fucking Putnam, so be it. I need to see my Siren.

Following my usual path up the side of the house to her balcony, my feet hit the floor quietly as I move to the French doors leading to her bedroom. When I reach for the handle and find it locked, I'm relieved. Thank fucking God, it's about time she started locking this shit. Then again, it's not like a simple handle lock could keep out dangerous predators, or me.

In seven seconds flat, the door snicks open, and I step through to find the room dark and Skyla laying on her side, facing away from me. I frown at that. It's only nine at night, and Skyla isn't known to go to bed early. Quite the opposite. She can stay up until two, sometimes three in the morning, but try waking her up before six, and it's like trying to bathe a cat.

"Go away," she says stiffly, her words sharp in the otherwise silent room.

I cross the room, rounding the bed to stand in front of her.

Demise

My eyes have adjusted to the darkness, and I look down to see her brows knitted together, cheeks blotchy like she's been crying. White hot rage thrums in my veins. This distress has Asher written all fucking over it.

I crouch down to meet her eyes when she turns her head. It sends a rush of anger through my body that she would try to evade me, try to escape me. My fingers pinch her chin, forcing her to face me. She does so begrudgingly, but as long as I have those pools of emerald green on me, I'm just fine.

"What happened?" I ask.

She stares up at me, contempt heavy in her gaze. Though, it's not that deep. Just past the surface is hurt, pain. Looking at it feels like a million needles poking beneath my skin. I'm desperate to remove it, all of it, and replace it with nothing but contentment and peace.

"What. Happened. Siren?" I punctuate each word slowly, letting it show that I will not be taking whatever bullshit silent treatment she's trying to give me.

She stays silent for several more seconds before she blows out a heavy breath and whispers so softly that I almost miss it.

"Asher slept with someone else."

Piece of fucking shit. Maybe now she'll let me finally kill him. I release her chin and reach for my knife, flicking it open as I head for the door to the hallway.

"Where are you going?"

"To slit his fucking throat," I say with too much glee in my tone.

Skyla flies out of bed, plastering her body against the door as she shakes her head.

"No! Stop! I..." she closes her eyes, inhaling deeply before looking at me once more. "Before we were together, officially, I guess. After the ceremony, he slept with Mercy Lewis..."

Understanding dawns on me.

"You didn't know."

She frowns. "You did?"

I nod once.

"Am I the only idiot who didn't? You know who told me? It wasn't Asher!"

"Christopher?" I guess since they had dinner there tonight.

She throws her hand out at me and nods.

"Bingo! I just...it's not like he betrayed me or anything. We were hardly even speaking back then, but still, I hate it. I hate knowing that others have been with him. I hate that he was still whoring around after supposedly loving me. I just...I feel stupid."

I don't have comforting words. I'm not an emotional, touchy-feely kind of guy. That's more Liam or Ronan's department. Need me to dismember a body twenty-three different ways? Want me to skin someone alive and turn their skin into jerky for the pig farm I frequent? I'm your guy. This...stuff, I'm no good at.

Slowly, I pull her into me, and she comes easily. Her arms wrap around my waist as I rest my chin against the top of her head and pull her in close to me.

"I can maim him," I offer. "If you don't want him to die, I can at least make sure he'll never stray again. Can't fuck whores without a dick."

She lets out a quiet snort before looking up at me.

"The bad part is I know you're being completely serious."

I nod once, and she shakes her head.

"Why did you run out on me earlier? We were talking about something serious. You were letting me in, and then you just...bailed."

An uncomfortability sets in as the topic of Nate is brought

Demise

up once more. I like it best buried, cold, and dead in the ground, just like him.

"I'm sorry," she says, catching me off guard. "For not listening with open ears. You were telling me about something that I know is not easy for you, and I met you with hesitance. That wasn't right, and I'm sorry."

I swallow roughly but nod my acceptance.

"But," she continues, "I need the full story. I need to understand everything."

"Why don't you just ask Putnam?"

Her jaw clenches, and she nods her head.

"Fine."

Pushing away from me, she opens the bedroom door and slips into the hallway. I hear her footsteps sound through the hall before a door opens. Ten seconds later and two sets of footsteps are coming down the hallway.

Asher's hair is disheveled, as if he's been running his hands through it like usual when he's being a little bitch. His eyes land on me, surprise flashing in them before they harden, and he looks to Skyla.

"What's going on?" he asks.

Skyla closes the door behind him, locking it as if that could actually keep us in here if either of us wanted to leave.

"Vincent told me that I should hear about Nathaniel from you, so we're all going to talk because all of this animosity cannot last forever. Not if this is going to be forever," she says as she gestures around the room.

I agree. She really should just cut Putnam loose now. No sense in dragging it out.

Predictably so, Asher's posture changes at the sound of my bond brother's name. His eyes drop to the ground, and he shrugs his shoulders as he speaks.

"He was found unconscious in his dorm room. He slipped in the shower, hit his head, and never woke up."

"That is the furthest thing from the truth, and we both fucking know it, Putnam!" I seethe.

Asher's eyes dart up to mine, fear like I've never seen him wear before absorbing all the color in his irises.

"That's all that I know firsthand," Asher defends. "I'm sorry you lost him, really, I am. He was a good guy, a hell of a lot better than you, but you need to cut this shit that I'm the one who killed him."

"Just because it wasn't your hands that took his life, doesn't mean you're not responsible," I speak lowly.

Asher looks genuinely confused for a moment and it pisses me the fuck off. Maybe that dumbfounded look works for him with some people, but not with me, never with me.

"Stop," Skyla intervenes. "This isn't helpful. Asher, do you know why Vincent thinks you're to blame?"

He opens his mouth to speak before he pauses, looks to me, looks to Skyla before his eyes go back to the ground.

"I saw him the night he was killed. My father had me meet him in the tunnels for a meeting with him and some of the Elders. When I came out of the church, I saw Nathaniel in the cemetery with a girl."

Rage attempts to consume me as he spins his bullshit. I'm waiting for him to stray from the truth, begging for him to tell a lie so I can cut out that piece of shit tongue.

"It was his girlfriend," Asher continues as he turns to face Skyla.

"Elise," I fill in. He deserves to know the name of the girl whose death he's responsible for as well.

Asher glances to me, nodding as he speaks,

"She wasn't a part of the Brethren. She was an outsider.

Relationships between members and nonmembers are taboo... relationships between Legacies and nonmembers are—"

"Prohibited," I cut off.

"Why?" Skyla asks.

Asher shakes his head. "Why are any of the rules in place? Because decades ago, someone decided it and made it so."

"What happened?" Skyla pushes.

He shrugs. "As you can imagine, having a relationship with an outsider was bad, but bringing them onto campus? On our sacred grounds? I told Nathaniel both of them needed to get the fuck out of there before anyone found them, and then I went home."

I let out a bitter laugh, and I feel my fingertips twitch in desperation for my knife. What I wouldn't give to jam it into his carotid right now.

"There seems to be some holes in your story, Putnam. Like the part where you narc'd on Nate to Daddy dearest and had him and Elise taken out."

Asher's face screws up at that.

"What are you talking about? I never told my father shit. I went home, went to bed, and when I woke up the next morning, news was spreading that he was dead."

My next dig pauses on my tongue as I study him closely. It's my job to read people, to study them, and right now, I do not like what I'm seeing. I don't like it because no matter how hard I look, I see nothing but sincerity in his eyes.

"How did the Elders find out, then? How did he get caught?"

"I don't know, maybe he didn't get out of there in time. Maybe someone else saw but didn't confront him like I did. You really have thought for all these years that I was the one to snitch?"

"You are your father's son," I throw out with far less heat than I intended.

The jab doesn't seem to affect him as he stays quiet for several seconds before huffing out a short breath.

"Fuck, no wonder you've been at my throat all these years. If I thought you were responsible for Liam's death, I'd have killed you a long time ago."

I don't like him understanding me; it's like he's trying to relate and compare the two of us, which is fucking ridiculous.

"Yeah, well, your last name affords you a certain amount of protection. You're the future king of this fucked up world. If I took you out, your father would send every enforcer out there after me. I chose my survival, not yours."

We both stand there, silently staring at one another. My head is racing with a million and one scenarios. Of course, I've scoured every database and security camera from that night. For months I poured over footage after footage. At 9:37 PM, Nate was, stupidly, walking hand in hand with Elise towards the graveyard. At 9:52 PM, Asher slipped out of the church and through the graveyard before coming across them. They spoke for thirty-eight seconds before Asher walked away. Two minutes later, the feed was cut. No amount of scrubbing and file repair has been able to pull anything else from it. The feed was lost, and therefore, so was the truth. Is it really possible that Putnam is telling the truth? That he went about his business and someone else's hands hold Nate's blood on them? I'm not completely convinced yet, but Skyla sure seems to be.

"See? All of this hate...it was for nothing. Asher didn't do anything wrong. Your anger and hate is misplaced."

I stare at my siren, more irritated with her than I've ever been before, when Asher intervenes.

"Is it, though? Granted, I personally am not the one who damned him or took him out, but my father is, right? My family is. My name is a curse, an omen of death. The entire Putnam lineage has blood-soaked hands that will never wash clean."

All so, so true. Then again, if we are talking about the amount of bloodshed, I'd say the Griggs family lineage is right up there with Putnam. At the end of the day, we are all their puppets. It started with the lead puppeteer Thomas Putnam in 1693, and it has descended down to our current master, Christopher.

I stare at Asher, unsure what to make of this new version of him. The one that accepts blame, despite him not being the direct culprit. The version that sympathizes with others and is self aware of his family's wickedness. Fucking hell, Skyla is some miracle worker. She brings out the absolute best in the most lost of causes. It's a phenomenon that deserves to be studied and explored.

Slowly, Asher puts out his hand to me, but I just stare at it. He doesn't seem offended. Instead, he just waits, his hand extended and a sincere look on his face. My eyes dart to my left to see Skyla watching me with a pleading look. So, I do it for her.

My hand slides into Asher's, squeezing harder than necessary as we shake. He does the same to me before we release and rest our hands back by our sides.

"I'll let you guys get some sleep. See you in the morning," Asher says as he leans down and places a kiss against Skyla's cheek.

"Stay," she says as she catches his hand.

Asher's eyes come to me before bouncing back to hers.

"Are you sure? We haven't gotten to talk about the whole... dinner situation."

Skyla shakes her head.

"And we don't need to, not tonight. Tonight, I just want you, both of you. Please."

"Of course," I answer for the both of us.

What my siren wants, my siren gets.

Asher and Skyla move to the bed as I kick my shoes to the side and shrug my leather jacket off. I slide in on the other side of Skyla and wrap my arms around her waist. She presses her ass against me as her head rests on Asher's chest, a soft, content sigh escaping her lips.

Chapter Sixteen

Ronan

"You've delayed long enough. It's happening; I'd suggest you make peace with it," Christopher snarls through the phone.

My jaw hardens as I stare out the kitchen window, staring off into the backyard.

"All I was saying is that it isn't the best time. Asher's initiation, the rest are following close behind. Why take the spotlight from them?"

"Because I deem it so! The engagement party is happening; it's already planned. You will be happy. You will be charming, and you will make it down that goddamn aisle this time."

Something twinges inside me at the way he says *this time*. It's not exactly hurt; my trauma from Madi's death took a while to heal, but slowly, it did. Instead, it's the reminder of all that I've lost, all that I have yet to lose, and all that has been stolen before I could even properly savor it.

Speaking of, my only beacon of hope these days strides into the kitchen, hair mussed and a sleepy smile on her face as she crosses the room and wraps her arms around my waist. I smile back at her, resting my hand over hers.

"Do I make myself fucking clear?" Christopher snaps.

"Crystal," I say stiffly.

Skyla's eyes watch me carefully, concern shifting in them as she takes in my expression.

My brother huffs, and with that, he's ending our call. I lower my phone away from my ear, pocketing it before fully turning to face Skyla.

"What's wrong?" she asks.

I shake my head and force a smile.

"Nothing, baby. I'm good."

"No, you aren't, and now you're lying to me. What's going on?"

A heavy sigh escapes me as I lift my hand up, cupping her jaw tenderly as my thumb glides across her silky skin. My fingers move, tangling into the back of her head and holding her hair tight as I pull her into me. She meets me easily and just with one simple touch of her lips, all of my worries melt away. Nothing can trouble me. Nothing can harm me. Not when I have her in my arms. With Skyla, things just...fit; they make sense.

When we break apart, she looks up at me breathlessly, her eyes flicking back and forth between mine.

"You're scaring me," she admits, anxiety heavy in her tone.

A million things run through my mind, but something completely unrelated spills from my lips instead.

"I want to take you somewhere, for the night. Think your guard dogs will allow it?"

A short chuckle escapes Skyla as she shakes her head.

"You act as if you aren't as protective as the others, like you're not as bad as them."

"Oh, I can promise, baby, I'm worse. Much worse. I just do a better job of hiding it."

She gives me a dry look as she raises an eyebrow.

"You're more protective than Vincent?"

Well, fuck. Of course not. That guy is goddamn certifiable.

I roll my eyes and press my lips to hers once before I speak.

"Pack warm; snow is coming today. We'll leave in two hours."

"Okay," she smiles, a light of excitement filling her beautiful green eyes.

She scurries off out of the kitchen and up the stairs. I love that she's excited. I am, too. In a house literally brimming with boyfriends, it's hard to get some time away, to just be together one-on-one. Normally, I don't mind, but right now, I need this, we need this.

Three hours later, I'm bobbing and weaving in and out of Boston traffic. Goddamn, the drivers around here are fucking psychotic. Not that Salem is all that better, but it's a hell of a lot smaller. Anytime I come into the city, it's a guaranteed headache and a half a dozen close calls.

Skyla doesn't seem to mind, though. She's been controlling the radio, not playing one song for longer than thirty seconds before she's on to the next. I think it would drive anyone else crazy, but I'm happy to sit back and watch her smile and sing horribly off-key.

Finally, we pull up to our destination.

"The Boston Park Plaza," Skyla reads the hotel's sign.

I nod and pull up to the valet. He opens my door quickly as

I pop the trunk, and the bellhop grabs our bags. The brisk December air is practically bone-chilling as I make my way around the car. I reach for Skyla's door, nearly getting sideswiped in the process.

Fucking asshole.

She smiles up at me as we round the car, and I hand the valet my keys. The doorman steps to the side, bowing slightly as we step through the automatic revolving door. When we step into the lobby, warmth wraps us up like a hug as a manager jogs over to us with a thousand watt smile.

"Welcome back, Mr. Putnam. We are so pleased to have you here."

I give him a quick nod and a tight smile.

"Thank you. Is our room ready?" I ask.

"All checked in. We have you in the penthouse suite," he says as he hands me two keycards.

"Thank you," I say as I take them, steering Skyla towards the elevators.

At least, I try to. Her eyes are everywhere, bouncing from the Italian restaurant to our right, Strega, over to the marbled floor of the grand lobby. A cozy seating area beside the bar makes you feel instantly at home, and the extravagant lighting throughout gives it that touch of elegance.

I hit the elevator button, and the doors open instantly. We step inside, and she looks over to me with a smile.

"This place is gorgeous. How were you able to already be checked in, though?"

"Perks of being the boss," I shrug.

"You own this hotel?" she asks with wide eyes.

Glancing at her, I smirk. "I own thousands of hotels, baby. This is one of my favorites, though."

She blinks at that and shakes her head.

"I had no idea. Is it technically owned by the Brethren or...?"

I shake my head. "This is my money. I had a sickening large inheritance when my father passed, and not a care in the world to spend it on anything for myself. So, instead, I invested."

"I know that I came from a privileged upbringing, so this will probably sound odd, but exactly how rich are you?"

A laugh escapes me as the elevator doors open and we make our way to our room.

"Rich, rich," I tease as we come to our suite.

I swipe the card over the reader and the door unlocks with a whir. Our bags are already up here, ready and waiting on the bed. I always wonder how the hotel staff manages to ensure your bags are in your room before you arrive.

Skyla's eyes trace over the clean interior of the room all the way over to the terrace. She practically jogs over to it, throwing the doors open as she steps outside.

The sky is dark grey, releasing lazy snowflakes as if waiting for Skyla. A megawatt smile spreads across her face as she lifts her arms out by her sides and begins spinning. I lean my shoulder against the wall as I watch her.

"I've missed the snow," she says with a laugh.

"You like it?" I ask.

"Love it. London doesn't get too much. It typically melts before you can even enjoy it."

"Well, New England gets absolutely buried in snow every year. You'll be sick of it before you know it."

She turns to me, white snowflakes beginning to stick to her loosely curled hair as she shakes her head.

"Not possible."

I smile at her, stepping out onto the terrace with her. She sticks her tongue out, catching a snowflake on it, and I do the same. Skyla giggles in delight when I'm successful, and it pulls a smile out of me just at the sound.

My phone begins buzzing in my pocket, and my smile vanishes in an instant. Skyla notices and cocks her head to the side as I silence it.

"So, what do you want to do?" she asks, clearly trying to distract me.

"Well, it's probably best if we don't leave the hotel. Boston is a big city, easy to be spotted and not realize it."

She frowns at that and nods. "I didn't think about that."

Frustration flares inside me. I hate that this is the best I can offer her. Hidden rendezvous, stolen touches. She deserves more, she deserves everything. At least Asher can give her more when they are together. Then again, maybe not. Christopher is already concerned with how close they are.

"C'mon, let's get some lunch. The Italian restaurant downstairs is great."

Skyla nods, stepping back into the room as I shut the doors behind us. I lead her out of the room and back downstairs where they take us to a private table in the back. As soon as we sit down, my phone begins buzzing again. I silence it, only for it to start up again and again.

Fucking hell. Not now. Not today.

Skyla frowns. "Who is it?"

I shake my head as I reach for her hand across the table.

"No one important."

She raises a questioning brow at that and clearly isn't going to let it go.

"It's Annie," I say.

"Williams?" she says.

I nod.

"Why is she calling you?"

My mouth parts to speak before my words die on my

tongue. Conveniently, our server comes over and takes our order before disappearing. When we're alone once again, she's right back to it.

"Ronan, why is Annie calling you?"

"Probably to discuss the engagement party," I say carefully.

"Engagement party?" Skyla echoes.

I grimace and nod.

"When?" she asks numbly.

"New Year's Eve. Christopher thought it would be a great time for a party," I say with a sneer.

Skyla's face remains impassive, but I don't miss the shimmering across those bright green eyes.

"So…uhm, so that's it?" she asks, her voice tightening as she speaks, cracking on that last word.

"I don't want to talk about it tonight, baby. Tonight, I just want it to be about you and me."

"So, tomorrow will be about you and Annie?" she throws out.

I frown at that, and she closes her eyes letting out a shaky breath.

"I'm sorry. I…I know you don't want this. I just…it's selfish of me to want to keep you all, huh?" she asks with a watery smile.

"No," I rush as I stand from my chair, coming to kneel beside her as I cup her face. "It's not selfish at all, baby. It's what I want, more than anything in the world. All I want is to be by your side. Our circumstances are…trying, but that doesn't mean we should give up, ever."

"What's there to fight, Ronan? We both know the outcome if you don't go through with it. As much as it would kill me to watch you marry someone else, it's better than losing you from this earth."

I press my lips against hers, pulling back only half an inch to speak.

"Don't give up on us, don't stop fighting, because I sure as hell won't. I'll fight for you with my dying breath, Skyla. Even if I have to marry her, I'll never love her. My heart will never belong to anyone but you."

"What will that even look like? Steph is right, huh? You'll be married to her, have a house, maybe a kid or two, and then what? Work late at the office?" she asks, using her fingers to create air quotes. "I'll be your mistress? Sure, we know there is more to it than just sex, but regardless, you'll be cheating on your wife with me?"

"So be it," I gruff. "I have no doubt she will do the same; it's more common in these arrangements than you can probably imagine. She means nothing to me, Skyla, absolutely nothing. I'll treat her with respect, of course, but that will be the extent of my care for her. She's not like Madi, she was never...kind, or good. She's a selfish brat who enjoys ruining others' lives for sport."

She frowns at that. "What do you mean?"

I shake my head. "The stories I could tell you about Annie Williams and her time and Gallows Hill would horrify you. You think Bridgette is bad? She's a saint in comparison."

Skyla's nose wrinkles at that. "Then why, out of all the women in the Brethren, did Christopher pick her for you?"

Even I don't know the answer to that. The Williams family has something my brother wants, desperately. I just don't have a fucking clue what it is.

"Can we table this for today? Please. I promise I'll tell you everything I'm able to another time but for now, can we not talk about any of the bullshit back in Salem? Can we just...be?"

She stares at me in concern for several seconds before slowly nodding. Remarkably, our food is already done and our server places it in front of us before stepping away. We eat in silence for a few moments before we begin talking about swimming, a safe topic for the both of us. I tell her about my Olympic trials, and she tells me about the competitions she was able to compete in before her father put a stop to it all.

I'm not surprised he did. The Brethren don't like distractions. The only reason my father allowed me to go as far as I did is because I was fucking spiraling from Madi's death, the weight of my responsibilities, and that he wanted to see as little of me as possible. For a daughter of the Brethren to have a hobby for herself? Something that could potentially be a *career*? That's a hard limit for them.

After eating, we decide to go for a tour through the hotel. I show her the cozy library, the state-of-the-art gym, and some of the conference spaces before we come across the ballroom.

As soon as we step inside, her mouth parts and her head turns up. Grand chandeliers eat up the cathedral high ceilings, pristine white pillars lining the room. It's a gorgeous room, the hotel's largest selling point. A lot of weddings, parties, and events take place here, and for good reason.

Skyla begins wandering through the room, admiring the gold accents every few feet before we wander up to the balcony level overlooking the ballroom. Her hands brace on the railing as she stares off across it.

"It's so beautiful," she says softly.

I come up behind her, resting my head on the top of hers as my hands wrap around her waist.

"You should see it all decorated, full of laughter and dancing."

A small smile touches her face.

"I'd love to."

"You and Asher could use it for your official wedding. If you want."

She turns to look at me, a slight dip in her features.

"We don't need an official wedding. We already have a marriage certificate. Signed, sealed, and delivered."

I shrug. "It matters to the Brethren. Though Asher let it slip that you two are already married, traditionally speaking, it's what's done."

She's quiet for a moment as she nods.

"Will you marry Annie here?"

I can't help but scoff as I shake my head.

"Fuck no. The wedding will probably be somewhere in Salem. I'd never take her here."

Skyla tilts her head to the side.

"How come?"

I unwind my hands from her waist and lift one to cup her cheek as I speak.

"Because now I've brought you here. Anyone else will pale in comparison. Every step you take, every inch of this world you touch instantly becomes imprinted with you. It wouldn't be fair to anyone to even attempt a competition with you, because they'll always come up short."

She lets out a sarcastic laugh and shakes her head, turning her face away from me, but I don't let her. My hold on her cheek tightens as I force her to face me once more. I don't speak but I can see the understanding in her eyes. I'm not trying to butter her up, I'm not whispering sweet nothings to inflate her ego. I mean it, all of it.

Skyla swallows softly as she wraps her arms around my neck, leaning into me. I close the remaining distance between the two of us, our lips pressing against each other as our bodies collide. There isn't more than a quarter inch of space between us at any given moment and it's fucking perfect.

One of my hands dives into the back of her hair, holding a tight grip on her, while the other goes to her throat, cupping it delicately as I deepen the kiss. She doesn't want it delicate today, though. I feel her teeth sink into my lower lip, tugging for a moment before she releases me and does it again and again. Our tongues tangle together in a lust induced haze that has us both scrambling for more.

Skyla drops to her knees, her hands making quick work of my belt before she's dragging my pants and boxers down to my ankles. She sucks my cock into her mouth and down her throat, forcing a guttural groan to rip through me.

"Fuck, baby. Just like that, such a good girl."

Those green eyes fly up, landing on me as she continues sucking me, her tongue wrapping around the tip of my cock before trailing down to the base. I feel her hand come up to cradle my balls, and it forces me to toss my head back on a moan.

My hips begin thrusting as I force myself deeper and deeper until she's choking and gagging on me. She pulls her head back to breathe for a moment, but that's all I allow her before I'm forcing my way back down her throat once more. Her eyes begin to water, and drool begins to drip down my cock. It's a sloppy blow job, and I love every goddamn second of it.

I feel my balls begin to tighten, but I need more of her before I'm finished. Forcing myself away from her, she releases my cock with an audible pop before I'm dragging her to her feet. She looks up at me in a daze, seeking direction, but I don't speak. Instead, I grab her leggings, yanking them down and over her shoes before tossing them to the other side of the room.

In the next moment, I grab her ass and lift her into the air, backing us up until her back is plastered against one of the pillars. Lining my cock up to her entrance, I waste no time in sinking myself into her. She squirms for a moment, trying to adjust to me, but I don't give her much time before I begin savagely thrusting into her. She whimpers and wiggles on me, but the pouty moans that begin pouring from her sweet lips tells me she's enjoying this just as much as I am.

"Fuck, Ronan," she moans.

"Excuse me? What's my name?"

"Daddy," she corrects, sending a satisfying thrum running through me as she does.

"That's right. That feel good, baby? Daddy making you feel good?"

"Mhmm," she mutters as I snap my hips, hitting her g-spot with my tip before I do it again and again.

"FUCK!" I grit between clenched teeth as I thrust again, each one more punishing than the last. "How are you still so goddamn tight? Like a fucking virgin every goddamn time."

"Daddy," she moans once more, grinding herself against me in a needy way that has me ready to cater to her every desire.

"What do you need, baby? Tell me. You need me to play with this pretty pussy? Want me to rub your clit?"

"Please," she whimpers.

My hand moves down, my thumb rubbing against her swollen clit as I begin rubbing quick, tight circles against it. She shudders against me in response, when the sound of the door echoes through the ballroom.

We both freeze, Skyla's wide eyes coming to me in panic as several sets of footsteps begin echoing as well.

"Goddamnit, I will never get over how gorgeous this room is," a redhead says loudly.

I see a manager with her, as well as three other women.

"Red," the blonde chides with a laugh. "It is perfect, though. I think people are going to love it."

"Where will the dance floor go exactly? We need as big as you're able to allow," the one with the purple hair interjects.

The manager smiles patiently as they begin discussing the

layout of the room. My eyes move back down to Skyla, making sure we are hidden as best as we can be behind this pillar. The best thing to do in a situation like this would be to pull out of her, get dressed, and try to sneak out of here. Honestly, though, that doesn't sound like the fun thing to do.

Slowly, I begin thrusting again. Skyla gives me a look like she thinks I'm insane, but she doesn't protest. I lower my mouth to her ear, speaking so softly I doubt she can hardly hear me.

"Don't make a fucking sound, do you hear me?"

She nods her head, and I smirk, pressing a quick kiss to her lips as I pick up my pace. My eyes keep moving from the group downstairs back to Skyla's. My fingers grip the flesh of her ass tighter, holding her closer to me to fuck her deeper. Her mouth drops open, and I quickly cover it with my hand to muffle whatever sound is about to escape her. Thankfully, it's fairly quiet, but that doesn't really matter when I watch the group walk just beneath us.

The brunette with long hair begins speaking, gesturing up to the level we are currently on.

"I think we are going for gothic, dark romance vibes. Some black drapery would really pull that look together up there."

"Oooo, yes! I love that," the blonde agrees.

"And the silks for the aerialist can go right here," another voice says.

My thrusts quicken but miraculously manage to stay virtually silent, and I feel Skyla's pussy throb around me. Her eyes are lust drunk, filled with equal parts fear and excitement. My little exhibitionist. I suppose I'm one, too, because I wouldn't be all that mad if they took a hard enough look up here and saw me buried in my girl like this. Obviously, it's safer for the both of us if that doesn't happen, but still, it's one hell of a rush.

My thumb begins rubbing her clit once more, and she's teetering on the edge. I toy with the idea of edging her, dragging it out just a little longer, but one more throb of her pussy forces an orgasm out of me that I didn't even know was within reach. I breathe through it, but I can't stop my cock from jerking and coming inside her. I quicken the pace on her clit as I fuck her through my own orgasm, pushing her to reach her own.

Her body shakes and jerks as she practically convulses on me, only a slight groan slipping past my hand. Everyone in the room stills, looking around curiously as I plaster my body against hers, hiding ourselves as ecstasy slams through me again and again.

Thankfully, they lose interest quickly as the redhead begins speaking again, all of them making their way out of the room.

"Okay, let's talk bartenders because if last year is anything to go off, our readers can throw it back."

All the women laugh their agreement as they step through the door. Once the sound of it shutting echoes through the room, I remove my hand from Skyla's mouth. We both take several labored breaths before we share a grin.

"Well," Skyla says. "That was fun."

Chapter Seventeen

Wesley

I'm so wrapped up in my work on my laptop that I don't hear anyone come in until Liam clears his throat. My eyes flash up to him, shutting my laptop at the same moment. He casts me a suspicious raise of his brow as he moves through the kitchen to grab a drink.

"What are you up to?" he asks.

"Just some work stuff."

"Uh huh, and is that work stuff for the military that you're supposedly out of, or work for my father?" Asher asks as he comes into the room as well.

"What do you mean?" I ask carefully.

Asher rolls his eyes as he leans against the counter from across from me.

"It means, you're sketchy, Wes, and I don't like sketchy in my home or around my wife."

"Or your boyfriend?" I challenge, nodding my head towards Liam.

Asher's jaw tenses, but he doesn't speak.

"Just admit that you're jealous, Ash. No shame in it. I'm definitely more experienced than you; it's understandable that you'd be worried I could sneak your bottom right out from under you...no pun intended," I goad.

Fire flashes in Asher's eyes as he reaches for Liam, hauling him to his side. He crushes his lips against Liam, keeping his eyes on me the entire time. I give him a bored glance as their tongues tangle together before Asher rips himself away. Liam blinks like he's in a daze before a satisfied grin spreads across his face.

"I like this kind of pissing match. Your turn, Wesley," Liam says as he makes an exaggerated kissing face.

Asher rolls his eyes and smacks the back of Liam's head as I laugh.

"Don't worry, kid. I'm not out to steal Liam, I've got Skyla."

"We've all got Skyla," Liam interjects.

I frown at that. I don't like the way he just said that. Apparently, neither does Asher if the look he shoots Liam is anything to go off. Liam thinks on his words for a second before his eyes fill with panic.

"Fuck, that's not what I meant. I love her; you guys know that. I just meant he wasn't special for having her...wait, fuck. That's not what I meant either! Shit...don't tell Sky, alright?" Liam grumbles as he runs his hands through his hair.

"Don't tell me what?" Skyla asks as the door sounds behind her, Ronan following in the room after her.

All three of us simultaneously light up at the sight of her, though Liam is the first to close the distance. He practically gallops over to her like a jackass before he's crushing his lips against hers. When he pulls away, he lifts her up into his arms, spinning her around until she's giggling, asking him to put her down.

"Missed you, babygirl!"

Demise

"It's only been a day," Skyla laughs.

"It was a day too long," Liam pouts.

She rolls her eyes as her gaze lands on Asher. He holds out his arms for her, and she moves to him quickly, allowing him to pull her in for a hug and a brief kiss before looking up at him.

"Hi," she smiles.

"Hey, princess. How was it?"

"Good," she says as her eyes land on me.

"Hey, little one," I smile softly.

"Hi, Wes. Have you guys been playing nice while we were gone?" she teases.

I grin at that. "Oh yeah, we are the best of friends now, isn't that right, Asher?"

He gives me a flat look as Ronan snorts and claps my shoulder.

"Oh, I'm sure."

I look up at him with a guilty smirk because he knows me way too fucking well.

"Where is Vincent?" Skyla asks, her eyes tracing over the room.

"You honestly think he's gonna willingly hang out with us when you're not here?" Liam laughs.

"I'm here, Siren," Vincent says as he steps into the room, placing a kiss against the side of her head before effectively stealing her from Asher's grasp.

"Where the fuck did you come from?" Asher grumbles.

"If you don't think I have a tracker on her at all times, then you're a fucking idiot."

"A tracker?" Ronan echoes.

"Yeah, a tracker?" Skyla says with raised brows.

Vincent nods. "When you were taken it, almost fucking killed me, Siren. Now, something like that will never happen again."

"Where exactly is this tracker?" she argues.

"It's best you don't know," he says as he presses another kiss to her forehead and faces the room.

We all give him puzzled looks before Liam is the one to speak up.

"So, are we all supposed to pretend that isn't some creepy ass shit?"

Ronan lets out a heavy sigh and shakes his head.

"I guess."

I watch Skyla closely and am intrigued to find her not looking up at Vincent with disgust or outrage as any normal person would. Instead, she's looking at him almost tenderly, like she understands him better than anyone else does. Probably because she does.

"I was thinking," Ronan says, grabbing the room's attention. "Christmas is in a few days, and I think we could all use a vacation."

"Vacation?" I ask.

He nods. "Skyla loves the snow, so I rented us a cabin up in New Hampshire through the holiday."

"Really?" she practically gasps.

Ronan smiles at her sweetly. The kind of smile I haven't seen him use in years.

"Of course, baby. Any objections?" he asks the room.

Asher scoffs. "Like any of us could say no when she's making those puppy dog eyes."

Liam and I chuckle and nod as Vincent wraps his arms around her tightly, nuzzling his head into her neck. I guess that settles it, we're going to New Hampshire.

Demise

The drive to New Hampshire takes longer than it should, mainly because we got stuck behind half a dozen people who clearly are not from around here. An inch of snow on the road, and they were driving like the road was going to suck them up whole.

Skyla invited Stephanie to join us but when she facetimed her, Stephanie was in the airport with a regretful look on her face. The call was brief. She just said that she was sorry to say goodbye like this and that she had to get back home. We all know there is more to it but none of us wanted to upset Skyla by prying, so we just focused on the drive, keeping ourselves busy.

When my GPS finally announces that we're here, a group cheer echoes out in the car. Liam and Asher are in the back, Vincent is in the middle row with Skyla, and Ronan is in the passenger seat beside me. The place is huge, a giant log cabin mansion placed in the middle of the woods. Town is at least a twenty minute drive in the other direction. It's completely isolated, perfect for all of us to take a breath and just exist.

The place already has over six inches of snow on the ground, and the forecast calls for a snowstorm tonight, so hopefully, this will be enough snow to keep Skyla happy. I guess I spoke too soon, or I guess thought too soon, because before I can even finish my sentence, Skyla is scrambling out of the car and diving into the snow. Vincent follows after her, as if the snow itself poses a threat to his 'siren.'

Her bare hands scoop a large amount of snow, compacting it into a ball before she tosses it at Vincent. The snow explodes against his chest, and he looks down at it in surprise before his eyes slowly lift to hers. That giddy smile on her face falls as the gravity of what she has just done sinks in for her.

Better run, little one.

She takes off running, and Vincent chases after her, scooping up handful after handful of snow. He misses the first throw but hits her in the back with the second.

"Hey!" Liam shouts as he scrambles out of the car. "That's my girlfriend!"

He's laughing like a lunatic as he scoops up a snowball of his own, hitting Vincent in the back of the head with it.

He turns around with murder in his eyes as he switches targets. Liam's teasing smile disappears as he mutters to himself.

"Oh shit."

In the same moment, Asher slips out of the car. At first, I think he's going to intercept Vincent, but instead, he takes off in the other direction towards Skyla.

"Hey! Ash! What the fuck?" Liam whines as he tries to dodge Vincent's snowballs.

"Sorry bro, gotta save the Princess," he says as he scoops Skyla up into his arms and begins running with her to better cover.

Ronan lets out a derisive huff before he looks at me.

"These kids wouldn't last five minutes in a real war," I smirk.

"Fuck no, they wouldn't. Should we show them how it's done?" Ronan asks.

I grin. "Thought you'd never ask."

We move together as a unit, moving carefully and quietly. It's easy to do, though. Vincent and Liam are pelting each other with aggressive snowballs, Asher and Skyla are furiously creating a stockpile of ammunition, which leaves Ronan and I to settle on top of the hill.

Without a word, we both begin creating a wall. We work quickly and effectively, and once our wall is well over three feet tall, we begin making snowballs. I'm on my tenth one before I look to see Ronan is on his twentieth. Shit.

"You keep loading me up; I'll nail them," I say as I grab the first snowball, aiming for Liam because, honestly, he's such an easy target.

His head whips to us, outrage on his face.

"What the fuck?"

I deliver another at the same time Vincent does before he directs his vicious gaze towards us.

"Shit, Griggs is coming for us. More ammo!" I call out as Ronan hands me two more.

I hear Skyla's squeals of delight and notice she's on her back in the snow, Asher covering her body with his as he dry fucks her into the ground.

"No fucking during a snowball fight!" I holler out.

Asher doesn't move his mouth from hers, just lifts his middle finger in the air as he begins peppering her neck with kisses.

"Fuck this, I'm on that team," Liam says as he takes off running towards them.

"Me too," Ronan says from beside me as he abandons his post and runs down the hill. Traitors, every last one of them.

Vincent and I hold each other in a stare off when we hear another one of Skyla's squeals echo in the woods. Then, we do the right thing and take off running for her. By the time we make it down to the bottom of the hill, Asher already has her pants off and his head between her thighs, Liam has her shirt lifted up while he is sucking on her right nipple, Ronan on her left. Vincent quickly claims her mouth, sinking to his knees in the snow and burying his cock in her mouth.

Looking over her, so completely full, so completely worshipped, I can't help but feel like the odd man out. I'm the one that joined this relationship dynamic late in the game. I'm the one that has spent the least amount of one-on-one time with her. Honestly, some days, I question if she even wants me or if she just felt obligated to include me.

That feeling only lasts for a moment or two before her eyes land on me, her arm lifting up towards me as she beckons me closer. I close the distance quickly, and when I'm beside her, I feel her hand reach for my belt. Undoing it quickly, I pull my cock out for her, and she begins stroking it softly. My head falls back as I moan my approval, hums and groans of pleasure sounding from all of the guys. Asher pulls his face away, sinking his cock into her pussy as he and Vincent find an equal rhythm while Ronan and Liam stroke their cocks. Goddamn, it's amazing that a group with this many guys, each of them has such pretty fucking cocks. Such a lucky little one.

Her hand is so fucking cold but so soft. I look down and see Ronan has slowed in his movements, his eyes firmly set on Skyla's hand wrapped around my cock. He seems to watch in fascination as she drags her hand up and down, twisting gently before doing it over and over again.

His eyes come to mine, a new level of heat in them that has my cock jerking in her hand. Ronan's eyes snap down to my cock, not missing the movement before he shakes his head and goes back to sucking on her perfect dusty pink nipple.

I'm not like Liam, hoping that my best friend will come around and fall in love with me. Deny it all they want, but that is exactly what is happening. I wouldn't be opposed to regularly hooking up with Ronan, though. He's fucking hot, has a nice cock, and it would give my little one a break. If we don't start

Demise

fucking with each other from time to time, she won't be walking for much longer. That's a guaranfuckingtee if the way Asher savagely fucks her is anything to go off.

At least he laid down his coat for her before he stripped her half naked. What a guy.

Liam's eyes are on Asher's, jealousy and lust mixing in his eyes. One look and you can tell he wishes he was fucking Skyla while also getting fucked by Asher at the same time. Very possible with desire and a healthy amount of lube.

I can tell by the look on Vincent and Asher's faces that they are close, and with the way that Liam is panting, he isn't far behind. Sure as shit, within seconds, Asher is coming, Vincent and Liam right along with them. I watch as ropes of Liam's cum cover her tits while Skyla drinks Vincent's release down and Asher slumps over on her.

Like a well oiled machine, despite me being a new addition, Asher, Vincent, and Liam move to the side, allowing Ronan to take her mouth and me to take her pussy. I lean forward, scooping up some of Liam's cum on my fingers before holding it up to Skyla.

"Taste him, little one."

She opens her mouth, and I let her suck on my fingers. She moans around them, the way she swirls her tongue around me has my cock raging hard. I can't help but thrust inside her in the next moment, her pussy absolutely soaked from Asher's cum. That makes it so much fucking hotter.

Skyla whimpers as I do before Ronan stuffs her mouth full. We find a smooth rhythm, working her and ourselves up to the edge. My legs are practically shaking with anticipation as I begin playing with her clit.

"Oh my god! Wes, yes! Right there," Skyla exclaims.

"You feel so good," I say through clenched teeth. "Thanks for getting her nice and soaked, Asher," I say with a smirk.

He snorts but doesn't speak as him and the others watch us with a close intensity. I watch as Ronan's grasp on her cheek tightens before his body stiffens, and he comes down her throat. In the same moment, Vincent leans over, slapping her clit so hard it rips a scream out of her. Just like that, though, she's coming hard around me. Her pussy grips me like a vice, and it's just what I need to follow right behind her.

My own moans are stolen from my chest, echoing into the otherwise silent woods as I fuck Asher's cum deeper, making more room for my own.

When our orgasms have passed, I pull out to look down at the mess we've made of her. Cum is literally leaking out of her pussy, so wet and fucking perfect. As soon as Ronan pulls away, I scoop her up into my arms and begin leading her to the door. Ronan stands, shoving his cock back into his pants before grabbing the door for us, entering the security code he was given while Liam, Asher, and Vincent grab the bags.

As soon as we step in, I gawk at the size of the place. It's a forested mansion. The second story overlooks the main living area, with an open concept and a huge wood burning fireplace marking the statement piece of the room.

"It's so beautiful," Skyla smiles as her eyes take in every detail.

Ronan comes over to stand beside me, pushing some of her hair out of her face.

"You like it, baby?"

"Love it," she grins as he presses his lips to hers in a sweet kiss.

The guys come in with their arms full of bags, shoving each other through the narrow doorway before spilling inside.

"Holy fuck! Thanks, Daddy Warbucks," Liam shouts to Ronan.

Ronan scoffs and shakes his head as Vincent dumps the

Demise

bags on the floor and practically rips Skyla from my arms, whispering something into her ear as he begins carrying her up the stairs.

"What the fuck?" I call out to him. "Where is he taking her?" I ask the room.

"Probably to shower or something. Vincent likes to baby her," Asher says.

"Don't we all?" Ronan challenges.

Asher shrugs his agreement as we all get settled into our temporary holiday home.

Chapter Eighteen

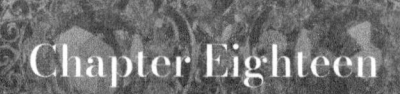

Skyla

Vincent carries me carefully up the stairs and across the open concept hallway of the cabin, seemingly on a mission.

"Where are we going?" I ask.

"To clean you up and warm you up. It was fucking stupid of Putnam to strip you down in the goddamn snow," he gnashes.

"Hey," I say gently, resting a hand against his thrumming heartbeat. "We agreed the rivalry thing was over, right? We are turning over a new leaf?"

Vincent narrows his eyes at me as he pushes through a bedroom door.

"I never agreed to like the guy; I just want him dead a little less."

I do my best to hold back my smirk. It's a start.

The room is pretty bare, but it is huge. Two nightstands, two matching dressers, and a four poster king-sized bed takes up the space. Vincent keeps moving, walking us into what looks like the ensuite.

"How do you know where everything is? You just got here," I say as he sets me down on my feet.

He doesn't look at me as he turns on the shower while he speaks.

"If you think I'm letting anyone take you anywhere without knowing every detail of the layout, entry points, escape routes and nearest resources, then I'm afraid you haven't been paying attention, Siren."

I can't help but smirk at that, stepping up behind him and wrapping my arms around his waist. His movements freeze before he sinks into my touch and lets out a heavy exhale that I'm sure he's been holding for longer than he'd ever let on.

"Vincent Griggs," I say as I smile against his back. My hands trail up, resting just over his heart as I continue. "Forever my protector."

His hand covers my own, and he squeezes it gently.

"In this life and the next," he promises, his words hitting me square in the chest.

He's so passionate, so devoted. He's completely off his rocker crazy, but I think that's one of the things I love about him most.

I let out a small sigh of contentment and press a kiss to the back of his shirt before he turns to face me. His hands come to the hem of my shirt before pulling it all the way off me. My shoes and pants are the next to go. He takes such care with me, every touch, every move. It's so thought out, so methodical. Like he's doing his best to be as gentle as he can. Like he doesn't know how to be gentle, but he tries for me.

He pulls off his own clothes before stepping into the shower, dragging me in with him. The water pours down his tattoos, creating an almost glassy like display of them. God, I'll never get over how gorgeous they are.

Vincent reaches for the shampoo bottle on the side of the

shower, squirting a large amount into his hand before he forces me to turn away from the spray. I do as he directs before his fingers dive into my hair, massaging my scalp. A satisfied groan leaves my mouth as his fingers work their magic. I don't know how long I stand there for, limp and pliable, as he kneads every inch of my head, neck, and shoulders.

Finally, he finishes, pulling the shower head off the wall and bringing it over to rinse the soap out. Somehow, this feels even better than the rubbing part. Once my hair is rinsed, he lathers it with conditioner before grabbing the body wash. He hangs the shower head back up before covering both his hands with the soap and running them up down my body. Vincent Griggs is nothing if not extremely thorough.

As his hands move and glide against my skin, I can't help but sink further and further into his touch. The gesture isn't sexual or suggestive. He isn't doing this in hopes I'll get him off, I don't even think he's trying to get me off. This is care in its most basic form. A human taking care of another in the most selfless and simplest of ways, and I love him so fucking much for it.

"I love you," I say softly as he washes between my thighs.

He's crouched down in front of me, his eyes coming to my own as his hands keep working.

"I love you, Siren, eternally."

I smile at that as he stands, wrapping my arms around him and holding him tight to me as the warm water pours over us both.

Demise

After our shower, Ronan was nice enough to bring up Vincent and my bags. We both got changed into some comfy clothes and made our way into the kitchen to find Wesley rifling through the cabinets, typical.

"Find anything good?" I tease.

Wesley looks over his shoulder at me and shakes his head.

"Nothing. I get that it's a rental property, but c'mon. Not even crackers?"

Vincent lets out a derisive snort but doesn't say anything as he begins doing something on his phone. Wesley leans over the giant kitchen island, resting his elbows against the counter as he smiles at me.

"Any chance you want to come to town with me? Stock up for the week?"

"Sure," I smile as my eyes roam around the house. "We should get some Christmas decorations too! I'd love to find a tree," I say as I look at the perfect empty space beside the fire.

"Fuck yes!" Liam cheers as Asher groans.

"Skyla, you haven't had the pleasure of seeing Liam during Christmas time. May I introduce to you, Father Christmas."

"Fuck off," Liam laughs. "Who doesn't want to get into the holiday spirit? Caroling and Christmas baking, lights, movies. It's magic!"

"Don't forget about Santa," Ronan says dryly.

"Well, how could I forget the fat guy?" Liam laughs.

I can't help but chuckle and shake my head at him as he pulls out his phone and music begins playing. "Rockin' Around, The Christmas Tree" begins blaring as Liam reaches for me, pulling me into a swing dance. He spins me around the room, dipping and twirling me as the others watch us in amusement.

Liam and I laugh before he dips me, pressing his lips to mine before pulling away.

"We should probably stock up on mistletoe, just to be safe."

I grin at him and nod before he pulls me back to my feet.

"Alright!" Liam exclaims. "Food, decorations, and a tree!"

"There are plenty of trees outside," Vincent drawls as he pockets his phone.

"Yeah, Mr. Lumberjack? You gonna go cut one down?" Liam asks.

Vincent shrugs. "I'm sure they have a chainsaw in the garage. We need some firewood anyways."

"Ooo, Skyla, look at this tough and rugged man you bagged. Nice," Liam smiles as he holds out his fist for a bump.

I raise a brow at him as I shake my head.

"Liam...no."

He pouts while everyone else laughs, well, everyone but Vincent, of course.

"I'll help with the firewood," Ronan volunteers.

Vincent nods before all eyes fall on Asher. He looks at us before sighing.

"Fine, I guess I'll help with the tree and shit too."

"If I'm Father Christmas, that would make Asher the Grinch," Liam whisper-yells across the room.

Asher flips him off in response before he digs into his wallet and hands me a black card. I furrow my brows before grabbing it. The name Skyla Putnam is printed across the front. I look up at him and smirk.

"Just couldn't help yourself?" I tease.

"You're my wife; it's my responsibility to take care of you."

"Yeah?" I ask.

He nods as he closes the distance between us. His thumb and forefinger grip my chin, forcing my face to meet his as he places a quick peck against my lips.

"And I like it."

"What a coincidence, I like spending your money, too!"

Demise

Liam says. "Any chance you got a black card in that wallet for me? I'll put out, I swear."

"No one in this room doubts that for a second," Ronan deadpans.

Liam gives him a wicked grin as Wesley claps his hands together.

"Alright, you guys go fuck around in the woods, we'll head to the store."

"Ready...BREAK!" Liam cheers, this time only pulling a chuckle out of me.

I swear his jokes are getting worse by the day.

We hit three different shops just for all the Christmas decorations Liam wanted. We went to the grocery store first and got practically every item off the snack aisle, all Wesley's fault on that one. Then we got enough supplies for breakfast, lunch and dinner while we're here since you can't exactly order delivery where the house is. Don't know who will be cooking them, though. Let's be honest, probably Ronan.

After that, the first store we went to didn't have the right lights Liam wanted. Then the next didn't have enough variety of wreaths for the inside of the house. Finally, the last was able to give us, or rather him, everything he was searching for. I love Christmas time, or at least I thought I did. Compared to Liam, though? I'm Mrs. Grinch, right alongside Asher.

We're heading back to the car, Liam quite literally skipping in front of us as he hums "All I Want For Christmas Is You." To be fair, the song is like an earworm, and for some reason, being played on loop in every single department store. I'm not sure if it's just an American thing because, while of course I've heard the song, I haven't heard it fourteen times in three hours before.

When we get back into the car, Wesley begins driving when Liam sighs dramatically.

"Shit! We forgot presents. You can't have Christmas without presents."

"Says who?" I ask.

"Says...everyone," he counters like it's common knowledge.

I shake my head and smile as I look out the window. The snow covered grass is so pure, so untouched. It's like a snow globe moment. A picturesque perfect moment frozen in time.

Wesley reaches over the center console and intertwines his fingers with my own. That grabs my attention as I look to him and smile. He lifts my hand and places a kiss to the back of it as he takes the next turn.

"I don't think materialistic presents are what makes Christmas, Christmas, Liam," I say as I turn to look at him.

Wesley takes another turn, sending a four-foot-tall snowman Liam insisted on getting slamming into him. He shoves it off himself quickly as he speaks.

"You're right, sexual favors should do just fine. What do you say we all swap coupons?"

"Like 'good for one blowjob?'" Wesley teases.

"Exactly! See, Wes is on board. I'll even make an extra one just for you." Liam flirts with an exaggerated wink.

Wesley raises his brows in intrigue as I interject.

"I don't know, I think he'd rather have Ronan's coupon."

Liam's mouth parts in surprise as Wesley fights back a smile and shrugs.

"No fucking way. You and Ronan? Since when?"

"It's not like that," Wesley deflects.

"Yeah, they don't have feelings for each other. They just like getting each other off," I say with a waggle of my brows.

"Fuck, that's hot. Can I come next time? I promise I'll just watch from the corner!" Liam says as he lifts his hand in a scouts honor gesture.

Demise

Wesley chuckles at that as he looks at Liam in the rearview mirror.

"I always say the more the merrier, but good luck getting Ronan on the same page."

"Fucking Putnam men, am I right?" Liam agrees with a clap on Wesley's shoulder.

I can't help but snort because, oh my fucking God, there is no way they are bonding over the difficulty to get fucked by their best friends. How is this my life? Honestly, don't answer that because it's too good. I don't want to question it.

Chapter Nineteen

Asher

After Ronan and I chopped over two dozen logs and stacked them in the house, we went in search of Vincent. He was gone for over an hour and a half, and we found him deep in the woods, hacking away at a monster of a tree. I asked him how the fuck he thought that was going to fit in the cabin, but he said he'd make it work. Said that Skyla would want the biggest one we could get. Whatever.

It took all three of us just to get the fucking thing inside, and when we did, he came to the acceptance that we needed to hack off over four feet of the trunk just so it would stand up inside. We were able to find an old tree stand in the garage, and while it isn't the sturdiest thing, it works.

Several hours after we finished, Skyla, Liam, and Wesley finally showed up. I was starting to think we'd need to go find them, which would have been fucking hard since we all took one car to get up here.

When they pulled up, though, it all made sense. Liam practically bounced out of the car, and when the back door was opened up, all hell broke loose. Ornaments, lights, and more

Demise

fake pine décor than we knew what to do with came spilling out; thankfully, nothing was made of glass.

One look at the haul they bought, not even counting the groceries, and I knew Liam had found a way to put a sizable dent in Skyla's limitless credit card. Fucker.

It took us almost the rest of the night to unload everything, get it put away, or hung up and make dinner. And by make dinner, I mean we opted for a couple of frozen pizzas that they picked up. After we ate, we all sat down to watch a movie, though everyone didn't last long.

Ronan was the first to go to bed, followed by Wesley. Vincent tried to act like he wasn't tired, but by the second *Santa Clause* movie, his eyes were staying closed for longer than they were open before they stopped opening in general.

Now it's just Liam, Skyla and I. Liam is sitting in the middle, one hand on Skyla's knee and the other on mine. When he first put it there, I felt almost everyone's eyes on me, but I just ignored them. I like Liam's hand on my knee, it's not a fucking crime.

Slowly, I feel Liam's hand begin to raise, moving higher and higher up both Skyla and my leg as he draws casual patterns against us. I lift my brow in question at him, but he innocently pretends to be watching the movie. Skyla is giving him a mirroring look before she looks at me and grins.

I can't help but smile back at her before Liam reaches the apex of her thighs, seconds before he reaches mine. I'm not ashamed to admit that I'm fucking hard. I've been hard since Skyla came out in her yoga sleep shorts and tank top, I stayed hard when Liam started touching me, pressing his body into my side, and I'm raging fucking hard now that his fingertips are caressing the outside of my cock.

"You ready to go to bed?" I ask Liam and Skyla.

Liam looks at me and pouts like a goddamn child, I swear.

"I'm not tired."

I lean into him, my eyes level with his as our noses brush.

"That wasn't the question."

Heat fills his green eyes as he practically springs to his feet, yanking Skyla to hers and tossing her over his shoulder as he runs through the house. For some fucking reason, I run too. Chasing after her, after him, after...them.

Mine, all fucking mine.

I climb the stairs easily and I just barely see Liam dart into one of the rooms down the hall. The door is left open, and when I get inside, I slam it closed before locking it. Skyla is already laying on the bed and Liam is sitting on the edge next to her when I close the distance between us.

I grab Liam by the throat, squeezing tightly as I bring my face to his.

"You've been a goddamn tease tonight, you both have," I say as I shoot a look over to her.

"Me? What did I do?"

"You're too fucking beautiful, too sexy. You leave me no choice."

"I like where these no choices are leading," Liam smirks.

I shove him away, releasing my hold on him as I reach over and grab Skyla's shorts, yanking them off her body before forcefully parting her legs.

Her cunt is glistening and pretty and pink for us, my mouth waters just looking at her. I look to Liam.

"Get over there and eat my wife's cunt."

Skyla's mouth drops at that as Liam practically scrambles across the bed. He dives face first between her thighs, and I spread them wider for him, allowing him to fucking suffocate on her. Skyla moans as Liam's tongue runs through her before he circles it around her clit. I grab a fistful of her hair and lower my face to hers as I speak.

"That feel good, princess? You like having your boyfriend eat your cunt while your husband watches?"

"Yes," she pants. "But I'd like it better if my husband ate my cunt *with* my boyfriend."

My eyebrows shoot up in surprise as I look down to see Liam nodding his head, his mouth currently latched onto Skyla's clit, ripping another moan from her.

Slowly, I grab the back of my shirt, pulling it up and over my head before I toss it to the side. I push down my pants next, only leaving on my boxers as I climb onto the bed. Liam scoots to the side, allowing enough room for me to join him. While he's focused on her clit, I go a little lower. My tongue circles her asshole before I drag it through her wet cunt, tongue fucking her before I start the movement all over again.

"Oh fuck! Shit, more," she begs.

"You hear that? She wants more," I smirk to Liam.

He releases her clit, a wicked grin on his face as he nods. Together, we begin savagely eating her. You know that clip of that popular comedy actor savagely eating the watermelon and then walking away? Yeah, like that. Except neither of us plan on walking away.

In the haste of it all, Liam's tongue brushes against mine, and the next time his tongue flicks down, I'm the one to run mine over his. Sloppy kisses are exchanged in between licking Skyla's pussy, and I can tell the minute she notices because her legs begin to squirm, forcing Liam and I closer.

"Oh my god! Yes! Lick my pussy together, kiss, touch. FUCK! You both are so fucking hot," she moans.

One more brush of our tongues together over her clit and she shatters apart. We lick and suck her through it, but when her body stops shaking, I need more. My mouth presses to Liam, his tongue covered in Skyla's cum. As if the taste of him couldn't get any better.

Our hands are everywhere, his neck, my chest, his arms, my cock. Fucking feral and desperate for each other and our beautiful girl. Tearing myself away from Liam, I sit up as I shove his face back towards her.

"Again," I demand.

"Oh, I don't know if I can come again this soon. I—"

Skyla's protests are cut off as Liam begins eating her out once more while I slip behind him. My hands move to his basketball shorts, pulling them down and taking note that, yet again, he isn't wearing any boxers. I'm not sure he even owns any, honestly. He arches his back, his ass a perfect heart shape. I swear to God, the only person that might have a better ass than him is Skyla, and that's a fucking compliment because hers stops traffic, literally. I've seen someone get rear-ended while she crossed the street.

My hand runs over the side of his ass, squeezing tightly before I give it a hard slap. He jerks at the move but moans into Skyla's pussy which causes her to whimper. So, naturally, I do it again and again, pulling moan after groan out of each of them.

I pause for a moment, moving to the other side of the room where Liam's bag is. I begin rifling through it until I find what I'm looking for. Bottle in hand, I climb back onto the bed, covering my finger with lube before I circle his asshole.

Liam moans again, louder this time, as I slowly start pushing inside the tight muscle. He throbs around my finger, his ass practically thrusting onto me. So, I add another.

"Fuck," he grumbles against Skyla's pussy lips.

"That feel good?" I ask as I leisurely work my fingers in and out of him.

He nods incoherently as I continue. I can tell when he gets fully adjusted to the intrusion because his hips are thrusting aggressively, practically begging me for more.

Demise

"Please, Ash. Please. More," he murmurs against Skyla.

"Get our girl off first," I say.

He nods his agreement. His fingers coming to play with her as he begins sucking on her clit while I finger fuck him. Skyla finds her second orgasm of the night, shattering apart on Liam's finger as I curl mine up to massage his prostate.

"Oh my god," Liam grits through clenched teeth as Skyla's whimpers soften.

I lean forward, still keeping my fingers buried in him as my other hand comes to wrap around his throat. I whisper against his ear, my eyes on Skyla as I speak.

"You want more, Liam? Want me to take this tight little ass? To fuck it? To make you completely mine?"

"It's all I want," he practically begs.

"That okay with you, princess?"

Skyla nods as she attempts to rub her thighs together.

"Please, for the love of god, fuck him."

I let out a short chuckle at that as I lean back, releasing Liam's throat and pulling my fingers out.

"Fuck my wife, Liam. I want you inside her while I'm inside you."

Liam nods, lining his cock up to Skyla before sinking inside her. They both let out pleasured groans as I cover my cock with lube. I fucking love anal, I usually prefer it, honestly. So, this shouldn't be any different. Why does it feel different, though? Warring feelings rage inside me. Dark whispers of how wrong this is, how bad it is. All of the horrible things my father has spoken over the years about queer people ring in my head.

Blowing out a heavy breath, I decide that I don't care. Fuck the labels, fuck the stigmas, and absolutely fuck the Brethren. I'm taking what I want, what we all want and I'm not going to feel shame for it for one goddamn second.

Lining the head of my cock up to Liam's ass, anticipation

thrums in my veins as I slowly sink inside him. Once I'm fully seated, ecstasy like I've never known fills me. Relief and pleasure mix together in an intoxicating cocktail that is so satisfying, so addictive, I'm ready to OD on it and die the luckiest fucking bastard that ever walked this Earth.

"Oh god," Liam whimpers.

"Are you okay?" Skyla asks.

"S-so good. S-so fucking good," he stutters. "Being buried inside of you while full of Ash it's...it's..."

"Heaven," I grit between clenched teeth. "It's fucking heaven."

Liam nods, and Skyla moans when Liam's thrusts pick up. I set the pace. My thrusts that started off soft and gentle quickly give way to rapid savagery. With each one, I can't tell whose moan is whose, whose tremble is whose. It's as if, in this moment, we have all blended together into one ball of pure pleasure. It's a feeling I want to milk for hours upon hours, getting lost in these two.

"You like getting fucked, Liam?" Skyla asks.

"Fuck yes, I do," he groans.

"How does it feel for you, Ash? You like topping him?" she says, her pretty eyes on me.

"Fuck. Yes," I say, punctuating each word with a thrust that has Liam moaning like a whore.

My whore.

"I wanna try," she whimpers as Liam fucks her hard.

"You want to fuck him, princess?"

She nods as Liam lets out another moan.

"I'd fucking love that, babygirl. I want you to peg me. You peg me while I suck off Asher. Fuckkkk," Liam whimpers.

My cock throbs at the idea.

Or while Liam fucks me.

"Fuck! I'm sorry guys, it's too good. It's too much. I gotta cum," Liam blabbers.

I thrust deeper than ever before in him, plastering my chest to his back as I growl into his ear.

"You will not," I snap. "You're gonna make Sky come once more, and then I'm gonna fill your asshole while you fill her cunt, got it?"

"I'll try," Liam grits.

My hand smacks the side of his ass, sending him jerking into Skyla as he lets out another pleasured groan.

"You'll *do*. Fuck her, Liam. Fuck her hard and raw."

His thrusts increase in speed, though the rhythm is off, it doesn't seem to matter. I watch as Skyla's mouth opens, her eyes squinting shut as she begins to tremble.

"Oh my god. T-too much. It's too good. I'm gonna...gonna... gonna—"

Her screams echo through the room, her body shaking and convulsing as Liam follows right behind her.

"There you go," I praise him. "That's a good boy. That's my good boy. You're doing so good fucking my wife while you take me. You want me to fill this ass up, baby?"

"Yes," he moans as he rides out his release.

"Kiss me," I demand.

He tries to twist himself to face me, and I meet him the rest of the way, our lips crushing together and becoming my undoing. My cock throbs inside his tight ass, my cum flooding him as my orgasm crashes into me like a goddamn freight train. I fuck him deeper and harder, trying to make every second last before we all collapse into a pile together.

All I can hear is our heavy breathing and the thundering of my pulse. Our skin is sticky with sweat, the smell of sex heavy in the air, and I've never felt more satisfied in my entire fucking life.

Chapter Twenty

Vincent

This morning, I woke up on the couch. I don't remember falling asleep; I try not to often, but every once in a while, my body has no choice, and I shut down. It's a dangerous habit that is going to get me fucking killed one day.

When I woke up to the empty room and Skyla wasn't there, I panicked. I began searching each room until I found her tangled in bed, fast asleep with Liam and Asher. My heart rate steadied a bit, but I had to get out of there because I don't think I'll ever get used to seeing my woman with other men, even if it's them. I tolerate it for her, but I'll never like it.

I spent the remaining hours of the early morning catching up on work. I have two tasks that are urgent. I'll need to head out as soon as we are back in Salem. It was difficult enough coming up with a reason that these targets wouldn't be taken care of immediately; having my appendix taken out seemed to do the trick, though. I scroll through my private email server, pulling up the forged hospital records and notes before sending my approval. They'll be uploaded into the Mass Gen hospital

Demise

records, and as far as anyone who is willing to dig will know, I've been there this whole time.

As soon as I hear movement in the house, I'm on my feet in hopes of finding my siren. When I walk across the walkway, I look down to see Skyla in the kitchen stirring something in a bowl. A smile almost touches my face as I look at her before two thick arms wrap around her waist and haul her into a chest.

Ronan.

Makes sense, he's basically our resident cook, same with Wesley on occasion. Ronan also has no problem staking his claim with Skyla at any moment, anywhere. I don't doubt he scooped her right out of bed from Asher and Liam and carried her down here before she was even fully awake. She is only wearing an oversized dress shirt that hits her mid-thigh. Probably his as well.

I'm not sure why he assumes he has some superior claim over her. Is it because he technically had her first? Sure, maybe he did, but I saw her first. I was the first person besides her father and his men to see her, first person to watch her set foot on this campus. If anyone has a claim, it's me, and rightfully so.

When I step into the kitchen, her eyes come to mine, practically sparkling in the early morning sun.

"Good morning," she cheers happily.

The ghost of a smile touches my lips as I nod my head, closing the distance between us as I press a kiss to her temple.

"Good morning, siren," I murmur against her skin.

She leans into my touch, forcing my inky black heart to beat a little harder than usual. Swear to God, without her, I know it would stop beating right on the spot. I honestly don't know how it worked all these years without her.

"We're making pancakes, eggs and bacon," she says. "Are you hungry?"

I shrug my shoulders as I take the kitchen island seat closest to her, reaching my hand out to hold her hip so that I can maintain some point of contact at all times. The heat of her body grounds me, the feel of her soft curves in my hand calms me. It's a peace I'll never tire of, never stop treasuring.

One by one, the rest of the guys start filing in. Sleepy, Happy, and Grumpy. I'm not sure what that makes Ronan and me. Skyla could definitely be Snow White but with golden hair. There were seven dwarfs in that fairytale, and let me tell you, five is more than enough.

Sleepy takes a step towards Skyla, wrapping his arms around her waist as he buries his head into the crook of her neck.

"Come back to bed," Liam whines.

She smiles and shakes her head.

"It's ten in the morning."

"And we went to bed at three. Come back to bed," he tries to reason.

She gives him a smile as Grumpy leans in, placing a quick kiss to both of their lips before he goes and takes a seat on the couch. He's gotten more affectionate with Liam, at least in front of the rest of us lately. Based on the position I found them last night, something tells me they are a lot more affectionate behind closed doors. Good. Maybe now Liam will stop bitching and whining about Asher topping him.

To round out the crew, Happy strides up to Skyla, all smiles with a freshly showered look and a new set of clothes for the day.

"Good morning, little one," he says as he steals a kiss as well.

I force my eyes away, my fist clenching on my thigh so I don't do something like hit the son of a bitch. Ronan and Liam, I had to tolerate. She was already dating them before she even considered me.

Then Asher was her fiancé turned husband, hard to kick him out of the picture, though don't think I didn't try. This motherfucker though...I don't like him. I know I don't have any good reason to, but something just feels...off. I can't explain it, but you bet your ass I've been spending any amount of free time I have to dig into him. If he's hiding something, I'll find out what it is, and soon.

"Good morning." She smiles like the blissful angel she is. "What does everyone want to do today?"

I shrug, as does Asher and Ronan.

"Whatever you want," Wesley says. "This is your trip."

She frowns at that. "No, it isn't, it's all of ours, right? It's our Christmas, our vacation."

"He's got a point, babygirl. If this was my vacation, we'd all be in Cancun at a nude beach sipping mai tais under the sun," Liam answers.

I scoff at that and shake my head while Skyla laughs.

"Okay, that is a vivid picture you just painted."

"Yeah?" Liam smirks. "All of your men naked around you, gorgeously tan in a tropical location?"

She wrinkles her nose up. "I was thinking more like the whole nude beach part. Hundreds of people way past their prime who don't give a shit what anyone thinks anymore, naked with sand everywhere."

Liam's face screws up at that as he crosses his arms.

"Well, when you put it like that, it doesn't sound nearly as hot."

"That's because it isn't," Asher drawls out lazily while scrolling on his phone.

Liam leans into him, whispering something in his ear that forces him to put the phone down and give him a heated gaze. I turn back to Skyla to see her watching them carefully as Wesley speaks again.

"What about snowboarding? Or skiing? Have you ever done either?"

She looks to him, shaking her head.

"But I've always wanted to learn."

Wesley nods. "Skiing it is."

"None of us brought any snow clothes that heavy duty, though," Liam interjects.

Ronan lifts an eyebrow to him.

"You all knew we were going to a snowy cabin in New Hampshire in the dead of winter, and no one thought to bring snow gear?"

Everyone except Wesley shakes their head as Ronan sighs.

"I did," Wesley shrugs.

"Okay, Mr. Boy Scout. We know you did. It's no wonder you had three bags for yourself alone. Always prepared."

Wesley nods his agreement. "Always. I'm sure the place will have some things for sale, and Skyla has that new fancy black card."

"Fuck you," Asher snaps. "That's for her to use, not you fuckers."

"Aw, what about me?" Liam teases. "I'll be such a good boy for youuuu."

Asher's eyes narrow as he smacks Liam's ass, hard. Liam winces, causing Asher to smirk.

"Sure, if you're a good boy, but no one else."

"If I suck your cock, can I get free shit too?" Wesley smirks, causing Ronan to sigh, Skyla to giggle, and Asher to roll his eyes and flip him off.

Great group dynamic we've got going on here.

"Alright, shitheads. Eat up and get ready. We'll take off in two hours," Ronan says as he turns off the burners on the stove, makes two plates, and drags Skyla into his lap at the dining room table.

He stabs a piece of pancake drowned in syrup, her favorite, before holding it up to her. She takes a bite of it before happily chewing, trading kisses in between bites for each of them. I roll my eyes as I dish up my own plate, scarfing down the food before deciding to go take a shower.

Once I got out of the shower, everyone else was just finishing their food. Wesley was doing the dishes while Liam, Asher, and Skyla took a shower. Hopefully, separately, or there is no way in fuck we will be getting out of here in two hours.

I pack my essentials, zipping up a small backpack as Wesley drops his bag onto the counter, filling it with protein bars, chips, bread, and God knows what else.

I lift a brow at him as he looks at me.

"What?"

"We're going snowboarding, not backpacking through Europe for a week. Why do you need so much food?"

Wesley shrugs as he zips up the bag.

"When you've gone six days without a scrap of food in the middle of the ocean, tell me you won't always be prepared in the future. A hunger like that...makes a man do some crazy fucking things."

Why the fuck would he be in the middle of the ocean with no food? He's a Navy Seal. Shouldn't he have a team, be on a ship or some shit? Shaking my head, I leave him to his over-the-top prepping as Liam, Asher, and Skyla come downstairs. Skyla is wearing a pair of black ripped leggings, a sweatshirt, and a pair of snow boots. I frown as I look at her.

"Where is your snow coat, siren?"

She shrugs. "I guess I didn't pack it. No big deal, I can get one from the ski lodge, right?"

Shaking my head, I shrug off my coat, slipping it through her arms before zipping it up to her neck. It's four sizes too big for her, and you can hardly even see her hands out the bottom of the cuffs, but she looks fucking adorable, and most importantly, she's warm.

"What about you?" she asks.

"What about me?"

"You need it," Skyla counters.

"Not as much as you do. Wear it until we get to the lodge, I'm fine."

She opens her mouth to argue before nodding her head, lifting up onto her toes, and pressing a kiss to my lips that I take the opportunity to deepen.

"Aw, no fair. You can have my coat if you kiss me like that," I hear Liam complain. followed by a thud and an 'Ow.'

We leave a few minutes later, and the drive takes less than thirty minutes to get to the ski resort. It's absolutely packed, and my eyes scan our surroundings a thousand times over, always watching, always waiting. I notice Wesley doing the same, along with Ronan. All of us on high alert while the two stooges and my siren laugh and push their way inside the lodge.

We are all able to get snow gear and rent boards. Skyla looked hesitant and honestly, I wish she would have gone with the skis; they are safer, especially when learning, but she insisted on getting a board. She also insisted on giving me my coat back, which I was less than thrilled about. Then again, it smells like her now, her scent practically encapsulating me, so I suppose I can live with it.

By the time we are all checked out, it's well into the late afternoon. We'll probably only be able to hit a few runs before the sun goes down, but it's what Skyla wants to do, so here we are. We grab our boards and find a more secluded area that we can give Skyla lessons. That turns to shit real quick when Ronan, Wesley, and Asher are all trying to teach her different things at once. She looks overwhelmed and frazzled as hell. I wait for her to need me, to ask for my help. When Ronan and Asher start arguing, Wesley playing peacekeeper, she looks over to me.

Request received.

"That's enough," I boom. "She's got the hang of it. We'll keep her safe, let's go."

I push past them, wrapping my arm around her as I lead her towards the ski lift. When we come up to the bench, she scoots to the very left, I take the middle, and Liam attempts to take the right. I say attempt because as soon as he takes a seat beside me, I shove him off. He face plants into the snow as the chair begins moving up the hill.

"Ow! Hey! Griggs! What the fuck!" he shouts from behind us.

A short chuckle shakes my chest, and Skyla smacks my arm.

"Why did you do that?"

I turn to face her, only her pouty mouth visible behind her new snow goggles.

"Because I don't get nearly enough siren time, so I'm making it."

Her pinched expression softens as her arm pushes into mine.

"You're so needy, God," she drawls sarcastically, a smirk spreading across her face.

Leaning forward, I press my lips to hers, our tongues tangling together as we are carried up the mountain. We don't stop until we hear the chair attendant shout at us. Tearing myself from her mouth is literally painful, but somehow, I manage, getting off the chair first as I help her.

We move to the top of the mountain and wait for the rest of them. Asher, Ronan and Wesley are on the chair right behind us, and three chairs behind them is Liam by himself. Before he can even get to us, I can hear him cuss me out, and it's actually quite amusing.

"Motherfucker! Why didn't you let me ride with you guys," Liam snaps.

"Because I don't like you," I say flatly before I turn to Skyla. "Alright, are you good? Remember everything we taught you?"

She looks a little hesitant as she stares down at the hill, but she nods, nonetheless.

"I think so. How do I stop again?"

We all share concerned looks before she shakes her head.

"Never mind, it's fine. Let's just go."

"No, we won't go until you're—"

I don't get to finish my sentence before she pushes off, down the mountain she goes.

Shit.

I follow after her, bobbing and weaving through people in an attempt to catch up to her. She almost loses her balance, crouching down a little to correct herself, which saves the balance but picks up her speed. She's catching up to a person in front of her, and instead of trying to slow down, she swerves right. Hard right.

I do my best to mimic her path, but before I can reach her, she shoots off into the trees. I hear one of the guys shout from behind us, but I don't have the time or care to focus on who. Doing my best to keep my eyes on her, I fly off into the tree line, leaning in and out of the path, doing my best to avoid any trees or uprooted branches.

She's screaming, flailing her arms wildly as she attempts to stop.

"Hold on!" I shout to her as I change course, coming up to a small ledge that I use as a ramp.

It gets me the coverage that I need to get closer, but it's not quite enough, and the snow has started picking up. It's amazing how far you can travel on a board, and though it's only been minutes. I'd say we are already on another side of the mountain. Unfortunately, this side seems to be getting pounded with a lot more snow a lot faster than the resort side.

White blurs my vision, Skyla's hot pink jacket being the only thing I can focus on. I find another jump and take it, flying through the air so far, I jump in front of her. In the next second, I turn, slowing myself down as she crashes into me. I wrap my arms around her and hold on tight as we begin tumbling down the steep embankment.

Her screams echo through the valley, panic filling me as I do my best to keep my hold on her and slow us down. My eyes scan the area for possibilities, but I come up empty, especially when I see a cliff quickly approaching. A body suddenly comes flying from my left, cutting in front of us before grabbing my jacket and yanking hard. It's enough of a change in direction to slow down our momentum, but our bodies are still sliding towards the cliff.

"Vincent!" Skyla shrieks as I feel the ground give way beneath us, nothing but air now.

Before the freefall sensation begins, a hard jerk catches us. I hold onto Skyla with everything I have as I look up to see Liam holding onto my jacket, his body straining to keep us dangling off this cliffside while wedging himself behind a rock for an anchor.

"Still don't like me?" he strains.

I feel his hands start to shake as he attempts to hold on, but the weight is too much. What's worse is he's holding me, not her. My mind races with possibilities to get out of this when another figure comes flying beside Liam, stopping on a dime before crawling to the edge and reaching for Skyla. My body flexes and strains, attempting to lift her as close to him as possible.

Finally, Wesley is able to slip his arms beneath hers and haul her up and off the cliff edge. They collapse in a heap, my adrenaline thrumming in my veins when I think about how close I was to losing her.

Without Skyla's added weight, Liam is able to pull me up the rest of the way. As soon as I'm not dangling, I crawl to safety, perching myself behind the rock beside him as I throw my back against the snow and breathe.

Our chests are heaving, faces tilted to the snowy sky as we pant.

"Thanks."

"No problem," he wheezes.

"Vincent!" Skyla shouts over the howling winds.

"I'm here," I say. "I'm okay. Are you?"

"I'm fine! I'm so sorry. I lost control and—"

"You're fine, little one. We need to get off this fucking cliff, though," Wesley shouts.

We all nod our agreement and carefully undo our boards, lifting them up and over our shoulders as we begin trekking up the hill. Seconds later, Ronan and Asher come in hot, stopping short when they see us.

"Thank God!" Ronan says as he unclips his board and rushes over to us.

"We gotta keep moving! Into the trees!" Wesley says.

Asher undoes his board, and together, we all move making sure to keep Skyla in the center in case she slips, or the ground gives way. Once we are in the tree line, visibility is a little better, but not much.

"Where the fuck did this storm come from?" Asher shouts.

"We're on the south side of the mountain now. We have to find shelter until it calms down. None of us are equipped to board through unmarked trails in this."

Our heads begin to swivel as we search for a place to wait out the storm until Liam shouts and points up the hill.

"There! Up there! Is that a chimney?"

I squint in an attempt to see through the snowflakes before I nod. I'll be damned, Walcott is on a roll today.

"Let's go!" Ronan says.

Slowly, we all begin making our way up the mountain, taking care with each step we take. The cold is biting despite our gear, and I notice it starts affecting Skyla especially. Her legs begin to shake, and her arms are tucked in tight to her chest. Wesley lifts her up, tucking her into his chest as he carries her. Ronan steps in front of them, attempting to block out the wind, and I do the same on their right while Asher stands to their left. Liam is behind them, staying close just in case.

The closer we get to the chimney, the clearer it becomes. It's a shack, like a small hunting cabin. Shelter is shelter, though. I don't think any of us will be picky. Ronan is at the door first, and of course, it's locked. He puts his shoulder into it several times before he assesses where the weakest point is. Then he lifts his boot up and kicks the bastard in. The door flies open, and we all file in, quickly closing the door and scooting a desk to the side in front of it to keep it in place.

The place is bare bones, and the musty smell in the air tells me no one has been up here in a while. There is a three-cushioned couch in the middle of the room in front of a bear skin rug, a small wood-burning fireplace, and a kitchen the size of a postage stamp. I peek my head into the single bedroom to find a mattress no bigger than a full, and a toilet and shower combo bathroom.

Wordlessly, Ronan begins loading the fireplace up with some of the pre-cut kindling, digging into his backpack but coming up empty.

"Top pocket of my bag," Wesley says through chattering teeth.

Ronan moves behind him, unzipping his backpack to pull out several lighters. He gets the kindling lit before he slowly begins building the fire. Asher and Liam are sifting through the kitchen, and I'm doing the same in the bathroom and bedroom. All I was able to find was two blankets, two pillows, an old pair of wool socks, and a tube of toothpaste. Of course, there is no power. Wouldn't expect there to be for a hunting cabin or whatever this place is used for. They probably only have it turned on when they plan to be here, and based on the dust collection, it's been a year at least.

"Find anything?" Wesley calls out from the living room, where he's now sitting with Skyla in his arms.

"A can of black beans that expired two years ago, a pot, and a single set of silverware. Oh, and two mugs," Liam says.

"Better than nothing," Ronan says as he gets the fire roaring and closes the door.

I bring one of the blankets out, wrapping it around Skyla and Wesley. She smiles up at me weakly as she watches the fire with a distant stare. Squatting down in front of her, I run my fingers through her hair.

"Are you okay?"

"I'm sorry," she whispers, her voice tight.

"Why?" I ask as my fingers begin massaging her scalp.

"I lost control...I tried to slow down and stop...I almost got us killed, and now we're stuck in this run-down cabin in the middle of a blizzard."

I tug on her hair a little, grabbing her attention as I shake my head.

"I don't care about any of that. All I care about is that you're safe. That's all any of us care about, right?"

The guys all agree, and she nods.

"I guess f-frozen water isn't exactly where I excel," she chatters with a weak smile.

I smirk and nod.

"Let's keep you in the liquid stuff moving forward."

A shivering huff leaves her as she nods.

"Liam, grab the packets of apple cider out of my bag and the water. We need to warm her up."

"You brought water?" Asher asks.

"And apple cider?" Skyla adds.

"Of course, you never know."

"What else do you have in there, brother?" Ronan asks as he takes the bag from Wesley.

"Enough supplies for the six of us to last at least four days," he says as he holds Skyla tighter.

Ronan begins sifting through the bag before his eyebrows reach his hairline.

"Fuck me, that's the last time I give you shit for being prepared."

Wesley nods with a laugh as he presses a kiss to Skyla's head. Asher and Liam make quick work of heating up the water over the wood stove.

When the water is warmed up, Liam pours it into a cup and brings it to Skyla. She greedily takes a sip before letting out a relieved sigh. She tries to hand the cup to Wesley, but he shakes his head, then me, and I do the same. Skyla offers the warm drink to all of us before Asher speaks.

"We don't want it. You need to warm up first."

"That's not fair. We either all drink it, or none of us," she argues.

We all share uneasy looks before Wesley nods and takes the cup from her, taking a small sip before handing it to me. I do the same and pass it to Ronan, and so on, until the cup makes its way back to her. Liam is already heating up more water, and Skyla sighs happily as she rests against Wesley's chest.

"Feeling better, little one?" he asks.

"A little," she nods.

"You know, there is a sure-fire way for all of us to get warm quick," Liam says.

"Liam." Ronan groans.

"What?" he asks with his hands raised. "You all were thinking it; I just said it."

"No, I think you were the only one thinking about sex at a time like this," Asher scoffs.

"Well, I was," Skyla admits.

We all look at her in surprise, and she shrugs.

"It's survival 101. You get wet or cold, you get naked with others, right?"

Liam laughs and points to Skyla.

"See! My girl gets it, thank you, babygirl."

Wesley's hand rests on her knee, slowly sliding up her thigh as he speaks.

"That what you want? You want all of us to get naked, keep you warm?"

She shrugs almost bashfully before meeting all of our eyes. She settles on me last, probably because I'm definitely the least enthused about group activities, but if she's involved, I'm in.

Guess we're having an orgy in the middle of a blizzard.

Chapter Twenty-One

Skyla

Wesley's hand traces up my thigh, rubbing against my pussy, though honestly, I can't feel much through all these clothes. Pushing out of his hold, I push to my feet in the middle of the room. Wesley is sitting, Vincent is crouching in front of me, Liam and Asher are to my left by the fireplace, and Ronan is to my right near the door.

"Can I get some help?" I ask as I gesture to my clothes.

All as one, they begin circling me. Vincent's mouth is the first on mine; then I feel hands everywhere. Unzipping my jacket and unbuckling my snow bibs, someone takes my shoes and socks off while another pulls the bibs and my thermal shirt off. All of this happening while Vincent never leaves my mouth for longer than a second.

Once more and more skin is exposed, more and more mouths are on me. They are trailing every inch of me, and it's so dizzying I can't even keep track of who is who. I don't care either; they are all mine, so what does it matter?

A chill runs through me when the last article of clothing leaves my body. It's quickly replaced when the first naked body presses against me. I turn away from Vincent to meet Liam's lips. Of course, he is the first one to strip naked.

His hands cradle me gently as his tongue swirls around mine. I feel one mouth on my neck while the other comes to my breasts. Then another between my legs, forcing my leg to hook over his shoulder as his tongue runs through me. I moan into Liam's mouth, and he smiles against me.

"Good girl. You like it when Wesley eats your pussy, babygirl?"

I look down to see Wesley staring up at me; his mouth latched onto me as his tongue circles my clit. I dig my hand into his hair and pull as I nod. Another mouth begins kissing down my back, covering my ass before his hands are gripping me tightly. In the next second, he's licking me all the way through, his tongue circling my ass.

The sensations are so good, but it's too much. I don't know what way is up or down as ten hands and five mouths absolutely ravage me in the middle of this abandoned shack. I feel my orgasm creeping up on me, but it hits me like a freight train. I don't even try to be quiet as I scream out my release. I feel my pussy pulse and throb to the point that my cum actually leaks down Wesley's face. He greedily licks it up, happy to clean up the mess I've made, or rather the mess they've made of me.

When I come down from my high, the room is still for a moment. Only a moment, though. In a flash, Vincent has me in his arms. He's sitting down on the couch with me facing the room as I sink down onto his cock. He slides right in, and I moan once he's fully seated in me. His hand wraps around my throat, his other hand coming to play with my nipple as he begins bouncing me.

"You all love to share her so much. You like watching her get fucked?" he goads.

"Fuck yes, we do," Liam says as he begins stroking his cock.

Demise

Asher does the same, and Wesley looks to Ronan, a heat in his eyes that he doesn't return. I don't miss the disappointment on Wesley's face before an idea comes over his features. He moves over to Liam and Asher, looking between the two of them before settling his eyes on Asher. He frowns at Wesley, but not before Wesley crushes his lips to his. I expect Asher to shove him away, but to my surprise, he doesn't. Instead, he drags Wesley closer, their tongues tangling together in a messy way that has my pussy throbbing.

Liam wastes no time inserting himself, all of their mouths mashing together in a sloppy three-way kiss. Their hands are everywhere, moans echoing out of each of them before Wesley is the first to drop to his knees. He sucks Asher into his mouth, pushing him to the back of the throat and forcing Asher to drop his head back in pleasure. He bobs on his cock for a few moments before moving to Liam, repeating the same motion.

"Goddamn, that's good. Suck my fucking cock," Liam moans as he thrusts against Wesley's face.

My eyes move to see Ronan watching with a hard-set jaw. He doesn't look happy, not at all, actually. I slowly bring my eyes back to see Wesley suck both Liam and Asher into his mouth. They groan as they begin making out, their hands both forcing Wesley to take them deeper and deeper.

"Christ, siren. Your pussy is literally leaking down my cock," Vincent grumbles as his hand moves to start playing with my clit.

"They are so fucking hot. Would you ever touch any of them?" I ask, not even trying to hide the hope in my tone.

"What? Four boyfriends playing together isn't enough for you?"

Four?

I turn back to see Ronan tearing Wesley away from them before shoving his own cock down Wesley's throat. Ronan's hands hold his head tightly as he fucks his face with a violent rage. Wesley gags and chokes on his cock, but Ronan doesn't seem to care; this isn't an act of passion or lust. This is an act of punishment, and fuck me, punishment has never been so goddamn erotic.

"This is my fucking mouth," Ronan grits out. "No way in fuck am I going to sit back and let you suck off my fucking nephew!" he spits, smacking Wesley's cheek as he speaks.

Wesley jerks at the slap before he moves his head faster and faster.

"You want to get your cock sucked? That's fine, but the only people who will feel this mouth are me and Skyla, understood?"

Wesley nods his head before pulling away. His breathing is ragged, voice raspy.

"In that case, Liam, why don't you be a good boy and come suck my cock."

Liam glances to Asher, seemingly asking for permission, before Asher nods, moving across the room to Vincent and me.

"Enjoying the show, princess?" he smirks.

"So, fucking much," I smile as Asher rubs the head of his cock against my mouth.

"Open up," he says, pushing his way down my throat.

He stands to the side so I can still watch the others, bless him, and fuck me, what a sight it is. Ronan is standing, still face fucking Wesley, while Liam is practically laying on the ground, sucking Wesley with wild abandon. The moans echoing in this cabin are so much, it feels as if the whole place will come crashing around us. I don't fucking care, though. This is too good.

"That's it," Asher grits out as he pushes down my throat further, forcing me to gag and choke. "That's my good fucking girl."

Demise

I nod my head in agreement as I hear the grunting of Ronan and Wesley continue before they both come. Ronan down Wesley's throat and Wesley down Liam's. In a flash, Liam jumps to his feet and crosses the room, grabbing Asher by the cock and pulling him out of my mouth.

My pussy spasms at the way he so casually handles his best friend's cock before Liam spits Wesley's cum into my mouth. Surprise hits me, but I tilt my head back further and open my mouth more, running my tongue across my lips so I don't waste a drop. When I swallow it down, I look over to see Ronan collapsed on the floor, Wesley leaning between his legs as he shakes his head.

"That has to be the hottest fucking thing I've ever seen."

"Yeah?" Ronan asks, tilting Wesley's head up to look at him.

Taking all of us by surprise, Ronan presses his lips to Wesley's. It isn't a wildly passionate kiss, more like a soft peck, but I physically see Wesley's cock twitch and begin to harden up already. Their kiss deepens as Wesley lifts his hand to hold Ronan in place.

Wesley's teeth sink into Ronan's lip before he is turning around, laying on top of Ronan and grinding his cock against his.

"Fuckk," Ronan moans as Wesley's length grinds against his.

"I need to be inside you, princess," Asher says, and without any negotiating needed, Vincent pushes me to stand.

I feel incredibly empty without him in me, but it only lasts a few seconds before he forces me to my knees and bends me over. Vincent's mouth latches onto my ass, licking and swirling his tongue in and around. My eyes roll into the back of my head as Asher slides in front of me, laying on his back as he slips his cock inside my pussy.

"Fuckkk," I moan.

"There's my girl. Is Griggs eating your ass, princess?"

"Uh, huh," I whimper.

"You want him to fuck it next?"

"Yessss," I moan when Vincent slips a finger inside me.

"It would be my fucking pleasure, siren," he grumbles into my ear.

Vincent paces his rhythm with Asher perfectly, for being enemies, they sure work amazing together. My eyes move up to see Ronan and Wesley still tangled together, but now it's Ronan that is kissing up and down Wesley's body, getting dangerously close to his cock. Wesley's eyes hold mine, a smile filled with excitement and hope in them.

When Ronan gets just to Wesley's cock, he pauses for a moment, his eyes finding mine. I give him an encouraging smile before Vincent adds another finger, and I moan once more. When I open my eyes again, Ronan has Wesley's cock in his mouth, his head gently moving up and down his length while Wesley takes hold of his head.

"Fuck, Ro. Just like that. Goddamnit, are you telling me we could have been doing this for years, and we haven't?"

I hear Ronan hum around Wesley's cock, but he doesn't say anything as he continues. The stimulation of the room in its entirety is almost too much. It feels like I'm watching my favorite movie while also being the star of the show. So much pleasure, so much feeling. It's overwhelming, and yet I never want it to end.

From behind me, I feel Vincent pull out his fingers before the sound of spitting echoes in the room, followed by the feeling of warm spit on my asshole.

"Keep that back arched for me, siren. We don't have any lube, so this is the best you'll be able to get."

Demise

"Yes, we do," Wesley grunts. "Liam, inside pocket, bottom left," he says as he points to the backpack.

Liam practically sprints over to it, retrieving the bottle and handing it to Vincent. He pops the top open and dumps a healthy amount on his cock and my ass.

"I'm ready," I pant.

Vincent presses the tip of his cock against me, slowly sinking into me inch by inch. I cringe for a moment, the pain burning as it rips through me before pleasure gives way.

"Fuck, babygirl. You're taking them beautifully. I'm so fucking proud of you," Liam praises.

I look up at him and smile.

"Come here, baby. Let me take care of you."

"I've got a better idea," he says as he lays down beside Asher, cupping his face as he begins kissing him.

My pussy pulses as I watch them before Liam's hand lifts, playing with my clit. I shudder at the much needed distraction from Vincent stretching me. He rubs tight circles against me before his hand slips down, his finger tracing over Asher's cock, thrusting in and out of me. Without a word, he rests his finger against Asher's cock, forcing his finger inside of me at the same time.

I feel my mouth drop open, this new sensation unlike anything I've felt before, as Asher curses. When Asher pulls out, Liam adds another finger, letting Asher set the pace and rhythm. Liam honestly isn't doing much except for stretching me more and more. When he adds a third finger, I think that I'm going to fucking die, but after a few moments, it doesn't hurt as much.

"I think she's ready," Asher grits out.

"Ready?" I echo.

"Come here, baby," Asher says to Liam, gesturing to his chest.

Liam seems to know what's going on because he scrambles over to him easily, forcing Vincent to lift me up and plaster me to his chest for a moment. He pushes my hair away from my neck as he lets out a ragged breath against my skin.

"What's happening?" I pant.

"They are about to stuff you full, siren. You ready?"

"Full?" I question as Liam lays his back against Asher's chest, shifting slightly to line their cocks up in the same position before Vincent pushes me back down.

Asher wraps his hand almost all the way around both his and Liam's cocks, covering them in more lube before lining their heads up to my pussy. My eyes bulge in surprise.

"No, there is no way," I gasp. "Both of you? Together? You're never going to fit."

Asher gives me a mischievous smile that shouldn't be as sexy as it is.

"Oh, we'll make it fit, princess."

With that, he pushes their tips inside me, stretching me like I've never been stretched before. My mouth opens, and a scream tears out of me. It's a mixture between pain and pleasure, if I'm being honest. Vincent, Asher and Liam all still as I breathe through it.

"If it's too much, we'll stop, babygirl," Liam says softly.

I inhale and exhale several times before I shake my head.

"Just go slow."

Asher does as I ask, him and Liam slowly lifting their hips at the same time before lowering them again. It takes several minutes before it doesn't feel like I'm being ripped in two, and once I can relax a little bit, Vincent begins to move again.

"Oh my god," I moan, this unfamiliar feeling filling me from my head to my toes.

"Fuck, Ash. Your cock feels so good against mine," Liam moans, dropping his head back against Asher's shoulder.

Demise

"Of course it does, baby. You and me together wrapped up inside our girl. It doesn't get better than this," Asher agrees before he lowers his voice. "You two are everything to me, you know that?" he says to me before looking at Liam, placing a kiss against his neck.

Liam moans and nods, his voice matching the same tone.

"I love you," he admits. "I love both of you so fucking much."

My eyebrows raise, and I feel Asher's thrusts falter out of rhythm before they pick up again.

"I love you too, baby. Both of you," he says as his eyes come back to me, full of devotion.

I lean down to kiss him, moving my mouth between the both of them as we all move against each other. I feel Vincent's hands on my hips tighten, and his cock begins to throb inside me.

"Fuck, siren. I need you to come."

Liam's hand goes back to playing with my clit, Asher and Liam's thrusts picking up pace, forcing matching pleasured faces on each of them. Movement from across the room catches my eye. Somehow, I missed Ronan and Wesley switching positions, Wesley currently sucking Ronan again before they meet my gaze and stand, crossing the room to us.

Both of them are stroking their cocks as they look down at us.

"Look at what they are doing to you, baby. You're taking all three of them so well." Ronan smiles.

"Th-hank you," I say with a soft smile of my own. "Did he make you feel good?" I ask him, gesturing to Wesley.

Ronan looks at him and smirks before nodding. "Always does."

"Same goes for you now, too," Wesley adds as he lets go of his cock and covers Ronan's hand with his.

Ronan releases his hold and lets Wesley stroke him before he does the same for him. They stroke each other's cocks, going back and forth between looking at each other and looking at me until Vincent smacks my ass, grunting out his release.

"Goddamnit! Fuck!" he curses as his cock begins throbbing inside of me, his hot cum coating me as he falls apart.

"Shit, shit, shit, shit," Liam says as he tries to keep it together.

Asher nips his earlobe as he whispers to him.

"It's okay, fall apart for me. Fall apart for us."

Liam's hand moves at practically supersonic speed against my clit before he moans like a fucking porn star. His cock twitches once, sending Asher over the cliff with me right alongside them. We all scream and moan, humping and grinding against each other to wring every last second of pleasure out of this moment as we can.

In the next second, Ronan and Wesley both make sounds of their own.

"Look at us, little one. Smile for me."

I do as he says, my orgasm still crashing into me as Ronan literally roars. Warm ropes of their cum cover me, starting at my face before trailing down to my breasts. I think the sight of me absolutely covered in their cum only makes them come harder, because their orgasms seem to last forever.

Once we come down from the pleasure, Vincent very carefully, but very painfully pulls his cock out of me. Then Liam does the same before Asher. When I'm completely empty, I collapse on my stomach, laying on Liam's chest as Vincent slouches over me. Our bodies are slick with sweat and cum, but none of us care right now. We lay there like that for several minutes, only the sound of our heavy breathing in the room.

Carefully, Vincent stands, peeling himself off me before I

roll onto my back. Liam climbs off Asher before looking down at me.

"Such a filthy little girl. Look at you; you're a mess."

I nod as I let out another ragged breath.

"Let me help," Liam says as he sticks his tongue out and begins dragging it all over my body, licking up the trails of cum left behind by Ronan and Wesley.

I let out a soft moan at the feeling, and it must spark something in Asher because he sits up and settles himself between my thighs.

"I'll take care of this mess, princess," he says before he runs his tongue through me slowly.

Instead of licking me up like he normally would, he's pushing it back in, tongue fucking the mixture of Liam and his own cum deeper and deeper into me.

"Ash," I moan. "What are you doing?"

"With any luck, pushing this cum so deep in your cunt you'll have no choice but to give us a baby."

"I'm on birth control," I laugh as my laughter turns to a moan.

"Doesn't hurt to try," he murmurs against my thigh before doubling his efforts.

"Shit, now that's a sight I want forever burned in my mind," Liam says as he licks his lips. "My man licking and pushing my cum back into my woman."

"Don't forget his own cum too," Wesley adds.

"Even fucking better," Liam agrees.

Ronan bends down, rubbing my stomach gently as Asher continues licking my pussy.

"That's a beautiful mental image."

"What is?" I ask.

"You round with our baby," he says, those blue eyes drilling me into place.

"Our?" I question.

"All of ours, siren," Vincent says.

My eyes come to his, the most possessive of the group, the one who hates sharing me. The one I constantly worry will realize I'm not worth sharing and disappear on me. To hear that even he is all in, one day, for anything the future holds makes my heart soar.

Asher slowly pulls away, pressing a gentle kiss to my pussy.

"There, that should do it," he says with a nod.

I can't help but laugh as I hold out my arms for him before gesturing to all of them. One by one, they all lay down on or beside me, all of their hands touching mine, our bodies cuddled close. I know that, without a doubt, I'll never feel more complete than I do right now.

Chapter Twenty Two

Skyla

The next morning, I can hardly walk. Okay, that's a bit of an exaggeration, but I am so fucking sore it's crazy. Not to mention the way my back is absolutely wrecked from sleeping on the floor all night. I guess someone could have slept in the bed and another on the couch, but it felt too right to all be together. I'm kind of regretting that choice now, though.

When I woke up, the kitchen counter was filled with snacks from Wesley's bag. I chose a protein bar and a piece of bread before drinking a little more water and getting dressed. The blizzard has died down to a barely there snowfall, and the light streaming through the windows gives us a little hope. Still, no clue how we are going to get off this mountain. I'm just going to try not to die in the process this time.

Once we are all dressed, we say goodbye to our safe haven shack. Without it, there is no doubt we all would have frozen to death last night. It also doesn't hurt that we made some good memories in it, ones that will definitely be living rent free in my head until the end of time.

We strap into our boards as soon as we step outside, the cold already biting its way through our clothes.

"Alright, everyone, stay safe. Stay together. Let's try to head east back towards the lodge or at least as close as we can," Wesley says as he pulls out a compass like the boy scout Ronan accused him of being.

Everyone nods as we pull on our goggles, and Vincent comes over to me, cupping my face in his hands before delivering a bruising kiss to my lips. When he pulls away, his tone is firm and harsh.

"No more giving me a goddamn heart attack, siren. If you feel like you're going too fast, turn sideways. If you're going slow enough, fall on your ass, alright?"

I nod my head. "I promise."

"Good," he says before giving me one more peck. "I'll be right behind you."

"And I'll be right beside you," Liam says. "After all, I am the one who saved both of your asses yesterday with my sick ass skills."

Liam flexes his arms, kissing his bicep in a way that has everyone groaning and rolling their eyes. Vincent smacks the back of his head as Wesley pushes off.

"Let's go," he says as he leads the way.

Asher follows after him, followed by me, Liam, Vincent, and Ronan. It is so much easier without the intense wind, the blinding snow, and the panic that was practically clouding my vision. We keep the pace nice and easy, and when I feel like I'm going too fast, I move my board sideways, and I slow right down. One time, I got a little wobbly and almost took Liam down with me, but we're fine; everything is fine.

It takes us about fifteen minutes, but finally, we find our way back onto the main slope that I deviated from in the first place. Relief practically pounds inside me when I see the bottom of the mountain. I love the snow so much, but from the inside of a cabin or a car or something. I've tried snowboarding and almost got everyone I love killed. I think we are going to chalk it up to it being not for me.

When we get to the bottom of the hill, we all unclip ourselves from our snowboards and hand them to a couple of attendants before grabbing our boots. Ronan heads inside to oversee everything is taken care of while the rest of us head for the car. Wesley already turned it on and has the heat going before we even get to it, so when we slide in, it's nice and warm.

I practically sink into the back seat between Liam and Asher, their arms wrapping around me as Vincent slides into the middle and Wesley into the driver's seat. Ronan comes out only a minute or so later, and when the door shuts, Liam shouts into the car.

"Let's get the fuck off this mountain!"

Hear, hear.

We spent the next few days in a lot more relaxing ways. We watched Christmas movies, drank buckets of cider and hot chocolate, ate so much delicious food, thanks to Ronan and Wesley, and fucked practically nonstop. If I thought I was sore on that mountain, it has nothing on how I feel on our drive home.

Christmas came and went; we all slept in on Christmas morning and sat around the tree. There was no gift exchange, apart from Liam handing out hand scribbled one oral session coupons to everyone. Vincent crumbled his up so fast and threw it at Liam's head before he could even walk away.

However, I noticed not just Asher tuck his away, but Wesley too. Liam must have made a good impression. Even Ronan didn't trash his, which took me by surprise.

Since we came down from the mountain, there hasn't been anything remotely flirtatious or sexual between Ronan and Wesley. Somehow, I truly think the nature of their relationship is physical. Heat of the moment kind of thing. Obviously, I'm not going to pry and possibly put pressure on a delicate situation, but I'd be lying if I said I wasn't a little disappointed. I love watching Asher and Liam's relationship bloom.

Each night, I spent the night in someone else's bed, but every night, Liam and Asher shared their own. I even asked Liam this morning if they had sex just the two of them, and he said they hadn't, no particular reason, just that the moment hadn't come yet. I wanted to ask why the hell not, because when we were all together, it was like goddamn fireworks, but again, I left it alone.

It was hard to say goodbye to the cabin. I begged Ronan to rent it again next year and the year after that. I want to spend every Christmas here, every holiday. It feels like...home. More than any home I've ever lived in has felt.

Now, we're almost back to Salem, and like a lead ball, something heavy and foreboding drops into my stomach. My chest tightens and it becomes harder to breathe the closer we get to city limits. It was a nice little break from reality while it lasted, but unfortunately, all good things must come to an end.

As soon as we got home, Vincent changed into a new pair of clothes, kissed me and hopped on his bike to take off. He said

Demise

that he had some work to do and that he'd be gone for a few days. I'm not going to lie; I hate that I don't know all that he does. Mainly that, I don't know where he goes. Obviously, what he's doing is dangerous. It's how his parents died; how many eliminators before him have no doubt died. The thought of losing him is...I can't think about it.

We spent the evening unpacking and getting settled in the house again. Ronan and Wesley have all but moved in, each of them taking up residence in a room at the house, which seems to be fine by Asher and is obviously preferred by me.

The next morning, Wesley drives me to school like usual, except this time, Asher and Liam accompany me. I steal a quick kiss from Wesley behind the tinted windows before he parks upfront.

When we get out of the car, Liam and I are holding hands while Asher walks with his arm around my shoulder. Everyone is staring and whispering, rightfully so, I suppose, and I know we should probably be more discreet. Then again, it's not like Christopher doesn't already know and approve, at least of the whole 'them fucking the same woman' thing. The whole love bit would be our downfall, honestly, but for some reason, I don't fear him, not as much as I used to. But that doesn't mean I'm going to be seen all over Vincent, Ronan, and Wesley to top it off. I do have a little thing called self-preservation.

We are walking through campus when a body comes charging at us out of nowhere. We all are slow to react, and they collide right into me, a familiar voice ringing in my ears.

"I missed you bitch! Where have you been? I called you like a hundred times this weekend alone," Maggie says.

"Oh, sorry about that. We were up in New Hampshire for Christmas; it was a busy weekend," I say with a small smile as I glance at Asher and Liam, both watching me with their own guarded smiles.

"Based on those smirks, I'd say busy is short for filthy, and you know I want all the details. Thank you for hand delivering my bestie, boys, but your services are no longer required." Maggie grins as she drags me away from the guys.

"What the fuck?" Asher growls as Liam rests a hand on his chest, telling him to relax.

Asher pushes him off quickly, looking around for a moment before his shoulders relax. I smile sadly at them, hating that they have to adjust their dynamics once more. They can't just be who they are, who they want to be here. Not with all of these eyes, all of these whispers. We are back to reality, and in the Brethren...with Christopher as his father...it wouldn't go over well.

"Sooo, give me the horny details. I can feel something vibing between Asher and Liam, are they fucking yet?"

"Shhh," I hiss as I cast a look around us.

Maggie's eyes are the size of saucers, her mouth parted as she stares at me.

"Holy fucking shit. I was just teasing. No way, Asher is gay?"

"SHH!" I say once more, rolling my eyes as we step into our first class. "Jesus, you're so loud. We will talk later, but not here."

"Okay, cranky," she huffs. "Have you had an orgasm yet? No one can be cranky if they've come. Want me to help you out?" she says with a waggle of her fingers and a raise of her eyebrows.

I laugh at that. "Nooo, thank you. My roster is officially fullll."

Maggie faux pouts before she glances around the room and lowers her voice.

"Well, between you and me...so is mine."

I raise my eyebrows at her in surprise.

"Oh really? Do tell."

"You know Maryia Sewall?"

I think for a moment. "That girl you hooked up with at the back to school bonfire?"

She points at me and nods.

"We're sort of dating," Maggie shrugs, a blush touching her cheeks.

My mouth drops as I shove her softly.

"Mags! Since when? Wait. Now you give me all the horny details." I tease.

Maggie smirks. "Don't think I won't. We've fucked around a few times since the bonfire; for a while, I thought she was just experimenting with me, you know? Which was fine since I was still hung up on...you know."

Bridgette.

I nod as she continues.

"But her family came over to my place for our Christmas Eve party. We spent some time together, and she admitted that she's had a crush on me for a while and wanted to see where things led. I mean, both of our futures are pretty bleak, but we're happy. Plus, she has one of the most delicious cunts I've ever tasted, and when I get her to squirt I—"

"Okay, maybe that's enough horny details." I laugh.

Maggie rolls her eyes and nods, but I don't miss the brief flicker of sadness that comes over her.

"What does Bridgette think? Of you and your girlfriend?" I test.

Maggie's head whips up, and she shrugs.

"That I'm disgusting, that it's a sin. That she doesn't want to be within ten feet of me, or she's worried she'll catch a disease."

I frown at that. "Are you sure that's actually how she feels or just what she's saying because she's scared?"

"Scared of what?" Maggie complains as she tosses her hands out by her side. "I've been patient, so fucking patient. Every fucking time with her, it's like one step forward, three steps back. I'm done."

Maggie shakes her head, opening her mouth to speak before closing it once more.

"Maryia is good for me. She makes me happy. I make her happy. We are good together. Not some toxic forbidden bullshit. I like *Maryia*," she says, emphasizing her name like it's for her benefit. Like she is forcing her heart to believe what her head wants so badly. If I've learned anything, though, it's that the heart wants what it wants, no matter who or how many. We don't get to choose…it…it chooses us.

Liam jogs into class, followed by an older man I've never seen before. The man settles in at the desk in the front of the room as Liam comes up the steps, scooching into his normal spot beside me. I smile at him, and he winks at me before squeezing my knee. Someone else also darts in at the last second. Andrew Hutchinson.

His head is down, hair a frazzled mess as he quickly takes a seat in the front row. Liam and I share a curious look before the professor calls our attention.

"Good morning, everyone. I'm Professor Danforth. I'll be taking over this class."

Taking over because Professor Corwin is gone. Because he was beaten half to death by two of my boyfriends before the sweet golden retriever boyfriend to my left squished his head like a grape with a lamp, and my other boyfriend burned his body to a crisp.

God.

That feels like it's been months since that happened, when in reality, it's been weeks.

Disassociation for the win, I suppose.

Chapter Twenty-Three

Liam

Skyla and I are having lunch at our normal table when Bartlett comes over with Maryia Sewall. The pretty little brunette's cheeks are flaming red, close to the color of Bartlett's hair. She glances at me and Skyla nervously before looking back to Bartlett.

When they sit down, I notice how Bartlett's hand shifts like she's resting it on Sewall's leg. Interesting.

I glance at Skyla to see if she's clocked this development, and she just nods and smiles before speaking.

"Hi, you must be Maryia. I'm Skyla Parris," she says as I nudge her.

"She means Putnam."

She rolls her eyes and gives me a look.

"Excuse me, are you Asher now?"

"Nope, just protecting my best friend's interests."

"Well, do me a favor and don't." She laughs as she faces Sewall once more.

I watch as the girl's brown eyes dart between Skyla and I before landing on Skyla once more.

"Nice to meet you. Maggie has told me nothing but wonderful things."

"Likewise." Skyla smiles demurely.

"How long have you been together?" I ask.

Sewall's eyes panic as she looks to Bartlett before shaking her head.

"Oh, uh. We aren't. I'm not...We're just fr—"

"Easy, Bambi. We're safe; you can trust them," Bartlett pacifies softly.

"Bambi?" I scoff.

"Yeah, with those pretty little doe eyes, how could I call her anything else?" Bartlett smiles before giving me a wink.

Sewall gives her a shy smile before shrugging. I watch as Bartlett whispers something into her ear, dragging it out before placing a quick and discreet kiss to her neck that has her giggling and relaxing a bit more. Aww, look at them, young love. They remind me of a young schoolgirl with her first crush and the much older, experienced partner ready to teach them everything. I mean, they are the same age, but I'm taking a wild guess that this is Sewall's first time dating a woman, so Bartlett is definitely the experienced one here.

"Where is Asher?" Skyla asks, pulling my attention away from the lovebirds.

"He had to stay back and work on a group project." I shrug as I take a huge bite of pizza, not giving a fuck when sauce smears across my chin.

Skyla rolls her eyes and laughs. "You're an animal."

I grin at her, but my grin quickly falls away when a familiar head of sleek black hair steps up to our table. I stand in an instant, putting myself between Bridgette and Skyla.

"What do you want, Brenton?" I growl, my normally cheerful tone long gone.

Demise

She stops short, surprised at how quickly I got up as she stares up at me, a flicker of unease in her eyes.

"I-I just wanted to talk to Skyla."

"Yeah, well, she doesn't want to talk to you. Do us all a favor and fuck the hell off," I snarl.

She winces, clutching her wrapped up hand. Shit. Asher really must have done a number on her with that fork if it's still injured.

Good.

I feel Skyla stand behind me, and though every instinct is telling me to push her back into her seat, I let her step past me.

"What do you want?" Skyla asks coldly.

Bridgette swallows roughly, her fingers twisting together as she speaks.

"I just wanted to...apologize. I've been...well, the worst to you, and you didn't deserve it. I don't have any excuses. Chalk it up to petty, mean girl bullshit. I thought you were taking something that belonged to me. I thought..." she trails off, closing her eyes and letting out a breath as she shakes her head.

"I thought I knew what I wanted, but clearly, I didn't have a clue," she says, her eyes flicking to Bartlett for half a second before her gaze comes back to Skyla. "Regardless, I was terrible, and I don't expect you to forgive me, but if there is anything me or my family can ever do for you...name it, and it's yours."

Skyla watches her with furrowed brows, not speaking for several seconds.

"You're serious?" she asks dubiously.

"Yes," Bridgette nods, her eyes drenched with sincerity. It's a really odd look for her, not gonna lie.

"Well, thanks...I guess?" Skyla says.

"I really am sorry. I don't want to be that person anymore. I want to change, and...change starts within."

Change starts within? What the fuck is that? A bumper sticker?

"Sure," Skyla says, hesitance lacing her tone. "Well, good luck with that. Try not to break any plates over people's heads."

Bridgette grimaces at that and nods, casting one more look at Bartlett. It's a look of pain, regret, and longing. When she sets her eyes on Sewall, her expression bleeds into fury. The evil, crazy bitch Bridgette is back in full force as she stares at Sewall like she wants to set her on fire. With her jaw clenched, she turns on her heel and stomps out of the cafeteria, several people staring after her with curiosity.

Skyla sits down, blinking several times before she looks to the rest of us.

"That just happened, right? I'm not imagining things?"

"Yeah," Bartlett murmurs, her eyes still glued in the direction where Bridgette disappeared to.

Sewall leans into her, shaking her out of her daze. Bartlett gives her new girlfriend a fake as fuck grin before she nods and takes a bite of her pasta.

What an absolutely confusing and tension filled lunch.

I'm sitting in my econ class, bored out of my fucking mind, when I decide to text Asher.

Me: What are you doing?

His reply comes surprisingly quick.

Asher: Listening to Professor Noyes drone on about fuck knows what.

I huff my amusement at that as I respond.

Me: Prayers be with you brother. Feel like ditching?

Asher: What did you have in mind?

I smirk as I type out my reply.

Me: You, me and an empty coat closet. Maybe a dark corridor.

I wait for his text, but it doesn't come. My teasing smirk slowly slips from my face, and I pocket my phone. I was just joking, fuck. *Kinda.*

My phone buzzes in my pocket, and I try to ignore the way my heart kicks up, hoping it's him.

Asher: Meet me at my dorm room. Now.

I don't even finish reading the text before I'm out of my seat. My econ professor asks me where I'm going when I call out over my shoulder.

"Shit my pants, see you tomorrow."

The class thunders with laughter as the professor shakes his head in disgust. Most people would be embarrassed to say something like that, but it's the perfect excuse. No one is going to stand there and argue with a guy they think just soiled himself.

I haven't been to the dorms in forever. I've practically moved into Asher and Skyla's place. We all have, none of us ever willing to be far from our girl. It doesn't take me long to get there, though. Since it's the middle of class, no one is around, thank fuck, because the less people that see me or him, the better.

It's not like people aren't used to us being attached to the hip anyways, but things are different, and I know others can tell. I'm not looking forward to the first Brethren function we all have to be at. That I'll have to be in a room with him and pretend. Behind Skyla, he's quickly becoming everything to me.

When I reach his door, I find that it's already propped open. I push inside to see the lights are off as the door thunks shut behind me. Confused, I look around for Asher, but come up empty until a body comes out of nowhere, plastering me against the wall, hand around my throat as his deep voice rumbles in my ear.

"This what you were hoping for when you texted me?" Asher says.

"Something like this." I smirk as his grip on my throat tightens.

"Yeah, what is it that you want? Tell me," he says as his lips run up and down the side of my throat, nipping at my ear lobe in a way that has my breath catching.

"Christ," I moan. "I was hoping you'd want to see me, that you'd want to touch me. Maybe even fuck me."

His chuckle reverberates in my ear, sending a shiver to run through my body.

"I always want to fuck you, Liam. All you have to do is ask."

"Really?" I gasp in surprise as Asher's other hand reaches around, palming my cock over my jeans.

"Get on the bed, now," he demands before releasing his hold on me.

I do as he says, practically bouncing on it before I go for my jeans. I undo them in record time as Asher prowls over to me, pulling his shirt up and over his head before his hands move to his jeans. He undoes his belt with one hand as he pushes them down with the other, revealing his rock hard cock. Goddamn, I'll never get tired of seeing him naked or the fact that his hard on is all for me, all because of me. It has pre-cum already leaking from my tip.

Demise

"Take your shirt off," Asher says as he strokes his cock. "I want to see all of you."

I grab the back of my shirt and pull it over my head before tossing it to the side. His eyes rake over me, his gaze lust drunk and intense as he pauses on my cock. I watch him sink his teeth into his lip before he closes the distance between us. He climbs onto the bed between my legs and rests his hands on either side of my head.

His hazel eyes are so fucking pretty, those three golden flecks in them making them practically hypnotic as he cups the side of my face tenderly.

"Look at what you do to me," he says as he grinds his cock against mine. "This isn't me; this has never been me, and somehow, this is who I become now when you're near. Just your scent gives me a raging fucking hard on, and all I can think about is getting you just like this," he accentuates with a thrust of his hips.

He sucks in a sharp gasp through his clenched teeth as his eyes pinch tight before they come to me again.

"You and this pretty bedazzled cock are going to be the death of me."

"You think my cock is pretty?" I tease, though even I can admit that my tone is lacking its usual lighthearted nature. This moment feels too raw, too intense.

Asher crushes his lips to mine, our tongues battling for dominance before he bites my lower lip so hard, a drop of blood blooms to the surface. His tongue flicks out, licking it up before he drags his body down mine, covering my chest and stomach with kisses.

"So. Fucking. Pretty," he says before pausing just before my cock.

His eyes come to mine, that same heated look in them as he closes his mouth around my head.

"Fuuuck," I groan as I thrust into his throat. Not because I meant to but because I can't fucking help myself.

Asher takes me well, his tongue swirling around me as he pushes me all the way down his throat before coming back up again and repeating the motion. Over and over, waves and waves of pleasure crash into me. His tongue begins playing with one of my piercings, causing a shudder to run through me as he chuckles around my cock.

His mouth comes off too soon for my liking before he's scattering kisses across my balls and lower. His hands go to my thighs, pushing them up, forcing me to grab hold of them as he continues.

"Jesus CHRIST!" I yelp when his tongue circles my asshole.

He flattens his tongue and begins swirling it around the sensitive skin. I've watched him eat Skyla's pussy and asshole more times than I could count, and he seems to be devouring me with the same amount of enthusiasm as her. Lucky me.

"That feel good, baby?" he asks as he begins tongue fucking me.

Fuck, I love it when he calls me baby. I love it way more than I should.

"Yes, Ash. Fuck, yes," I whimper.

He continues eating my ass, his hand lifting up to play with my balls before he pulls away and looks at me with a smirk.

"You ready?" he asks.

I don't know why, but for some reason, I'm kind of nervous. I've fucked countless men before. I've also gotten fucked by countless others. This is not new territory. I've even been fucked by Asher before, and it was amazing. Skyla was there, though. It was different. The dynamics were different. This feels so...personal, so intimate. Right now, it's just me and him, and I'm practically shaking with anticipation.

I give him a shaky nod as he lines the tip of his cock against me, pushing in with a savage thrust that has my back bowing. Asher stays buried inside me, letting out a satisfied chuckle that turns animalistic as he begins thrusting.

"Ohhh, fuck, baby. This ass is something else," he says as he snaps his hips hard.

I whimper as pain runs through me for a moment before pleasure gives way.

"You like that?" he asks through clenched teeth. "You like it rough, don't you?"

Another hard thrust has a 'yes' ripping out of me.

"Of course you do. Such a good boy for me. You gonna take my dick? Gonna let me fucking ruin this asshole?"

I nod quickly. "Whatever you want, it's yours."

"Fuck yes, it is," Asher grits as his hand comes to my cock, wrapping around it as he begins stroking me.

I feel my body physically melt into the bed as his strokes match his thrusts perfectly. He lets go for a moment, putting his hand up to my face as he speaks.

"Spit on it."

I do as he says, gathering up all of my saliva and spitting into his hand. He then moves his hand to my cock, stroking it quickly as he fucks me deeper than before.

"There we go. That's it. Tell me how good I feel inside you. Tell me how bad you want my cock," Asher growls.

"It's so good, Ash. You're stretching me so fucking good. No one has fucked me like you do."

"Fuck no, they haven't, and they never will. My cock will be the only one you'll crave from here on out."

I nod, my eyelids fluttering closed as pleasure threatens to suffocate me. I feel a sharp slap sting across my cheek, forcing my eyes open.

"Eyes on me, baby. Do you understand me? You're fucking mine. I fucking love you. Do you get that?"

I reach my hands out, resting them on Asher's bare ass as I force his thrusts harder.

"I love you, Ash. You and Sky are all I want."

"Good," he practically seethes before he closes his eyes, letting out a ragged breath as he nods. "Good."

Our bodies move together in a perfect rhythm, his hand practically choking the life out of my cock in a way I could only crave. He's so perfect. This moment is perfect. Together, we are...perfect.

Asher's pace begins to quicken, his forearms flexing as he holds me tighter and tighter.

"Liam, I need you to come. I need you to come, okay, baby?" he grits.

I nod my head as that familiar feeling begins to tingle inside me while Asher jerks me faster and faster.

"Fuck." He winces. "You gotta come for me. Right now, okay? Okay?" he pants before his face contorts, and he lets out a groan.

I feel his cum flood me, and I follow right along with him, my cum shooting across his stomach and hand. He doesn't stop, continuing to milk every ounce he can out of me as he fucks his cum deeper and deeper into me.

When he stops, he practically throws himself on top of me, resting his head against my heaving chest. His cock stays buried inside me and it's fucking perfect. I wish we could stay like this forever.

My hands begin running through his hair, gently massaging him as he lets out a soft sigh of contentment and closes his eyes.

"Do you think Sky will be mad?" he murmurs against my skin.

"Jealous? Absolutely. Mad? No way in hell," I answer.

Demise

He lets out a short hmph as he nods his head and looks up at me.

"I hope you don't have any plans today because, in about twenty minutes, we're doing that again."

Well, fuck me. Literally, please. Fuck me.

Chapter Twenty-Four

Skyla

When I get out of bed the next morning, I think I'm the first one up. Well, except for Wesley. I swear he's almost as bad as Vincent. He texted me sweet dreams last night at two in the morning and good morning at four. He said that he'd be home soon, and I hope so, because I miss my broody overprotective psychopath.

Wesley is working on his laptop at the kitchen island, a cup of coffee beside him when he looks up at me, smiles and closes his laptop.

"Morning, little one."

"Morning," I say as I slide into his lap. "Whatcha doing?"

"Just looking over some surveillance footage for a friend."

I raise a brow at him. "What kind of friend?"

"The paying kind." He smirks.

Letting out a chuckle, I laugh and nod.

"What are you doing up this early?"

I shrug. "Couldn't sleep. Was thinking of going to the pool. I haven't been in a while."

"That will be good for you. Want me to drive?"

Demise

"If it's not too much trouble?" I ask with a shy smile.

He kisses my temple and nods.

"No trouble at all. I'm happy to. Besides, I hear road head is excellent this time of the day."

I stand up and push his shoulder, shaking my head as I walk away. I slip into my room, grabbing my outfit for the day as well as all of my swim stuff before throwing it into a duffel bag. When I come back down, Wesley is ready and waiting by the door. He opens the door for me before ushering me out to the car.

Wesley tells me a ridiculous story about when he was getting road head in high school, and the girl's braces got caught on his pubes. Suffice it to say they were lucky he didn't crash.

When we get to the university, he sneaks a quick kiss before getting the door for me, waiting until I step inside the building before he drives off. As soon as I step inside the building, the smell of chlorine permeates my senses, and I feel at peace. I don't know why I haven't come here in so long. Maybe between being forcefully married or, more accurately, raped, stalked, and kidnapped while juggling five boyfriends, I just haven't had enough time.

As soon as I push through those doors, it's like I never left. I'm not shocked to find the school's resident swimming God. Ronan's arms stretch out as he cuts through the water, his shoulders like boulders of muscle propelling him forward.

I smile as I step inside, taking a seat at the edge of the pool as he comes up to the end. He must be able to sense someone is here, though, because his head pops up and looks straight at me. Lifting his goggles up, he wipes at his face before grinning.

"Good morning, beautiful. Just what do you think you're doing in my pool?"

"Well, I heard that you give private lessons. I could really use the one-on-one time," I say with mock seriousness.

"Oh really?" he feigns. "Well, you're in luck. My six AM appointment cancelled. Ready to start now?"

"Born ready." I tease with a smile. "I'll just go change."

"No need," he says. "I like to get nice and familiar with my swimmer's bodies," he says before dragging me into the water.

My pajama pants and sleep shirt are soaked instantly as my head slips underwater for a moment. When I push to the surface, I splash him, wiping the chlorine from my eyes.

"What the hell, Ronan?" I sputter as I look at him.

He just grins at me and pins me against the wall, his hand bunching up the waistband of my pants before pulling them down. They float away as Ronan lifts my tank top, freeing my breasts as his hand comes to palm one, his thumb rubbing against my nipple.

"There we go," he grumbles. "That's much better."

"This isn't very sanitary," I argue with a smirk on my face.

"You're right," he nods before he grabs me by the hips and hauls me out of the pool.

My ass barely lands on the cement edge before he's pushing my stomach down, forcing me to lay on my back. His mouth latches onto me, wrapping my thighs around his shoulders as he buries his face in my pussy.

I moan as I reach for his hair, gripping tightly as I grind my pussy against him.

"The cameras," I moan.

"Cut the feed and set up a loop in case anyone checks."

"Why?" I ask breathlessly.

"Don't need my brother watching me with a microscope, and it's easier to eat my baby's cunt whenever I want," he says as he flattens his tongue and licks through me.

I shudder at the move and scoot closer to him.

"Play with those pretty nipples, baby. Play with them like I would," he says against my sensitive flesh.

Demise

"The doors." I remember, looking up at the unlocked passageways.

"Who is coming in here at six in the morning?" he counters.

"Who knows? Is that a risk you're willing to take?" I argue.

A wicked grin spreads across his face.

"Kind of. I remember what a good time you had being daddy's little exhibitionist."

Memories of that day in the hotel flash before my eyes at the same time Ronan slips a finger inside me.

"Play with your tits," he repeats. "Make daddy happy."

I do as he says, cupping both of my breasts before I begin tweaking on my nipples.

"Like that?" I moan as he slips a second finger in.

"Yeah, just like that. Such a good girl. You like daddy finger fucking you while you play with your tits, baby?"

"Uh, huh," I mutter as his tongue drags across my clit, sending a shudder to run through me.

"Of course you do, my perfect girl. I want you to come on daddy's fingers, then I'm gonna fuck you until you see stars in this pool."

"Okay," I happily agree, letting out another moan when he rubs against my g-spot.

"That's it. Relax for me, baby. Let me have my fun with you."

Pleasure pulses inside of me as I continue pulling on my nipples, rolling them between my fingers and tugging on them the way I'd want Ronan to. It feels so good that I don't feel my orgasm coming until it crashes into me. Wave after wave of pleasure takes over me as I squeeze Ronan's fingers. His mouth comes down to cover his fingers, lapping at my pussy until he licks me clean before pulling them out.

His lust fueled gaze locks with my own, and he begins dragging me back into the pool when the sound of his phone rings.

He closes his eyes and curses before pushing out himself, jogging over to his discarded clothes as he fishes out his phone.

"Hello? Yeah, I was just doing some laps in the pool. Alright. Yeah, I'll be there soon."

He hangs up the phone and gives me a regretful look.

"Sorry, baby. I gotta go. Raincheck?" he asks as he comes over to me, scooping my floating discarded clothes and dropping them on the concrete beside me. Disappointment fills me, but I nod as he helps me up.

His hands cup my face, holding me tenderly as his mouth presses to mine. It's a kiss that has me sinking into him, making me instantly dizzy when he pulls away.

"Come have lunch with me. You order in while I eat out," he says.

I let out a short laugh and shake my head as I smack his chest.

"Oh my God. You need to stop spending so much time with Liam; his shitty pick-up lines are rubbing off on you."

Ronan chuckles as he heads to the showers to rinse off, and I start getting dressed into my swimsuit. It's a lot more difficult to get on now that I'm already wet but still, so worth it.

I'm in the middle of a lap when Ronan leaves, waving goodbye. A morning spent getting finger fucked by my hot older boyfriend and finishing it off with a nice cool swim. Name a better way to start the day.

As soon as my class lets out, I'm practically sprinting to Ronan. I already told everyone that I was having lunch with him today, which they all knew what that was code for.

Demise

Excitement thrums inside me. We haven't hooked up at school in forever. It was too dangerous before. Even what we did this morning would have been too much of a risk. Now that we don't have a stalker watching our every move, we can actually relax. At least a little.

I may or may not have thrown my hair into some slutty pigtails, folded my skirt up a few inches, and am currently folding my white blouse up to really sell the whole naughty schoolgirl thing. I think he's going to fucking love it, and I can't wait to see what he'll do to me with these pigtails.

Slipping into the pool building, I push through the doors and look over the empty space, inhaling that sweet chlorine smell before grabbing the door to his office. When I do, I'm not at all prepared for the sight I'm greeted with.

Annie Williams is perched not on his desk but in his *lap*. There she is, sitting pretty, arms around his neck like there is no more natural place for them. I feel my heart physically sink to the ground as I look at them before Ronan turns to face me.

"Skyla." His eyes widen, a hint of alarm in his voice.

Yeah, he should be very fucking alarmed.

"Skyla?" Annie says with a wrinkle of her nose. "Oh! You're his niece."

Ronan sneers. "She is not my niece."

Annie rolls her eyes. "She married your nephew, same thing. How are you, sweetheart? You can call me Aunt Annie," she giggles, forcing her tits into Ronan's face as she does.

He tries to resist her, or at least tries to make it seem like he does, but he doesn't move very far away from her.

"Will we see you tonight?" Annie asks me.

"Tonight?" I hedge.

"RoRo, did you not tell her yet? So typical of you." She laughs as she playfully swats his chest.

RoRo?

"Our engagement party at Putnam Manor. It's tonight. You have to be there, after all, we're family now," she says, batting her three-inch long fake eyelashes.

Her tone is sugary sweet, but there is a level of malice to it.

Engagement party? Tonight?

I know Ronan told me that it would be after the holidays, but I didn't think...I didn't expect...it's happening already?

I feel my throat begin to tighten, hot tears burning my eyes as I do my best to banish them away.

"Right, of course. Almost slipped my mind. My husband and I wouldn't miss it for the world. Congratulations, you two. You're an adorable couple," I say, somehow managing not to vomit as I do.

Ronan's blue eyes are drowning in pain, but conveniently enough, his hand is still resting on her hip. It's been there since before I walked in, and he can't even do the courtesy of removing it. Unfuckingbelivable.

"I know, right? He's a bit of a fixer-upper, but give me a few months, and I'll have him better than ever." She smiles.

I'm speechless, for too many reasons, but I don't have it in me to voice any of them.

"Can I speak candidly, though?" Annie asks.

I grit my teeth together as I nod.

"Sure."

"It's a nice party, black tie. You'll definitely need to change...that," she says as she gestures to my outfit.

"Oh, of course." I play along. "Asher loves it when I dress like his dirty little slut before he fucks me in closets around campus."

"Oh," Annie says, clearly surprised by my lack of discretion. "Well, I suppose whatever it takes to keep your man satisfied. You wouldn't want him to stray," she says, her nails digging into Ronan's arm, a clear territorial move on her part.

"No, we certainly wouldn't want that," I agree before I turn to leave. "Sorry to interrupt, I'll see you both *tonight*," I bite out.

Ronan doesn't try to follow me, nor do I expect him to. Each step I take feels hollow, numb. I'm barely able to pull my shirt down and take my hair out of the pigtails before I stumble, dropping to my knees. I sit there for several seconds, only able to hear the sound of my heart beating.

"Skyla? Are you okay?" Maryia asks, coming over to me in concern.

I look up at her, handing her my phone with a shaky hand.

"Can you call my husband? I need to go home."

She nods quickly, finding Asher's number and calling him. Within minutes, Asher, Liam, and Maggie are all surrounding me, asking me what's wrong, but when I insist that I just want to go home, they concede. Asher lifts me up into his arms and carries me to the car while Liam follows closely behind. Liam unlocks his car, climbing into the driver's seat while Asher sets me into the back and slides in beside me. He hauls me into his chest and begs me to talk to him, but I don't want to talk. I don't know what to say. So, I just sob instead.

Chapter Twenty-Five

Ronan

I'm holding a neat scotch that I haven't touched all night. Quite the opposite to my very inebriated fiancée. This is her sixth or seventh dirty martini, and it shows. I'm not sure why she feels so untouchable. Maybe because she is engaged to a Putnam, or maybe it's because she's a Williams. Elder family or not, there is no room for embarrassment in the Brethren, and she is most definitely an embarrassment.

Annie tries to stand up straight but ends up crashing into me, her drink spilling over her glass as she giggles.

"Ooopsies. Sorry, fiancéééé," she drags out, giggling once more.

I swear to Christ, I've never met anyone that giggles as much as this woman. She knocks back her glass before signaling one of the servers. I catch her hand, though, lowering it to her side.

"That's enough," I say lowly.

"Pfft, I've only had two." She defends.

"No, you've had six, possibly seven. You're drunk, sloppy, and embarrassing me and your family. Go to the bathroom,

Demise

sober up, and come out like the respectable woman you are expected to be," I snap before shoving her away from me.

Hurt flashes in her eyes, but I really don't give a fuck. In the small increments of time I've spent with Annie Williams, I've learned several things. She's extremely self-centered, her condescension knows no bounds, and she's honestly just a fucking bitch.

"Move!" she snaps at a woman and man in front of her, shoving the woman several feet away.

See? Bitch.

My eyes scan the room, in search of that beautiful head of blonde hair and those piercing green eyes. I don't doubt she'll be here. It would look bad for her and Asher if they didn't. After all, we're family. If they don't arrive soon, people will talk, and Christopher will not be happy about that.

Speaking of Satan himself, he slithers across the room, holding out his hand for me to shake as if we aren't fucking blood.

"Ronan, congratulations," he says with a head nod.

"Thank you," I say stiffly.

Christopher's eyes roam over the crowd before he faces me.

"Where has your fiancée run off to?"

"Bathroom," I say curtly.

He nods. "And my son? Have you seen him?"

"No, not yet. I'm sure he'll be along," I say as my eyes come to Liam.

His gaze has come to my own a few times, hardened and judgmental as he looks away to focus on what his mother is saying. I catch Wesley's eye in the corner. He's laughing and schmoozing with a group of people when his smile falls away. A look of indignation crosses his face as he shakes his head and looks away.

It's obvious why they're upset with me. If the roles were

reversed, I'm sure I'd feel the same. They don't get it, though. They should, but for some reason they don't. The party wasn't supposed to be for another two weeks. Christopher only informed me of the date being moved up this morning after I left Skyla in the pool. I planned to talk to her at lunch, but of fucking course, Annie had to beat her to it. The way I wanted to snap her thin fucking neck when she smiled and sneered in Skyla's face. And the heartbreak that etched across my sweet girl's face...it's an image I'm not sure I'll ever be able to remove from my mind.

As if I conjured her from my thoughts alone, the doors open, and Skyla appears. She's wearing a white fur shawl and a blood red gown that looks absolutely breathtaking on her. Asher is by her side, her arm tucked into his as he escorts her through the room.

"Finally," Christopher mutters before waving Asher towards us.

He nods his acknowledgment, sending me a brief but scathing look while Skyla looks anywhere but at me. They stop a few feet short of us, Asher holding out his hand to my brother first.

"Father," he greets before turning to me. "Ronan, congratulations."

"Thank you," I say numbly while Christopher takes Skyla's hand, kissing the back of it as his eyes roam over her.

Her hair is in an updo, wrapped up with a sparkly hair piece holding it together. Her lips are the same blood red as her dress, and her eyes have a shimmery shadow on them that make those green gems absolutely pop.

"My darling daughter, you look absolutely breathtaking," he says as he pulls her from Asher's grasp, forcing her to do a spin.

Demise

I notice the way Asher's hand flexes, like he's trying to reach for her before he closes his fist by his side.

"You must honor me with a dance," he says, dragging Skyla to the dance floor.

She casts an uneasy glance to Asher but makes sure to smile and nod.

"I'd be honored."

They stop in the middle of the room, my brother's hand resting far too low for my liking on her back as he begins leading her through a waltz. She twirls around the room effortlessly. Everyone can't help but to watch her. She has this presence about her that forces you to pay attention, whether you want to or not.

"Where is your bitch fiancée?" Asher asks, keeping his eyes on Skyla and his father.

"Bathroom trying to sober up," I say blandly.

Asher huffs. "Trading Skyla for a boozehound. Nicely done."

My head whips to him, lowering my voice as I do.

"I haven't traded Skyla for anyone. You know as well as I this is nothing more than a business transaction."

His head turns to face me, an unimpressed look on his face.

"Maybe to you. Not to her," he says as he points to the bathroom. "Most certainly not to her." He nods towards Skyla, who is putting on the show of her life.

If I didn't know any better, I'd think she was enjoying her time with Christopher. My eyes never leave her, I'm practically willing her to look at me, just for a second. She doesn't, though. She's perfected the art of pretending I don't exist at all.

"You should have told her," Asher said with a shake of his head. "Warned her."

"It was sprung on me. I ran out of time. I was planning to—"

"Yeah, well, your plan went to shit. I didn't see you picking her up off the ground, holding her while she cried over this fucking joke," he says, glaring at the elaborately decorated party. No doubt all Annie's doing.

My heart aches to hear how hurt Skyla was today, how hurt she no doubt is now. I wish I could steal a moment with her, reassure her that she is my everything. That no one will ever take her place. It's not ideal, but it's the world we live in. I will have to marry Annie Williams, but that doesn't mean I'll stop loving Skyla, that I'll stop seeing her. If she'll have me. It's complicated, but doable. If she wants it too.

"Will you distract Annie for me? I want to talk to Skyla," I say as I spot Annie making her way towards us, looking a hell of a lot more put together than she was before. Not sure how she managed that, but I don't really care.

Asher snorts condescendingly as he looks to me out of the corner of his eye.

"You're fucking delusional. You've already made her cry enough for one day, for a lifetime. Stay the fuck away from my wife," he seethes as the song ends, and he weaves through the crowd to collect Skyla.

A white manicured hand slides up my arm, digging in as she forces my attention to her.

"Better?" she asks.

My eyes roam over her out of obligation as I give a stiff nod. She seems to preen under my approval, which is fucked up since I didn't even give her so much as a compliment. My indifference must be all she needs to feel valued. Poor girl has no idea what it's like to truly be appreciated. Or maybe she doesn't care either way.

I notice the moment she sees Skyla. Her mouth purses and her eyebrows raise as her eyes roam over Skyla from top to

Demise

bottom. My shoulder pushes into hers, reminding her to fix her face, and like the good little daughter of the Brethren, she does.

"So good to see you. Thank you for coming to celebrate us." She smiles at Skyla, resting her head against my chest.

Skyla's eyes remain on her, a perfectly practiced smile on her face as she nods.

"We wouldn't have missed it for the world. Are you having a good evening?"

"The best. How could I not with this amazing man by my side?" Annie says as she looks up at me, batting her eyelashes dramatically.

"We're so happy to have you join the family, Annie." Christopher smiles, that wolfish grin spreading across his face.

She smiles demurely at him, though you'd have to be stupid not to clock the suggestive gaze she gives him in return. Maybe she'll decide to hell with me and go for my brother instead. It would save me a lot of pain and heartache if she did.

"I couldn't imagine life getting any more perfect now," she says, winding her arms around my neck and dragging my mouth to hers.

I resist for a moment but remember all of the eyes on me. The one pair I care about most is reason enough to rip myself away, but I know it's not the right move.

Skyla, forgive me.

Annie's lips are thin and cold. She presses our faces close together to the point where it's uncomfortable. A turning in my stomach spreads to every inch of my body, and when she finally allows me to pull away, I discreetly wipe my mouth.

However, when I look up, I see Asher watching with unrestrained rage, Christopher with approval, and Skyla gone. My head whips around to see the hem of her dress slipping around the corner. I feel myself take a step towards her before I take a breath. Chasing after your nephew's wife at your engagement party is the exact thing I shouldn't be doing. So, I find an out.

"Annie, have you been given a tour of the art room at the manor?" I ask, knowing it's one of Christopher's favorite things to boast about.

Predictably so, his face lights up, and he slides up beside her.

"I'd be happy to show you. The Putnam family has been collecting for over three hundred and fifty years."

She gives me a tight smile before it melts into something more convincing, her arm slipping in the crook of Christopher's.

"I'd be delighted."

"This way, beautiful," he says, his eyes taking extra time on her cleavage as he leads her up the stairs and down the hall.

As soon as they are out of sight, I head after Skyla. I only make it a few steps before Asher catches my arm.

"Where the fuck do you think you're going?"

"I need to talk to her," I say.

"No, you need to leave her the fuck alone. Don't you see how hard this is for her? You chasing after her is only going to make it worse."

I shake my head. "I need to apologize, Asher. Explain...I don't know. I have to do something."

Asher stares at me for several seconds before letting go of my arm reluctantly. It's not exactly his acceptance, but I know it's the closest I'll get from him. Turning around the corner Skyla disappeared behind, I peek my head in each room as I pass by, all coming up empty.

When I come to the back door, I hesitate for a moment before looking outside. My feet move across the concrete patio, the rustling of the maze bushes catching my attention.

Of course.

Demise

I make quick work of jogging down the stairs to the gardens, entering the maze as I begin weaving in and out of the pathways until I find her. My heart practically seizes in my chest when I see her sitting on the ledge of the fountain; her head hung low, and the soft whimpers of her cries hanging in the night air.

Her head whips up when she hears my footsteps, quickly wiping away her tears as she sniffs.

"What are you doing here?"

"Looking for you," I say as I come to sit beside her, giving her enough space but allowing myself to be close enough that she could reach me if she wanted to.

"This is your engagement party, Ronan. You should be inside with your fiancée," she says bitterly.

I nod. "If I remember correctly, you and I seem to have a habit of spending engagement parties in the gardens instead."

Her mouth twitches in what could be a smile or a frown, I'm not too sure, before she shakes her head.

"Just go. Please. I can't be in there, smiling like I'm alright. Watching her dig her fucking claws into you, kissing her. Do you have any idea what that did to me?" she chokes out, clearly holding back a sob as she does.

I swallow roughly, my hands aching to reach for her.

"I'm sorry, baby. I never want to hurt you. We all have a part to play here. Trust me, I'd rather spend any amount of time with anyone else. She's vile and conniving and—"

"Your future wife. You'll be married soon and have vile and conniving babies," she finishes.

I grimace at that and shake my head.

"I don't want that," I say lowly.

"You don't have a choice, though, right? 'We all have a part to play,'" she says, using air quotes as she does.

"If I could do something, anything, you know I would, right?" I ask.

She's silent, and it fills me with an insurmountable level of panic.

"Baby," I say as I reach for her hand, gripping it like she'll be ripped away from me any minute. "Please, believe me."

"I believe you," she says, her voice soft and thick with tears. "It doesn't change anything, though. I've lost you, and I...I just...I—"

A growl tears through my chest, anger and pain mixing inside me as I yank her over to me. She barely has enough time to catch herself, her legs forced to straddle me as my hand goes up her dress, bunching it up around her hips.

"Ronan," she gasps as I pull my cock out through my slacks and push her panties to the side before sliding into her.

Her moan is louder than it should be, but I thrust into her deeper, craving another.

"Ohhh," she shouts, as I do it again and again, savagely fucking her as rough as I can.

"You haven't lost me. I haven't lost you. You can't quit me, baby. You understand? You're mine, and I'm yours. We will never not belong to one another, okay?" I punctuate with another sharp thrust.

"Fuckkk," she moans.

"She doesn't mean shit. You're everything, Skyla, absolutely fucking everything," I groan as her pussy pulses around me.

"I hate her," she cries, a tear rolling down her cheeks as she bounces on my cock.

"Me too, baby. Me too."

"You're mine. She can't have you," she moans as her eyes come to mine.

"She never will," I promise. "Not in a way that counts. Not in the way you do."

She nods her head, milking the cum out of me with her groans and whimpers.

"Fuck, baby. Ride daddy's cock. Show me how much you love daddy."

"So much," she mutters.

"I know. I love you, baby. Forever."

Another tear rolls down her face, and I catch it with my tongue, running a long line up her cheek before pressing my lips to hers. I feel her body shake, and I feel my own orgasm beginning to build. Our bodies are so in tune with one another, so connected. There is no way anyone could stand a chance at comparing to Skyla. To think otherwise is just plain idiocy.

"Ronan, Ronan, Ronan," she shouts as her orgasm takes over her.

Her movements fall out of rhythm as her legs shake and her back arches. I curse under my breath as my cock floods her pussy. I fuck her deeper than before, intent on pushing my cum further and further into her before our movements still all together.

She rests her head against my shoulder, letting out a shuddering breath as she sighs.

"We'll get through this together," I say. "Okay, baby?"

Skyla doesn't respond, concern weighing heavily inside me as she slowly lifts herself from me. I watch her adjust her dress, wincing as she takes a step. No doubt she feels uncomfortably full, my cum leaking down her legs.

"Asher and I are going to leave. I know that you don't love her, but I can't pretend to sit back and smile and be happy for you. Even for show."

My mouth stays in a flat line, and I nod my understanding

as she turns on her heel and slips out of the garden. I sit there for several seconds, running my hands through my hair. I wonder how the fuck I'm going to go back in there and pretend that everything is alright, let alone marry a woman that I can't fucking stand, knowing that it's breaking the only person that means anything to me in this life.

Chapter Twenty Six

Skyla

I step inside the party, laughter and music practically deafeningly loud when I bump into a woman. Oh, not a woman. The woman. *Annie.*

"Ow! Watch where you're fucking going," she sneers at me.

My mouth drops open, unable to hide my shock.

"Excuse me?" I ask.

"Excuse me?" she mimics before narrowing her eyes at me. "You heard me. If you would stop being a pathetic lovesick bitch, maybe you'd be able to watch where you're going."

I shake my head, scoffing at her as I speak.

"I don't know what you're talking about."

"Please," she snaps. "The tacky slutty schoolgirl thing, the little heart eyes you give him any time you're in the same room as him. You've got a little crush on your husband's uncle. Fucking disgusting of you, honestly. I wonder how your poor husband would feel if he knew?"

I don't react, allowing her to see absolutely none of my emotions.

"You think I like Ronan?" I laugh derisively before shaking my head.

I don't like him, I love him.

Indecision muddles her eyes before she tilts her head to the side in question.

"Yes, I do. You're so obvious about it. You're just an inexperienced little girl. You could never give him what he needs."

Really, I try to do my best to hold in my amusement at that statement. After all, I'm the one with Ronan's cum dripping down my legs. I don't respond as she lifts up her white dress, exposing her ass cheeks that have very defined fingerprint bruises developing.

"He likes it rough. As soon as you left that office, he couldn't bury himself inside me quick enough," she smiles before pulling down her dress and sashaying off towards the kitchen.

I know she's full of shit. She has to be. I trust Ronan, and if anything would have happened between them, he would have told me. I know it. That's not to say something won't happen eventually. He'll be expected to produce an heir, and that means he'll have to sleep with her at least once. What if he finds out he enjoys it? What if they do it more than once? What if...

"Hey, are you okay?" Asher asks, rounding the corner before reaching out to cup my face.

"Can we go? I need to go."

He nods. "We've made our appearance. That's all that matters. C'mon," he says as he laces our hands together, leading me through the throngs of people.

Liam and Wesley both catch my eye, and I watch as they both dismiss the people they are talking to before they begin following us. When we are all outside of the house, waiting for the valet, Asher speaks quietly to them.

"I'm taking my wife home for the night."

They both nod their understanding, handing the valet their tickets as well when Asher's car pulls up. He tips the valet driver and opens my door for me before climbing into his own seat. I look out the window, seeing sympathetic looks on Liam and Wesley as Asher pulls away and makes our way home.

Somehow, Liam and Wesley beat us home. As soon as Asher parks, Wesley is at my door while Liam reaches for my hand. I take it as I walk numbly into the house before settling in on the couch. Liam crawls behind me, pulling me into his lap as Asher and Wesley sit on either side of me. We all sit in silence for several minutes before Liam speaks.

"Are you okay?"

I shrug. "It's our life, right? First Ronan. You and Vincent will be next. I'm sure Christopher is already plotting for Wesley," I say bitterly with a shake of my head. "It's what I get for falling for five men, right?"

"Hey," Wesley says as he squeezes my hand. "One day at a time. There are ways for us to stay together."

"Like what?" I ask. "You guys come over here after work, get a quick screw in before you go home to your wife and kids?"

Liam's face twists up at that as he forces my head back to make eye contact with him.

"You know it wouldn't be like that."

I shrug my shoulders. "I don't know what to think, what to expect. I just..." I pause, my voice catching. "She's awful," I say as tears begin pouring down my face.

Liam holds me closer to him, shushing me softly as the sound of the door opens and closes.

"Baby?" Ronan calls out. "Baby, where are you?"

Asher's jaw clenches, but it's Wesley who stands up, intercepting him before he can reach the couch.

"It's not a good time," Wesley says.

"What did she say to you?" Ronan asks. "She was bragging to me, telling me she had a little chat with you."

Before I respond, the door opens and closes again, Vincent stepping into the room. As soon as he sees me, his body goes rigid but I spring out of Liam's lap and run to him. I jump into his arms, and he catches me midair, burying his head into my neck as he grips the back of my hair and inhales.

"Fuck, I've missed you. What's wrong, siren?"

His gravelly voice gives me a comfort completely unique to him, and I cherish it, burrowing in deeper against him as I sob. He rocks me gently before turning to face the guys.

"What happened?"

"Ronan's engagement party was tonight," Liam says with a heavy breath.

"The fuck?" Vincent snaps.

"It was a last minute thing. Christopher told me about it this morning," Ronan defends.

"And apparently, Ronan's bitch fiancée said some shit to Sky," Asher continues.

Vincent forces my head away from his chest, holding eye contact with me as he speaks.

"What did she say, siren?"

I shake my head. "That I could never be enough for Ronan. That she knows I have a 'crush' on him and that I could never compare to her. She also said they fucked this afternoon after I left. Showed me fingerprint bruises on her ass cheeks and everything," I smile weakly.

"What?" all of the guys snap, staring at Ronan with murder in their eyes.

"That's a load of fucking horseshit. I made her leave literally minutes after you left. Sky, you don't honestly believe her, do you?"

I shake my head. "But you'll have to fuck her one of these days, and she is pretty. Wouldn't be able to hold it against you if you liked it and—"

"And absolutely nothing," Ronan intervenes. "She's a fucking liar!"

"It doesn't matter even if you had," I say dejectedly.

Ronan looks at me helplessly before Vincent presses a kiss to my forehead.

"I'll fix it, siren."

Then, he sets me on my feet and steps out of the room. Ronan takes the opportunity to close the distance between us, but honestly, it's been a long day and I'm fucking tired. I hold my hand up to him, effectively silencing him as I shake my head.

"I'm being irrational, I get that. We all knew this was going to happen eventually, I was just hoping it would be later than sooner. I'll get over it, I will. I just…need some space."

Moving past him, he tries to reach for me when Wesley grabs his arm, pulling it away. When he tries to push against Wesley, Asher is there reinforcing him as Liam comes up to my side.

"What can I do?" he asks.

I smile at him sadly. "Want to come take a bath with me?"

He nods, his hands running through my hair.

"I'd love to."

Liam and I soak in the bath in silence for over forty-five minutes, and it's absolute heaven. After, we get dressed into our warmest pajamas and head downstairs for a late night snack.

Ronan is down there, his head in his hands, while Wesley and Asher talk quietly from the kitchen. As soon as I step into the room, all eyes are on me as Ronan stands to his feet. His mouth opens like he wants to say something before he shakes his head and sighs.

In the next moment, Vincent steps inside the house, pulling off black gloves and stuffing them into his back pocket. His eyes come straight to me as he nods.

"Problem solved."

My brows furrow at that.

"What?" I ask as Asher shakes his head.

"You didn't..." Asher says hesitantly.

"Didn't what?" I ask as I look between the guys.

Understanding dawns over each of their faces as I turn back to Vincent.

"What did you do?"

He shrugs. "I fixed the problem. Ronan is no longer engaged."

I look to see Ronan's face blank, devoid of any emotion.

"What do you mean? How?" I ask.

Vincent strolls up to me casually, cupping my cheek as he looks into my eyes.

"He can't be engaged to a corpse."

"Jesus," Ronan grumbles under his breath.

My eyes widen at the realization.

Demise

"You killed her? You killed Annie Williams?"

"Technically, yes," he says. "Officially, she was still drunk from the party, fell down the stairs, and cracked her head open."

I wait for horror to fill me, disgust or anger. I wait for that fight or flight urge to run rampant inside me, demanding I get myself away from this psychotic maniac as fast as possible. Instead, I just shake my head.

"What if you get caught? What if—"

His finger comes to my lips, silencing me immediately.

"I never get caught, siren. You had a problem, I fixed it. Just say thank you," he says before pressing his lips to mine.

For some moronic reason, I kiss him back. Not only do I kiss him back, though, I enjoy it. I feel thankful, grateful even. It's one thing to have a man who will protect you. It's another who will so easily kill for you. Not for your protection, but for your peace, for your heart. The fact that he went over there without another word, murdered a woman just so she wouldn't marry one of my other boyfriends...you can't make this shit up.

"You okay?" Wesley asks, and I tear my mouth away from Vincent to see him nod.

"It's better this way," Ronan says, a coldness to his eyes as he crosses the room to Vincent and me, holding out his hand for him.

Vincent doesn't move for several seconds before he shakes Ronan's hand. He doesn't say thank you, but he doesn't need to either. You can see it written all over Ronan's face. I can also see the morality battle he's currently fighting. Ronan is kind and caring. He doesn't wish death on those that don't deserve it. Was Annie awful? Absolutely. Did she deserve to die? Probably not. Will I cry at her funeral? Absolutely the fuck not.

Chapter Twenty-Seven

Wesley

News of Annie Williams' death spread quickly, and her father was out for blood. He insisted that it was murder, but when the tox screen came back and her blood alcohol level was .25, he was silenced almost immediately. It's an embarrassing look, a soon_to be bride dying from being too shit faced and stumbling down the stairs; at least, that's how everyone views it.

I'm sure Vincent poured more liquor down her throat to get that BAL up. She was buzzed during the party but seemed to sober up rather quickly. Unless she went home and started slamming vodka shots, I doubt it was all her own doing.

Honestly, I expected Skyla to flip when I realized what Vincent had done. To everyone's surprise, not only did she not freak out, she seemed kind of grateful. It just showed that our girl has a much darker streak than I think any of us anticipated. One that honestly might just be her saving grace if she wants to survive in this world.

I'm currently waiting to pick her up at the university. Adjusting to this more relaxed pace of living has been an adjustment. When Ronan called me about coming back to Salem, I almost didn't answer the call. I had been discharged for two years, unbeknownst to the Brethren, and I planned on keeping it that way. There was something in his voice, though. Something desperate, and I knew he needed me.

Little did I know, I'd end up finding the love of my fucking life. Yeah, I said it. Skyla is the love of my life. I don't care how improbable that seems, and fuck no, I haven't told her. Where would I find the time in between the stalker, the kidnapping, and the four other guys always attached to her hip? We barely got started before she was taken, something I still feel responsible for and probably always will. I'm always meticulous, my guard is never dropped, but she...she is the exception, and it's dangerous for us all.

The unfortunate thing about being back in Salem is that the Brethren believe I am their own personal PI. I mean, to be fair, being born into an Elder family means I am whatever the Brethren wants me to be until I'm rotting six feet under. Sometimes, I think it was a mistake to come back. I flew under the radar. I was offered an opportunity to leave Salem, an opportunity not many were given. My father was a large factor in that. He and my uncle were both SEALs when they graduated from Gallows Hill, and they said it made them the leaders they are today.

Like so many, my mom died when I was young. Officially, it was a car accident, but everyone in the Brethren knows the truth. My parents supposedly had a rough marriage, and it's no coincidence that the police were called the night before my mother was found dead in the street for a domestic disturbance.

My father had his heir and no use for my mother. Poof. Gone.

I haven't even spoken to my father since I've been back in Salem, and honestly, I prefer it that way. We never had any semblance of a relationship, and neither of us try to pretend otherwise.

The singular reason I haven't slipped off in the middle of the night and faked my death begins walking towards me, forcing my heart to skip a beat in my chest as I slide out of the driver's seat. Her face lights up as she sees me, and I can't help but match her grin.

"Good afternoon, Mrs. Putnam," I tease.

She rolls her eyes as she slides into the backseat. "God, not you, too."

"What's the matter? You don't like being Asher's wife?"

"No, it's actually pretty great," she smiles as I shut her door and climb back into the car.

"Where to?" I ask.

"Wherever you want."

I lift a brow in the rearview mirror.

"Liam is having dinner at his parents' house, Asher and Ronan are at Christopher's, and Vincent is off doing...whatever Vincent does. I'm all yours."

I grin at that. "Finally," I say before I put the car into drive and take off. We drive for a few miles before I turn onto the freeway, earning a curious glance from Skyla as I grin.

"Where are you taking me, sir?"

"You'll see." I smile as I merge.

Snow flurries begin sticking to my windshield, and I turn on the wipers. Skyla is already wearing a thick winter coat and a hat with cotton gloves, and I have an extra pair of snow gloves in the console for her. Perfect.

"Sooo," Skyla draws out slowly.

I look to her in the rearview mirror, my brow raised in question.

"Sooo?" I mimic.

She smiles and shakes her head as she leans forward.

"Sooo, has there been any development? Between you and Ronan?"

"Like?"

Skyla shrugs as I turn to look over my shoulder at her.

"Little one, are you asking if I've fucked my best friend?"

A blush blooms across her face as she shrugs once again.

"Inquiring minds want to know."

"You want to know," I tease. "Sorry to disappoint, though. We aren't like Liam and Asher."

Her bottom lip sticks out just a bit in an adorable as fuck way that makes me want to bite into it.

"You could be," she hedges.

I grin and shake my head as I focus on the road.

"What is it with you and trying to get us all to fuck?"

"I like it," she says as she pulls her hair over her shoulders, running her fingers through it as she speaks. "Name me a woman that has five boyfriends and then tell me she doesn't want her boyfriends to be boyfriends."

I let out a short chuckle at that.

"Well, I think you're well on your way with that wish when it comes to Liam and Asher."

A giddy smile crosses her face as she nods.

"I know, right?"

Smiling, I merge into the fast lane, passing the Nissan that was refusing to do more than fifty as she continues.

"Come on. That kiss in the shack wasn't nothing, and neither was the way he willingly went down on you," Skyla says in almost a pleading tone.

Flashes of that night play in my head like an erotic fever dream. She's not wrong, he did kiss me and suck my cock like he'd been the one doing it all these years. Honestly, it felt even better than when Liam sucked me off because it was Ronan. He definitely didn't wake up this morning and think about how he was going to give his first blow job, how he was going to kiss his best friend. He looked at me with such a want, and when he gave in...it made it all that much sweeter.

Shaking my head out of my horny daydream, I shrug.

"I don't know, too early to tell," I say cryptically.

She releases an exaggerated sigh and leans back into her seat.

"Fine, I'll be patient," she says with a defiant grumble.

Yeah, sure, she will.

The thing is, I wouldn't be opposed to pursuing anything with Ronan as well as Skyla. Granted, I'm not sure I could ever have the same feelings for him that I do for Skyla, but I care about him. I like to see him happy, and I've wanted him to fuck me with that beautiful cock of his for years now. We don't have to date or be in love or any of that. If he would be down, I'd love to fuck around from time to time. Share Skyla together, just me and him like we did at the house. I'd call him daddy all he wanted.

Shifting my position in my seat, I go to adjust my cock when I catch Skyla smirking at me.

"What?" I ask.

"Got a problem up there?"

I huff. "I'm fine."

Her head tilts to the side. "Want me to take care of it?"

I lift a brow at her, and she unbuckles her seat belt, crawling through to the front seat. I grip the steering wheel extra tight as I snap at her.

"Jesus, Sky! What the fuck are you doing?"

When she reaches the front, she buckles in like a good girl before pulling her hair out of her face.

"Helping out," she says as she leans over the center console, unzipping my zipper and pulling out my raging hard cock.

I glance down to see a bead of pre-cum on my tip, and she flattens out her tongue, licking it off before smiling up at me.

"I hear road head is excellent this time of the day," she teases before pushing my cock down her throat.

It takes everything in me to keep my eyes open as I let out a string of curse words. Her tongue licks and twists up and down my cock as her mouth tightens around me.

"Fuck, little one. Just like that," I groan.

She hums around me, sending a rush of pleasure through me. Her mouth comes all the way to the tip, pulling off me for a second as she speaks.

"Talk to me, Wes. Tell me, what's got you so hard?"

Chuckling, I grab ahold of her beanie, pushing her further down on my cock until she gags, then I push her another inch or so.

"That's my girl," I moan. "I was thinking about that day in the bedroom. You, me, and Ronan. Thinking about how fucking amazing you felt, and then how much I loved sucking Ronan's cock with you."

"Mhmm," she mumbles, nodding her head in agreement.

"I was thinking how I'd love to do that again. Think you'd do that for me? Would you share your daddy's cock with me?"

I glance down to see her eyes are already on me as she eagerly nods. I smirk at that.

"Such a sweet girl sharing her daddy time. Think we could get daddy to suck my cock again?"

Her mouth releases my cock with a pop as she nods.

"Leave it to me," Skyla says, a malicious smile spreading across her face.

I release the back of her head, gripping her throat and dragging her to meet my lips. I keep my eyes on the road as we kiss, our tongues tangling together before I rip her away and push her down on my cock once more.

My hips begin thrusting, my hand coming to the back of her head once more as I begin fucking her face.

"Good girl, little one. Good. Fucking. Girl," I grumble as I punctuate every word with a thrust down her throat.

She moans and whimpers around me as she nods her head and reaches into my boxers, massaging my balls. It's just what I need to throw me over the edge. I feel the building of my orgasm begin, my body starts shaking, my breathing coming in choppy before I lose it.

I feel my cock throb down her throat, my cum coating her mouth as she swallows me down like a goddamn porn star. I guess when you have four boyfriends and a husband, you basically are one.

Skyla swallows one more time before sitting up, licking her lips once more. I grin at her, reaching across her and grabbing the lever to her seat. It drops almost flat in an instant, and she squeals in surprise as I speak.

"Take your leggings off, little one. Let me play with that pussy."

Her eyes dilate as she quickly rips off her leggings and panties, shoving them to her ankles as she spreads her legs. Such an eager little thing.

Reaching over the console to her, I rub my fingers through her, pleased to find her absolutely fucking drenched. I play with her pussy for a moment before I shove my fingers inside her, pulling them back out as I hold my fingers up to her mouth.

"Taste," I say.

She does so happily, letting out a little satisfied moan as she does.

I grin at that. "You like tasting yourself, sweet girl?"

Skyla nods, a bashful blush tinting her cheeks as she releases my fingers.

"A lot."

My cock throbs at that.

"Maybe we need to find you a girl to play with. I bet you'd love eating pussy. Or having those soft lips on your pussy," I say, pushing my fingers inside her and taking an interest when her pussy pulses around me.

"Maybe," she mutters. "I've never been with a girl before."

Her pussy pulses again, and I grin.

"But you want to, or you're curious. Your cunt is practically milking me with just the idea of it. What about that pretty redhead friend of yours?"

"Maggie?" she laughs. "She's my best friend. Sounds messy."

"Oh, it is, trust me, but you'd love every fucking second of it."

Skyla laughs as I begin thrusting in her.

"She has a girlfriend."

"And you have four boyfriends and a husband," I point out.

She shakes her head no, and though I'm a little disappointed, I go with it.

"Just a fantasy, then." I decide, dragging my fingers through her before settling on her clit.

"Close your eyes, little one. Picture Maggie or some hot actress. Any woman in the world you want playing with your pussy. Imagine her soft lips pressed against yours, her smooth body grinding against you, and her sweet tongue circling this clit," I whisper lowly.

Skyla lets out a moan, her head resting against the headrest as I move against her clit faster.

"Imagine she has you pinned in this seat, nowhere to go or move. All you can do is breathe through it as she begins licking, sucking, and finger fucking this pussy."

Another soft whimper comes from her lips as she lifts her

hips against me, seeking more friction that I'm happy to provide.

"Yeah, you love that, don't you, sweet girl?"

She nods shakily. "I do. I want it," she begs.

"Only in fantasy?" I test.

"Uh, huh," she agrees.

Just checking.

"Play with your clit, little one. Play with it like you'd play with hers," I say as I slip my fingers back inside her.

She obeys me instantly, her fingers moving expertly against herself as she cries out and bucks her hips.

"Fuck! I love it."

"She's so wet for you. Practically dripping," I say as I pump my fingers in and out of her. "What are you gonna do?"

Her breaths are choppy, her voice shaky as she speaks.

"I'm gonna make her com-me. I'm gonna...gonna...fuck!" she moans as her orgasm crashes into her.

Wave after wave of pleasure hits her as she groans and squirms in the seat, not settling down for at least thirty seconds before she lets out a shaky breath and closes her eyes.

I watch her with a hunger fueled look, my cock already stiff as a fucking board.

"Please," I beg. "Please make that fantasy a reality someday, little one."

She lets out a lighthearted laugh as I pull my fingers out of her, and she pulls up her leggings. She doesn't say no, but that laugh definitely wasn't a yes. I pop my fingers into my mouth and begin sucking off her taste, savoring it for the remaining few miles we have.

Chapter Twenty-Eight

Skyla

When Wesley exits, I have no idea where we are or what we're doing. Honestly, it could just be that I'm still in a post-orgasm haze. I've never had a more enjoyable car ride and probably never will.

He pulls off to the side of the road and parks, reaching into the center console to grab a pair of snow gloves. Now that we aren't moving, I can see how quickly the snow is falling, and I can't help but smile.

"Where are we going?" I ask as he hands me the gloves.

"Just come on," he says as he adjusts his pants once more before opening the door, jogging around the front of the car to grab mine.

I slip on the gloves over my cotton ones as he tucks my arm through his and begins walking me down the street. He begins trying to match my pace as I match his before we begin gently pushing each other and laughing. It's so easy to spend time with Wesley. He has this very protective and strong nature, but it can just as easily melt away, leaving space for this other light-hearted and goofy side.

A few more steps and, I finally understand why we are here. Dozens and dozens of food trucks block the road, hundreds of people moving from truck to truck with baskets full of food. My eyebrows raise as I look up to Wesley and smile.

"What is this?" I ask.

"The seventh annual food truck fair." He grins.

Of course, why didn't I think of it before? There was no way Wesley's idea of a first date wasn't going to include hordes of food. My perpetual snacker.

We move through the walkways for a bit before stopping at a street taco truck. We both order two and start munching when we come across a falafel truck. Wesley orders us one to share and that's pretty much how we spend the next two hours. We laughed, cracked jokes, told stories about us growing up and ate. My God, did we eat.

The portions aren't huge, thank goodness, but still, after the apple cinnamon churro, the strawberry cheesecake on a stick, chili dog, onion ring tower, and deep-fried cheese wedge, yep, you read that right, I can hardly walk.

Slowly, I practically waddle over to a bench beneath a twinkle lit gazebo. It overlooks the river, and I smile as I stare out over it, my stomach and heart equally stuffed. Wesley takes a seat beside me, wrapping his arm around my waist in an attempt to hold me closer to him.

My eyes instinctually look around.

"Shouldn't we be careful?" I ask.

He shakes his head and smiles. "I've got us covered. Don't worry."

I open my mouth to ask how but decide maybe it's better if I don't know. I'm starting to see the bright side to women being left out of things in the Brethren. It's a hell of a lot less stressful.

"Thank you for today," I smile. "It was a lot of fun."

Demise

"Thanks for coming."

I drop my smile in faux concern.

"I didn't have a choice. You were driving."

He grins and shakes his head, leaning in to press his lips against mine. When he pulls away, his blue eyes are practically twinkling, his blonde hair holding several large flakes of snow.

Suddenly, his gaze becomes a little more serious as his fingers intertwine with my own.

"I know our relationship is unconventional, and you're obviously in a different place with each of them than you are with me, and I don't care, but I...I love you," he says, forcing my heart to do a cartwheel, back flip, and beat out of my chest all at once.

"I've loved you from the moment I laid eyes on you. Each day spent with you, that love has grown more and more; all I see is you, all I breathe is you. You're my entire fucking world. Nothing matters but you, and I hope you'll let me prove it every day for the rest of our lives because I can't picture a life without you."

He lets out a short breath and shakes his head as his eyes come back to me.

"I've made mistakes, big ones. But even through all the mistakes in my past and all the mistakes I'll no doubt make in the future, I'll never stop loving you."

I swallow roughly as I look at him. Is it crazy for me to feel the same way? Already? We've only known each other for a few months, and already I'm head over heels for this man when I have four others who also hold a piece of my heart. Yes, abso-fuckinlutly, yes.

"I love you too, Wes. I've loved you for longer than I think I even realized. The instant your lips touched mine, I knew that you were that missing piece to the puzzle. The one I didn't realize was missing until you were right in front of me, and everything was so clear. You were always meant to be here."

"And I always will be," he says as he cups my face, bringing me in for a sweet and tender kiss.

I melt into him, lazily wasting minutes, or maybe it's hours, getting lost in him. It's never a waste when it's time with him, though.

It's been three days since Wesley's and my food truck date and, honestly, I'm just now getting my appetite back. I was able to eat a small chicken salad for dinner, but that was pretty much it. There is no time to think about anything but the task at hand currently.

I woke up at four in the morning just so I would have enough time to put everything together. I'm just finishing the last swirl of icing on the cake when Ronan walks in, dressed and ready for the day. Meanwhile, I'm in my sleep shorts, tank top, my hair is in a messy bun, and there's a streak of cake batter across my cheek.

Ronan's eyes widen as he scans the living room and kitchen. It took me thirty-five minutes just to inflate all of the balloons with one of those helium tanks in the garage. Even longer, embarrassingly enough, to string together the happy birthday banner currently tacked to the wall and then this German chocolate cake…let's not even talk about it. Why Asher has to love one of the most troubling cakes I've ever made is beyond me. Then again, I'm not exactly a world class baker, but at least I tried!

Ronan looks at me, a sweet smile melting across his face as he crosses the room.

"Baby, how long have you been up?"

I glance at the clock and grimace.

"Three hours."

He shakes his head. "All for Asher's birthday?"

I shrug. "It's a big day. He has his ceremony tonight, and I can only imagine whatever that will entail will be...less than pleasant," I say with a wince. "Then he has to go to a party at his dad's house and pretend to be happy about officially becoming a member. I thought the least I could do was blow up some balloons and bake him a cake."

He stares down at me as he tucks a piece of hair behind my ear.

"You're really sweet, do you know that?"

Ronan lifts my chin, bringing my lips to his, when footsteps sound through the kitchen. I scramble away from Ronan, grabbing one of the confetti cannons I bought before handing him one. I get ready to shoot it when I see that it's just Wesley. He holds up his hands in surrender, and I lower my celebratory weapon.

"What's going on?" he asks.

"It's Ash's birthday. Here," Ronan says as he hands Wesley a cannon before grabbing another one for himself.

Another set of footsteps come down the stairs. Wait, two. Excitement runs through me as I nod at the guys. They take up their aim just before Liam and Asher stroll into the room, both with a melancholy look on their face. As soon as the confetti cannons go off, Liam's downcast expression falls away. He looks around, wide-eyed with excitement, as he begins bouncing up and down while Asher remains shocked.

"Happy birthday!" I smile before setting the cannon down and running over to Asher.

Confetti is still fluttering around us, even more going off when Liam gets a hold of one, shooting it off into the air.

"Oh, these are fucking badass!" He laughs.

I wrap my arms around Asher, and he hesitates for a moment before closing his arms around me as well.

"Happy birthday, baby," I say again, smiling as I pull away to look at him.

Instead of a smile or excitement like I half expected, he looks confused. His eyes roam around the room, from the balloons to the decorations and finally to the cake. His head tilts to the side as he shakes his head.

"What's all of this?" he asks.

My own smile falters as my brows knit together.

"It's your birthday...I wanted to do something special. Do you not like it? I can take it down if you—"

"No," he cuts off quickly. "It's perfect. It's..." his words trail off, and I notice a slight gloss to his eyes as he blinks hard and looks at me. "It's the nicest thing anyone has ever done for me."

I smile at that and kiss his cheek. "If you think that's nice, just wait until you see what I got you for your birthday. Spoiler alert, it's something that goes on my body that you'll hopefully take off with your teeth."

That seems to pull a smile out of him. He lets out a short chuckle as he shakes his head and brings my lips to his, holding me there for several seconds before pulling away.

"That better be a promise," he practically growls.

"You can count on it." I wink as Liam begins talking excitedly.

"Ooo, for my birthday, can I have a huge cake?! Each layer a different flavor?! Oh, and one of those balloon arches. They look so badass. And—"

"You'll get what I give you and like it," I say sharply, smirking at him as he gives me a goofy grin.

"Fineeee," he drags out before practically bouncing over to us, planting a huge kiss against Asher's lips. "Happy birthday, babyboy!"

"Babyboy?" Asher asks with indignation.

"Yeah, Skyla's nickname is babygirl. You're babyboy. It's cute, right?" Liam asks.

"Adorable," Asher scoffs, though there is no way he can hide that hint of a smile at his lips.

"Alright, birthday boy, babygirl," he says, facing me. "I think it's time for a little birthday throuple love, unless you fine gentlemen want to join?" Liam asks Ronan and Wesley.

Ronan lifts an unimpressed brow. "I put up with a lot for Skyla, but I think you can count me out of my nephew's birthday throuple love session."

"Ooo, good point." Liam nods. "Wesley? Care to show Asher how well you can suck a cock?"

An amused laugh bubbles from Wesley as Asher gives him a pinched look. Wesley swaggers towards him, getting so close to Asher that his chest brushes against his.

"Don't act so disgusted. I remember a moment in that shack that you loved my mouth on your cock," he says, tilting his head to the side.

"Oh my god! I almost forgot about that," Liam exclaims. "Fuck, that was hot. Round two?"

Wesley's eyes don't leave Asher's, clearly fucking with him as he runs his tongue over his lips.

"Nah, you both have fun spoiling your boy. Maybe just a kiss for the road," Wesley says as he grabs the back of Asher's head and crushes his lips to his. Asher resists the entire time, but it doesn't stop Wesley from stroking his tongue against his, trying to pry at his restraint.

When Wesley finally pulls away, he sinks his teeth into his lip once more and smirks.

"Take him out of here, too grumpy for my liking."

"With pleasure," Liam says as he laces his fingers in Asher's, dragging him out of the kitchen and back up the stairs.

Asher reaches for me, and I go along with them, laughing at the very jealous look Ronan is giving Wesley right now. Let's just be honest, Wesley did that 10% to fuck with Asher and 90% to fuck with Ronan.

Chapter Twenty-Nine

Asher

After a hot as fuck three-way with Skyla and Liam, we all climbed into the shower and got cleaned up for the day. The sex was amazing, and distracted me for a little bit, but the reminder of what tonight will bring has my good spirits falling quickly.

I'm not exactly sure what will happen tonight, maybe that's what scares me the most. I've been hounding Ronan for weeks, and the most he's ever given me is 'it's different for everyone.' I don't like the fucking sound of that.

We spend the day at the house, soaking up all the possible time together, mainly because I know once I leave this house, nothing will be the same. Skyla talked on the phone with Vincent for hours, I guess he's in Europe right now, and he won't be home for a few weeks. That's all he would tell her. She tried to fight the tears, but you could tell it was not what she wanted to hear.

She has this connection to Griggs that's unlike any of our others. Not that it's more powerful or important, just more unique. When they are together, it's like a codependency kind of thing. Like they can finally both breathe, like a comfort only they can provide to each other and my heart hurts that my girl is so broken up.

Ronan was nice enough to make us a late breakfast, and we ordered an early dinner before it was time for me to leave. The others are meeting us at my induction party later tonight at Putnam Manor.

Oh, joy.

Slowly, I move to the car, dressed in a pair of jeans and a dark grey henley. Ronan said that they would have my robes in the tunnels for the induction. When I climb inside the car, my leg is shaking. I can't help it; needing something to focus on. I bounce my knee over and over again as I stare out the window, keeping the rest of my body rigid and still.

"Hey," Ronan says, forcing my eyes to him. "It's gonna be alright. Stay silent, stay obedient and disassociate. It'll be done, and then it'll be smooth sailing from there."

"What was your task?" I ask.

Ronan grimaces as he shakes his head.

"Ronan, please," I beg. "I've got some fucked up shit running through my head right now. At least give me something to mentally prepare myself for."

He clears his throat, sniffing roughly as he blinks his eyes shut. When he opens them, a blank mask is covering his features as he speaks.

"A member's daughter was caught with her boyfriend. He was going down on her or something. They hadn't had sex, but her father was furious. It was my job to dole her punishment."

I listen intently, waiting to hear.

"Her father believed that if she was ready for that, then she was ready for the full thing."

Oh, fuck.

"I had to rape her, in that room, in front of everyone, and they wouldn't let me stop until they said enough."

He closes his eyes once more, shaking his head as his voice comes out rough.

"She was fifteen, Ash," he says, his voice cracking. "Not a day goes by that I don't think about that night, that I'm not haunted by it. Her screams and pleas."

A shiver runs through Ronan as he shakes his head faster.

"I wouldn't wish that on anyone, ever. I...I hope yours won't be like that."

My stomach sours, twisting as I see the look of shame and heartbreak on my uncle's face. What kind of fucking disgusting society were we born into? Blackmailed into staying in? Though, we know the only true escape is death.

"Me too," I rasp.

Ronan nods, and we ride the rest of the way in silence. When we arrive on campus and park, my tremors begin to intensify. My entire body begins to convulse with fear. I hate that I can't stop it. I'm not a bitch. I'm not a coward, but I'd be lying if I said I wasn't the most terrified I've ever been in my entire life.

"Hey," Ronan says as he shuts the car off, rubbing his hand up and down my back. I curl into myself, shaking uncontrollably as I try to breathe through it.

"It's alright," he says. "Get it out now. Get it out."

I choke on my breaths, this car feeling too small, too suffocating. Gritting my teeth, I do my best to pull myself together. Closing my eyes, I try to think of calming things. I think of the smell of Skyla's hair fresh out of the shower, the way Liam rests his head on my chest just before he falls asleep, my mom. The way her hugs used to feel, so warm and comforting.

Slowly, my shaking eases, and I can breathe again. Inhaling

deeply, I blow out the same breath before sitting up. Ronan pats my back as I do, looking at me with concern.

"You good?"

I nod.

"Whatever you just did, whatever you're thinking, keep thinking it. You'll be alright, and tonight, we'll go home and forget this fucking mess, yeah?"

"Yeah," I say roughly as he opens his car door.

I do the same, and together, we make the trek through campus to the old church. I've been to the tunnels easily over a hundred times in my life, but for some reason, tonight I'm noticing things I never have before. The paintings hanging in the church, the cobblestone walkway, how several of them are broken or missing, and the ominous lighting as we open the passageway to the tunnels. A foreboding feeling like I've never felt before takes over, but I do my best to push it down.

When we reach the end of the walkway just before the first room, a man comes out holding a burgundy threaded robe like all of the other Elders possess. He bows his head, holding it out to me, and I nod my thanks as I begin stripping down. Once I'm naked, I slip the robe on, and the man takes my clothes, disappearing into the shadows while Ronan knocks on the door.

Slowly, it opens, and we slip inside, signing in and pressing our bloody fingerprint beside our entry. Once the second door opens, voices instantly carry through. It's amazing to me how each room is virtually soundproof despite being built hundreds of years ago.

As soon as I step inside, all conversations die, and every pair of eyes focus on me. I walk towards the middle of the room, shoulders back and face impassive as Ronan takes his place on the side of the wall. There isn't a table in here like there is for meetings, and there isn't a stone slab like there was when they had Skyla in here. That's a good sign, I suppose.

Demise

All the Elders are standing along the wall, each member beside their respective family and bond brother. My father steps up to me, all smiles as he reaches out to shake my hand before pulling me in for a hug that is so foreign to me, all I can do is freeze.

When he pulls away, he smiles towards the room.

"Brothers, what a joyous day, for not just me, but all of us. A new member, a new Elder and your future leader, my son," he beams proudly, a look unlike anything I've ever seen before.

All heads bow in respect to me as I keep my face stoic and still.

"Asher Putnam, do you swear your allegiance to the Brethren? Do you swear to honor our ways, fulfill our practices, and protect our secrets?" my father asks.

"I swear," I say hollowly.

"Do you swear to slay our enemy when given the chance and keep our people safe?" He continues.

"I swear."

"Do you swear to enforce all law whenever deemed necessary, no matter the task?"

My stomach twists at this one, but still, dutiful as ever, I respond.

"I swear."

My father nods approvingly before gesturing to the man at the door. I hear the door opening, but I stay facing my father, knowing all eyes are on me. Suddenly, the sound of muffled screams ring throughout the room. A woman's screams.

Christ.

The door shuts before a woman with curly brunette hair is thrown at my feet, a white gag tied around her face and black mascara streaks running down her face. She's wearing a white nightgown that is stained with red around her legs. I chance a quick glance to her before looking directly at my father once more.

"This *woman*," my father spits, "is a disgrace to the Brethren. She has failed to give the Ingersoll family an heir after three pregnancies, and thus, her husband has deemed her unworthy."

My eyes move to Jackson Ingersoll, the scrawny bean pole of a man. He looks at his wife with such indignation, such disgust. The cold hate in his eyes chills me to the bone. They are kidding, right? She's clearly having a miscarriage, apparently it being her third, and her husband deems her unworthy?

"Your task is simple. Release your brother from his bonds to this unfit woman. Set him free so that he may find a suitable wife to carry on the coveted bloodline," my father says.

My eyes move to Jackson, back to my father, and down to this poor woman. His words are clear, and that fear I had inside me before is back tenfold, but I don't let it show. I can't.

I swallow roughly as I speak.

"Method of choice?"

Her sobs rip through the room, whimpering and groaning as she holds her stomach tightly.

An evil smile curves my father's face as he looks at me.

"Your hands will do."

I nod curtly once as he steps to the side in front of Ronan. My eyes catch his, and nothing but devastation can be seen in his gaze as he looks at me. Ronan squeezes his eyes closed, shaking his head in condolences. To her or maybe to my morality. Possibly both.

Looking down at this woman, my heart seizes in my chest. The likeness to my mother is uncanny. Then again, maybe that's my own sick and twisted mind playing tricks on me. Her eyes, though, they're the same shade of hazel. Her hair is even a similar color of brown.

Demise

My gut twists and turns as I look at this unfortunate woman who did nothing wrong but be born into this fucked up world. Nothing wrong but experience the loss of a child not once but three times over, and now, she is losing her life through no fault of her own. And I have to be the one to do it.

Emotion is choking me from the inside out. I can't breathe, I can barely even see. I do a remarkable job of not letting it show. Slowly, I lay her down, easily overpowering her thin, willowy limbs as I straddle her chest.

Tears are pouring down her face as she attempts to fight me off, but she barely moves me. It doesn't stop her from fighting; she's so strong. Stronger than she probably knows, stronger than every man in here probably knows. Then again, the way her husband is looking at her tells me he might very well know. Another factor that no doubt has played a part in her untimely demise.

I lean down slowly, forcing a sneer on my face that I hope is convincing enough as I press my lips to her ear.

"I'm sorry. Close your eyes."

When my head lifts back up, I conjure a smile that would make the devil himself proud as my hands wrap around her thin throat. Her eyes shut as a muffled whimper escapes her before I squeeze. She does her best to keep them closed, but I clench my hands around her as tightly as possible, forcing them to spring wide open. They burn into me deeper than any brand ever could. I can feel the terrified look etching its way into my mind, saving itself for all of my nightmares, all of my thoughts from now until eternity.

She gags and gasps, attempting to breathe, but I only hold on tighter, strangling her until my entire body begins to shake from the impact. Still, like the fighter she is, she hangs on, those pleading hazel eyes plucking at something buried deep inside. Something horrific.

So many memories of my mother with a similar look, my father's hands wrapped around her throat, come to the surface, tearing me from the inside out.

I can't take it anymore. I can't. I can't.

Squeezing my own eyes shut, I clench my jaw tight and jerk my arms sharply to the left, the sharp pop of her neck breaking echoing throughout the room. Instantly, the strain in her gives way, her entire body going limp and head lulling to the broken side. I feel my hands shaking and no matter how hard I try to stop them, they won't.

So, I stand, forcing myself to do it slowly so it doesn't look like I'm desperate to pry myself off this woman's body. But I am.

I don't realize that my chest is heaving, my breathing erratic as I look around the room, doing a full circle as I meet the eyes of every man in this room. I linger on Jackson's for several seconds, a vindictive smirk on his face as he stares at his dead wife before my gaze comes to my father. That same sinister smile from before is practically splitting his face in two as he steps forward.

He pulls a small black box out of his robe pocket, opening it up to show me. Like a carbon copy of every other Elder ring, that big embossed 'B' surrounded with Latin script.

Maleficis esse mori.

Death to witches.

I don't see any witches in this room, though. All I see is a room full of egotistical cowards and one innocent woman who paid the ultimate price of their ways.

Regardless, I pluck the ring from the box, sliding the smooth metal onto my ring finger. I never got a wedding ring, obviously, and I don't need one. No Elder wears one. This is more important. A direct vein running from this finger to my heart, signifying my truest love, my truest devotion will always be to the Brethren.

My father nods approvingly, all Elders chanting much like they did in the woods that night.

"Maleficis esse mori."

All as one, they stop and my father nods.

"Welcome to the Brethren."

I stood in the shower for over an hour. Far longer than anyone wanted me to, but I couldn't help it. I had to scrub my hands twenty-two times, and even then, I couldn't remove it. It's worse than blood; it's more permanent than that. This heavy feeling has penetrated into my hands, and like an inky black tar, it can't be removed.

I can still feel her throat in my hands, the sound of her neck cracking lives in my ears forevermore. Those eyes...that look of terror and pain. That will surely never leave me, ever.

When I was finally able to pry myself out of the scalding water, I slip on some clothes that I brought with me. I have to go to this fucking party. Make an appearance. Even if the only thing I want to do is crawl beneath a fucking rock and rot.

Like she is.

Shaking my head, I make my way out of the tunnels and find Ronan waiting for me outside the church. He claps my shoulder, and I move out of his hold, continuing to move forward. I hear a heavy sigh escape him, but he follows after me silently.

When we get in the car, I look out the window, focusing on

nothing and everything. Ronan climbs into the driver's seat, starting it up and turning out onto the road when he speaks.

"I'm proud of you."

A bitter laugh tears through me as I look at him.

"Proud? Of me? For what?"

"You held yourself together well and—"

"No, I didn't," I bellow. "I fell apart in that room. I'm falling apart right now. Just because you don't see it, doesn't mean it's not happening."

Ronan is quiet for a moment before he nods.

"You're gonna be a great leader one day, Asher."

I want to laugh at him, that's not the compliment he thinks it is.

"I'm saying," he continues. "You'll be good for the Brethren, better than your father. You have the capability to be ruthless out of loyalty, but the moral compass to discern what is right and wrong. Your father doesn't have that. You will be better."

I take little comfort in that as Ronan drives through Salem. When we get to my father's place, I don't even wait for the car to stop before I open the door. I decide to use the side entrance through the kitchen so I don't have to deal with the whole goddamn welcoming committee. I just need to find Skyla.

As soon as I push through the door, an aggressive whisper hits my ears.

"You will knock off this attitude or so help me," a woman says before I recognize her as Calista Brenton, formerly Calista Bartlett. Maggie's mom.

The bright red hair is the only thing they have in common. Her mom has been under the knife so many times she's beginning to look like a ventriloquist doll. She apparently has enough movement in her face to make a scowl, though.

Demise

Harry Brenton is standing beside his wife, a matching scowl on his face as Calista continues.

"You have the audacity to disrespect one of Harry's business partners' sons? You're lucky we're even finding a match for you! Left to your own devices, you'd be living on the street within a month."

Maggie shrugs like she's bored.

"I'm sure I could find a kind woman to let me stay in her bed for a night or two."

My eyebrows shoot up at her antics. Liam's parents hate his sexuality, too, but he never goads them like that. Rage flickers in Calista's eyes as she winds back her hand, smacking Maggie across the face. Maggie's head whips to the side and I push fully through the door.

"That's enough!" I snap.

Calista and Harry both startle at my presence, bowing their heads like the good little subordinates they are.

"Mr. Putnam," Harry says as Calista keeps her head bowed.

"What's going on in here?" I ask as I step in between Maggie and her mother and stepfather.

"Just a little family matter. Nothing to bother you with. Congratulations." Calista smiles in a way that I'm sure secured Bridgette's father after her husband had a mysterious heart attack in the middle of the night.

"I am concerned. I'm concerned you just struck my wife's best friend. Lay another finger on her, and I'll have you buried six feet under before you can even move your bought and paid for lips," I snarl.

Calista shrinks back, flinching as I speak before Harry steps in.

"It won't happen again. Our apologies for bringing this ugliness to your party."

"See to it that it doesn't," I say, offering my arm for Maggie while keeping my eyes on her parents.

Maggie's arm loops through mine and we push out of the kitchen, pausing in the hallway when she pulls her arm from me. She's looking anywhere but me, her long sleeved arms crossing over her green dress.

"Thanks," she murmurs.

"No problem," I say as I turn to look for my wife.

Maggie's arm catches mine, holding me back for a second.

"Don't tell Skyla, okay? She'd only worry."

I nod my head, pulling away from her hold as I begin wading through people. It's not in my nature to insert myself in others' business. If Skyla asks me, I'll never lie to her but I'm not going to send her into a spiral if I can help it.

I see her just across the way, talking to Hutchinson and his grandfather. I waste no time in crossing the room, desperate to rip her away from this place and forget the fucking world.

Chapter Thirty

Skyla

Liam got dragged away almost the second we arrived at Putnam Manor. Wesley quickly followed behind him to chat with some middle-aged man and his wife. So, that just left me. I shoot off another text to Vincent when a voice clears beside me.

Looking up from my phone, I notice an older man with white hair sitting in a wheelchair, smiling up at me.

"Hello." I smile politely as my eyes scan the room for Asher, though who knows when he will be done with...whatever he's doing.

"My god, the resemblance really is uncanny," the man whispers to himself.

I frown at that as I turn my head to the side.

"Pardon?"

"Your mother, why, you're practically her twin."

I nod and smile for a moment.

"I'm sorry, I didn't catch your name."

"That's because I didn't give it to you," he says with a sharp smile and a slight shake of his head.

I feel my own smile fall before he lets out a short laugh, offering his hand to me.

"Only teasing, sweetheart. Horris Hutchinson."

I take his hand, shaking it once before he places a chapped lip kiss to the back of it.

Gross.

"Pleasure to meet you. Skyla Putnam," I say, knowing how happy Asher will be to find out I'm using his name to introduce myself.

"Oh, everyone in Salem knows who you are, Mrs. Putnam. You're practically famous."

"Well, I assure you everything you've heard is completely false," I tease, causing him to let out another laugh.

"Sharp witted one, aren't you? Tell me something, are you a good girl?"

I'm thrown by his question, my smile turning suspicious as I narrow my eyes.

"I suppose it depends on your definition, but I like to think so."

He nods thoughtfully at that.

"Good, you're too busy to get caught up in messy business like your mother."

My brows furrow at that. "What do you mean?"

He doesn't answer me, instead, his eyes roam over me curiously before his eyes catch on my scarred palm, the one with the Brethren emblem forever engraved onto me. His eyes move to my other hand, assumingly searching for the cut from that night.

"Tell me, did you bleed black?"

"What?" I ask.

"Bleed black, did you? Course you didn't. They wouldn't have let you live more than a second later if you had. Still, though...fascinating."

"Wait, what does bleeding black have to do with anything? That's impossible. No one's blood is black."

"No one except those that have sold their soul to the devil," Horris counters.

My eyes stay narrowed as I look at him for several seconds before I swallow.

"Are you saying—"

"I'm not saying anything, just making polite conversation with a darling girl," he interrupts.

"No," I snap quickly, sucking in a deep breath before blowing it out. "Are you saying that my mom was a...witch?"

"All I know is what I hear. There were rumors for years, no one could ever provide evidence, but her death was quite... convenient."

"Convenient? How?"

"Well," he says, sitting forward in his chair as he lowers his voice. "Right around the time of her death, the Coven was growing in strength. Luther knew there was a mole. A handful of days later, your mother ends up dead, and you are sent away."

"Coven?" I echo. "Like a group of witches or—"

"Grandpa! There you are. I've been looking for you everywhere," Andrew says before his eyes come to me.

Shock splashes across his face before his trademark red cheeks appear.

"Oh, hi, Skyla. I see you've met my grandfather."

I nod. "Hi, Andrew.

"It's been...a while," he says hesitantly.

A while since I thought he was my stalker, and we only figured out he wasn't because Corwin assumingly held him at gunpoint and forced him and his family to flee the country to throw us off his track.

"It has," I agree.

He takes a step closer to me, lowering his voice as he whispers desperately.

"I'm so sorry about everything. I heard what happened. The fact that Professor Corwin had been torturing you like that. The fact that he was the one that approached me in the parking lot that day," he says with a shake of his head.

I nod and smile, appreciating the condolences, but far more interested in what his grandfather has to say. I move to look around Andrew when an arm slides behind my back, that clean familiar smell washing over me as Asher presses a kiss to the side of my head.

Looking up at him, I smile before turning to wrap my arms around him.

"Are you okay?" I whisper into his ear.

"No," he responds hollowly, causing me to frown as I pull away.

There's a vacancy in his eyes. He stares down at me warmly, or as warmly as he can, but there is noticeably something off, an emptiness hiding something horrible.

"What—"

"Kiss me," Asher demands before he's leaning forward, pressing his lips to mine.

I go to him easily, his kiss bruising against me as he lets out...whatever he can. I'll happily hold the burden of his pain. Whatever he needs.

When he pulls away, he lets out a ragged breath, inflating himself in the next moment, his shoulders back and a look of contentment on his face. Though, I'd wager it's a load of shit.

"Apologies for the interruption gentlemen, if she was your wife, I'm sure you'd understand."

Horris laughs at Asher's joke while Andrew just stares at him, a hint of malice to his gaze. See? Stalker vibes. Just a little bit. I know, in reality, he's just being kind in my name. Andrew has only seen what others have, the horrible things Asher has done to me. Outside of the guys and Maggie, no one knows how good he really is to me. Now, at least.

"It's more than alright. Congratulations. You are a fantastic addition to our society." Horris nods to Asher. "Mrs. Putnam, it was such a pleasure. Come along, Andrew. I think I'd like to retire for the evening."

"Wait. Do you think I could ask you some questions...about what we were discussing?" I say cryptically.

Horris smiles kindly as he leans forward and shakes his head.

"Better that we not. Enjoy the party," he says as Andrew, on cue, begins pushing his grandfather out the party and to the door.

"What was that about?" Asher asks.

I turn to him, my heart sinking as I speak.

"Have you heard that people think witches bleed black?"

Asher's brows immediately knit together as he hushes me sharply. He shakes his head as if to say not here before he glances around the room. When his sweep is done, he leans in to press a kiss to the side of my head.

"Not here. We'll talk at home."

I nod slowly, more on edge than ever as a couple of people approach us, congratulating Asher on his official membership. He smiles through each congratulation, the façade becoming harder and harder to recognize the longer the night drags on.

After sharing an awkward and tense moment between my father, Christopher, and Asher, we only had to stay for another twenty minutes or so before Asher tells us we're leaving. We climb into the car, Ronan driving, when I turn to face him.

I open my mouth to ask him about the witch thing when I see his put together façade crack and crumble, giving way to a shaking mess. His arms are quivering as he rests his head in his hands, struggling to breathe as he does.

"Asher? Asher! What's going on? Talk to me," I beg.

He reaches for me, grabbing onto me like I'm his lifeline as he falls apart. What on earth happened to my husband?

"Hold him, Sky," Ronan says from the front seat.

I do as he says, and Asher comes to me easily, snaking his arms around my waist as he buries his head into my neck. He doesn't cry, but he does let out labored breaths, sucking them back in with as much strength as he can seemingly muster.

"What did they do to you?" I whisper softly, brushing his hair out of his face.

He shakes his head, his pain drenched eyes coming to mine.

"Don't....I...I can't. Ever. I can't talk about it. I can't—"

"Shh," I say, forcing his head back against me. "It's okay. You don't have to. I've got you, okay? I've got you, and I love you, and I won't let anything hurt you."

He nuzzles into me deeper, a pained look on Ronan's face as he watches us from the rearview mirror. Thankfully, it doesn't take us long to get back to the house and when we do, Ronan is there to open all of the doors for us.

Asher is able to get himself out of the car and into the house, but only just. Like a zombie, he marches through our home, heading straight for the staircase. I follow him quickly, trailing after him as he steps into his bedroom. I share a concerned look with Ronan who is also following us before he leaves us at the doorway, shutting it with a soft snick and drowning the room in darkness.

Light isn't needed right now, though. Not when Asher is already crawled into his bed and I'm slipping in right beside him. He curls into me, much how he did in the car and together, we just lay there in perfect silence.

Chapter Thirty-One

Skyla

The next morning, I woke up to Asher still wrapped around me while Liam is wrapped around him from behind. They are both sound asleep, and I don't want to wake either of them, so I slip out of bed as quietly as I can. When I reach the door, I'm amazed that they are both still passed out as I grab my phone and close the door.

I wait until I'm in the backyard, hopefully far enough away from everyone that I won't bother them. And they won't bother me.

The signature facetime ringtone echoes in the morning air as I wait and wait for a connection. Finally, it goes through, Steph's panicked face filling up the phone.

"Sky? Is everything okay? What happened?"

I don't bother trying to reassure her that everything is fine because, honestly, I'm not so sure that it is.

"Was mom a witch?"

She looks stunned at my question for several seconds before she speaks.

Demise

"What? A witch? No, of course not. Why would you think that?'

"Apparently, that's what people in Salem think, or at least suspect. It's what Horris Hutchinson thinks."

Her eyes squint before understanding dawns on her.

"The eldest member of the Hutchinson family? He's still alive?"

"And kicking," I answer. "He asked me if I bleed black."

Steph's brows furrow at that. "Why on earth would he even ask that? If you did, you wouldn't be standing here. Especially after the ceremony."

My eyes bug out at her response. "Steph, no one bleeds black! What the fuck is this shit?"

Her mouth opens and closes before she shakes her head.

"It's just what we were taught growing up, hun. What we were told was the truth. You'd be amazed what Brethren kids are taught and warped into believing."

"I'm sure it's extensive, but I want to know exactly what happened to Mom. Horris said that the Coven was becoming stronger right around the time Mom died. Did she help them? Was she one of them? Give me something here, Steph. While you're safe, tucked away in London, I'm in the goddamn lion's den and I can't even get a straight answer out of the one person I'm supposed to trust wholly."

She closes her eyes, letting out a deep breath as she shakes her head.

"Your mom was not a witch, Skyla. Trust me. We were both born and raised inside the Brethren; our lineage traces back to the right side of history."

"So, she could have picked it up?" I challenge.

"She didn't," Steph snaps. "She would never. Her death came at a high pressure time in our world, and no doubt was a cause because of that pressure. Your father was always a short tempered prick, as was Putnam. I've told you before, you can't convince me it wasn't one of them."

I shake my head, running my fingers through my hair as I look at her.

"Why did you keep all of this from me? All these years?"

"What would it have changed, Sky? No matter how much you hate Henry, you still have to see him. You still have to play the part. I knew if you heard the truth, you wouldn't be able to do what it takes to survive, and I need you to survive. I can't live without you."

Shaking my head, something still feeling off in my gut, I blow out an irritated breath.

"So, that's it then? There is nothing more to tell me? Nothing more that you know?"

She shakes her head sadly, and I wish I could believe her. I really do. Maybe I don't because I already feel so betrayed by this person that I always thought to be open and honest. Maybe I don't because I'm emotional and desperate for some kind of sense to come out of all of this. Or maybe I don't because I know deep down, there has to be way more to it. To my mother's death, to the Brethren, to this supposed 'Coven,' whatever that is.

Clearly, I won't be getting anything more out of her, though. Shaking my head once more, my finger goes to the end call button.

"I gotta go," I say as I hang up the phone.

"Wait, Sky—" she calls out as the signal goes dead.

"Who was that?" Ronan asks, making me practically jump out of my skin as he steps onto the back porch, two mugs in his hands.

I let out a heavy breath, watching as the frigid morning air displays the path before it dissipates. Ronan offers one of the mugs to me and I take it happily, tasting the comforting flavor of apples and cinnamon on my tongue, hold the sedatives this time.

"Steph," I answer as I take a step.

He nods. "Everything okay?"

I don't answer for a moment, my mind running wild with thoughts and questions before I look up to him.

"Do you think my mom was a witch?"

Ronan's face doesn't react for a few seconds before he responds brusquely.

"No."

I wait for him to elaborate but when he doesn't, I lean forward.

"Noooo?"

"Why do you think she was?" he asks.

"Something Horris Hutchinson said last night. He made it seem like everyone thinks she's one. Like people expected me to bleed black at mine and Asher's ceremony." I say with a scrunched up nose.

Ronan is careful with his words as he nods.

"There were some who...had theories. My father was crazed back then, intent that we had more witches among us. For years, he had women slaughtered for just looking a little off. The hysteria from the trials didn't die in 1693, it evolved."

"So, your father was the one who killed my mother?"

His head moves back and forth. "I'm not sure. That's who I suspected when it happened, but then again, he never did his own dirty work. It's more likely he sent an eliminator after her."

"Like Vincent's parents?" I ask.

He gives me a pained wince and nods.

What's worse? The idea of your father, father-in-law, or boyfriend's parents being responsible for your mother's death? I'll give you a spoiler, all of them fucking suck.

"Why are you so sure that my mom wasn't a witch?" I ask, pushing again.

"Her maiden name isn't in the book," he says simply.

"Book? What book?"

His jaw sets like he realizes he said something he shouldn't have. I watch as he seems to have an internal battle with himself before he speaks.

"Thomas Putnam's journal."

"He had a journal? And you've read it?"

He nods. "I have. The first entry was written in 1682, and the last page was in 1699, a few days before his death."

"He kept the same journal for almost twenty years?" I ask.

He nods. "It wasn't like a daily entry or anything. Only his innermost thoughts. It's a family treasure. Christopher keeps it practically stitched to his hand, much like my father did. When we were young, and my father would go to the country club or something, Christopher and I would break into his office and read it. I was a lot younger, so it bored me, but Christopher became obsessed with it, much like my father and his father before him. I wouldn't doubt that he has the entire thing committed to memory."

"What's in there?" I ask.

Ronan looks out over the backyard before gesturing to the house. I move inside with him and once the door is shut, he begins speaking again.

"Most of the entries are personal, speaking about his family, an unnamed woman he was in love with, things like that. However, when his daughter Ann was essentially responsible for the trials in 1692, he rarely wrote about anything but that."

"Like what?" I ask, oddly curious and desperate for more information.

"Lists of suspects and the reasoning behind it. People that were tried and acquitted, those that were tried and executed, and those that were tried and died before they could see judgment."

My nose wrinkles up at that.

"That's awful," I say with a shake of my head. "And he had family names listed in there?"

Ronan nods. "All of whom were executed or banished from Salem Village. Though, they never really left."

"The Coven?" I guess.

Ronan tilts his head to the side curiously.

"What do you know about the Coven?"

"Besides what the name implies...nothing. I'd guess it's the group you all have hinted about since I got here. The ones that the Brethren are constantly fighting against."

He doesn't agree. Then again, he doesn't deny it, either.

"I want to know more," I say.

Ronan winces. "It's better if you don't. If the wrong people find out you're digging, it'll make you look suspicious. Make no mistake, my brother is even more deluded than my father was. If he even suspects you have an interest in witches or—"

"I don't have an interest in witches. I have an interest in finding out what happened to my mother, into what these families I'm living alongside are capable of. I'm interested in uncovering the truth."

"The truth is all a matter of perspective," Ronan says cryptically.

Wesley moseys into the kitchen, a sleepy smile on his face that quickly falls away when he senses the tension in the room.

"What's going on?"

We are both quiet for several seconds before Ronan speaks for me.

"Skyla is asking questions about the Coven. She wants to know more."

Wesley is already shaking his head when Ronan continues.

"And I think she has a right to."

"What?" we both ask simultaneously.

"We all got to learn our history; it was practically beaten into us. You were not given that advantage. So, let's rectify it."

I nod, a little shocked he gave in so easily.

"Get dressed. We'll leave soon," he says as he looks at me.

"Where are we going?" I ask.

"The town's library."

Chapter Thirty-Two

Ronan

I lead Skyla through the library, Wesley close behind her as we come to the front desk. The librarian smiles at us but does a double take to me before a look of unease passes over her. I reach into my wallet, pulling out a few hundred dollar bills that I slide over to her.

"You were just about to take lunch," I say.

She slowly takes the money, slipping it into her purse as she nods.

"Of course, Mr. Putnam. Nice to see you."

I nod, but don't say anything as Skyla looks at me. There are a few people in the library, though a majority of them bolt as soon as they see us. It's a shame my family has such a negative reputation in town, but it does help when one is looking for privacy.

Guiding Skyla through the stacks, I come to the town records, letting her take over from there. Her eyes scan over book after book as she begins pulling them. Wesley steps up, taking them from her as she stacks them higher and higher until he can hardly see. Then we move to historical fiction, where she grabs a copy of *The Crucible*.

Honestly, I can't believe that the library has that in here. It's basically viewed as propaganda. It paints the Salem townsfolk in a terrible light, and there is little accuracy to any of it. At least going off Thomas Putnam's journal and the teachings of the Brethren.

We find a table to sit down at, and Skyla dives in, cracking open book after book. Her finger moves along the pages, digesting every morsel of information she possibly can. Wesley and I watch her patiently, both of us clearly on edge, but ready to do whatever it takes to make her feel a little more at ease. At least an hour goes by before she finally looks up.

"Did you know it wasn't just women that were accused of witchcraft? Some men were as well," Skyla says as she looks up from the book she is currently reading.

I nod. "From Thomas's point of view, some husbands were forced into witchcraft by their wives. Regardless, he felt they were a threat."

"Clearly, he believed everyone, young or old, was a threat," she says bitterly. "You can't tell me either of you believe in all this, though, right? I mean, from my perspective, it sounds like it was a couple of young girls who were bored and ended up crying 'witch' for attention. I mean, did they accuse Tituba of witchcraft because she was actually a witch, or just because she came from a different culture?" she scoffs.

I stay silent as Wesley speaks.

"History is always a shade of grey, right? All we have to go off is snippets of the past. Unless we were there, we will never fully know what happened."

Skyla frowns at that.

"I guess, but believing in witches the way the Brethren clearly do? Like spells and flying on brooms and bleeding black." She shakes her head. "Doesn't it seem a little farfetched to you?"

I nod. "You're not wrong. Like Wes said, I think the past is open to interpretation. We have to do our best to collect the information and make our best educated guess."

Skyla looks between us for a moment or two and nods.

"Sorry, I don't know why I got so obsessed all of a sudden. I guess Hutchinson put me on edge last night. I hate that I don't know what happened to my mother, how she spent her last moments. When he offered up a small amount of information about her, good or bad, I just wanted to know more."

"I'm sorry I don't have more comfort to give you," I say.

She smiles sadly and shrugs as she begins gathering up her books. Wesley and I grab the rest, and we begin putting them away together. Her arm stretches up, attempting to put the book in place, when Wesley grabs it from her, sliding it into place.

"Thanks," she smiles as she turns to face him.

He slowly backs her up against the bookcase, a smirk on his face as his finger comes underneath her chin.

"No problem."

Wesley pauses for a moment, looking both ways before leaning down, pressing his lips to hers. She makes a soft sound of surprise but easily sinks into the touch. Her arms wrap around his neck as their kiss turns more heated.

Today, Skyla is wearing a plaid skirt with dark tights and a white sweater. Or at least she was. Wesley's hands move down her body, going between her thighs, when a sharp rip sounds out inside the quiet library. I whip my head around, making sure the librarian hasn't come back yet. I know I saw a few college students a couple sections over. They could come this way any second, but that doesn't seem to be stopping them.

In the time that it took me to turn around and scope out our surroundings, Wesley had ripped a hole in Skyla's tights and shoved his cock into her pussy. He has her right leg lifted, hiked up to allow better access as he begins fucking her against the bookshelf. A few books fall from the force of his thrusts, but that doesn't stop him.

Her mouth drops open, her head falling to the side as she looks at me. Those eyes practically beckon me, and before I know what I'm doing, I'm coming to her. My hand comes to the side of her cheek, keeping her head turned as I crush my mouth to hers. She hums her satisfaction against my mouth, my tongue stroking against hers before I whisper against her lips.

"Such a bad girl letting Wesley fuck you in public like this," I tsk.

"She's a good little slut, aren't you, little one?" Wesley says with a cocky whisper.

Skyla nods, her face turning to look up at the ceiling as I look at Wesley and shake my head.

"This isn't smart," I tell him softly.

"No," he agrees. "But it's fun."

Wesley's free hand reaches out for me, palming my already hard cock through my jeans. I choke back the moan that begs to run through me at the feeling, but he seems hell bent on getting more of a rise out of me. His hand runs up and down against me, forcing my cock to strain uncomfortably against my pants.

He never stops thrusting into Skyla, but his eyes also never leave mine. Carefully, his fingers move to my belt, slowly undoing it. My heart is beating out of my chest, every fiber of my being extremely on edge. Still, though, I don't stop him. I tell myself it's because Skyla loves it, and I hold onto that reasoning tight enough to allow me to be okay with what comes next.

Once he has my belt undone and my jeans unbuttoned, his hand slips inside my boxers, gripping my cock. His hand is so

Demise

warm, so firm. I throb into his hand as I bite back a groan when he begins stroking me. His blue eyes are so intense, filled with so much want. It fills me with warring feelings that I don't know how to process. Thankfully, I don't have to before Skyla is speaking.

"Are you touching him?" she whispers before letting out a moan that is way too loud.

I smack my hand over her mouth, keeping her muffled as Wesley begins fucking her faster. He jerks my cock a little faster too, and I find my hips slowly thrusting with him.

"Fuck," he grumbles low. "You feel so good," he says, his eyes on Skyla before they come to me. "Both of you."

That pulls another moan out of Skyla that my hand helps keep quiet. Wesley stares at me so intently, I don't know how to look away. He tugs me closer and closer until our chests are practically touching, a private little triangle formed between us. I drop my hand from Skyla's mouth, and he leans forward, making out with her for several seconds before turning to me with ragged breaths.

"Kiss me?" he asks.

My stomach flips at that request, and I hesitate. My eyes drop to his lips, lips I have tasted before. Once. There were a lot of things that happened in that shack that I never thought would. A lot of things I swore to myself were just in the heat of the moment and would never happen again. Now he's here, asking me to break one of those rules, and for a moment, fuck me, I consider it.

His pink lips are wet and plump, small teeth indents from Skyla on his lower lip that makes them all the more enticing. A kiss, though...it feels too personal, too exposing. My best friend has sucked me off for years, and things have never been weird. It's been a pleasure thing, a release, and he sucks cock better than any woman I've ever met, so that didn't hurt.

Wesley seems to be able to read my mind, or at least able to tell the minute I decide I won't be kissing him. So, he turns away, his hand falling away from my cock as he cups Skyla's face. My cock twitches at the loss of contact, every instinct in me screaming to grab my cock and start jerking it while I watch them. How could I not? They are so fucking hot together.

Luckily, I don't have to. Wesley falls over the edge, his orgasm ripping through him surprisingly silent as he pumps in and out of Skyla. As soon as he's finished, he pulls out of her, stepping to the side to make room for me. Gladly.

"Hi, baby," I smile as I grab my cock, lining it up to her wet pussy.

"Hi." She smiles when I push inside, her face twisting up with pleasure as I rest my head onto her shoulder, biting down because, goddamn, she feels so good.

She's so tight, so wet, and it's even more of a turn on to know that it's not just her that's all wet but Wesley's cum. Every thrust pushes it deeper and deeper into her, and something about that spurs me on.

"There you go, Ro," Wesley encourages softly. "Fuck my cum deep into our girl. Get her nice and pregnant for us."

I grumble at his words, snapping my hips aggressively as I do.

"S-so good," Skyla moans. "A-almost...t-there."

"Need a little push over the edge?" Wesley asks before lowering to his knees.

Skyla and I both watch him curiously before we feel him. For a moment, my vision spots, and I black out. That's the only way to describe what it feels like to have Wesley's mouth attached to where I'm fucking Skyla. His tongue swirls over her clit before coming down to meet my cock. I intentionally slow my thrusts, looking down as I watch Wesley's tongue drag along the side of my cock. He opens his eyes as I thrust back inside her, giving me a quick wink that has a new passion taking over me.

"More," Skyla begs, to which Wesley happily obliges.

His tongue begins flicking against her, devouring her whole while I fuck her raw. His tongue even slides along my cock, pushing into her at the same time I do. It forces my movements to stutter, and I close my eyes, cursing under my breath as he does.

I feel Skyla's pussy begin to tremble and I'm right there with her. My pace becomes urgent as I push inside her before the wave of my orgasm hits us together. I feel my cum begin to coat the inside of her walls, and Wesley is right there, practically feral as he tries to lick inside her. Like he's desperate for a taste.

Before I can think about it, I pull my cock out of her early, turning and shoving it down Wesley's throat. His eyes open in surprise as a rope of my cum splashes against his tongue. He closes his mouth around me, bobbing his head as he draws out the last of my orgasm. My hand comes down, digging into his hair because fuck, I want to keep his mouth on me forever.

He has other plans, though. As fast as he took me, he releases me, turning his attention to Skyla as he latches his mouth onto her pussy. His tongue swirls and licks through her, like he's desperate for the taste. Her, him and me mixed together into a combination that sounds like the best thing he's ever tasted, if his moans are anything to go off.

When he pulls away, he looks up at us from his knees, a small dribble of cum falling down his chin. Instinctively, I reach out, gathering it with my thumb before pushing my thumb into his mouth. His mouth parts in surprise, but he closes around me, his tongue swirling around my digit in a way that already has my cock hardening.

"Good boy," I growl.

Chapter Thirty Three

Skyla

"Stupid motherfucking piece of shit," Asher grumbles as he tries and fails to wrestle with the balloon arch.

I glance across the kitchen at him, shaking my head as I finish Liam's five tiered cake. Each layer is a different flavor, per his request. We have streamers, confetti cannons and a huge balloon archway. At least, we will if Asher ever finishes assembling it.

"Why the fuck does he have to be so high maintenance?" Asher grouches as I giggle, making my way over to him.

"Because he wouldn't be Liam if he wasn't, and you love him for it," I say as I give him a hand, helping stabilize the base so he can fasten each side.

The balloon arch is a mix of blue, white and black balloons since blue is Liam's favorite color. I also made the icing of each layer of his cake a different shade. From darkest to lightest on top. I gotta say, with all the birthdays around this place, I'll become a not so bad baker in no time.

"Love him a little less for this shit," he huffs before we stand back and admire our handy work.

I hold out my hand to high five Asher, and he begrudgingly meets me halfway.

"Alright! Let's go wake up the birthday boy." I smile.

Asher nods, a hint of sadness in his eyes. I don't ask about it; I don't want to spoil the mood, but I can't help but wonder if it's about tonight. About what Asher experienced two weeks ago on his own birthday. He still hasn't told me what happened, hasn't told anyone. He says he never wants to talk about it, and as much as I want to pry and forcibly help him heal, I know it's not what's right. So, instead I support him how he deems fit, which lately has been a lot of blowjobs. If he wants to chase away his demons with a little, or a lot, of oral, then so be it.

When we creep inside Asher's bedroom, we find Liam passed out on his stomach, softly snoring. I shake my head and smile to see Asher giving him a similar adoring smile. He gestures for me to go to him on one side of the bed while he goes to the other. Together we both carefully slide into bed, Asher slipping behind him as he begins peppering his neck with kisses.

Liam groans in his sleep, turning on his side enough for me to slide beside him and capture his lips with mine. That's all it takes to wake him up. I feel his lips begin moving against me, his eyes flying open before another moan releases from him.

"Fuck," he murmurs against me. "What a way to wake up," he chuckles as he turns his head to look at Asher, wrapping his hand around his neck and bringing his lips to him.

I can't help it, my pussy throbs when I watch them. My husband and boyfriend, happy and unapologetically together. As if they can hear me, they break apart, both landing their hungry gaze on me. Liam is the first to reach me, though.

"I've missed you," Liam moans into my neck.

I chuckle. "We made love last night, baby."

"I know. It's been forever," he whines.

Liam sucks in a sharp breath against me, bringing his eyes up to mine as he moans. Glancing over him, I see Asher behind him, slowly pushing a finger inside Liam.

"Whatever you want, it's yours," Asher murmurs against Liam's neck, resting his lips there for several seconds before placing another kiss and another.

"I just need you two, however I can have you," Liam moans.

"Mmm, I've got the perfect idea," he says as he withdraws his finger, earning a sad whimper from Liam as he continues kissing me.

Asher rolls off the bed, shuffling in one of the side drawers before he's back.

"Sky...think you're ready?"

I break away from Liam, looking at Asher and dropping my mouth in shock. Asher is holding a bottle of lube in one hand and a dildo attached to a harness of some sort in the other.

"Is that a—"

"Strap on?" Liam finishes for me.

Asher nods in a devilish way that promises nothing but naughty, good fun.

"Think you're ready, princess?" Asher asks again.

My eyes come to Liam as I shrug nervously.

"Is that something you'd want?"

"Are you fucking kidding?" he blurts out, rolling to his hands and knees in record time, arching his back as he sticks his ass out. "Fuck me, babygirl."

Excitement rushes through me as I move behind Liam as Asher meets me. He helps me into the strap on, fastening and adjusting the straps as needed until I'm ready. Then he takes the lube, flipping the cap open and squirting some onto Liam's ass. He jerks at the cool liquid but doesn't say anything. Then Asher squirts some more into his hand, lathering up the tip of the dildo, especially before looking at me.

"You good?"

I nod as I look down, unsure what to do with my hands.

"Grab his hips," Asher encourages.

I do as he says, holding either hip much like they do with me before I line the tip of the dildo to Liam's ass.

"There you go," Asher says. "Nice and slow. Liam is going to be a good boy and open up for you, isn't that right?" he asks as he grips Liam's neck roughly.

"Yes," he nods, and Asher rewards him with a brutal kiss before tearing away from him.

"That's what I fucking thought," he says through clenched teeth, his arousal bleeding into unfiltered aggression that somehow makes him hotter than normal.

There is a little resistance at first, but when I push my hips forward, the dildo slides in, and a moan escapes Liam.

"There she is," Asher says as he begins stroking his cock. "What a good girl you are," he praises as I keep pushing until I'm fully seated inside Liam.

"Oh my God," he moans.

"Now take it out, almost all the way before pushing back inside," Asher directs.

I nod, doing as he says. This time when I push inside, there is almost no resistance, and the groan Liam lets out has me eager to do it again and again.

"Hold on," Asher says as he reaches between me and the dildo, pulling down a piece before pushing it into me.

I gasp at the feeling, noticing that when I thrust into Liam, the toy also thrusts into me.

"Oh my god," I moan. "What is this?"

"It's a dildo for you too, princess. You didn't think I'd leave you out, did you?"

"Does it feel good, babygirl?" Liam gasps as I thrust into him.

"Yes, you?" I whimper.

"So fucking good," he grumbles into the pillow.

I start to catch a rhythm, and I find myself craving more. For him, for me. Just more. My thrusts become more hurried and aggressive, pulling cry after cry of pleasure out of both of us.

"Fuck! You two are beautiful. You like my wife fucking you, baby?" Asher asks Liam, running his hand down his spine, sending goosebumps racing across Liam's skin.

"Yes," he groans.

"Would you like it better if I sucked your cock while she did?"

His head whips to the side, eagerly nodding.

Asher lets out a humored chuckle as he taps the side of Liam's ass.

"Sit up for a second."

Liam practically throws us both backwards, but somehow I'm able to hold onto him. My arms are wrapped around him, our bodies pressed flush as he turns and begins making out with me. His lips are so soft, tongue so nimble as it caresses mine while Asher climbs onto the bed. Only, he doesn't climb to the side. Instead, he lays down on his back right beneath Liam's knees as he pushes his own pants down.

His cock springs free and Asher's hand rubs it once or twice before he speaks.

"Come choke on my cock while I choke on yours."

Liam goes to him eagerly, his mouth wrapping around Asher's as Asher wraps around him. They both make a muffled moan as I spread my legs a little further and grip Liam's hips again. I take my thrusts slow, allowing them the time to work each other up properly.

It doesn't take long though, before their blowjobs become sloppy and hurried. My hips begin thrusting as I start chasing my own orgasm, a power like I've never felt before thrumming inside me. I've never gotten to experience this position, this level of dominance. It's invigorating, turning my boyfriend into a wanton mess just for me. I don't know how I'll ever want to do anything else because this right here is fucking addicting.

"That feel good? You like Ash sucking on your cock while I'm in your ass?" I say to Liam.

He nods and wiggles his ass into me as I fuck him deeper.

"How about you, Ash? Like sixty nining with your boyfriend?" I ask.

Technically, they don't do labels, so I could be pushing the limits here, but I can't help myself. Asher pulls Liam's cock out of his mouth for a moment as he practically growls.

"Fuck, yes I do. We have the best boyfriend, princess."

"We really do." I agree as Asher sucks him back into his mouth, moaning as he deep throats him.

Altogether we move, skin on skin, spit dripping, cock slobbering. The sounds of this room are absolutely disgusting and yet so fucking delicious.

I fuck Liam harder and faster, chasing the high I know is so close as my pussy begins to pulse around the small dildo inside me. A few more thrusts and it sends me over the edge. I'm whining and screaming my release as Liam whimpers around Asher's cock, following right behind me. Just the taste of Liam must have been all it took for Asher though, because his groans echo as well, both him and Liam drinking down each other's cum until they release one another, ragged breathing being the only thing you can hear for several seconds.

Slowly, we all pull apart, laying in silence on the bed. Liam is the first to speak, turning to look at Asher and me with a cheeky grin.

"Happy fucking birthday to me."

Chapter Thirty-Four

Liam

After the amazing morning with Skyla and Asher, the five tiered cake and the fucking balloon arch, there was no way the rest of the day could live up to it. All good things must come to an end and all that depressing shit. Now, much like a few weeks ago, the others are getting ready for the party tonight, only this time, I'm the guest of honor. And I couldn't be less thrilled.

The ride to campus was quiet. Ronan didn't try to speak, and neither did I. I wouldn't know what to say even if I tried. I have no idea what awaits me tonight, only that I'm sure I'll never be the same after it. If Ash is anything to go off, that is.

Ever since his birthday, he's tried to pretend, put on a good show. There is something shadowing him, plaguing his dreams, monopolizing every ounce of space in his mind. It's heavy and dark and, fuck, he won't let anyone in.

I begged him to tell me what happened at his ceremony to help prepare, and he begged me to never ask him again. The way he looked at me broke me in two, and for him, I dropped it. Suffice to say, I'm shit fucking scared.

Demise

The walk through campus is long and quick all at once. Like a blur, I blinked and somehow found myself waiting outside the meeting room door, burgundy robe on and finger freshly pricked from the sign in sheet. I inhale deeply through my nose, exhaling deeply once more before nodding to the man at the door. He nods to me, pushing it open and revealing the room.

There is a table in the middle of the room, not like the one they use for meetings, or the stone one used during Asher and Skyla's ceremony. This one is different, industrial, medical almost, with a black folded over cloth on the end.

My eyes roam the room, meeting the eyes of every Elder, including the newest Elder, Asher. My eyes come to my father, and he lifts his chin, as if to say straighten up. I do so instinctually, no matter how much I fucking hate the bastard. Finally, my eyes come to Asher's dad, and he smiles at me warmly as Ronan moves to stand behind him.

"Welcome. What a joyous day for us to all be reunited in this holy room so soon. Gaining new members, new brothers, is a gift that can only be given to us by God himself."

A collective nod waves through the room as Christopher turns to me.

"Liam Walcott, do you swear your allegiance to the Brethren? Do you swear to honor our ways, fulfill our practices and protect our secrets?" he asks.

"I swear," I nod.

"Do you swear to slay our enemy when given the chance and keep our people safe?" he continues.

"I swear."

"Do you swear to enforce all law whenever deemed necessary, no matter the task?"

Fear clenches inside me at that. I don't like the sound of

that, not at all. Fuck, God, if you're there, please help me through this. I'll do something...anything. Just...help.

"I swear," I hesitantly answer.

Christopher's mouth twists up like he didn't like my delay, and I dart a quick glance to see my father mirroring his expression.

Shit.

Despite my hesitance, Christopher seems to forgive it because he nods to the man on this side of the door, ordering him to open it. When he does, a man steps inside carrying a woman. A limp woman. He lays her on the table before he begins strapping her wrists together beneath the table. Her legs are next, forcing her white nightgown to ride up and more than a few Elders to lean forward in appreciation.

Fucking disgusting.

Her eyes are glazed as her head lulls to the side. Her long black hair reaches almost to her hips, and the untamed curls looked caked in something. Based on the smell of her, I'd say it was vomit.

"Behold! A witch!" Christopher hisses, causing an uproar to sound through the room.

The woman's eyes can't move, though, it's like she's imprisoned inside her own body. This is a witch? This is the thing that our parents, our Elders, have been warning us about for all these years?

"She was a nasty one. Gave some of our own a rough time when they selected her, so not to worry," Christopher says to the room before his hardened eyes come to her. "She's been subdued."

That's obvious. She looks as if she's been hooked up to a drip for days. Based on the condition of her, she could have been kept for longer. I know as well as any that there are many cells down here, and I've always been told to pretend

Demise

like you don't hear the screams. How could you ignore it, though?

Christopher's hand goes to the black cloth, unwrapping it to show a gilded wrapped dagger. He hands it to me, handle first, and I take it slowly, looking down at it before up to him. I know what comes next, and fuck, I'm not ready.

"Liam, this woman has been convicted of witchcraft, what do we, as the Brethren, do next?"

"Death," I answer hollowly. "Death to witches."

"Maleficis esse mori," the room chants.

Christopher nods in approval as he gestures to her.

"Cut out her heart and take a bite! Feast on the wicked to show you hold no fear!"

I feel my face go pale, I know everyone can see it, and I don't care. Feast on what? He wants me to...to...cut out her heart and *eat* it? Just the very idea of it has my stomach turning.

The entire room stares at me with anticipation, but I can't move. I can't breathe.

"Son," a voice sounds from the corner of the room.

My head whips around to see my father staring at me with malice in his eyes. He doesn't say anything else, but his intent is clear. Do this, now. Do not embarrass me. Do not embarrass yourself. Do the Walcott name justice.

Turning back to the drugged out woman, I take a wobbly step towards her and then another before I'm next to her chest. With shaky hands, I reach out to her nightgown, ripping the front of it open.

Her breasts spill free, and I notice them littered with bruises and hickeys as several men holler out in appreciation. I can't help but turn away, my entire stomach turning in disgust. Witch or not...this is wrong. To even imagine what she's been through over the last...however long is unthinkable. If this was Skyla, if this was my mother... I...

"Are you having difficulties, brother?" Christopher asks, displeasure heavy in his tone.

I look up to him, my eyes burning as tears begin to fill my eyes.

"Are you not capable of protecting our people?"

I don't speak, not knowing what to say, as Asher shoots me a panicked look. He's begging me to do something, but I can't. I'm frozen, no matter how hard I try to move my hands or my mouth, they are both glued in place.

Anger ignites in Christopher's eyes as he sneers, stepping toe to toe with me as he lifts a gun to my head. I quiver under his hold as he turns his head to the side and scoffs.

"If you cannot do something as simple as rid the world of evil, then you have no place in the Brethren. Choose your allegiance now. NOW!" he thunders, the flick of the safety being turned off echoing in the silent room.

"I," I pant shakily, blowing out a choppy breath. "W-will. I-I can," I say a little easier this time.

Christopher watches me through narrowed eyes before taking half a step back, lowering his gun by his side as he gestures for me to continue. I know that I have no choice. I know that to refuse is to sign my own death certificate, and fucking God help me, as selfish and disgusting as it is, I choose life. I choose Skyla, I choose Asher. I choose me.

The dagger plunges into her chest, forcing her back to bow despite being heavily drugged. A spine chilling scream erupts from her as several men step forward, helping to pin her down as I continue dragging the knife through her. I'm hacking through chunks of flesh, bone and muscle as I attempt to make my way through to her heart. In minutes, I have her entire chest cracked open, a river of bright red blood pouring out of her body cavity. So much for witches bleeding black.

I grab her heart into my hand. A squelching noise rips out

of her mouth as her body begins seizing. The warm, wet organ slips in my hand, forcing bile to rise up inside me as I begin cutting it out. Blood squirts me across the face before shooting out across the room. A commotion sounds behind me because of it, but I don't focus on them, I focus on the task at hand with everything I have.

When I cut the last vein, freeing the slippery mass, I turn to face the room, holding it up in victory as the Elders roar in celebration. It's a sound similar to a football game when the home team scores a touchdown. Varying expressions of ferocity take over each Elder as they cheer me on. Ingersoll looks downright feral as he mimics savage biting gestures. Egging me on.

I don't look down at the woman bleeding out, she's gone now, whether she deserved it or not I...I'll never be able to say. Instead, I lower the heart to my mouth, biting off the smallest piece I can manage, and rip my head away, blood seeping from the organ down my face.

Another round of thunderous cheers practically shakes the room as Christopher takes the heart from me, sinking his teeth into it as he rabidly shakes his head, then gives it to Henry Parris, who does the same, and so on and so forth. Even Asher and Ronan take a bite, though they swallow it quickly with grimaces of disgust.

That was probably the smart move. I'm still chewing the gummy tissue, the flavor burrowing its way deeper and deeper into my tastebuds. Oh God. With all of my willpower, I forcibly swallowed the mushed up piece of heart, my stomach violently turning as I do. I feel it heave and attempt to push it back down, but I will it to stay, breathing through it until my throat is clear.

Christopher pulls out a ring, sliding it onto my finger before grabbing my arm and lifting it up into the air, much like the winner of a fight. Everyone is to their feet now, apart from

Horris Hutchinson in his wheelchair, as they surround me, slaps of congratulations coming to me from all angles. Their bloodlust high really knows no bounds. I've never seen a single Elder behave this way, let alone all of them. My own father even comes up to me, cupping my bloody cheeks as he shakes me.

"I'm so proud of you!" He smiles, honest to God, smiles. I've never seen the man smile a day in his life. And he's proud of me? For what? For killing a woman that, let's be honest, may or may not have been a witch? For cutting her heart out and eating it along with all of these sick fucks?

I'm numb in shock, and thankfully, everyone begins filing out of the room, no doubt to go get cleaned up for the party. Ronan swoops in, grabbing me by the arm as he practically yanks me out of the room, Asher hot on our heels. We walk for a while before he pushes us into a room I've never been into. It's a bathroom with a full walk in shower, a deep soaker tub with a sink and toilet.

Ronan quickly turns on the water to the shower and I numbly walk towards it. Asher undoes my sash, but I don't reach for it, instead, I let it fall to the ground. When I step into the water, it feels cold. I try to turn it up, but still, I feel nothing. Hotter and hotter, I try, but nothing gets through.

I feel Asher's hand come to my back, and just at that single touch, I collapse. My body hits the tiled floor as I curl up into a ball and sob. Asher tosses his robe to the side, diving to the floor beside me as he gathers me into his arms. I come to him quickly, letting out sob after sob as I cling to him. He shushes me softly, kissing my forehead over and over again as he rocks us.

"It's okay. It's okay. You're safe, baby. You're safe."

"She's not," I choke out. "She's dead. I killed her!" I rasp before another pitiful sob tears through me.

Demise

Asher cups my cheeks, holding me tight as he looks into my eyes.

"You made a choice. She was going to die regardless, as soon as the Brethren saw her, she was done. You had a choice to live or die tonight, you chose to live. You chose to stay. Stay for Skyla, stay for me. You did the right thing, you hear me?" he asks.

I don't speak, and he winds back his hand, smacking me across the face.

"Do you goddamn hear me? The right choice is always to keep yourself safe, to keep yourself with me. You don't feel guilty for one fucking second, alright? I almost lost you in there, Skyla almost lost you. I could feel it, practically see it and—"

Asher's voice wavers for a second as he bites his lip and shakes his head.

"Don't you ever fucking do that to me again, alright? You never force me to witness you with a gun to your head again, Liam? We won't survive it. I—"

His words break off as he shakes his head and holds me tighter than before, rocking us quickly as his shoulders shake silently. I feel my tears begin to dry up, and my eyes come to see Ronan watching me with a brokenness in his gaze. He shakes his head in sorrow, like he wishes he could fix things, protect us. He's always been able to before, ever since we were babies, he's always looked out for us, but now...this...this is something no one could have prepared me for, no one could have protected me from.

Looking up to Asher, I pull his head down to mine, smashing our lips together. He doesn't move, but then again, I don't need him to. I just need to feel...something, anything. So, we sit there under what feels like freezing water, our mouths pressed to one another for countless minutes, hours, whatever it is, trying to feel, to cope and then to bottle this night way the fuck up.

Chapter Thirty-Five

Skyla

Wesley and I are chatting with some of his acquaintances, maintaining an appropriate distance, of course, when I spy Liam's parents. Well, more specifically, his mother. She practically floats through the room, all dressed in white.

I know the instant that she sees me, because she changes direction and heads straight towards me. It immediately puts me on edge. I've never spoken to her before, but I have heard some nasty stories from Liam growing up. Granted, a lot of those stories stemmed from Liam's father, but his mother sat idly by as her husband beat him for stepping a toe out of line, so in my mind, she's as much to blame.

Still, though, wanting to make a good impression, I turn on my charm, giving her a warm smile as she approaches us.

"Skyla, darling. It's a pleasure to finally meet you," she says, pulling me in for air kisses.

I kiss beside her cheeks as I smile and nod.

"It is so good to meet you, Mrs. Walcott. Liam has told me so much about you."

Her eyebrows shoot up her forehead, well, as far up as her injections allow her.

"You and my son talk often? Often enough to talk about family?"

I physically feel my eyes widen, and I kick myself as I scramble to try to answer before deciding to play everything casually. Nodding with a soft smile, I continue.

"He's my husband's best friend. He's always around."

"Uh, huh," she says, her eyes raking over me in suspicion. "Well, we simply must get to know one another better, maybe not on a night where all eyes are on me and my family. Lots of schmoozing to do, as you can imagine," she titters, and I struggle to find it in me to laugh along with her.

This night is about her? Her family? Not just Liam? I don't know how she could be so delusional, or maybe she has her head in the sand but honestly, joining the Elders isn't the honor everyone thinks it is. It's more like officially sealing your fate. Guaranteeing you will serve the Brethren until your dying breath. Sounds like an even more need for mourning than a celebration, personally.

"Let's do brunch, tomorrow? At the country club. I'll tell them to have our table ready by noon," she says as she floats away, drifting in and out of each conversation she comes by before settling in with a flock of mother hens. Or at least that's what I call the gossiping group of mothers in the corner. Their eyes roam over each person slowly, methodically, with nothing but pure judgement in their eyes.

A few more minutes go by before I see some Elder men begin to file into the room. My father and Christopher are two of the last to enter. They both make eye contact with me and nod, my father going so far as to smile. At me. I don't know why, and honestly, I don't care. The sight alone is unnerving.

My eyes continue scanning the room in search of the guys, but I come up empty.

"They'll be here soon. Relax," Wesley says to me softly.

I don't make eye contact with him, unsure of who could potentially be watching us right now.

"I'm trying. It's hard to relax when you don't know what's happening."

Wesley nods as he lifts his drink to his mouth.

"They'll be fine."

"Why didn't you have to go?" I ask.

"Hm?"

"Tonight. Or the night of Asher's ceremony. You're an Elder, technically, right?"

Wesley shrugs. "My father holds the Elder seat for the family."

My brows knit together. "Right, but Ronan still has to go despite Christopher holding his seat. He goes to every gathering and ceremony. So, why don't you have to?"

He pauses for several moments, his tongue running along his lower lip before he finally speaks.

"Christopher and I have an understanding."

My face screws up at that as I look at him.

"An understanding? What could—"

"Drop it, Sky," he says quickly. "Please," he tacks on, softer this time.

Begrudgingly, I nod, not because I intend on dropping it, but because it's not the time or place.

Relief swells my chest as Liam, Asher, and Ronan all walk in together. That relief shrivels up and dies when I see the look in Liam's eyes. His face is all smiles, bright and infectious as ever, but those eyes. His sweet green eyes, that make anyone feel like the most important person in the room, are dull, lifeless, practically black.

I cross the room before I can talk myself out of it, forcing myself to hug Asher first when all I really want to do is cradle Liam gently and ask what I can do.

Asher accepts me happily, holding onto me for several seconds longer than anticipated before he whispers into my ear.

"He needs you."

I nod against Asher's shoulder, smiling to Liam as I put on a show for the people around us.

"Congratulations!" I grin, pulling him in tight. "Are you okay, baby?" I whisper into his ear.

He shakes his head as he pulls away, that same smile on his face, but the pain in his eyes has nearly doubled.

"Thank you." He smiles. "Enjoy the party," he says as he begins making his rounds, much like his mother.

Asher and Ronan hang back with me as we all keep our eyes on Liam.

"Is he okay?"

"No," they answer in unison.

I nod. "Will he be okay?"

They both hesitate before Ronan faces me, shrugging his shoulders with a disappointed head shake. Meanwhile, Asher hasn't taken his eyes off Liam, like he can't. Like he's afraid to. What the fuck happened to my sweet golden retriever boy?

Liam lasts longer at his party than Asher did, a lot longer. We are two hours deep into the party, and he is currently telling an extremely animated story to his father and some of his friends. Asher, Wesley, Ronan, and I so very obviously want to go, but Liam is practically the life of the party. At least, he appears so.

Demise

Maggie comes up to me, bumping her shoulder against mine and I smile before turning to watch Liam once more.

"Is he alright?" she asks.

"No," we all answer.

She nods. "He seems off. A little too happy."

My eyes clock movement to the right, stunning me speechless. Liam's mother is practically shoving Maryia towards him, okay not practically, but literally. When they get within a foot or so, she shoves her, hard. She stumbles into Liam's shoulder, and he turns just in time to catch her, giving her a kind smile and a nod. I see the look on his mother's face, though. I see the look on her parents' faces as they hang back a few feet. Their plotting practically leaves an odor.

"Jesus," Maggie scoffs. "Of course my girlfriend is being arranged to your boyfriend," she mutters just under her breath.

"You don't think that's what's happening, do you? I mean, you've been introduced to a lot of men at parties like these, and you're not engaged," I defend.

She chuckles. "Because I'm an insufferable cunt. Intentionally so. Mads...she can't help but be sweet and charming. It's who she is; it's who Liam is. Honestly, from an outsider's perspective, they are kinda perfect for each other."

I frown at that, and Maggie bumps my shoulder once more.

"Relax, she's not into him. She just came all over my tongue in the bathroom before she voluntarily ate my pussy until I saw stars. Trust me, she's gay as fuck." Maggie chuckles as she looks at her with equal parts adoration and ravenous hunger.

Her words bring me a little relief before I see Maryia take a step back for comfort, and Liam's mom shoves her into his chest once more. Liam catches her again but this time, he settles his hand around her waist, holding him to her as he whispers something into her ear. She gives him a sweet smile and nods before sinking further into his touch. I like Maryia, I really do. She's super sweet and seems to be good for Maggie. But, if she doesn't stop rubbing herself all over my man, we're gonna have a fucking problem.

"Easy girl," Wesley teases. "Your claws are showing."

"No, they aren't," I gnash at him, causing his brows to raise.

"C'mon," Asher says. Let's go for a walk."

He holds out his arm for me and though I don't want to go anywhere, I take it, looping my arm through his as we begin moving through the throngs of people. A new song starts up and dozens of people rush to the dance floor, including Liam and Maryia. My stomach turns, and Asher jerks my arm quickly, forcing me to look away.

My eyes roam around the room, resting on Christopher's office before I turn to Asher.

"Does your dad keep a journal? Like the one Thomas did?"

Asher frowns. "Thomas? Thomas Putnam?"

I look at him confused. Ronan knew about it. Asher doesn't?

"Yeah, Ronan told me that he kept a journal. Him and Christopher used to read it when they were kids. It's supposedly your father's prized possession."

I watch as Asher's face pinches in thought before understanding dawns on him.

"Black, leather? With a Brethren B stamped into the front?"

"Sure?" I nod just in case as we pass the office.

"Yeah, he keeps it tucked away in his desk. Never let me get near the thing, but I always find him reading it pretty much nonstop. Makes more sense now." He nods.

My mind can't help but wander. His desk? As in, the desk that is a mere ten feet away? And growing further.

The library wasn't all that helpful for me, then again, I'm not really sure what I'm looking for. Sure, it gave me all the cut and dry historical facts about this town and the trials, but there is something else, something missing. I can practically feel it, and I'm desperate for answers.

"I'm actually going to use the restroom," I smile.

Asher's eyes narrow on me. "Are you okay? Do you want me to come with you?"

I shake my head as we move towards the bathrooms. Yes, plural, because of course a mansion of this size needs three restrooms downstairs alone.

"I'm alright. Just need to catch my breath for a moment."

Asher gives me a sympathetic nod of his head.

"I'll wait right here."

"No," I say, attempting to sound calm and relaxed. "Go schmooze or whatever you have to do so we can get the hell out of here. With or without Liam, I don't want to be here anymore."

He lets out a derisive snort and he nods. "Agreed."

Asher turns and heads back the way we came, weaving in and out of people. I only wait until he's fully out of sight before I slip off into the kitchen. There are a couple of servers that pretend as if I'm not there, but I ignore them in favor of the servant's entrance to Christopher's office that I've noticed before. You heard me right, a servant's entrance for an office. How disgusting can you be?

"Excuse me? I believe Mrs. Walcott is looking for some assistance. She wanted more hors d'oeuvres to be passed out."

The two servers quickly jump to attention, grabbing the trays and hustling out of the kitchen, giving me the perfect opportunity to slip inside the office. Honestly, I'm amazed it's unlocked. Then again, who would be stupid enough to sneak into Christopher Putnam's office in the middle of a party? Apparently, this girl.

When I step into the office, the heady scent of scotch and

cigars permeates my senses. I look around carefully before stepping up to his desk. I don't know why I'm so nervous, I haven't done anything technically wrong. Yet.

My hands shake as I open the first drawer, finding nothing but a few silver pens and papers. The next drawer, more paperwork. Same with the final drawer. I'm ready to give up when I notice a paperweight on the bottom of the drawer jiggle as I pull it fully out. Curiously, I reach in, lifting it out and testing the bottom of the drawer. It has a little give, and when I lift it up, there it is.

Just like Asher described it. Black, leather with an engraved B and old as hell looking. I mean, it's literally over three hundred years old. I'm surprised it's still together, let alone in the condition it's in.

For some insane reason, I reach for it, picking it up as my fingers begin thumbing through it. Page after page is filled with elaborate cursive handwriting, eating up every centimeter of space. The first date I notice is November 2nd, 1692. The next is November 5th, 1692. It's no wonder the thing is so fat. He was writing in it several times a week. Probably more, for twenty years.

Looking down at my blue gown, I'm thankful I decided to wear a corset with the ballgown. Grabbing the journal, I slip it under my skirt, tucking it just beneath the bottom of my corset before looking down. You can see a slight bulge, so I grab a handful of tulle and fan it out in front of me, perfectly camouflaging it. This is so fucking stupid, but before I can talk myself out of it, I'm slipping back out the servant's entrance, closing the door behind me.

My heart pounds in my chest as I move through the party, catching nearly everyone's eyes. I know it's my own paranoia, but it feels like they are all watching me, that they all know I've done something terrible. I'm just thankful no one stops me.

Demise

When I make it back to the guys, I notice Liam has now joined them, Maryia still around his arm, as Maggie conveniently is cozied up beside her. All eyes come to me as I rejoin the group.

"You good?" Asher asks, clearly picking up on my off demeanor.

I nod and he narrows his eyes like he doesn't believe me. "I'd like to go home now."

Asher nods, and Ronan and Wesley move together, heading for the door when I pause to look at Liam. He nods to Maryia before meeting my gaze.

"I need to take Maryia home first."

Of course he does.

"I got her," Maggie says before lowering her tone with a laugh. "I mean, you are literally all over my girlfriend, bro."

"As if I had a choice," Liam grits through his clenched teeth before shooting an apologetic look to Maryia. "Sorry, no offense."

She shakes her head. "None taken. You know I'm...spoken for."

Maggie laughs a little louder this time, nodding her head.

"That's one way to call being absolutely pussy whipped."

Maryia's mouth drops open in outrage but when Maggie gives her a teasing smile, she blushes, shrugging her shoulders.

"At least let me make it look like I'm taking her home for our parents," Liam says as he begins guiding Maryia out of the party.

Maggie and I loop our arms together as Asher waits for us a few steps away. I move as carefully as I can, feeling the journal moving with each breath I take as Christopher and my father intersect us.

"Are you kids off?" Christopher asks, almost in a jovial way.

What the fuck is up with him and my dad today?

295

"We are. Skyla isn't feeling well, and I have a big presentation in class tomorrow," Asher answers.

Christopher nods. "Good man. I hope you feel better soon," he says to me before leaning in and pressing a lingering kiss to my cheek.

Fear ratchets inside me. The item I'm currently concealing on my body is his most prized possession. Does he know I have it? Can he sense it? That's ridiculous, of course not. Then again, the Brethren is filled with nothing but surprises.

When he pulls away, there is no suspicion is in his gaze, only that creepy way that he always watches me. My father leans in, giving me a matching kiss on the other cheek before they nod at us and turn as one, like the weird little culty duo they are.

Asher turns, leading the way for us, when I feel Maggie stop walking. Her eyes are on a woman in a bombshell red dress with sleek black hair down to her ass. I'd recognize that hair anywhere, and when those bright blue eyes snap towards us, or more accurately so, Maggie, I can practically feel the tension from here.

An old white haired man has his arm around her, his hand dangerously low to her ass. Bridgette looks uncomfortable with it, but also like she's been in this position a million times. She gives Maggie a sad shrug as she turns back to face the conversation.

"Mags?" I ask carefully.

She doesn't respond, I don't even think she sees or hears anyone but Bridgette. Bridgette and that man.

"Maggie?" I ask again, forcing her gaze to snap to me. "Are you okay?"

She closes her eyes for a second, shaking her head before looking to me again, pasting on a fake as fuck smile.

"I'm great. Never better. Let's go."

Demise

I hesitate for a moment until I feel the journal slip a little further. I can comfort my friend from the safety of Asher's car, or maybe on facetime. I know I have to get home immediately, and I also know Maggie doesn't want to talk about it, so we're gonna put a pin into that little moment because the way they looked at each other...that's not how you look at an *ex*-lover.

All of our cars pull up to the valet, and we begin filing in, though Maggie and Liam make a clean exchange of Maryia like she's smuggled goods before he jumps into the car with Ronan and they take off. Asher, Wesley, and I are right behind them, and Maggie's car is the last to leave.

I rest my hand against the bottom of the journal the entire way home, and when we get to the house, Liam makes a beeline for his room, shutting his door with a loud bang. I look to Asher in concern, but he just shakes his head.

"Let him process."

"Process what?" I ask.

He hesitates for a moment before speaking.

"He'll tell you if he wants to, if he's ready."

I frown at that, but nod as I grip the front of my dress, or more accurately, the journal a little tighter as I make my way up the stairs. When I turn into my room, none of the guys say anything, and I'm grateful because I swiftly lock the door, pull out the journal and begin devouring every single page.

Chapter Thirty-Six

Vincent

It's an hour or so before sunrise when I make it back to Salem, driving straight over to Skyla's house. I didn't even stop off at one of my properties for a change of clothes. As soon as I turned eighteen, I began buying up property all over the world. Some in my name...most not. Like fuck was I ever going to stay on campus willingly.

I need to see her, though. I feel like my flesh is about to literally crawl off my body. Two weeks...it might as well have been two years. I refuse to be gone from her for this long again. Next time, she's coming with me. I don't give a fuck what anyone says about it.

There were several people of interest I was sent to investigate overseas. A majority of the time I was in Monaco, France and two days in Spain. All points of interest were eliminated days ago, but Christopher forced me to stay put to let the heat die down first. It made no sense other than he didn't want me in Salem. Which I don't like one fucking bit. The calculated motherfucker has to be up to something.

I forget all about that in one breath. As soon as I set eyes on

Demise

my siren, it all floats away. I sneak through her balcony doors like usual, though I could technically use the key from the front door. I like it better this way. She is the person I want to see first, not some fucker downstairs with his hands down his pants.

She's sleeping heavily, her chest slowly moving up and down, her breathing virtually silent. I'm surprised she's alone. With four other boyfriends, it's a rarity to ever get alone time with her, and for her to sleep alone? An extinct concept, or so I thought.

As her eyelids flicker, I curl myself around her, gently stroking my hands through her hair as she dreams. I hope it's a beautiful one. One where she is in the water, getting lost in how long she's been in with no sign of getting out. I hope in her dreams I'm there, always within arms reach. I hope that we're away from Salem for good, and I hope the Brethren is burned to a crisp at her hands like the queen she truly is.

I purposefully drag my fingers a little close to her face, startling her awake. Those bright green orbs flash to me, filled with alarm before recognition flickers in them and they soften.

"Vincent?" she whispers softly.

I nod as I continue running my fingers through her hair. I don't get the chance to finish my movement before she is on top of me. Her mouth presses to mine before frantic kisses are spread across my face and down my neck. I arch into her touch, letting out a soft groan as I lift my hips and grind my rock hard cock against her thigh. I've been hard since I first saw her laying here, and touching her only made that problem worse.

She grabs the waistband of her shorts, sliding them down and off her legs as she grabs my jeans, beginning to unbutton them.

"I've missed you so much," she whines. "I need you."

"I'm all yours," I say as I let her take the wheel.

Her hand slips inside my pants, pulling out my cock. Her breath catches softly, and I know that she found her surprise.

"What—"

"Do you like it?" I ask.

Her eyes stare down at my cock, seemingly in awe. The intricate design of a siren is wrapped around it, her name scribed up the tail that stretches all the way down to the base.

"You tattooed your cock, for me?" she asks, seemingly stunned.

I frown at her. I'm not sure why she's surprised. As if there was anything in this world that I wouldn't do for her. I would have had the guy cut out my goddamn heart and tattoo her name on it if I thought it would bring a smile to her face.

"Of course. It's yours."

She frowns, shaking her head in disbelief. "I just...didn't that hurt?"

"No."

Yes, like a motherfucker. I don't want her to know that, though. She'd get all sad and sympathetic, and that's not what this moment is supposed to be about.

When she looks up at me again, her frown is gone but replaced by two glossy eyes, brimming with tears that are about to fall.

"Why is this the sweetest thing anyone has ever done for me?" she asks on a choked sob.

"Shhh," I hush. "Don't cry, siren. Just come here. Come ride your cock."

She looks at me and nods, straddling me before slowly sinking herself down. When she's seated, we both let out a moan. Goddamnit, I've missed this. Missed her. I haven't been able to even jerk off since I got this thing, trying to let it heal. I knew it was the perfect time to do it, because there was no time ever again that I was going to go without having my siren for over two weeks.

As she lifts up, I see her look down, watching me sliding in and out of her wet cunt. She throws back her head and cries out.

"Oh my God. That is so fucking hot."

"Yes, you are, siren. Fuck me like you missed me."

Her hips begin gyrating, and I hold onto her tightly as I help guide her. I feel her hand reach back, cupping my balls as she begins massaging them. Another shock of pleasure runs through me at the feeling and I begin thrusting harder to compensate.

"Fuck," I grumble.

"Am I doing okay?" she asks, like the silly girl needs to ask.

"You do more than okay from just fucking breathing, siren. Do you have any goddamn idea how much I used to watch you before? How often I'd jerk off just to the sight of you?"

She scrunches up her nose as her thrusts slow.

"Like, stand around a corner and stroke your cock."

"Fuck yes," I agree.

She shakes her head as her pace continues.

"What the fuck is wrong with me, why do I find that so hot?"

"Because, you were made for me," I say as I smack her ass cheek, encouraging her to go faster.

She obeys me immediately, bouncing on me so quickly that her tits begin smacking each other. I raise my tattooed hands, lifting her sleep shirt up and over her head before throwing it to the other side of the room. My hands come to cover her tits, squeezing as my thumbs play with her nipples.

They are instantly hard for me, the sweetest shade of pink, and I pull her towards me, dragging one of her nipples into my mouth. My tongue swirls around the hardened peak and Skyla moans in response.

"More," she begs.

I obey her instantly, I always will.

My mouth moves to her other nipple, sucking and nipping at that one as I continue tugging on the other with my fingers. She's so pliable for me, so willing, and the fact that she likes a little pain with her pleasure? It makes her fucking perfect for me.

"Cut me, Vincent," she whimpers.

My eyes meet hers, mouth still latched around her as she moans.

"Use me, make me bleed. Make me come like only you know how to."

One of my hands drops to my jeans, fumbling around for the switchblade I always keep on me as I pull it out. I haven't used it since I cleaned it, so it's safe to use on her. And when she begs me so beautifully, how can I say anything but no?

"Where?" I ask.

"Wherever you want. Mark me, make me yours."

"You've always been mine, siren. Always."

I start with a small slit on her upper left thigh. Her thrusts have stopped as she sits there with bated breath as I drag the tip of the knife against her fleshy skin. Her teeth sink into her lip like she's hurting, but the lust drunk look in her eyes tells me she's as addicted to receiving the pain as I am to giving it.

A thin red line blooms in the wake of my knife before I pause and move to the other thigh. I repeat the motion, and this time, a choked cry escapes her. My eyes glance to hers in warning. I'll stop if she needs me to, but my cock is fucking pulsing inside of her from this act of trust, of obedience. It has me ready to come and fucking hard.

Twin trails of blood begin running down her thighs as I toss

Demise

the knife to the side. I can't stop myself from playing with it. My fingers smear the blood against her perfect creamy thighs, marring the flawless skin with that deep, inky red. My fingers rub against it more and more until the tips are completely covered. I suck them into my mouth, relishing the taste of her as I begin thrusting.

She whimpers, but begins bouncing, her eyes on me as she watches me closely. When I've sucked my fingers clean, she grabs my hand, rubbing it against the other leg that has become wet, smearing blood all over my fingers once more before shoving them back in my mouth.

I can't help but moan around my fingers, the taste of her almost better the second time. She groans and whimpers as she rides my cock, her pussy pulsing as I lick my fingers clean.

"You're so fucking sick," she moans.

"So are you, siren," I counter.

"Fuck, yes, I am. Do it again, play with my blood like you like to," she cries.

I rest my hands on her thighs, actually surprised when I feel my entire palms wet. She's bleeding more than she should be, probably because she's the one on top, flexing her legs. In a flash, I flip us, pinning her to her back as I lift one leg over my shoulder and fuck her raw and deep.

Her eyes roll into the back of her head as my hand comes to cover her mouth, pinning her to the mattress as I do.

"This what you want, siren? Want to be fucked hard by your man? Blood soaked and so fucking horny?" I ask as I slip my hand to her throat.

A bloody handprint covers her face. My bloody handprint. I don't give a fuck what it says about me, it's the most beautiful thing I've ever seen. Hesitantly, she sticks her tongue out, running it along her bloodied lip. She pulls her tongue back in, tasting herself before she sticks it out again.

Eagerly, I shove a finger into her mouth, forcing her to suck her blood off my finger. As soon as her tongue wraps around my digit, that's all I can handle. I lose it, lose my fucking vision, my mind. I lose everything as I fall over the edge, roaring out my release as my cum floods her.

Her pussy pulses around me, squeezing tight before she comes. Her whimpers are so loud, even around my finger, they still seem to shake the walls. Her pants are hurried and desperate as she moans and grinds against me, milking every ounce of her orgasm that she can before her body collapses in defeat, mine right there alongside her.

We lay there for a few seconds before I push myself to stand, lifting her into my arms and carrying her to the bathroom. I start up the shower and move us inside to the bench where the water can't reach us yet. I sit there and hold her for several seconds, pressing a soft kiss against her shoulder as she sighs.

"I've really missed you."

Moving some of her hair away from her neck as I place another kiss to her, I murmur against her skin.

"If I'd have had to suffer another day without you, I'd have gladly offed myself."

She whips around to face me, disappointment in her eyes.

"Don't joke like that."

"I'm not joking. Being away from you…it was some of the worst torture I've ever endured."

"Why did you have to be gone for so long?"

Wish I could tell you, still trying to figure that piece out myself.

"Work stuff. Why are you sleeping alone? Do I need to kill someone?"

She smiles sadly and shakes her head, probably thinking that I'm joking. I couldn't be more serious, though. I don't give a

Demise

fuck who it is. If anyone ever inconveniences my siren, I'll gladly slit their throat and present their severed head like a prize at my siren's feet.

"Liam's induction was last night, and...he's not okay."

I nod. I'd imagine not. I've already heard through the grapevine about Asher's. Even I was surprised he was able to go through with it. He's not soft like Liam, but he's also not a desensitized killer like...well, me.

Liam though...he's as squishy as they come. He wasn't meant for this life, or at least, he doesn't have what it takes. He's still breathing, so clearly I underestimated him. He'll probably never be okay again, though. That's the point. If you kill for the Brethren, it is the ultimate ammunition to keep you subdued and subservient. You step a toe out of place, and if they don't send an eliminator after you, they'll send the police for your crimes. Blackmail at its finest.

"What about the others?" I ask.

She pauses for a moment, and it puts me on edge, like she's choosing her words carefully. I don't like that one bit.

"I was tired, sad for Liam. I just wanted to be alone."

I narrow my eyes in suspicion, not believing what she has to say for a fucking second but allowing her to believe she's fooled me. For now.

"And now?" I ask.

She smiles, leaning her head against my shoulder.

"Now, I never want you to let me go."

"I never will, siren."

Chapter Thirty Seven

Skyla

After the shower, Vincent and I went back to bed for a few more hours. My eyes open as sunlight streams in through my balcony door, Vincent fast asleep beside me for once. I smile down at him as I slide out of bed, wincing as I do. My thighs are sore...like a lot. Vincent tended to my cuts so sweetly and patiently but still, the dull, sharp pain is there, and it is persistent. Worth it.

Carefully, I slip on a baggy pair of sweatpants and a tank top as I slip out of the bedroom. My feet carry me towards the stairs for half a second before I look down the hallway, Liam's door practically calling to me. I turn and head towards it, hoping he's ready for some company.

It's true that I slept alone last night because Liam was upset. I also slept alone because I stayed up until two in the morning reading Thomas Putnam's journal. I haven't been able to finish, obviously, but I'm currently reading entries during the witch trials. I made it up to the point his daughter, Ann, was having unexplained fits and cried 'witch.' Just from the history books, I know things are about to get bad fast.

Demise

I hid the journal underneath a loose floorboard beneath my bed. If I'm honest, I wouldn't be surprised if Vincent finds it. It seems like something he'd be especially good at. I'm just hoping he won't even bother, that he wouldn't have picked up on anything off this morning.

Who am I kidding? This is Vincent we're talking about.

My feet pause outside Liam's door, and for some reason, a wave of nervousness rolls through me. Maybe I'm just worried that he won't want to see me, that he'll kick me out. Maybe I'm not his favorite person anymore; maybe I'm not what he needs.

Still, I have to try. My hand rests on the doorknob, and when I turn it, I'm surprised to find it unlocked. Slowly, I push inside the dark room. The curtains are drawn, all lights off as Liam's still figure lays in bed. His usually soft snoring can't be heard, and it has me furrowing my brows when he speaks.

"What do you want, Sky?"

His voice is so hollow, so...bare. It's devoid of any of the emotion and playful tone it usually carries. Hesitantly, I cross the room, coming to his side as I speak.

"I just wanted to check on you. How are you feeling?"

"Like death," he mutters against his pillow, not looking up at me or even moving as he speaks.

Worried, I reach for him before I think better of it. Instead, opting to stand there awkwardly because what do I do...how do I help?

"Should I leave you alone?" I ask.

He's quiet for several seconds before he lets out a heavy sigh and lifts the blankets in invitation. I take the gesture happily, sliding into bed beside him as I lay on my side to face him. We stare at each other for several minutes, just watching one another. If we have to do this all day, then it's what we'll do.

I watch as a single tear escapes his eye, slipping down his

face, over his nose, and to the other cheek before hitting his pillow. My heart aches as I lift my hand, brushing the tear away.

"Baby," I whisper hoarsely. "What did they do to you?"

He doesn't speak, instead, he just swallows. We stay like that for another minute or so before his voice comes through, the softest whisper I've ever heard.

"I killed someone."

Oh, my poor sweet boy. Closing the distance between us, I wrap my arms around him, burying him into my chest as I shush him softly, running my fingers through his hair as he continues.

"A woman...I...I killed her. Brutally," he says as his body shakes.

I hold him tighter as his arms wrap around me and he falls apart. His body shakes as sobs rip through him, the sound of his cries literally breaking my heart to pieces.

"It's not your fault, Liam. You were doing what you could to survive," I whisper against him. "You are so kind, so loving. That wasn't you. It was who you needed to be, right?"

He cries for a few more seconds before he shakes his head.

"I tried to refuse. I couldn't...not after all she'd been through. Then..."

He pauses, like he knows he shouldn't say this next part.

"Christopher pulled a gun on me, said it was me or her, and like a fucking coward, I deemed my life more valuable than hers."

"No," I say.

"Yes," he snaps. "That's exactly what I did, because in that moment, all I could think about was you. I thought about how much pain you'd be in if I was dead, how much Ash would be. I was given a choice to do the right thing, and I didn't take it because of you two."

Guilt gnaws at me as he continues.

"And I fucking hate myself because, given the chance, I'd make the same choice again."

My heart aches and soars simultaneously. I press a kiss to his forehead as I rest my head against his.

"It's not like he would have let her live regardless." I try to reason.

He shakes his head. "That's not the point. If he had, it wouldn't have mattered."

I stay quiet for a moment as I nod.

"Does it make me a terrible person if I say thank you?"

He scoffs but doesn't say anything as I continue.

"Thank you for not putting me through the hell of losing you. Thank you for not putting Asher through the same. Thank you for not surrendering one of the loves of my life. Thank you for being selfish, for me."

His breaths are deep but more measured this time as he speaks.

"I don't know how to live with this...this guilt. This pain. I... I see her eyes, her face. Even when I blink, she's there."

I nod my understanding, though I truly can't understand until I've lived through what he has.

"You'll learn how to, and we will be here by your side to help you through it. All of us."

He nods as he holds me closer, burrowing his head into me before falling into a heavy sleep. I lay there for several hours, running my fingers through his hair, whispering reassurances, telling him how much I love him, and he sleeps, deeply.

I glance at the clock on the wall and decide I have to get up now if I'm going to make it to brunch with Liam's mom on time. I don't know how I got roped into that, but here I am.

Carefully, I slide out of bed, thankful Liam doesn't even stir as I slip out of the room, closing the door with a soft snick.

Tiptoeing my way to my bedroom, I find it empty. Vincent must already be up somewhere.

Moving to my closet, I select a turtleneck sweater dress and a pair of tights with over the knee boots. Liam's mother is definitely a judgmental one, so looking my best has to be a priority. Though, does it really matter if she likes me or not? She's literally trying to marry off my boyfriend to my best friend's girlfriend.

Still, I want to make a good impression because maybe, one day, things can be in the open, and if that day comes, I don't want my boyfriend's mother to hate me.

I flat iron my hair, do a respectable amount of makeup while keeping it neutral before grabbing my designer sunglasses and stepping out the bedroom door, running straight into Vincent.

"Oh, there you are."

"Where are you off to looking like that?" Vincent asks, his eyes running up and down my body.

"I think what you meant to say is, 'Wow, Skyla. You look beautiful this morning.'"

He lifts an unimpressed brow.

"Wow, Skyla. You look beautiful every morning. Now, where do you think you're going?"

"The country club. Liam's mom invited me to brunch, well, told me to go to brunch with her."

Vincent frowns. "I'm coming."

I laugh at that before I see that he's being serious.

"You can't."

"Yes, I can."

"No, you cannot invite yourself to have brunch with us, Vincent."

He rolls his eyes like I'm being unreasonable.

Demise

"I'll sit a few tables away, don't worry. You can still try to schmooze the wicked bitch of the northeast."

I frown at that. "Is she really that bad?"

He laughs, actually laughs. Vincent never laughs. Suddenly, all of my nerves are on edge as he nods.

"She's essentially the only matriarch left in the Elders... apart from you. Does that answer your question?"

Unfortunately, yes.

Lovely.

Liam always talks so highly of her. Well, now that I think about it, highly isn't exactly the word I'd use. More like he doesn't hate her like he does his dad, so I guess I just assumed she was a good person. My mistake, I suppose.

"Fine. But we're leaving now, and you're driving," I say as I brush past him.

"Anything for you, siren."

I tried to say goodbye to the guys, but none of them were downstairs. I don't know if they already left to start their day or slept in. I'll call them later. For now, I'm walking up to Salem's Country Club, feeling insecure as ever. I shouldn't though, posh superiority is what I specialize in. A London boarding school education really teaches you a thing or two. That, and having Henry Parris as your father.

The hostess smiles at me, guiding me through the restaurant before I can even give her my name or Liam's mother's. Which, I guess I should start calling her—

"Alison," I greet with a polite smile.

"Ah, Skyla." She smiles as she stands from her chair, giving me air kisses before taking her seat once more.

"Thank you for joining me," she says as she takes a sip of her coffee.

"Thank you for the invitation." I smile as the waiter steps in.

"Hello ladies, my name is Cara, I'll be your server. Can I get you anything? Coffee, tea, mimosa?" she asks me.

"I'd love a coffee, black. Thank you." I smile and nod.

She steps away with a nod and heads back to the kitchen as Alison makes a sound.

"I'd have thought you'd choose tea, given your upbringing."

I smile through the stereotype. Though yes, many people that reside in London drink tea, it's not a requirement. Steph and I always preferred coffee anyways.

"I've always preferred coffee," I say, and she hmphs but doesn't say anything.

Slowly, my smile falls as the server comes back with my coffee and takes our orders. I decide on half a sandwich and a bowl of soup while she tuts and gets a Caesar salad, no dressing, no croutons and no cheese….so, romaine lettuce.

"Always have to look good for our husbands, do we not?" she asks with a raised brow, the barb very clear.

I smile and nod. "Asher certainly has no complaints, thankfully." I throw back.

Her eyes rake over me, that plastic smile intact as she nods.

"I'm sure not."

An awkward silence descends over us before I try to break it.

"So, what do you do for work?"

She releases a condescending laugh like I'm hilarious.

"Sweet girl, I don't work. No wife of the Brethren, let alone an Elder's wife, works."

"Oh, I wasn't sure."

Again, awkward silence.

"Well, what do you like to do with your time?" I ask again.

She takes a sip of her coffee, resting it down to the table as she speaks.

"I organize a lot of parties for the Brethren, galas, functions. That's all me. Christopher hands me his card and says make it look nice," she gushes.

I'm almost sad for her that being Christopher's henchwoman is the most exciting thing she does with her time. I guess if she's happy though, that's what matters.

"Well, from the parties I've been to, you've done a wonderful job."

She nods her thanks as our food is placed in front of us. She gives mine a disgusted look, like she's mentally counting the calories, before shaking her head.

"So, I think it's best if we address the elephant in the room," she says as she daintily gathers a few pieces of lettuce on her fork.

"Elephant?" I ask.

"You sleeping with my son."

My eyes widen as she takes her bite, chewing slowly before swallowing.

"Sweet girl, you didn't honestly think the two of you were subtle, did you?" Alison laughs.

"I—"

"My question is, what will your husband think?" she asks, a hint of malice in her smile.

Is she trying to blackmail me? For what? What on earth would I have to offer her? Deciding that playing nice is over, I sit up straight, drop my smile and fold my hands in my lap. I give her a look that my father would surely be proud of as a condescending smile curves my face.

"My husband is *well* aware of Liam and myself."

Her lips purse at that as she shakes her head.

"Ah, I see they are *those* type of Bond Brothers."

"Excuse me?" I ask.

"The ones who share their women. The ones who use and abuse them until they are nothing but worthless trash who disappear. Careful, girl, your days are surely numbered at this rate."

Not sweet girl anymore, just girl. Alrighty then.

"Speaking from experience?" I jab.

She waves her hand in dismissal. "Hardly."

Her fork slams against her plate, gaining the interest of several diners, but she doesn't pay them any mind as she leans forward, lowering her tone.

"My husband cherishes me, unlike yours, apparently. Look around, how many Elder's wives are there? Just one, me. You know why that is? I keep my husband satisfied, and I keep my goddamn mouth shut. I live and breathe for the Brethren with a smile on my face. Anyone who tells you this isn't a game of survival of the fittest has already lost. They've all lost, all but me."

"And me," I say, pushing my shoulders back a little further as I sit taller in my chair.

She rolls her eyes at me and shakes her head.

"Not for long at the rate you're going. You've been a wife for less than three months and already your husband is auctioning you off like a common street whore. You'll be dead and forgotten in two months."

My mouth drops open in shock. "Is that a threat?"

"No, that's a fucking guarantee."

I stare at her for several seconds before I shake my head.

"Why did you invite me here? To threaten me? Blackmail me or something?"

"I invited you to educate you," she says as she shakes her head, flicking her blonde hair over her shoulder as those pale green eyes, Liam's eyes, come back to me. "And to warn you. Fall in line quickly and you might survive. Continue down this...path and—"

"You'll make sure I'm never found again?" I guess.

A malicious smile spreads across her face as she lifts a shoulder.

"I'll leave that job to your husband. Apparently, he has quite the talent for a nasty death."

My brows furrow at that. Did he have to kill someone for his initiation too? How does she know that? Something tells me her husband shouldn't have told her, let alone have her telling others. I go with my gut and swing.

"Huh, I'll have to chat with my father-in-law, oh, you know Christopher," I smile like I'm being silly. "I'm sure he'll be fascinated to know that not only is one of his Elders spilling induction secrets during pillow talk, but that his wife is then repeating such things in mixed company no less," I say as I make dramatic eyes at the people around us.

She visibly pales before anger takes over her face. I'm so over this conversation and company, so I stand, throwing my napkin over my untouched food.

"We'll see who winds up dead first, I suppose," I say as I turn to walk away.

Sharp nails dig into my wrist as she holds me in place. I do my best not to show weakness, but it feels like she's cutting me more than Vincent's knife ever could.

"Stay the fuck away from my son! He's set to be married soon, and you will chase away his fiancée!"

I scoff, shaking my head at her.

"Chase her away? Why would I do that when I prefer her

in bed with us?" I lie, ripping my hand out of her grasp and sauntering out of the restaurant.

I can feel her fuming, but she doesn't dare cause a scene. Not when I've just threatened her so beautifully. Honestly, no idea where that came from but I'm kind of proud of myself.

"What happened?" Vincent asks as he quickly steps beside me, opening the front door for me as we walk outside.

"She told me I'd be dead in months and I told her that I was gonna fuck her son and Maryia together."

"What?" he snaps.

I shake my head. "Let's just go. I'll tell everyone when we get home."

Vincent hands his ticket to the valet, but his body is turned, facing the restaurant. I can practically feel his body vibrating as he contemplates all the ways to kill Alison Walcott. She's not worth it, though. She's a deluded woman who feels a sense of superiority because her husband hasn't offed her, unlike every other woman, it would seem. Maybe Steph had it right. Maybe my father is the one who killed my mother. It seems to be a pattern among the Elders. Get married, have a baby, kill your wife.

If he did, I'll make sure that he suffers tenfold what she did. The lust to avenge her practically thrums in my veins the entire drive home, and I don't stop vibrating with rage until we get there.

Chapter Thirty-Eight

Skyla

Vincent called Ronan and Wesley when we were driving home. Asher was already at the house, and he was able to get Liam to come out of his room. I'm sitting on the couch beside Liam with Vincent on my other side, Asher sits on the coffee table facing me, and Ronan and Wesley stand to the side.

"She said what?" Liam snarls.

I nod with a sad smile.

"Sorry, baby. I don't think she likes me very much."

"I don't give a fuck. Who the hell does she think she is to threaten you? And I am NOT engaged. You know that, right, babygirl?"

"Of course." I nod.

"Well, if you do. I've acquired a knack for disposing of fiancées." Vincent shrugs and I shoot him a look as Ronan grimaces.

Despite Annie being awful, I know he feels guilt for it. After all, she was Madison's little sister. The family has now lost both of their daughters, and Ronan, my sweet teddy bear, hates that both of their deaths had something to do with him.

"Not helpful," I say to Vincent. "Maggie would never forgive you. I would never forgive you."

Vincent rolls his eyes. "Between your happiness or Bartlett's, do you really have to ask me whose I'd choose?"

"Liam and Maryia might not be the worst thing," Asher butts in. "He'll be forced to marry and produce an heir at some point. If it's Maryia, you guys can be together in the public eye, and behind closed doors, she can be with Maggie, and you can be with us."

Asher says us so simply, so easily. It makes my heart warm, and apparently Liam's too. I see a small smile spread across his face, the first one I've seen since his induction ceremony.

"There is more," I admit. "She said that you had developed a skill or something for killing," I say to Asher. "I think she was referring to your induction."

Asher's face turns to stone.

"How the fuck does she know that?"

"I'm assuming Liam's dad?" I guess.

"Elders are never supposed to share practices...ever," Ronan says.

I nod. "I figured, so I kind of threatened her. Told her I'd be telling Christopher about what a fat mouth her husband and her have."

Trailing off, I turn to Liam as I shake my head.

"I won't, obviously. I know that your relationship with them is strained but—"

"Fuck them," Liam says, cutting me off.

I turn my head to the side in surprise as his jaw clenches.

"My dad can burn in fucking hell for all I care. My mom, I....I thought she was better than that. These years in her position, in the Brethren, they've changed her."

He closes his eyes, shaking his head as a new fire forms in them.

"If it comes down to you or her, I will choose you."

"I don't want you to choose between me and your family, Liam," I say.

"You are my family, all of you," he says as his eyes move to Asher before Ronan, Wesley and even Vincent.

I smile sadly at that as he cups my face, bringing his lips to mine. He holds me there for several seconds before standing up.

"Where are you going?" I ask.

"To set the record straight with my mother. She will be apologizing to you, and if she steps a toe out of line again, I'll let Vincent cut it off."

Vincent perks up at that, the promise of bloodlust rousing him from his typical sour mood.

"Name the time and place," Vincent calls out as Liam bends down, placing a quick kiss to Asher's mouth before he's gone.

A heavy sigh comes from Wesley as he shakes his head.

"I need a drink. Anyone else?"

All of our hands shoot up, and he nods, moving to the kitchen and mixing cocktails.

After three of the strongest drinks I've ever had, I decided to lay down in my bed for a while. Wesley mixed apple cider, brandy, a swirl of caramel, and topped it with whipped cream...suffice it to say, I got a little more than buzzed. I ended up sleeping for a little over forty-five minutes, and when I wake up, I'm groggy as hell.

I don't feel like really getting up and doing...whatever I

have to do with my day. So, instead, I stay in my bed. That is until the memory of Thomas's journal comes to the forefront of my mind. Pushing myself up, I crawl beneath the bed, lifting the loose floorboard to find it exactly where I left it.

Cracking open the pages, the musty smell of parchment and ink permeates my nose. I thumb through it carefully as I find the next entry.

June 10th, 1692

Bridgete Bishop was slain as the early morning dew rose. With thy wickedness slain, God favorably looked down upon the town of Salem. For with the world now purged of her evil, we shall bask in his glory and the promise of a prosperous future. Let the word travel with haste that any man, woman, or child consumed with the darkness of evil shall too be slain, giving more room for God's divinity.

Holy shit, the way they celebrated innocent people's death is just....disgusting. They acted like it was God's will. Like God would be proud of them. I'm not sure what kind of bibles they were referencing back in the day, but from the ones I've studied, that doesn't add up.

My finger trails along the seam of the page, noticing a small rip. My brows furrow as I trace over it again and again. It's almost like...there is a page missing. Examining the seam, I'd guess several are actually. I flip over to the page before, noticing that the date is March 6th, 1692, three months before the next?

Flipping backwards and forwards, it appears Thomas was writing in this thing almost daily during the trials. So why the three month gap?

"What are you doing?" Ronan asks from the doorway stiffly.

I jump at his voice, scrambling to hide the journal, but it's too late. He crosses the room in a flash, gripping my hands with one of his as he grabs the journal from me. His eyes skate over it, going wide as realization hits him.

"What the FUCK! SKYLA! Are you fucking insane?" he roars.

I cower beneath him. He's never raised his voice with me, never yelled. The look in his eyes is a new one as well. It's unfiltered rage, it's a crazed look that chills me to my bones. Several pairs of footsteps run up the stairs, and as one, Vincent, Asher, and Wesley peel Ronan away from me.

Asher comes to my side, examining my arm like he's expecting to find bruises or something before he faces his uncle.

"What the fuck is your problem?" he snarls.

"THIS IS MY FUCKING PROBLEM!" Ronan rages as he shakes the journal in his hand.

Asher stares at it for a second before his eyes go wide. His gaze snaps to mine in disbelief, as does Wesley's, when Vincent speaks.

"What is that?" he snaps.

"This," Ronan says as he addresses the room. "Is Thomas Putnam's journal. My family's most prized possession, my brother's most prized possession. How the fuck did you get it?"

All eyes come to me as I lower my head.

"I found it," I mutter.

Ronan lets out a humorless laugh that is so unlike him as he shakes his head.

"You found it? Where? On his person? Because that's where it stays, always."

"It was in his desk...under a hidden compartment."

Asher shakes his head and Wesley winces as Ronan tips his head to the sky.

"How long?" he asks.

"How long what?" I ask.

His crazed eyes come back to me once more, clearly no patience in them.

"How long have you had it? When did you take it? How long has my brother already been, no doubt, searching for it?"

I guess I hadn't thought about when he would notice it missing, though I probably should have.

"Last night. At the party. I told Asher I was going to the bathroom but I...snuck into his office through the kitchen entrance."

A hurt look passes across Asher's face as he shakes his head.

"What were you thinking, princess?"

I run my hand through my hair and sigh. "I wanted answers about...everything. Things in the history books don't add up to the Brethren's practices."

"No, shit. Because they don't go off history, siren. It's a goddamn cult," Vincent says.

"It is not," Wesley, Ronan, and Asher defend.

He laughs bitterly and nods. "Sure, whatever. Delude yourselves."

"What kind of answers were you hoping to find, little one?" Wesley intervenes.

I shake my head. "I don't know. Something about my mom and her family, maybe?"

"This again?" Ronan huffs. "Horris Hutchinson mentioned the rumor of Skyla's mom being a witch, that's why she was killed."

Demise

Understanding passes across their faces and they all nod like it makes sense.

"You all knew about this rumor and didn't tell me?"

"What's there to tell you, princess? It's bullshit, just like half the rumors are in the Brethren."

"While the other half are truth," I point out. "I just wanted to make sense of everything. Get some answers on her death. I just...I don't know. I feel so out of my depth. I'm a pawn on a board I've never had the chance to fully study."

"Well, this is not the way to get your answers," Ronan says, shaking the journal in his fists as he huffs in anger. "I'm going to return this and hope to fucking God that my brother hasn't already figured out that it's missing," he says.

"I'll go with you for backup," Wesley says. "We'll come up with some bullshit story if we have to."

"We're gonna have to do something because of her stupidity," Ronan barks as he storms out of the room, his feet thundering down the steps as the front door opens and slams shut.

I wince at the slam and Wesley bends down beside me, rubbing his hand over my knee.

"He's not mad at you, little one. He's scared for you. We'll get it sorted. Did you take anything else?"

I shake my head.

"Alright. Just sit tight. We'll be back as soon as we can," he says.

I nod and he cups my chin, squeezing it gently as he presses a kiss to my forehead.

"Good girl."

With that, he takes off after Ronan, this door slam being a lot less aggressive. Vincent, Asher and I sit in silence for several seconds, and I finally chance a glance to Asher to see him looking at the floor.

"Let's go for a drive," he says as he stands up.

"To where?" I ask.
Asher looks to Vincent before back to me.
"To the Salem Witch Museum."

Chapter Thirty-Nine

Wesley

Ronan drives with both hands on the wheel. More like both hands strangling the wheel. He's fucking pissed, but I know him better than anyone, and I know that he's just masking right now. He's not mad at Skyla. In fact, I know a small part of him understands why she did it. No matter how dumb it was.

"It's gonna be okay, Ro," I say calmly as he shakes his head.

"Yeah? Have you figured out a way to sneak onto my brother's property, uninvited, sneak past his security cameras and staff, break into the house and slide the journal exactly where Skyla found it without setting off a single red flag?"

I stay silent for several seconds because no, not really. The only hope is that he's not home, which means his security team won't be. As far as the feed goes, that's one of the easier parts.

My fingers begin tapping away at my phone as I hack into his feed with ease. It only takes me seconds to record a small bit of feed and play it on an endless loop. Or at least a loop that will last nine and a half minutes before it notifies the security team.

"I'll cut the feed and motion sensors as soon as we get to the driveway. We'll have roughly nine minutes and thirty-two seconds until I have to turn it back on."

Ronan frowns as he looks to me before facing the road once more.

"How do you know that?"

"Because I'm the one who upgraded his system recently," I say as Ronan approaches Putnam Manor.

I already scanned the feed and thankfully, only the maid is here. She's currently folding laundry in the laundry room so that should leave us with enough uninterrupted time. I think.

"Three, two, one," I say before Ronan punches the gas.

The car takes off, soaring down the long driveway before coming to a sharp halt at the front steps. We both spring out of the car, choosing to leave the doors open as the quieter option before moving up the stairs. I inwardly thank the military for teaching me how light on your feet you can be, even for a guy my size, when your life is literally on the line.

Thanks to the maid, the door is already unlocked, and it takes virtually no effort to slip inside the house. Ronan and I work as a team, our eyes scanning the entire perimeter before moving forward. When we're clear, he hustles forward, moving into Christopher's office while I'm on his heels. He begins pulling drawer after drawer, all coming up empty with a false bottom, until he comes to one.

"Got it," he mutters as he lifts the false bottom. Ronan sets the journal in there and pauses, his brows furrowing.

"What the—"

I look over to see him shuffling through several pieces of paper before he holds up a photograph. He flips it around for me to see and the sight turns my stomach. Christopher and Henry are in it, completely naked, as they fuck a woman tied up. Her hands are tied to the bed, her mouth stuffed with

Henry's cock as tears stream down her face. That isn't the part that is particularly surprising, though. The shocking part is that it's not just any woman. It's Stephanie, and based on their appearance, I'd wager this was just from weeks ago when Stephanie was in town.

Ronan reaches inside again, grabbing out another photograph that is nearly identical. This time it isn't Stephanie tied up, but Giselle Parris. She's a spitting image of Skyla, but the photo is clearly much older than the one with Stephanie.

Ronan continues rifling through the papers inside the drawer before his entire frame stills. The last photograph he pulls up isn't a sexual one like I expect it to be. Instead, it's of Corwin, standing over Skyla as she sleeps in her dorm room. Ronan flips over the back to see a date scribbled onto the back of the photo in sharpie. October 14th.

What the fuck.

So, Christopher knew about Corwin well before anyone did. He knew what he was doing, and he didn't stop him, didn't intervene. I'm not sure why that surprises me, maybe because he seemed so confused and taken by surprise. I guess that's a testament to what a slimy fucking bastard he is, and if the other pictures are anything to go off, a fucking rapist too.

I glance down at the clock, my eyes rounding. One minute left.

"Now!" I snap, not having to explain myself as I peek out the door and bolt to the front entry.

I hear Ronan rustle the papers, setting the false bottom back and closing the cabinet before he's out the door. I make it to the car first, sliding into the open door as I fire up the car and take off. Ronan dives in just in time and slams his door shut as I speed down the driveway. My clock ticks on my phone, slowly counting down. Twenty-nine, twenty-eight, twenty-seven.

My hands white knuckle the steering wheel, pushing the

vehicle as far and as fast as I can. I just have to make it out of Christopher's perimeter, and we'll be in the clear. I whip the wheel hard to the right, speeding down the road until we approach the neighbor's house. For good measure, I drive another house down before I screech to a halt, grabbing my phone and pulling up the screen with Christopher's feed.

My finger practically smashes against my screen as I resume the live feed, and two seconds later, my alarm goes off. A ragged breath leaves Ronan and I simultaneously before we begin laughing. Not joy filled laughs, but shaky adrenaline fueled laughter because our bodies don't know how else to process this moment. I shake my head and put the car into drive once more, getting the fuck out of here.

We don't speak as I drive, and Ronan doesn't question me when I don't go back to the house, but instead my property in Peabody. I'm on edge, and I just want to go somewhere that I know won't have eyes on us.

When we pull up to the seemingly humble house, I enter in the passcode for the gate. The wrought iron gate swings open, allowing us inside. Just because it's a humble house, doesn't mean I don't take my security seriously.

Together, Ronan and I step out of the car once I'm parked and make our way inside the house. As soon as the door shuts, Ronan speaks.

"What the FUCK was all that?"

I shake my head. "I don't know. I guess we know why Stephanie disappeared practically overnight. Why the fuck didn't she say anything?"

"To who?" Ronan counters. "To me? Her rapist's brother? To Asher? Her rapist's son? To her niece that she's tried to protect from this shit world her whole life?"

All fair points.

Demise

"What's up with that anyways? They were recreating a memory from their time with Giselle or something?" I wonder.

Ronan shakes his head. "Something like it. Christopher was clearly infatuated with her, more than he's ever wanted to let on."

"Then why have her killed? Because let's not even pretend that it wasn't your brother or Parris."

He shrugs his shoulders. "For the only reason women always go missing, control."

I scoff and shake my head as I stare at the ground.

"And he knew about Corwin the whole fucking time, what the fuck is up with that?"

A thunderous look crosses Ronan's face as he shakes his head.

"I can't let that go. I..."

He trails off, closing his eyes with a disgusted sneer before he looks at me again.

"I'm gonna kill him, Wes."

I nod. "I know—"

"No," Ronan says, a dark lilt to his words as he speaks. "I mean it. We can't live under him forever. I'm going to kill him or die fucking trying."

I clap my hand on his shoulder, nodding in solidarity.

"I'm with you, brother. Until the very end."

He nods, his rigid stance shaking a little. I'm not sure if it's from anger, fear of what's to come, or something in between. I pull him into me. Wrapping my arms around him as I pat his back encouragingly. He tenses, and I wait for him to relax, but he doesn't.

Frowning, I pull away as I look at him.

"What's wrong?"

"What?" he asks nonchalantly.

I lift a brow and wait for him to explain before I shake my head.

"Am I not allowed to hug you? Comfort you?"

Ronan tries to brush it off, pocketing his hands into his pants.

"I'm not in the mood for your kind of 'comforting,' Wes."

I screw my face up at that.

"What the fuck? You think I was making a move on you?"

"When aren't you? Anytime I'm at the house, you're watching me. When we're with my girlfriend—"

"Our girlfriend," I correct.

"You're always approaching me, initiating things with me," he continues.

"I'm sorry, I've yet to hear a complaint," I fire back. "In fact, all I hear fall from your lips are moans when I'm 'initiating.'"

Something flashes in Ronan's eyes as he shakes his head.

"Things are getting too intense, I don't want to lead you on. It's best if we stop fucking around together. Just focus on Skyla," he says.

I tilt my head to the side curiously, taking a step towards him. Surprisingly, he takes a quick step back. Then another and another until I have him pinned against the wall. He's not a coward, he doesn't back down from anything, yet he seems hell bent on running far and wide from me right now. Interesting.

Slowly, I rest my hand on his hip, taking note of the way his breath slightly catches as I slip it beneath his shirt, dragging my fingers against his rippled abs until I reach his throat. I grip it tightly, keeping him in place as I keep my mouth just inches from his.

"I think things are getting too intense for *you*. I've never been led on, never expected anything. Ro, you've used me as your dirty little secret cock sucker for years and I haven't minded. Fuck, you cheated on Madi with me...often," I say, knowing that will strike a nerve.

He pushes against me, but I bring my other hand up, pinning his shoulder in place.

"Don't," he says. "Just...don't."

"No, you don't," I say. "I've always known the score. I've always been a lot more easy going about sexuality than you, and hey, nothing wrong with that. Don't act like I'm some kind of degenerate that is hopelessly in love with you, seducing you at every turn," I say, squeezing his throat a little harder with that.

He grits his teeth together, his voice coming out strained.

"What about right now? Are you telling me you aren't seducing me?"

"I don't know," I ask with a slight taunt. "I think it's only seducing if your cock is hard. Is your cock hard, Ro?"

He inhales sharply through his nose but doesn't speak, so I do a little investigating myself. Pressing myself against him, our slacks rub together, my cock finding his steel pipe in milliseconds. His eyes fall closed, a look of defeat on his face as I grind my cock against his.

"Want to explain that?" I growl into his ear.

He doesn't speak, so I grind against him again, and again, finally pulling a choked moan from him.

"Goddamnit," he groans.

"Why are you fighting it, Ro? Can't we just...be? Who gives a fuck what we call it. No expectations, no rules. As long as Skyla is okay with it, why can't we explore each other fully?"

His heavy breathing is the only sound in this house for several seconds.

"I'm scared of you, Wes," he admits.

I can't help but grin, just a little bit as I push my cock against his once more, not moving away this time as I drag my lips over his while I speak.

"You should be. I'm gonna fucking ruin you."

I force my lips against his in the next breath, not giving him a chance to push me away. If he wants to, he's gotta face me head on first. The way his tongue slips into my mouth tells me that's not what he truly wants, which I'll admit, makes me giddy as fuck because I've wanted Ronan for longer than I could say.

It started off as admiration. Then we had the drunken night where he wanted to know if it felt different to have a guy suck his dick. Him and Madi were dating for a year or so at this point, and as soon as that post nut clarity hit, he felt so guilty he avoided me for a week. On that seventh day mark, though, he showed up at my place, drunk off his ass, and begged me to suck him off again. To which I did. And then the next day, the next day and the next.

We were hooking up so often for a while there that he'd blow off dates with Madi and stay in bed with me. Usually, it was a blow job, and then we'd hang out before he'd ask for another. I never asked for more, but I never denied him either because...fuck, look at him.

I felt bad that we were betraying Madi, but it felt too good to stop. It felt so right. The situation is different this time, though. Skyla knows that I want Ronan, I think she knows that he wants me too, and she's fucking into it.

As if she couldn't be more perfect.

I'm ready to drop to my knees, ready to choke on Ronan's thick cock, when he takes me by surprise, him willingly dropping to his knees as he undoes my pants. He's scrambling like he can't get my cock in his mouth fast enough, and when he does, we both groan in pleasure.

"You like sucking on me?" I ask him as I begin thrusting into his mouth.

He hesitates for a moment before nodding.

"Of course you do. Fuck, Ro. Why do you have to keep fighting us? Can't you see how fucking good we are?"

He nods his head, sucking my cock down his throat.

"Fuck," I shudder. "I want you. I want you so fucking bad. It's all I've thought about for years."

Ronan releases me with a slobbery pop as he looks up at me.

"What do you want, Wes?"

My eyes meet his, my meaning clear. He swallows roughly before nodding his head once. I turn mine in surprise as he speaks.

"Get down here."

I slide down to the ground and Ronan covers my body with his against the hardwood floor. He undoes his pants, pushing them down as our bare cocks grind against each other. I feel his hand grab his cock, purposefully dragging it up and down my length before he releases it.

I'm about to beg him to continue when his hands come to my pants, fully pulling them down, my shoes coming off with them as he pushes my legs up. I'm surprised at how quickly he agreed, how eager he is. He gathers up a large amount of spit and drops it straight onto my asshole. He does it again into his hand, covering his tip as he lines up to me.

"No time for foreplay, this is gonna hurt," he warns.

"I love a little pain," I goad.

Ronan rises to that challenge, shoving into me with a sharp snap of his hips that sends stars dancing across my vision.

"Christ," he chokes as he pulls out and pushes into me again.

This isn't sensual love making. It's not a romantic moment. No, this is years of built up tension. This is raw fucking on the hardwood floors, dirty and hard, just the way I fucking love it.

His cock slides in and out of my ass like a goddamn jack

hammer and I begin jerking my cock to match his rhythm. I watch as his eyes flick down, watching me as he groans.

"Fuck! Daddy likes seeing you touch yourself."

"Oh, are you my daddy now too?" I grin.

Ronan surprises the shit out of me, smacking the side of my ass hard, forcing me to tense around him.

"Fuck, yes, I am. Now be a good boy and take daddy's cock."

My cock jerks at that. Shit. I guess I'm into this daddy kink. His hands come to my hips, forcing himself deeper and deeper into me. It's fucking heaven, it's everything I thought it would be and more. He's a fucking animal, and I love every goddamn second of it. Minutes blur together, this lust fueled haze lasting for so long and yet long enough that I couldn't even tell you how long he's been inside me. All I can say is I never want him to stop.

"Fuck, daddy," I groan.

"Yeah," he growls. "Cry out for daddy. I want to hear you call my name as you cum all over me."

"You want me to come on you?" I pant.

"Fuck, yes, I do. Paint daddy with your cum, baby."

I spasm at that, a hard thrust from him catching me by surprise, and before I can even blink, I lose it. Thick ropes of my cum paint Ronan's shirt and he fucks me harder and faster as I release all over him.

"Fuckkkk," he groans before his cock throbs inside me, and he falls apart.

His thrusts are jerky and uneven as he pants and groans through it. I swear to god, his orgasm lasts well over thirty seconds, and it's the most gratifying and sexy thing I've ever seen in my life.

When it finally ends, he slumps against me, his body plastered to mine, his cock still inside me. We lay like that for several seconds, just breathing and basking in the post orgasm bliss.

"We gotta tell Sky," Ronan murmurs against my shoulder.

I nod, pressing a soft kiss against his head.

To my surprise he doesn't outwardly react. He doesn't pull away and run. It's nice.

"Of course we do, and she's gonna be so fucking pissed she missed it," I smile.

A rough chuckle escapes Ronan as he nods, sighing softly as we continue to lay on the floor of my house in comfortable silence and complete release.

Chapter Forty

Skyla

Asher drives while Vincent and I sit in the back seat. I haven't explored downtown Salem all that much. I've gone shopping and been to a few restaurants, but nothing too extensive, and definitely not to the historic side of town.

Asher parks on the street, but I can already see our destination. A large sign hangs in front of it saying Salem Witch Museum. It's a large brick building that looks more like an old church than a museum. We all get out of the car and begin walking towards the entrance when Vincent's phone rings. He curses as he looks down at it, muttering an apology as he stalks off in the other direction.

"Looks like it's just you and me, princess," Asher says as he laces his fingers through mine.

I give him a weak smile and nod as we walk into the building. Instantly, the stale smell that typically occupies older buildings surrounds me. My eyes are still adjusting to the dim lighting in the waiting area when an older employee comes forward.

"Hello! Just two of you toda—"

She stops shortly, her eyes rounding as they bounce between Asher and I.

"Oh, Mr. Putnam. My apologies. I didn't realize you were coming. I—"

Asher holds up his hand, silencing her as he hands her a fifty dollar bill and moves past her. I follow along, but I give the clammed up staff member a soft smile. It doesn't seem to ease her, though. She looks uncomfortable with us being here, borderline terrified.

"Have you been here before?" I ask.

"Of course," he huffs. "There are only so many locations to go for field trips in Salem growing up."

"No need to get short," I throw back. "She seemed to know you well, I was curious."

"Everyone knows me," he says stiffly.

"Yeah, because you were a whore."

He gives me a disbelieving look.

"She was like seventy-eight. You seriously saying I fucked her?" he asks in outrage.

I shrug, doing my best to hold in my teasing smile.

"She was a pretty seventy-eight. Age is just a number."

He shorts, lowering his voice as he speaks into my ear.

"Is that what Ronan and Wes say so you'll jump on their old ass cocks?"

I let out a laugh and shake my head.

"As if they have to talk me into anything, I love every minute of it," I tease, and Asher swats at my ass before we come to the first exhibit. My eyes begin roaming around the room as I take it all in. I'm not sure what I was expecting, but wax figures depicting the events of the trials, from the first accusation to the hanging and pressing of supposed 'witches' and their accomplices, is not what I was expecting.

From the research I've done and the reading from

Thomas's journal, I feel pretty well versed in the subject now, but Asher explains every exhibit for me in detail. First, he'd explain the scene or event we're looking at, then he described the Brethren's version. Some of them line up perfectly. Others...don't. At all.

I look down at a plaque, three names standing out above all else.

Bridgette Bishop, Sarah Osbourne and Elizabeth Proctor.

It takes me a moment to figure out why those names sound so familiar, and then it clicks. My dream, from last year when I first came to Salem. The one where I was trapped in the cemetery on campus, running and running with no way out, surrounded by three headstones.

Bridgette Bishop, Sarah Osbourne and Elizabeth Proctor.

"These women...who were they?"

Asher looks at where I'm pointing as he nods.

"Witches. Bishop was the first to be executed from the trials. Osbourne died in jail before she could be hung. Proctor was acquitted. She was pregnant when her and her husband were tried, and so while he was sent to Gallows Hill, she was put on hold until she had the baby, but by the time she gave birth, the trials had ended."

"Wait...Gallows Hill. Like our school?" I ask.

He frowns like he's disappointed in me.

"Did you not know that the university was built on top of Gallows Hill? That the cemetery on campus is where all of the witches were buried?"

A chill runs through me. Nope, definitely missed that piece of information in the welcome packet.

"Where did she go?" I ask, still in absolute disbelief.

How fucked up is this society? As if I have to ask.

"Not far. Her husband wrote her out of the will while they

were in prison, so when she got out, she was virtually penniless."

I cock my head to the side. "Why would he do that?"

Asher shrugs. "He was in there because he was defending her and other members of their family. He died because of it; maybe he was hell bent on revenge, maybe he assumed she'd be executed too and he wanted their money left to their kids."

"They had kids?" I ask.

He nods. "All of them did. Those that didn't had brothers, sisters, uncles, nieces. It's why the Brethren was formed. What do you think happened once the trials had ended? You think everyone shook on it and decided to be friends?"

We move further through the museum as he continues, shaking his head.

"It was a bloodbath for months. Families of the witches were burning down homes, slitting throats in people's sleep. The townsfolk of Salem were in more danger post trials than they ever were before. They had to do something, power in numbers and all that."

"And thus the Brethren was born," I say.

Asher nods as we come to an exhibit of a woman yelling out at the townsfolk, a noose around her neck. She looks to be late thirties or so, wearing traditional Puritan clothes and an angry expression as she stares at one figure in particular.

"That's Thomas Putnam," Asher says, gesturing to the man who seems to be the focus of her ire.

"It is?" I ask as I assess the man.

Who'd have thought a man capable of such evil could be decently attractive? Then again, look at Christopher. He's horrendous but definitely not terrible to look at. Those Putnam genes have been strong for hundreds of years apparently.

"Who is she?" I ask.

"Sarah Good," Asher explains. "She was one of the first three that were accused."

"But not tried?" I ask.

"Oh, she was tried. She was heavily pregnant at the time of her arrest, so her execution date was postponed. The baby died shortly after being born due to the poor conditions in the jail and she was executed in July."

My heart hurts for that poor baby...that poor woman. There is no way all of these women were truly witches, right? I mean, what is a witch even? Especially in those times?

"Do you think they were all witches?" I ask as I turn to him.

He continues staring at Sarah, as if he were back in 1692 living it before he shakes his head.

"I don't know what to believe. The Brethren taught us they all were, that there were even more who weren't brought to light. History says they were all innocent. Is it too crazy to believe there is a middle ground?"

I shrug. "What really makes you a witch, though? Magic flying from your fingertips? Brewing up spells in cauldrons?"

"Take her for example," Asher says as he nods towards Sarah. "The words she screamed out right before her death to one of the ministers was, 'You're a liar! I'm no more a witch than you are a wizard! If you take my life away, God will give you blood to drink.' Twenty-five years later, he died of a hemorrhage, choking on his own blood."

My eyebrows knit together at that.

"Surely that's a coincidence?"

"Or a curse," Asher says with a shrug of his shoulders as we move through the rest of the museum.

My mind is racing, absorbing as much information as possible and not so discreetly searching furiously for my mother's maiden name. Thompson was nowhere to be found, at least

Demise

from what I saw. Which was equal parts disappointment and relief, I suppose.

We step outside to leave when my eyes catch on the street beside us. Several shops and restaurants are lined up, people milling about lackadaisically. My gaze moves to Charlie's Burgers & Brews before stopping on the shop beside it.

Before I know what I'm doing, I'm moving towards the shop. It's painted black on the outside, with intricate wood trim framing the large windows. In the window, the etched name of the shop sprawls across it, with glittering crystals and rocks on display.

Luna's Apothecary and Gift Shop.

"Sky, where are we going?" Asher asks as we cross the road.

"I just want to pop in here for a minute."

Asher shakes his head as he follows beside me.

"This isn't a good idea," he mutters.

I look back to him with a frown. "Why not?"

He shakes his head as I reach for the door, pulling it open. Instantly, I'm wrapped up in the warmth of the shop compared to the bitter cold of this January day. The walls are lined with wood shelves, glass vials filled with rocks, sand and plants filling the place on one side, and on the other, countless rocks and crystals take up the space. There are also several paintings on the walls, all of the moon and its different cycles. One catches my eye in particular. It's a woman standing beneath the moonlight, her arms lifted in what looks like celebration as the moon rises from the lake in front of her.

Turning, I look to see Asher is still outside, furiously texting on his phone. I frown, but continue browsing when a woman with long black hair steps out from the back. She has bright blue eyes and a pretty septum piercing. She looks to be in her mid to late forties, but that doesn't take away from her beauty. She's absolutely gorgeous.

341

Her eyes scan me over for a moment before she smiles.

"Welcome, anything I can help you find?"

"I'm not sure. I've never been here before. I was just browsing."

She nods as she comes closer, extending her hand to me.

"My name is Rachel. I'm the owner."

I find it a little odd that an owner would feel the need to introduce themselves, but maybe she's just overly friendly. I shake her hand and her head snaps down to our joined hands before she looks up at me.

"I'm Skyla," I say hesitantly.

She nods at that, releasing my hand before her smile is back in place.

"Well, Skyla, are you struggling with anything? Stress, anxiety, confliction?"

"All of the above?" I laugh.

She does as well as she brings me over to a small vial, grabbing it from the shelf and handing it to me.

"I like to call this my peace and harmony jar," Rachel says.

I take it from her, tipping it as I examine the brown wax sealed top with a strange symbol on the front.

"What's in it?" I ask.

"Vervain for inner peace and tranquility, jasmine for harmony and positive interactions, amethyst for peace to emotions, peppermint to soothe tension, and lavender to calm the mind and ease anxiety."

I nod as I examine each ingredient.

"What do you do with it?"

"You keep it on you. Some people get several of a certain kind and scatter them throughout their house or their car. Wherever you feel you need the support. You could also get a combination depending on your intention and need."

"Wow," I say as I look at it. "So, it really works?"

An amused smile plays at her mouth as she nods. "My family has been in the business for longer than I could tell you, we wouldn't be if it didn't."

I smile as the door opens; instantly Rachel's pleasant demeanor shifts as she looks at Asher.

"You're not welcome here," she says, her voice taking on a violently low lilt.

"Trust me, I don't want to be here," he grits out.

I frown between the two of them.

"Do you know each other?" I ask.

"No," Asher says while Rachel says, "Yes."

They both glare at each other before she speaks again.

"We have no tolerance for your kind on our properties. Leave," she says, reaching into her pocket and pulling out a small handful of some kind of powder, flicking it in Asher's direction.

He swats it away angrily. "What the fuck was that?"

"Cumin, it banishes away evil," she says with a lift of her eyebrows.

Asher sneers. "I'm not the one who worships the devil."

Rachel shakes her head, rolling her eyes.

"Typical Puritan man and your assumptions."

Wait.

"Are you a witch?" I ask, cringing at how that must sound.

If she isn't, I no doubt just offended her, and if she is…well, I don't really know.

Her narrowed eyes leave Asher before they come to me.

"I am."

"Sky, can we go? Please?" Asher butts in.

I open my mouth to say…something to Rachel when Asher interrupts again.

"Now, Skyla," he snaps.

I'm shocked at his attitude, but when I look in his eyes, I see the desperation in them, and I know it's for good reason. Nodding to him, I go to hand Rachel back the vial when she closes my hand around it and shakes her head.

"You keep it. In his presence, you'll need that and more."

I can't help but let out a laugh at that.

"Well, he's my husband, so trust me, I'm aware."

"Husband?" she asks sharply, eyes going wide. They move to Asher as she rakes her narrowed gaze over him judgingly before shaking her head. "You could do far better, love."

Asher makes an irritated noise in the back of his throat as he opens the shop door, waiting for me impatiently.

"Thank you," I say as I gesture towards the vial.

She nods. "You're welcome back anytime. Just leave your... husband at home."

I don't really know how to respond to that, so I turn and walk out the door. I feel Asher give her a look but by the time I turn around, he's facing forward, hurrying me out of the shop. His hand grabs hold of my arm, rushing me to the car.

"What's going on?" I ask. "What was all that?"

"Fucking witches," he snarls, reaching into my clenched hand and pulling the vial from it. He looks at it for a moment before throwing it to the ground, stomping his boot over it.

My mouth drops open as he shakes his head and keeps walking, yanking me along with him.

"Asher! What the fuck!"

"It's evil, Sky. Made with witchcraft. You don't need that shit infiltrating your life. We should have never stepped foot in a damned place like that," he says with a shake of his head as we approach the car, Vincent leaning on the side of it.

"Where were you?" Vincent asks me.

"In Proctor's shop," Asher gnashes as he unlocks the car, practically tossing me into the back seat.

"What? Why?"

"Fuck if I know!" Asher says as he climbs into the driver's seat, Vincent sitting in the back with me.

"Wait, Proctor? Like Elizabeth and John? From the museum?" I ask.

"From the trials," Asher corrects. "And yes. One of the only families that didn't get the fucking hint to leave Salem. If word gets out that we were seen in there..." he stops with a shake of his head. Instead of finishing, he fires up the car and takes off. We pass by the shop as we leave town, and I see Rachel on the sidewalk with a broom and a dustpan, collecting the debris from the shattered vial. I give her a sympathetic look as she shakes her head and looks back down to the ground.

Chapter Forty One

Skyla

When we get home, all the guys are already sitting around the living room looking absolutely livid. We don't make it through the front door two steps before they are laying into me.

"What the fuck were you thinking?" Ronan snarls.

"You idiots took her to that side of the town? Really?" Wesley says in contempt.

"I leave for three goddamn hours, and everything goes to shit!" Liam adds.

"She wanted the full history. I took her to the Witch Museum—"

"Stupid." Ronan interjects.

Asher throws him a look but continues on. "Then she took one look at the Proctor shop and practically ran to it."

"What?" the three of them collectively snap.

"It's not a big deal," I say, earning myself five scathing looks.

"Not a big deal, siren? You don't understand what those... people are capable of."

"Maybe I don't. Do you?" I counter.

Vincent scoffs. "I've encountered plenty of them, trust me, they are not your friend."

"Maybe they aren't my enemy either."

Ronan shakes his head. "Baby, you don't know what you're talking about."

"She was kind to me. I felt no malice or unease, unlike every other person in the Brethren apart from those in this room. Doesn't that strike you as odd? That maybe you guys are on the wrong side of things? That you've been turned against a group of people out of fear, not reason?"

"They're witches, babygirl," Liam argues. "They're bad news. They curse people, hurt people."

"Says who, Liam?"

He opens his mouth to speak before closing it, shaking his head. I understand that they are all concerned, I mean, they've basically been conditioned into believing one set way their entire life. Maybe it's time they break those mental chains, though, because if we are going off people like Christopher Putnam to give us the whole truth and nothing but the truth... we shouldn't. That man is more evil than any witch ever could be.

"Little one, we're just worried. You never know who is watching. If the Elders find out you went into Proctor's shop, they could jump to conclusions."

"Let them jump!" I snap before sighing. "I'm tired of the clouded truths, the hidden meanings. This world we have all been forcibly born into is fucked up and broken, and if you don't agree, then each of you are part of the problem."

They all stay quiet for several seconds before Vincent nods.

"She's right. None of us are under the impression that the Brethren are just or saints."

Soft murmurs of agreement sound through the room as Vincent continues.

"But, that doesn't mean that you go charging into a witch's shop in broad daylight. Do you have the answers you went in search of?"

Technically, yes. I suppose I did.

I nod, and so does he.

"Good. Come here," he says, pulling me into his arms. He holds me close to his chest and I wrap my arms around him.

I can practically hear each of the guys' thoughts. Feel their unease. Honestly, though, for guys that claim to hate what the Brethren is, what it stands for, they sure seem to blindly follow their rules and word.

The next day, Maggie, Maryia and I are leaving class for the day. They are talking about going to grab an early dinner when I butt in.

"Mind if I tag along? I saw this place yesterday downtown. It looked good."

They nod as we make our way to the parking lot, where Wesley is already waiting for me. I walk ahead, meeting him at the front of the car. He greets me with a smile, but it falls when he notices I don't try to get in the car.

"I'm going to get some food with Maggie and Maryia. I'll have her give me a ride home."

He doesn't seem to like that answer. His brows knit together as he turns his head to the side.

"Why can't I drive you?"

I smile and shake my head.

"Because we can't be together every minute of the day."

"Why not?"

Demise

I laugh at him, but he's not laughing.

"Wes, it's a few hours at best. I'll be fine."

He sighs and nods. "You're right. You deserve to have some time with your friends. Text me when you're on your way?"

"Sure." I smile, fighting the instinct to kiss him before I walk back to Maggie and Maryia.

"You good?" Maggie asks.

I nod. "I'm just over the protectiveness."

"I can imagine with five boyfriends," Maryia adds with a snicker. "Do you even get to pee alone?"

I shoot a look to Maggie and she shrugs.

"What? She's my girl. I'm not gonna keep secrets from her."

"Not even mine?"

Maryia frowns, shaking her head frantically.

"Skyla, I'd never tell anyone. Ever. I know what kind of danger you all could be put in. I swear."

I shoot one more scathing at Maggie before glancing to Maryia.

"It's okay. It's not that I don't trust you. It's just the more people that know, the more likely it is that it could get out."

She nods. "I understand, but trust me," she says with her eyes on Maggie. "We all have secrets we don't want getting out."

"Ouch," Maggie scoffs as she unlocks her BMW. "I'll have you know there are hundreds of women that would love to be with me."

A jealous flare flashes in Maryia's eyes as she climbs into the tinted out car. She sits in the front seat and grabs Maggie by the face, pressing her lips together brutally before pulling away.

"Trust me, baby, I know."

Maggie pulls her in, their tongues tangling together as their hands begin to roam. Meanwhile, I'm in the back seat, feeling both awkward and kind of turned on. I clear my throat, but that doesn't stop them. When Maggie's hands trail down to cup Maryia's breasts I know that it's about to go too far.

"Okay, you two are cute and adorable and hot and everything, but I'm kinda getting turned on," I laugh awkwardly.

They break apart and both of their eyes come to me as Maggie smirks.

"You're my best friend, Sky. You know you can always join my harem," she teases.

Maryia darts her gaze to Maggie, eyebrow quirked. "What harem?"

"The one I'm gonna build. C'mon, Mads. Wouldn't you love to see me play with her? Or maybe we all play together?"

Curiosity flashes in Maryia's eyes as her gaze comes to me and I panic.

"That sounds really hot, and everything but five is my limit, sorry babes."

We all bust out laughing and all of the tension evaporates just like that. Thank God, because I don't know how I'd explain it to the guys. Sorry, we were going to dinner, and then the next thing I knew, I was having a three-way with my best friend and her girlfriend. Yeah, that wouldn't go over well.

Well, maybe with Wesley since he's already suggested something similar. And Liam is always down for a good time anytime. The other three, though? Not a chance. Besides, I have more than any other girl could dream of. I honestly don't think I could handle any more complications.

"Alright, where to?" Maggie asks.

"Have you been to Charlie's Burgers and Brews? It looked good," I suggest lightly, or at least I attempt to.

Maggie and Maryia share a look for half a second before Maggie nods.

"Sure, Sky. Let's try it."

I nod, happy and confused with what I'm doing. I couldn't

sleep last night. I just kept tossing and turning, unsettling dreams morphing into each other between weird pieces of all the Salem history I learned and the encounter at the apothecary shop. The guys all forbade me to ever go back, but I just... need to. It's hard to explain. Besides, I feel bad she gave me a gift and Asher broke it. I need to pay for it at least. That jar was supposed to bring me peace, if it really worked, can't imagine what it'll bring me now that it was intentionally broken.

When we get to Charlie's, Maggie and Maryia sit on one side of the booth while I sit on the other. We chose a seat in the back, and once our orders are placed, they begin making out. I don't blame them. They have to keep things so secretive at school, in front of their parents. In front of...everyone. They have to take advantage of any chance they have to just be themselves without fear of persecution of punishment.

Noticing my perfect exit, I make a comment about going to the bathroom, to which Maggie waves me off as she buries her hand into Maryia's hair. Perfect.

Heading back through the restaurant and out the front door, I suck in a deep breath before letting it out as I turn to Rachel's shop. When I step through the door, that same warmth wraps me up as Rachel peeks her head out from around a shelf, surprise on her face.

"Skyla." She smiles. "I'll admit. I wasn't anticipating seeing you so soon."

"Yeah, I wasn't planning on coming back so quickly," I say with a weak smile of my own.

"Or ever, by the way your husband was acting."

I nod my agreement, and we stand there in silence for several seconds before I pull out some cash.

"I'm sorry that he broke the jar, and that you had to clean it up. I wanted to come pay for it," I say as I offer her a twenty.

She looks down at it and shakes her head.

"I don't want your money. No apologies needed."

"Please," I say. "It'll make me feel better."

Smiling, she shakes her head again and I sigh as I pocket the money once more.

"So, there isn't a chance I'm like, you know cursed? From the jar being smashed, that is?"

She purses her lips and shrugs, like she's trying to soften the blow.

"You weren't the one to break it."

"Does that change anything?" I ask.

Shaking her head softly, my heart sinks. Great. Now on top of everything else, I'm cursed.

"I'm sorry you got to see the ugly side of him yesterday," I say. "He can be stubborn, and he thinks he knows best, but he's a really good man. I don't want to see him with any blame or bad luck or anything."

She laughs at that. "Love, you did not just say that a Putnam is a good man?" she questions, spitting his name as she does.

I frown at that and nod. "He's nothing like his father, trust me."

Her lips purse at that as she stares at me, like she doesn't believe me. Reaching to the side of me, she grabs some kind of bundled thing and hands it to me.

"Go home and light the end. Burn this all around your home, yourself, two times around your husband. Goddess knows he needs it."

"What is it?" I say as I look at it.

Demise

"White sage. It cleanses and attracts positive energy. Something tells me you could use all the positive energy you could get."

I laugh at that, taking the sage from her as I nod.

"What, are you a mind reader as well as a witch or is it stamped across my forehead?"

She gives me an amused smile.

"Not a mind reader, love, but your aura is...messy."

I frown. "I think that's an insult."

She laughs. "No, it's not your fault, per se. It just tells me there is a lot going on in your life."

"You have no idea," I mutter under my breath.

Rachel shrugs her shoulders. "I'm an excellent listener."

That's apparent. I've felt a sense of ease and comfortability from her from the moment I met her. She's so warm and inviting. If the things going on in my life wouldn't endanger me or the people I love, I'd definitely open up to her. But, I know better. So, instead, I politely shake my head. There is something that's been burning in my mind, though I'm certain I know the answer already.

"Are you, by chance, related to Elizabeth and John Proctor?"

She doesn't seem surprised, but she does nod.

"I am a descendant of them, yes."

"Wow. So, your family has lived here for—"

"Well over three hundred years, yes."

She hesitates for a moment before she points to the back.

"I actually have some of Elizabeth's belongings. Would you like to see them?"

I nod, and she walks me back there, pulling out an antique looking jewelry box. When she opens it, a ring, a couple of stones, some buttons, and a few pieces of paper are inside.

"May I?" I ask as I gesture towards the box.

She nods as I reach for the paper, my eyes rounding as I read the words on it. My eyes flick up to the date before coming to her. She gives me a knowing nod and a disappointed frown. I can't read the words on the pages fast enough, finishing the final sentence before setting the papers down.

What the fuck did I just read? What the fuck did...

"While you're here," she says, shaking me out of my thoughts, maybe intentionally so.

She gestures for me to follow her, leading me over to the wall filled with rocks and crystals. Her fingers delicately trace over the shelving before she stops on a gold and grey rock.

"Pyrite Stone," she says. "It draws energy from the earth and transfers it to you, helping build a protection layer of energy around you. It helps block out negative energies, but also physical and emotional harm."

"It's pretty," I say as I examine the quarter sized stone.

"Carry it on you at all times, okay?" she says.

I nod, and she hands it to me.

"No," I say. "I'm paying you this time."

"Skyla. You don't—"

"I'm not taking no for an answer," I say with a shake of my head.

She smiles at me and nods but walks me to the register. Rachel goes to grab a necklace that has a little metal fastener in it. She twists it around the Pyrite Stone, holding it into place before handing it to me. It's a long chain. So long that you'd never see the stone in even the deepest V-neck. That's probably the point.

"Thank you," I say as I slip the sage bundle into my purse.

"Thank you," Rachel says as I turn to leave the store.

I'm almost to the door when she calls out.

"Could you come back tomorrow?"

I pause, looking over my shoulder.

"I have something coming in tomorrow. I think it would be perfect for you."

Intrigued, I nod my head, though I'm not sure how I'll slip away two days in a row.

"Sure, I'll be here around the same time."

"Perfect. See you then," she says with a nod and a smile.

I smile and wave as I step out the door and back into the restaurant. Maggie and Maryia appear to have finally come up for air and are eating their food while mine sits in front of my seat. I slide into the booth and Maggie looks at me.

"Where did you go?"

"Bathroom," I say.

"Mads just went to the bathroom, and she said you weren't in there."

My eyes widen slightly as I nod. "Yeah, all of the stalls were taken when I went in there, so I used the one next door," I say.

Maryia lifts an eyebrow. "There was only one stall."

I close my eyes and let out a breath when Maggie speaks.

"Hey, you don't want to tell us why you wanted to come to the old part of town and disappear for twenty minutes, that's your business. Just tell us to stuff it." She shrugs as she takes a big bite into her burger.

I give her a grateful smile and nod as I pick up my food and begin eating.

Chapter Forty-Two

Asher

Liam and I are hanging out at home playing video games when my phone rings. Glancing at the screen, I couldn't be more uninterested to answer when I see my father's name flash across it.

Groaning, I pick it up, and Liam pauses the game.

"Hello, father."

"I need you at my house in one hour. We have some things to discuss."

Cool. Just how I wanted to spend my afternoon.

"Yes, sir."

He doesn't wait for me to say anything more, instead, hanging up abruptly as I toss my phone on the couch.

"What's wrong?" Liam asks.

"He wants to meet me. Says we have some things to discuss."

Liam screws up his face. "That can't be good."

"Fuck, no, it can't," I laugh.

His hand comes to my thigh, squeezing encouragingly.

"It'll be alright. Want me to come with?"

I shake my head and drop a quick kiss to his cheek.

"It's good. I'm just gonna head over now. The sooner I get there, the sooner I can fucking leave."

Liam gives me a sad smile and nods.

"Good luck."

Pushing to my feet, I bend down to him, gripping his jaw as I pull his lips in for a kiss. He practically melts against me, a sweet little content sigh escaping him that goes right to my cock. Fuck. It's amazing how easy things progressed between Liam and I. One minute, we were best friends since birth. The next, he was making my heart flip with that smile of his and making my cock throb with just the smell of him. I never thought I could love anyone the way I love Skyla, but Liam... he's pretty fucking close.

When I pull away, just an inch or so, I rest my forehead against his.

"I love you," he murmurs.

I pull away to fully look into those soft green eyes, my thumb softly dragging against his jawline.

"I love you too, baby."

The smile he gives me fucking melts me and I know that if I don't leave now, we're gonna end up tangled up together on this couch naked, me deep inside him, pumping him full of my cum. Fuck, maybe I'll just plan on it for when I get home.

It's like he can read my filthy thoughts, because he gives me a wicked wink and an air kiss before I shake my head and walk away, smiling the entire goddamn time.

I make it to my dad's place in no time and when I pull up to the front of the house, I frown to see Wesley's car here. What the fuck is he doing here?

Climbing the front steps, I pause outside the door when I hear shouting.

"I don't give a fuck what your excuses are! This is not an

adequate report! You get me something on that girl, and you get it to me now, or I'll slit your goddamn throat!" my father booms.

"I'm working on it. She doesn't trust me enough yet," Wesley says tightly.

"I don't give a flying fuck. You've been her driver for months now. You should be listening, hacking, you know, what you do best, remember?" my father sneers.

"Yes, sir."

"Good, because that shit about Liam and Asher sharing her is something a monkey could have fucking figured out. She's hiding more than she lets on, figure it out before I no longer have a use for you."

A few more murmured words are exchanged before the front door opens and Wesley is there. His eyes widen when he sees me, but he quickly schools his expression.

"Hey, Ash. What are you doing here?"

"What the fuck are you doing here?" I throw back.

"Your dad wanted to meet up. Go over some things," he says as he shrugs and begins walking to his car.

I'm fucking floored and in total disbelief as I shake my head after him.

"About my wife?" I call out.

Wesley's feet stop for a moment before they continue. I'm half convinced to run over and slit his fucking heels, make that motherfucker stop walking and start explaining. Unfortunately, before I can, the door opens again and my father is there, practically yanking me inside the house as the door slams shut behind me and Wesley's car drives away.

"I told you an hour," my father says stiffly as he looks down at me.

"I was running early, my apologies."

He makes an unimpressed noise in the back of his throat as

Demise

he moves to his office. I follow after him as he takes a seat behind his desk.

"You know how I feel about eavesdropping."

"It was by mistake."

"Yes, I'm sure it was. I imagine you have some questions?" he asks.

I nod. "Why are you having Wesley dig up information on Skyla?"

"Because you have become too attached to her, as has your bond brother. My own brother seems far too close with the girl as well, and she doesn't hang out with anyone but that vulgar Bartlett."

I keep my expression neutral, not reacting to any of his words as he cocks his head to the side.

"I allowed Ronan to bring in Wesley to assist with the protection of Skyla, but Wesley has always known the score. I run the Brethren, I run Salem. Anything that occurs within this city limits, within my society, I have a right to know."

That son of a fucking bitch.

"So, he's been spying on us."

"For lack of a better term."

"And you knew about her and Liam," I say.

He nods. "I've had my suspicions about Ronan for some time as well, and Griggs...he watches her far too closely."

"You think I'm sharing my wife with all those men?" I scoff. "Liam is one thing, but my uncle? Griggs?" I shake my head like the idea is preposterous, hoping I'm a good enough actor.

My father watches me closely, shrugging his shoulders.

"You tell me, son."

He's baiting me. He already knows the truth, or at least he thinks he does. I don't give in, though. I shake my head.

"No, I would never."

"I'd hope that I raised you better than that. A bond

between a brother and his property is one thing but to lend her out to every man in the Elders...well, then I'd say you'd truly need to lend her to all," he says with a wicked grin that turns my stomach.

It would be a freezing day in hell before I ever let my father get his hands on Skyla, or any of the others for that matter. I nod to appease him before attempting to change topics.

"What did you want to discuss?"

He watches me with narrowed eyes before easing back into his chair.

"Now that you're an Elder, you need to start carrying your own weight. I want you to begin your role effective immediately."

"Which is?"

"Doling out punishments."

I lift a brow to him. "I'm not an eliminator."

"No. You'll be punishing our people. Only in extreme cases do we send an eliminator after one of our own. The rest falls on me, now you."

"Okay," I agree. "Do you have a list of people who need... punishments?" I grit out.

His smile spreads as he nods.

"As a matter of fact, I do."

My foot doesn't leave the accelerator the entire drive home. My hands are white knuckling the steering wheel, so much anger and warring thoughts in my mind. I don't even want to think about the punishments my father has tasked me with. I have to compartmentalize what I can, and right now, there is a single person who deserves all of my anger. Everyone else's too.

I texted Ronan that he needed to meet me at my house, and I checked to make sure that Liam was home. He said he was, and so was Wesley and Vincent.

Perfect.

When I pull up to my driveway, I barely get the gate open before I'm flooring it to the front door. Slamming on the brakes, I stop just before the stairs take out my bumper. Throwing myself out of the car, my feet pound against the ground as I climb the stairs, throwing open the front door and leaving it that way.

As I turn the corner to the living room, four pair of eyes swing to me, one looking a fuck ton more guilty than the others. I don't hesitate. My fist drives into the side of Wesley's face, a crack echoing through the room as everyone moves as one. Ronan forces us apart, Liam rushes to help Wesley, up and Vincent stands like he's ready to attack.

"What the fuck is your problem?" Ronan snarls.

"Ask the fucking traitor!" I gnash as I point to Wesley.

Ronan's brows knit together as Wesley sits up on the floor where I knocked his ass down. He better stay there, or I'll hit him again and again until he can't fucking get up.

"What are you talking about?" Ronan asks.

"Wesley! He's been feeding my father information on Skyla since day one. That's how my father knew about Liam and I sharing her. He also suspects you and Vincent. I'm sure that's no coincidence. My father told me he allowed him to come to Salem only to be his little fucking narc!"

Outrage and hurt slashes through Ronan and Liam's features, while Vincent just looks murderous. Before anyone can move, though, a sound catches us off guard.

"What?" Skyla says softly, betrayal overwhelming her features.

I shrug Ronan's hands off me as I turn to face my wife.

"It's true. I heard them myself and my father confirmed it." I turn to face Wesley, sneering down at him. "You're disgusting," I say as I spit at his feet.

Liam distances himself, abandoning his effort to help him to his feet and Ronan stays cemented in place, staring down at him in disbelief.

"So, Christopher knew. He knew about us, about the stalker...because of you?" Skyla asks, hurt choking her words.

"There is more to it, little one. Please," Wesley says.

"Answer the question," Ronan says stiffly.

"Yes," he sighs as Skyla takes a sharp inhale and nods, her watery eyes looking anywhere but him.

"I agreed to report back what I found before I even met you," Wesley goes on. "I thought I was going to be eavesdropping on Asher's spoiled wife. I had no idea you'd be...you. From the moment I met you, I knew I couldn't betray you like that."

"Then why did you?" Liam adds, hurt lacing his tone.

"I started feeding Christopher false info. Boring shit like her and Asher were fighting when they weren't. She was throwing temper tantrums with his credit card. Things that I knew Christopher wouldn't care about and ultimately keep her safe."

"Then what about me?" Liam asks.

Wesley winces. "He got suspicious. He saw you staring at her the night of their ceremony apparently."

Liam scrunches his nose. "Everyone in that room was staring at her."

"Not the way you were, I guess," Wesley says, causing Liam to stand more rigidly.

"You stand there and watch the love of your life basically

being assaulted by your best friend and tell me you won't flinch or react in any way!" Liam defends.

"I know," Wesley says with his hands raised as his eyes move to each person in the room before landing on Skyla. "I should have told you from the start, but please believe me. I've only looked out for you. Christopher told me to install new security cameras in the house—"

"So, you did," Skyla says numbly.

"So, I did, until I cut his feed the next day, telling him I think the stalker did it," he finishes. "Everything I've done, has been for you, little one. It may have not started that way, but one look at you, and I knew I had to do everything in my power to protect you."

"So, you knew Christopher knew about the stalker early on then? Yesterday, you were lying to me?" Ronan asks.

"Wait, what?" I say. "What do you mean?"

Ronan's gaze flits to me and Skyla before sighing. "Yesterday, when we returned the journal, in that same hidden compartment, I found...pictures. One of them being Corwin watching Skyla sleep while she lived on campus."

"I didn't know that it was Corwin, let alone that Christopher knew. When I told him about the situation, he acted surprised."

"Yeah, he's good at fooling everyone," Asher says bitterly.

"What were the other pictures of?" Skyla asks.

Ronan grimaces and Wesley hangs his head as Ronan speaks.

"It was Christopher and your father...with your mother."

Her nose wrinkles at that.

"She was tied up, clearly crying, and...there was an identical one of Stephanie. By the looks of it, I'd guess it was taken the last time she was here."

"What?" Skyla asks softly. "You learned this yesterday and you didn't tell me?"

"I was going to," Ronan says. "Then Asher told us you went to the Proctor witch's shop, and I didn't feel like it was the right time or place."

"But now it is?" she laughs. "So, my father and Asher's raped my mother, probably repeatedly. And Steph?" she asks, her sarcastic smile melting into sorrow.

She shakes her head. "I have to call her."

Walking away, Skyla begins heading towards the stairs when Wesley calls out.

"I'm sorry, Sky. I never wanted to hurt you. I've done everything to protect you. Please believe me."

"Well, she doesn't," Vincent snarls, hauling Wesley to his feet by the back of his shirt.

Skyla pauses in her steps, looking over the room as she shakes her head.

"I do believe you, that doesn't change the fact that you lied to me for months. You could have been honest. Instead, you were a coward, hoping you wouldn't get caught."

She closes her eyes, letting out a deep breath before looking at Wesley once more.

"I believe you, but I don't forgive you. Not right now."

With that, she turns and heads up the stairs, phone pressed to her ear before the sound of a bedroom door slams shut. Liam takes a step like he's gonna follow after her and I shake my head once. He gives me a sad nod as all eyes fall on Wesley once more.

"Well, well, well. What are we going to do with you now?" Vincent asks, an excited lilt to his tone.

"Nothing," Ronan snaps.

I glare at him, screwing up my face as I do.

"He's a fucking traitor. We should gut him out back like a pig," I say.

Ronan shakes his head. "He didn't betray us. He wasn't truthful, but he never compromised Skyla's safety. He made a mistake, but haven't we all?" he asks, his eyes heavy on me until I look away. Then they move to Vincent, who also can't stand the reminder. Finally, he comes to Liam, who shrugs his shoulders.

"I haven't made any mistakes with Skyla. I'm the perfect boyfriend."

I roll my eyes at that, and Vincent shakes his head as Ronan sighs.

"Wesley is not the enemy, Christopher is. The sooner we can agree on that, the sooner we can fucking destroy him."

Chapter Forty-Three

Skyla

"C'mon, c'mon. Pick up, pick up," I mutter to myself as I pace my room.

It goes to voicemail again, so I hang up and re-dial. The third ring echoes in my ear when she answers.

"Skyla?"

"Why did you leave Salem so quickly?" I practically word vomit.

"What?" she asks like she just woke up.

"You left, almost immediately after that dinner at Asher's dad's house. What aren't you telling me?"

The line goes quiet for a moment. I check to make sure the call didn't drop, or she didn't hang up. Nope, she's there. She's just silent.

"You calling me in a panic tells me you already have a suspicion," she says numbly.

My throat tightens with emotion as I attempt to hold back my tears.

"How long?"

She's quiet again. "For me, that was the first time. Your mother, though...she had it much worse."

A sob rips out of me at that, and I cry. I hear Steph begin to cry through the phone, too.

"I'm so sorry, Steph! Why didn't you tell me? I could have stopped them. The guys could have."

"It was too late, Sky," she cries. "I didn't want to leave you there, I just...couldn't be there for a second longer. I—"

"You don't have to explain," I say, pulling myself together as I take a ragged breath.

"How did you know?" she asks, sniffing loudly.

Sadness and pain is replaced by anger as I speak.

"They have a picture! Of you, of mom."

"Oh my God," she whispers to herself. "You don't think they'd leak it, do you? I haven't told Collin yet...I don't want to, ever. If you think they'll spread it, I need to, though. He has to know it wasn't consensual, that I would never."

"From the sounds of it, the picture does not depict consent," I assure her.

Another cry rips from her chest as she sobs. I sit on the phone for several minutes, just listening to her heart break.

"I always knew they were evil. I knew what they did to her, but to live it? To feel the...pain. The...disgust."

"It's unforgivable, it's despicable," I say.

She sniffs several times, exhaling roughly.

"I'm sorry, sweetheart. You don't need to listen to me fall apart."

I frown. "You don't owe me your strength, Steph. Not right now. I know that you're a strong woman, but it's okay to fall apart right now."

"No, no," she says as she banishes more and more emotion from her voice. "If I fall apart, I'll never pull myself back up, and that's not an option, so....so," she says matter of factly, like she's decided she will never cry again.

"Have you spoken to anyone?" I ask softly.

There is a long pause before she says, "No."

I nod at that. "I think, maybe you should try. You don't have to give over the top details, but...you need someone completely unbiased to dump on. You know I want to be here, but something tells me you won't open up to me the way you need to."

"You're right." She laughs derisively, like she hates herself for it. "All I've ever done is try to protect you from this world, Sky. I don't want you dragged into it even deeper."

I huff at that. "Trust me, I'm in it as deep as I can be."

"And I hate that for you. She would have hated that for you."

My heart aches at her words. I hate it for me, too.

"Anyway, how are you? Everything okay for now?"

Okay is relative. I just found out one of my boyfriends has been keeping a major secret from me since the moment that I met him. Also, just found out that my lovely father-in-law knew about my stalker and who he was the entire time, yet did nothing to stop him. Apparently, he is also trying to dig up information on me, for what, who knows. I can promise nothing good.

I don't say any of that, though. Mainly because, as sad as it is, the chaos and drama that is my life has actually begun to be quite typical. Little can shock me these days. The other part is I really can't find it in myself to hate Wesley, no matter how much I want to. He was in the wrong, absolutely, but...he didn't owe me anything in the beginning, and for him to risk everything to protect me before we were even together...I just...in a world this terrible, I can't afford to lose one more person that I love.

Demise

"We're fine," I say simply, and I can practically hear Steph's relief that more shit hasn't hit the fan.

"Good. That's good."

We're both quiet for a few moments before she speaks again.

"I love you, Sky. You know that, right?"

I frown. "Of course I do. You know I love you, right?"

"I'm the luckiest auntie in the world for it."

That makes me smile. We small talk for a few more minutes before she makes an excuse that she needs to get to bed. Truthfully, I just think she wants to cry a little more and doesn't want to do it with me on the phone, which I respect, but also wish she would let me be there for her like she has always been there for me.

A soft knock at the door comes and I anticipate it to be Liam. Whenever there is tension, he is always the sacrificial lamb they send. Maybe because he's never the one I'm angry with. Or maybe it's because he's able to diffuse any situation, no matter how intense. It's like a gift.

Instead of Liam though, it's Wesley. I'm honestly shocked they let him up here. I stand up a little straighter as he peeks his head in.

"Can we talk?" he asks softly.

"What's there to say, Wes?"

"So much," he sighs as he steps in fully, shaking his head as he runs his hand through his hair. "And nothing. I don't want to make excuses. I should have come clean early on, that's on me. No matter how much I thought I was doing the right thing, it doesn't excuse my behavior, and I don't expect you to forgive me."

I stay silent, watching him as he continues.

"But even if you hate me, even if you never want to see me again, even if you want Griggs to empty his clip into my head, I need you to know that I love you. That I'll never stop loving you, and even if I'm not with you, I'll never stop protecting you."

He waits for me to say something, but when I don't, he hangs his head and sighs, nodding before heading for the door.

"Where are you going?" I ask stiffly.

His eyes come to me, confusion heavy in them as he shakes his head.

"I'm pissed at you," I say, "obviously. You broke my trust, all of ours, and that is not something that can just be given back. Just ask Asher." I laugh bitterly. "But I understand where your head was at, even if I don't agree with it. You didn't owe me anything when you accepted your...position, and I'd like to think I know you well enough to know you wouldn't let anything happen to me or any of the guys going forward."

He shakes his head fiercely. "Never. Sky, I promise, no more secrets, no more hidden agendas. Full honesty, all the time."

I nod at that, though my stomach turns with guilt. We should all come to this conclusion together if we want a healthy, functioning relationship, and that includes me fessing up to where I was today and where I very much plan on going tomorrow.

Holding out my hand, he hesitates for a moment before linking our fingers together.

"C'mon, we all need to talk."

He nods and follows me willingly as we make our way downstairs. The guys are still in the living room, all with drinks in their hands as they talk. When they notice me, each of them stands to their feet, their eyes coming to Wesley and my hands in a curious way.

"No more secrets, no more bullshit. If this is going to work, we have to be open and honest, no matter what," I say.

Everyone nods their agreement, and I take a deep breath as I go on.

"And that includes me as well. Today, I told Wesley that I was going to grab some food with Maggie and Maryia, which I did, but I also went back to Rachel's shop."

"The witch?" Asher snaps.

"Skyla," Liam groans.

"What were you thinking?" Ronan thunders.

Vincent and Wesley stay quiet, but looks of disappointment are splashed across their faces.

"And," I continue, "I'm going tomorrow as well. I understand none of you may like it, but I'm doing it, it's happening, so I suggest you deal with it."

"Is this what you would deem healthy communication?" Vincent drawls.

I shrug. "I'm not lying about my whereabouts."

They are silent for several seconds before Ronan speaks.

"We're coming with you."

"What?" Asher bites out.

Ronan looks to him, nodding before his eyes come to me.

"I don't like it, but since you're clearly going to go regardless of our warnings, I want to be there for your protection. The band of idiots are welcome to join."

"Hey! Why the fuck am I lumped in? Have we forgotten? Perfect boyfriend over here?"

Vincent and Asher scoff as Ronan shakes his head, ignoring Liam as he looks at me.

"Deal?"

I nod. "Deal."

Chapter Forty-Four

Skyla

I'm standing outside Rachel's shop, looking inside with men literally flanking my every angle. I'm not sure if it's out of protection or so I'm not seen here. Maybe both. Either way, it's a little much. Together, the guys and I make our way into the shop until we are practically crowding the intimate space. Liam, being the goldfish he is, immediately walks over to the crystals, checking out all of the sparkling, shiny things, while Wesley picks up one of the jars, reading the label curiously.

Rachel comes from the back, a smile on her face that quickly dies as she notices the guys. All as one, they circle me once more.

"Skyla, when I told you to leave your husband at home, that included his friends."

"Where she goes, we go," Ronan answers.

She lifts an eyebrow to him, her mouth flattened into an unimpressed line as her eyes rake over each guy assessingly.

"They are with me," I say to Rachel. "They are my..." I trail off as Rachel nods once.

"Friends?"

"Yeah," I say, rolling with it.

"Mhmmm," she says, her eyes settling on Vincent.

I don't see auras, or feel them, whatever Rachel does, but even I can tell Vincent is giving off bad vibes. It's not because he's a bad person, he's just in ultimate protection mode. He can't help it.

"Is it okay that they stay?" I ask. "Please?"

Rachel opens her mouth before letting out a displeasing sigh.

"I don't have enough sage for this," she mutters under her breath as she lights two smudge sticks like the one she gave me and begins waving it around the room, lingering around Vincent and Asher for the longest before nodding.

"Did it come in?" I ask Rachel, hoping to diffuse the tension.

"Did what come in?" Asher questions.

"Rachel told me she had something coming in that she thought I needed."

"Yes," she says. "It's in the back. Come with me."

I step forward, as do the guys, when she holds a hand up.

"Not you all. You," she says, pointing to Liam. "You may come."

He points at himself, earning irritated glares from all of the guys as he steps up beside me.

"Why him?" Asher challenges like the petulant child he is.

Rachel shoots him an irritated look.

"Because you all carry a toxic energy that is fucking suffocating. He is the only one who has a pure aura. Your heart must not do well with your circumstances," she says as her eyes move to Liam with a pitying frown.

She has no idea.

Liam being Liam, though, eases the tension and grins.

"Did you hear that? Perfect aura," he teases to the guys, who all flip him off as one.

Liam cackles as he sweeps his arms out dramatically.

"After you," he says to Rachel, and she nods approvingly before leading us to the back room.

Shelves are stacked all the way to the ceiling on either side of us, filled with extra jars, crystals and stones, as well as herbs. A small table is to the left as we move deeper, assumingly where Rachel assembles everything. Finally, we come to a small office. She opens the door and allows Liam and I to step inside first. Confused, I do before my feet cement into place.

What. The. Fuck.

At first, I don't know what I'm looking at, because how can I be seeing this? This has to be a dream or a hallucination. Something. I grab the inside of my wrist, pinching hard. Shit, not a dream. That means...

"Mom?" I choke out, my eyes running over the blonde woman standing before me.

I've only ever seen pictures of her, but it's like she hasn't aged a day, and my god, people were not exaggerating when they said I look just like her.

Her green eyes instantly fill with tears as Liam whispers under his breath, "Holy fuck."

"My girl," she says before swallowing roughly.

That's all she can do before I'm rushing to her, full on body slamming her as I wrap my arms around her and sob. Her arms encase me as she begins to cry. Her smell is so calming, like a mixture of vanilla, coconut and a hint of sandalwood. I find myself nuzzling my head into her neck as if I can get closer to her, cling to her harder, and she does the same to me.

Our bodies shake with silent tears before she pulls back and cups my face, looking me over before shaking her head.

"My Goddess, you've grown into such a beautiful woman."

"So have you," I say with a choked smile.

"My girl. My perfect baby girl," she says as she cups my face.

I lean into her touch, a loud sob ripping out of me. Apparently, it was too loud because a commotion sounds, followed by several feet pounding through the shop's wooden floors.

"NO!" Rachel shouts. "You can't be back here!"

All the guys blow past her, spilling into the room to see what is the matter, but all stop on their heels when they see who is in front of me. Four pairs of eyes, all the size of saucers, as they stare.

"What the fuck is going on?" Ronan asks.

Wesley is shaking his head as Asher and Vincent continue to stare. My mom pushes me behind her protectively, standing in front of them with her shoulders back and head held high.

"She said leave."

"It's okay," I say softly. "These are...well..."

"We're her boyfriends, well, he's her husband," Liam says as he points to Asher before pointing to himself. "But I'm the favorite. It's a pleasure to meet you," he says as he reaches his hand out for my mom.

Hesitantly, she takes it, shaking it slowly before her eyes assess all of the guys.

"All of them?" she questions.

I've never felt so insecure as I do right now. The idea of her not approving of them, of me, of how I've chosen to live my life. It gnaws at my stomach until her eyes come back to me.

"So many strong men to protect my baby. Have they done a good job?" she asks.

I smile softly and nod, and so does she, holding me to her once more. We stay like that for several seconds before I speak against her white cotton shirt.

"Mom?"

"Yes, baby?"

"How is this possible? I mean, how are you not dead? Even Steph believes you are. My dad definitely believes so...everyone does. How are you...not?"

She smiles sadly, tucking a piece of hair behind my ear.

"That is a very long story."

"Please," I beg.

"Luther Putnam discovered me and your father. He sent Christopher and Henry to kill me and—"

"Wait," I say, feeling as if the entire world has shifted beneath my feet. "Are you saying Henry isn't my father?"

She gives me a watery smile and shakes her head.

"Oh shit, I didn't see that coming," Liam comments before someone, rightfully so, smacks him on the back of the head. "Ow."

"What do you mean?" I ask. "If he isn't, then who is? Where have you been all these years? How could you—"

"G, it's time," Rachel says urgently.

My mom closes her eyes, her shoulders sagging with disappointment as she leans forward, pressing her lips to my forehead. When she pulls away, she gives me a sad smile.

"I have to go."

"What? NO!" I shout, clinging to her.

"Skyla, I have to. We only have cover for so long."

"Who is we?" Ronan asks.

"Please, I feel like I just got you back, don't disappear on me. Please," I beg.

"I'd never," she says with a shake of her head. "I'm so sorry. Will you come to me this weekend? Stay as long as you want, make sure you aren't followed or tracked, okay?"

I nod unquestioningly, and she gives me another forehead kiss before slipping on a hooded cloak and slipping between the guys and out the back door. When the door shuts, the room is silent for several seconds. Rachel grabs a pen and paper from the desk, scribbling an address onto it before handing it to me.

"This is where she lives. Please, for the sake of everyone, make sure you tell no one. Not even Stephanie."

"You know who Stephanie is?" I ask.

Rachel nods. "And she can't know. It's not safe for your mom...or for you."

"You knew who I was the second I stepped foot into your shop, didn't you?"

She gives me a soft smile before pulling me in for a hug.

"I'd have recognized you anywhere. You don't know how long I've been waiting to meet you."

"Do you know who my real father is? Where he is?" I ask as I look up to her.

She nods as she looks around the room.

"Come this weekend, and you will get all the answers you are searching for."

I nod, glancing down at the paper in my hands. New Hampshire?

Chapter Forty-Five

Liam

I thought that discovering Wesley had been a mole for months was the craziest thing to happen to us this week. Then, we discovered that Skyla's dead mom wasn't so dead after all, and I stood corrected. Now, I'm sitting across from my father, who is handing me the Walcott family engagement ring, insisting I am now engaged to Maryia Sewall. This takes the fucking cake. Okay, well, I don't think it can actually trump dead, not so dead mom, but shit, I'm fucking livid.

"No," I say simply.

"Excuse me?" my father snaps in outrage. "What the fuck do you mean no?"

"I mean, no, I will not be marrying her. Thanks, but no thanks."

His jaw tenses, hellfire in his eyes as he stares down at me.

"This isn't a discussion. This is a, 'I tell you what to do and you shut the fuck up and do it,' kind of thing."

I glare at him, shaking my head.

"I'm not a little kid you can force into submission anymore. This is my life."

Demise

"Alison!" my father roars.

Like a dutiful wife, my mother rushes into the office, looking perfectly put together as always, while my father stands. I already know where he's going with this as he pulls a gun from his hip, putting it up to my mom's head. I jump to my feet as she squeals, but my father holds a tight grip on her by the front of her throat.

This isn't the first time he's played this card before. I don't love a lot in my life, at least that he knows of, but my mother is one of those things. Anytime I'd test my boundaries, it was always her who would pay for my insubordination. After a while, I stopped pushing back because seeing your mother's lip split or her kidney bruised because of you...that's a guilt I wouldn't wish upon anyone.

"Stop," I grit out.

"I don't think I will," he sneers as he speaks to my mother. "Alison, what the fuck have you done to raise such an insolent piece of shit? Can you believe your son doesn't want to marry the nice girl I picked out for him? He could do far worse, could he not?"

She whimpers, nodding quickly. "Speak!" he shouts. "Convince him, or I'll splatter your brains all over these goddamn walls."

"P-please, Liam. Please. She's a nice girl. A pretty girl. She'll make you s-so happy," my mom cries.

"Time to make a decision, son. Be a man and live with the consequences of your actions. Three, two, on—"

"Wait!" I shout, holding up my hands as I hang my head. I stare at the ground, my voice full of defeat. "I'll marry Maryia; just let mom go."

He makes a derisive noise from the back of his throat before he jams the butt of the gun into the side of my mom's head. She cries out as she falls to the ground, and my father moves to sit behind his desk.

"Both of you get the fuck out," he snarls. "And take the goddamn ring with you."

Sighing heavily, I pocket the ring and scoop my mom into my arms. She's sobbing, her hand covering her head as blood begins to seep between her fingers. I don't even bother to give my father a second look as I carry my mom out of his office and to her bedroom. Several staff stand by, acting as if they didn't see or hear anything.

"Get me washcloths and call the doctor, just in case," I say as I begin climbing the stairs.

My mom clings to me, sobbing into my chest when I lay her down on her bed. A staff member rushes behind me with a white washcloth that I press to the back of her head. Black mascara tears streak her face as she looks up at me.

"Why doesn't he love me?" she cries.

I shake my head. "He doesn't love anyone, mom."

She curls herself up into a ball, sobbing harder than before. I sit with her until the doctor comes before excusing myself in search of my girlfriend. My stomach is heavy, I feel as if I'm going to throw the fuck up everywhere. I'm sure this is how Ronan felt when Skyla found out about him and Annie Williams. After all, how do you tell the love of your life that you'll be marrying someone else?

I texted Sky that I wanted to take her for a drive. She agreed happily but one look at me and she knew something was up.

Still, she got into the car, and I drove her to the spot I first took her to overlooking the city.

When we park, Skyla pops open the door and gets out. I follow her as she climbs onto the hood and looks out at the view. Scooting beside her, I rest my forearms on my knees as we sit in silence.

"You're getting married, aren't you?"

I hesitate for a moment before looking at her. Her eyes are glimmering as she gives me a watery smile. All I find myself capable of doing is nodding once. Skyla flattens her mouth and nods as she faces forward once more.

"To Maryia?" she guesses.

"Yeah," I say, hurt and anguish warring inside of me as I do. She swallows roughly before facing me.

"She's really pretty, and kind. You could do worse," Skyla says with a smile that couldn't be any more strained if she tried.

"I could do a hell of a lot better, too," I say, cupping her face in my hands as I begin swiping away her tears.

A pitiful cry escapes her as she shrugs. "We knew it was coming."

"I'm so sorry, babygirl. I tried to fight it. I..." I break off because what the fuck am I supposed to say? There is nothing to say.

"It's okay," she says. "I just...maybe we could talk to her? See what her expectations are for the marriage. I mean she's with Maggie—"

"And I'm with you," I say, finishing her sentence, or at least I hope that's what she was going to say. "We will figure it out, all of us, together."

Skyla nods. "Do you have a ring yet?"

"Yeah. It's a family heirloom."

"Can I see it?"

I frown but reach into my pocket, where the velvet box still rests. Pulling it out, I hand it to Skyla. She pauses for a moment before popping it open. Her breath catches softly and I don't blame her. It's a three carat sapphire surrounded by forty diamonds. My great great great grandfather gave it to his first wife because sapphires were her favorite. It's been passed down every generation since then.

"It's beautiful," Skyla whispers. "I'm sure she is going to love it."

I can't help but sneer, shaking my head as I slide off the car. I turn around, grabbing Skyla's feet and dragging her to the edge of the hood. Snatching the box out of her hand, I shake my head.

"Liam, what's—"

I cut her off by dropping to one knee, holding her hand in mine as I hold the box in my other.

"Skyla, I don't give a fuck if someone loves it. I want you to love it. There is no one in the world I want to see wear this ring but you. It's belonged to you from the moment I set my eyes on you."

"Liam," she says, her voice raspy and tears brimming her beautiful green eyes.

I slide the ring onto her finger, resting it just above her wedding ring from Asher. It looks good beside it, a little untraditional, but it's perfect for her.

"I'm not even going to ask you to marry me if the circumstances were different. You don't get a choice, babygirl. We are endgame. Who gives a fuck what a piece of paper says. I am yours, right here," I say as I take her hand, covering my heart with it as I look up at her. "Forever."

A tear falls as her mouth lifts into a smile before she drags me to her, pressing her lips to mine. Our kiss is hurried and frantic, like we can't show each other how much we love one another fast enough.

Demise

"I love you, babygirl," I say in between kisses.

"I know," she says. "I love you too."

"I know." I nod as I pull away, gripping her neck tightly as I look at her. "We are going to make it out of this, together."

"Together," she nods.

I'm smiling like a fucking clown, thanking everyone that is congratulating me with a woman that is not my girl on my arm. Her hand is wrapped around my bicep, and her smile seems even more fake than mine, if you can imagine it. The new two carat diamond ring on her finger practically shimmers from the glitz and glamour that my family home has been turned into. My mom did always know how to throw a party.

I couldn't give her my family ring, not when it looked so perfect on Skyla's finger. So, I insisted she keep it, and I bought Maryia a new one, which she didn't seem to mind, seeing as she could barely stop crying when I gave it to her.

Even now, at our engagement party, she can hardly keep the tears at bay. Leaning down, I whisper into her ear.

"Hey, it's gonna be okay. Remember what we talked about. We're friends. I want my friend happy. Maggie will be welcome over anytime."

She gives me a grateful smile and nods. "I appreciate that. And same for Skyla. I really like her."

I grin at that and nod. "Me too."

Maryia giggles softly before sniffing back the next tears as my father comes up to us, my mother on his arm.

"Oh, would you just look at you two," she beams. "The couple of the decade!"

I nod my head but don't turn on the charm for them. They know where I stand among all this.

"Thank you for the wonderful party, Mrs. Walcott. It's beautiful."

"Oh, it's my pleasure, darling, and please, call me Alison."

Maryia nods graciously and my eyes can't help but drift away from present company. Skyla and Asher are currently slow dancing, spinning around and around in the room, smiling like a couple of lovesick fools. I can't help but feel envious, feel left out. No offense to Maryia, but I don't belong over here, I belong over there, with them.

"Excuse me a moment," I say, slipping past my parents as I make my way over to Skyla and Asher.

As soon as the song ends and the crowd claps, I whisper into Asher's ear.

"Coat closet off the mud room, now."

He turns to me as I head towards the back of the house. I can feel Asher a few steps behind me and Skyla a few behind him. I don't make eye contact with anyone as I weave through the crowd, casually separating myself from this God awful party before I reach the closet. Opening the door, I step inside as Asher and Skyla follow me in.

As soon as the door is shut and we are plunged into darkness, it's like an unspoken agreement is set into motion. Instantly, my mouth is on someone's. It takes me only half a second to recognize it as Skyla's. I feel Asher kissing up and down my neck as Skyla's hands move across my chest and down to my pants. Pulling my head from hers, I move to Asher, our tongues tangling as he cups my face and bites down on my bottom lip. He bites so hard I taste blood, but his tongue is quick to lick it away, groaning as he does.

"Fuck," he groans. "I do not fucking like that bitch all over you."

"Hey," Skyla chastises. "Maryia is nice and she's not all over him. She's playing the part."

Asher scoffs. "Why the fuck am I the only one not okay with someone else marrying our boyfriend?"

I grin at that, though no one can see me. I love it when he calls me that.

"I mean, to be fair, the two people I love married each other. Imagine how left out I feel?" I pout.

"Aw, you feel left out?" Asher teases. "Sky, how do you think we could make our boy feel included?"

I hear her soft chuckle, and I feel her hands on my pants, dragging them down to my ankles before a warm mouth wraps around my cock.

"Fuck," I sigh as I rest my head on Asher's shoulder.

He practically has to hold me up as I turn to complete Jell-O at the mercy of Skyla's mouth.

"There you go." Asher soothes. "Relax for us, let us take care of you."

His hand runs a trail down my back, squeezing my ass before forcing a finger inside me. I cringe with the lack of lube before he slips inside and all I feel is pleasure.

"You like that?" Asher asks, nipping at my earlobe as he does.

"Uh, huh," I moan.

"How is our girl doing? She taking care of you?"

"Fuck yes," I pant as I thrust against Skyla and Asher.

She hums around me before releasing me with a pop and standing up. I hear some rustling of clothes before Asher removes his finger, pushing me into Skyla.

"Fuck me, Liam," she says, her voice soft and breathy.

"Shit, don't have to ask me twice," I say as I lift Skyla's already bare leg. I feel around to notice that her dress is bunched up around her waist. Such a good girl for me.

My cock finds her wet cunt instantly and it's all too easy to slip inside.

"Fuckkk," I groan.

"Liam," she pants.

"Yeah, babygirl. Say my name," I say through clenched teeth as I begin fucking her.

In the next second, I hear a bottle open, followed by a squirting sound. Despite not being able to see, I still turn in search of the sound before I feel a cold liquid spread over my asshole.

"Shit!" I yelp.

Asher chuckles as he covers me with lube.

"Why the fuck did you bring lube to my engagement party?" I ask.

"Because," he says as his hands grab onto mine. "I figured you were going to need a reminder about who you belong to."

With that, Asher snaps his hips, thrusting inside me and making me see stars. It burns for several seconds, but that doesn't stop Asher from pushing inside me, rapidly fucking the shit out of me.

"Who do you belong to?" he grunts.

"You two," I moan as I fuck Skyla to match his pace.

"That's fucking right," Asher says tightly. "You're ours, right, Sky?"

"Yes!" she shouts, way too loud, honestly.

"Are you Maryia's?" Asher practically snarls.

Honestly, his jealousy is kind of wild. I haven't really seen him like this, at least not with me, besides some shit with Wesley. Pretty hot, not gonna lie.

"Fuck no. Just yours, Ash. Yours and Sky's."

His cock pushes deeper, hitting my prostate just right as he smacks the side of my ass. I clench around him and he groans.

"That's fucking right. Now be a good boy and fill up our girl. Come in her cunt while I come in this ass."

His filthy words spur me on and I begin fucking Skyla with wild abandon. I feel her orgasm coming several seconds before it finally hits, and when it does, she practically shakes the house with her screams. I cover my hand over her mouth to muffle it, but the next second, I'm falling over the edge, letting out my own moans of pleasure. Asher's hand covers mine like a chain reaction as I empty my cum into Skyla.

"Fuck, you two are so good for me. All mine, all fucking mine," he growls before his cock throbs in my ass and he comes.

"Shit," he pants. "Fuck yes! This ass is so fucking greedy for my cum."

I nod as he pushes his cum deeper and deeper, moaning through his release.

"Such a tight little ass. God, you milk my cock so good."

Slowly, all movements stop, and all that can be heard is heavy panting. Eventually, Asher pulls out of me as I pull out of Skyla. I give my pocket square to Skyla, and she uses it to clean herself up as Asher hands me his.

"Thanks," I smile.

"My pleasure," Asher chuckles, placing a quick kiss to my cheek as we do the best to clean ourselves in this dark closet.

When we are all set and righted as we can be, we open the door, wincing at the bright light before filing out of the closet. Skyla runs a hand through her hair and Asher and I straighten our ties before we all share a secretive smirk. Alright, this party isn't all bad, I guess.

Chapter Forty-Six

Skyla

My knee bounces anxiously as we drive down the road. It's a long drive from Salem to northern New Hampshire, probably for a good reason.

I can't believe she's alive. My mom. She's been alive all this time. There are a million things running through my head, thousands of questions. Yet, one stands out above the rest. Why did she fake her death? Or I guess, more importantly, why did she leave me behind?

Wesley is driving with Ronan in the front seat, Vincent and I in the back, and Liam and Asher in the center row. We passed the road that takes us to the cabin we stayed at for Christmas about an hour ago. I can't help but smile as I think about the memories we made over that weekend. I'd do anything to go back and relive it all over again. Maybe someday.

We can only stay one night before Liam has to have dinner with Maryia's parents, something he is most definitely not looking forward to. Ronan looked up some hotels near the address we were given and chose a suite so we could all be in the same room together.

Demise

I'm not sure what will await us when we get to my mom's house. Will my real dad be there? Are they still together? Where does Henry fit into this puzzle? I'm honestly a little irritated that she dropped several bombshells on me and then vanished. I'm trying not to jump to conclusions, to allow her the chance to explain herself, but being anxious is putting it lightly for how I'm feeling.

The GPS announces that we've arrived at our destination, but we all frown when we see that it's just a long dirt road off the highway.

"You sure you punched it in right?" Ronan asks Wesley.

Wes rolls his eyes and nods as he slowly turns down the road.

"What if this is a trap?" Asher asks.

The vehicle is silent as Wesley creeps down the heavily wooded driveway.

"I'm just saying." Asher continues. "She has ties with witches, clearly. Who's to say she isn't trying to hurt Skyla? Or one of us? Hell, all of us."

"She's my mother," I defend.

Asher turns to look at me with a shake of his head. "And if there is anything all of us can agree on, it's that parents suck, princess."

I frown at that, doing my best not to let Asher's negativity seep in. After a quarter mile or so, the trees break free and my jaw unhinges when I look out at the land before us. There are at least fifteen little cottages sprawling across acres and acres of cleared land. It's like a fairytale meadow or something. There are several large gardens with plants, fruits and vegetables growing. There are also several outdoor seating areas, like a large community center.

"What the fuck? Did we just walk into a commune?" Liam asks.

"Commune of witches," Asher adds.

"A Coven, morons," Ronan corrects.

"I don't like this," Vincent murmurs.

I turn to him and frown. "Why?"

"No good escape routes. The car could be easily sabotaged, then we are out in the open with no cover until the tree line."

I snort and shake my head because they are all being ridiculous...aren't they? Unease settles inside me as we pull up to the main parking area. We put the car in park as several people begin walking towards us. Oh god.

Wesley is the first to get out of the car, followed by Ronan and Asher. Liam lags behind a bit, and when I try to get out, Vincent forces me back into my seat. I glare at him, but he only shakes his head as he watches the guys intently.

"Who are you?" a man with a long brown beard asks.

"Just take a look at them, Anthony. You know who they are," a red-headed woman hisses.

"You are not welcome here!" another woman shouts.

All the guys stand tall, unmoving, when my mother walks through the crowd. More like she walks, and the crowd practically separates for her.

"I invited them," she says as her eyes scan the guys before she frowns.

"G," the redhead whispers so loud that even I can hear her. "You may have doomed us all."

She gives her a tight smile and holds her hand.

"Trust me?"

The woman sighs before nodding, and Vincent climbs forward to get out of the car, grabbing my hand so I follow behind. When my feet land, I hear a soft gasp escape, several people before my mother smiles, opening her arms for me. I run to her immediately, reveling in the feel of her arms around me.

Demise

We stay that way for an awkward amount of time for everyone else, but I don't think it'll ever be enough for me.

"Are you all staying the night?" she asks.

I nod. "Just tonight. Some of us have to return to Salem in the morning."

She looks disappointed by that, but she nods nonetheless.

"Where one goes, you all go?" she guesses.

I smile and shrug.

"Good. That's the best way to keep you safe," she says as she cups my cheek. "C'mon, I'll show you all around."

My mom's arm loops through mine as she begins walking us through the grounds, introducing me to anyone and everyone she possibly can. She also introduces the guys as mine. Not my boyfriends, not my friends. Just that, "This is my daughter, and these men are hers."

I kinda like it.

She points out the community garden, the little schoolhouse and all of the communal areas like sitting areas, fire pits and walking trails leading into the forest.

"So, are the rumors true?" I ask. "Are you a witch?"

We climb the short steps up to a cottage and my mother shakes her head from side to side like she's contemplating how to answer.

"Yes and no. The rumors you're no doubt referring to are false for that time of my life, but after living here for over sixteen years, I've adapted practices, yes."

"This is your Coven?" Ronan asks.

She turns to look at him and smiles.

"This is my family."

Pushing the door open, she pauses, turning to me.

"There is someone who couldn't wait a second longer to meet you."

This puts all the guys on edge, and I feel them practically surround me.

"Jonathan?" my mom calls out in the house.

A tall man, at least six foot five, steps around the corner of the cottage, his feet freezing when he sees us all on the front porch. He has green eyes, darker than mine or my mother's, with black hair that has been pulled into a man bun and a trimmed beard. There is a touch of grey encroaching in to show his age, but it's the kind smile that spreads across his face that helps put me at ease.

His eyes move from me to my mom before settling back on me. My heart is pounding in my chest, my breaths quickening as we just stare at one another. Something inside me knows exactly who he is immediately. Maybe he feels the same way too, because he practically sprints to me.

His arms wrap me up, lifting me into the air and spinning me in a circle. I wrap my arms around his neck as I hold on tightly, and he speaks into my shoulder. I can't quite hear him, but when he sets me down and looks at me, he repeats himself.

"Skyla," he rasps. "Is it really you?"

I smile softly and shrug my shoulders.

"Is it really you? Are you—"

"Your father," my mom interrupts. "Yes."

He smiles down at me before realizing we have an audience. He doesn't look surprised. No doubt my mom has already told him how their daughter grew up to be a trollop. No, I'm sure that's not what the conversation was. She's seemed quite accepting thus far.

"Jonathan Proctor," he says with his hand extended to Liam.

He smiles and takes it, shaking as he speaks.

"Liam Walcott."

Jonathan...my dad, still weird to think about, raises his

eyebrows in recognition as he moves through the guys. The next to offer up his hand is Wesley, then Ronan, lastly being Vincent and Asher, of course. Wait, Proctor? As in...

"There she is," Rachel smiles as she makes her way out of the cottage, wrapping me up into a hug.

"Are you—"

"Your aunt?" She smiles. "Yes."

"Why didn't you tell me?" I ask.

She gives me a dry look. "How should that conversation have gone? Welcome to my store. I recognized you instantly, you're a spitting image of your mother with a touch of your father, who happens to be my brother? Oh, and by the way, your mother isn't actually dead and has been heartbroken every day she hasn't been in your life? But keep it to yourself?"

"She's right," Liam says. "That's a mouthful."

Ever the comedic relief, everyone chuckles at that as Jonathan makes a sweeping motion.

"Please, come inside."

Rachel steps in first, followed by me, my mother, and all of the guys. I move to one of the several couches in the living room, taking a seat as Vincent and Asher quickly claim the seats to my left and right, ever my guard dogs. Liam, being the goof he is, doesn't mind sitting on the floor in front of Vincent and Asher, as Ronan and Wesley stand on either side of the couch, flanking us all.

My dad takes a seat on the other couch, dragging my mom into his lap. He begins nuzzling her neck and she smiles, giggling and pushing him away as he only drags her closer. I can't help but smile as I watch them. They look so at peace, so in love. I hate that I lost my mom for all of these years, but it helps a little to know that the years without each other have been filled with light and love.

"Ugh, get a room," Rachel grumbles as she comes out from

the kitchen, a lit smudge stick in her hand as she begins waving it around the room, and more specifically, my guys.

"You're in my house." My dad reminds her.

"Yes, and you have company. You can maul your wife later."

He sighs dramatically in a way that reminds me of Liam before he lets my mom sit beside him instead of on him, though it's clear she preferred it the other way. As Rachel comes up to us, she sprays something out of a bottle at Asher, Vincent, and Ronan as if they were misbehaving dogs.

"What the fuck? Again?" Asher snarls as Vincent stands to his feet.

I yank at his arm, forcing him to sit, which he does so begrudgingly.

"Smudge spray. Cinnamon, moon water, black pepper, vinegar and rosemary. Sorry. Someone had to do it, your auras are practically leaking into the house. None of us need that shit," Rachel says.

"You're not sorry," Asher grumbles.

"You're right, Putnam, I'm not." She smirks.

"Okay, that's enough," my dad says before Rachel rolls her eyes and puts her things down, taking a seat beside her brother.

"So," my mom starts.

"Sooo?" I question.

Awkward silence descends around the room for several seconds before Liam blurts.

"How are you alive? I mean, we all thought you died in a boating accident when Sky was three."

My dad grips her hand, and she nods with a sad smile.

"I did, kind of, and yet, I lived."

We all give her puzzled looks and she looks at her husband before continuing.

"I don't need to explain to any of you how the Brethren

Demise

works. Based on the amount of Elder rings in this room, it seems you know perhaps more than I."

All but Vincent glance down at their ring and nod morosely.

"When I was engaged to Henry Parris, there was another who vied for my hand."

"My father," Asher guesses.

Her gaze locks on Asher before nodding. "The resemblance between you two is quite frightening."

He frowns like that's offensive. "I'm sorry, trust me, I wish I'd have taken after my mother."

My mom smiles sadly. "She was one of my best friends. I was heartbroken to hear about her death."

Asher nods as she continues.

"Christopher had decided that he wanted me instead, and tried to convince his father, Luther, to switch brides. Give Isabel to Henry, and me to him. Thankfully, he didn't approve."

"Thankfully?" Ronan questions. "You preferred Henry?"

She nods hollowly at Ronan. "Henry is a nasty son of a bitch, but he doesn't hold a candle to the evil inside Christopher."

I feel Asher's eyes on me as I look at him and remember that day in his father's house. My back practically burns like the wounds are fresh at the reminder.

"Christopher didn't like that," Liam guesses.

My mom shakes her head. "He and Henry would play this...game. They'd tie me up and—"

"We know the rest," Wesley says with a sad shake of his head. "I'm so sorry you had to live through that."

She gives him an appreciative smile and nods.

"That went on for...months. I was desensitized, floating through life, until one day I met Jonathan," she says as she smiles at him. He grins down at her, giving her a quick kiss to the cheek. "Literally, we ran into each other at the grocery store, of all places. He knew who I was immediately, and I knew he wasn't a part of the Brethren. Fate kept pushing us together, running into each other at a park, at the dry cleaners, even restaurants."

"I may have been keeping tabs on her, a little," my dad admits.

"Stalking is the proper word," my mom corrects.

He scoffs but doesn't deny it. "She was so beautiful. I could see she had a pure heart, but it was shrouded in darkness. She was trapped, and...something told me I was the one that could save her."

"We fell in love," she says, staring into his eyes. "And I fell pregnant with you."

Her eyes meet mine, and I turn my head to the side softly.

"I'm sorry to ask, but how do you know Henry is not my father? If you were married to him, and he and Christopher were both forcing themselves on you, isn't it possible one of them could be my father?"

Ronan and Asher look at me with panicked expressions and my mother shakes her head.

"Christopher was forbidden from seeing me while he and Isabelle were conceiving...you," she says as she points to Asher. "And Henry is sterile."

"What?" I ask.

My mom nods. "We'd been in the process of conceiving for months, consensually or not, and I wasn't getting pregnant. We went to specialists who deemed him unable to father children."

"So, he knows he's not my father?" I ask.

"Yes, when I was pregnant, he knew it couldn't be his. I tried to hide the pregnancy as long as I could while Jonathan and I came up with an...exit strategy, I suppose. I was discovered before we could actually pull it off. He nearly beat me to death." She laughs on a sob before banishing it away.

"He told me we'd tell everyone that it was his. That way he's producing an 'heir,' and I get to keep my lifestyle. Like I wanted it," she adds.

"What happened?" I ask, desperate for more.

"Obviously, I told Henry I'd stopped seeing Jonathan, but... we made it work. I'd take you on a walk and he'd meet us in the park, or we'd drive out of state to have lunch, as a family. You even called him dada when you were just under two."

"One of my favorite memories," he says, his eyes glossy with memories of the past.

"He even dressed up as a doctor, paid off the real one, and delivered you himself," my mom laughs, smacking my dad's chest.

He lets out a gruff laugh, shrugs, and looks at me.

"I wasn't going to miss your birth or the chance to hold you, even for just a second, for anything."

I can't help but smile at that, the picture they're painting, the tones their voices carry. It sounds like there was so much love, so much joy in our lives together, whenever we could have it.

"On your third birthday, I snuck away with you to visit Jonathan. He gave you a tricycle and was pushing you on it at a park in Boston. I didn't know I was being followed by Christopher, but...I was, and he saw. He put everything together, sent his little informants to dig up information and took it all to Luther and Henry. I think he was hoping they'd kill Jonathan, but instead Luther just wanted me dead."

"I had a vision that day." Rachel admits.

"A vision?" I question. "Like psychic stuff?"

She shrugs as she continues. "It was your mother on a boat

with two men. It was dark and ominous and I knew death was lurking in those waters."

"So, Rachel and a few of her friends met me and placed a protective spell over me."

"And it worked?" Asher asks dubiously.

My mother doesn't take offense, instead she smiles at him and shrugs.

"I'm still here, aren't I?"

My guys all share disbelieving looks, but it doesn't really matter if they believe it or not.

"True to Rachel's vision, Henry and Christopher took me out on a boat late one night before Henry held my head underwater. I tried to fight back but he was so strong. For a moment there, Christopher even tried to stop him, saying he'd hide me. He was hysterical and I thought maybe I'd have a chance out of there. I wasn't scared to die, I was scared I'd never see you or Jonathan again," she says as she looks at me.

"But," she says as she clears her throat. "Henry reminded him it had to be done, and Christopher was the one to hold me over until my body went limp and he shoved me into the water. At least, that's what I think happened. The next thing I knew, I woke up borderline hypothermic in the back of Jonathan's car as he drove me to a hospital in rural Massachusetts."

"How could you have survived if your body went limp? If you had that much water in your lungs, you must have stopped breathing," Ronan asks.

"What I've come to find over the years is we are not always supposed to know everything that happens or why it does. Sometimes, we just have to be thankful for what we can, and understanding for what we can't."

"And then...you came here?" I ask.

She nods. "Jonathan bought this land before you were born.

We had a dream to have a self-sustained piece of paradise, just the three of us. But Henry moved you away to live with Steph, and I knew you were in good hands. I also knew that no matter how much it hurt, it would have been selfish to put you in danger by taking you. If they'd have caught us...I don't know what the Brethren would have done to you as well. I just...not a day goes by that I don't regret not taking you. Before you left or while you were in London. I tried to do what was best for you, but I—"

Her voice cuts off on a sob and she shakes her head before looking up at me.

"Sky, baby. I'm so sorry. I know you can't forgive me, but I love you so much. I've loved you from the moment I took that pregnancy test. There isn't a day that goes by that we don't think about you or talk about you. And now you're here, right in front of us," she says, her bottom lip quivering as she smiles. "Feels something of a blessing, right, Jonathan?"

"And then some," he agrees.

I don't realize I'm crying until Vincent intertwines our fingers, squeezing gently. Rachel cocks her head to the side curiously and it sets Vincent off.

"What?" he snaps.

She doesn't jump or react like most would. Instead, she just shakes her head.

"It's just interesting. The most negative of you all, the one carrying the most death, the most guilt, is the first to provide comfort and support. Practically absorbing her own hurt and putting it onto your shoulders."

"I'm just holding my girl's hand," Vincent says dryly.

"Yeah? That's it?" Rachel challenges.

He narrows his eyes at her as I stand and close the distance between the two couches. When I come to stand between my mom and my dad, I slump to my knees on the floor and cry. They both dive to the ground, wrapping their arms around me on either side as we all fall apart together. Just the three of us, like it always should have been. A family. My family.

Chapter Forty-Seven

Skyla

After an emotional day, we all had dinner at my parents' house and talked a little bit about our lives. And by our lives, I mean that Liam and I opened up. The rest stayed very tight lipped. They aren't as trusting, and I understand that. They can't feel the connection I feel. They are on guard, and I know it's only out of protection for me and themselves.

My mom walked us over to the cottage that they set up for us. The guys were vehemently against it. Ronan explained that we already had accommodations, but my mom insisted, and honestly, I was happy with it. I want to soak up every minute I possibly can with her, with my father, too. Begrudgingly, the guys agreed, and now as we are getting settled, I take a moment to pull my mom to the side.

"When can I tell Steph because…I can't keep this from her forever."

"You have to!" my mom urges. "Sky, you can't tell a soul outside this house. Your father, myself, and the entire coven would be in danger if you did."

"But it's Steph. She loves you and grieves you to this day more than I know. She deserves to know."

"It's not safe. You have to know that the Brethren has bugged everything from her home to her cell phone."

I frown. That's valid. Look at the dorm rooms, our home. We debugged it only for Christopher to want it bugged again. He always has his ear to the ground, or his henchmen. It's probably how he's become so powerful in the time he's been in control.

My heart breaks for Steph but I nod my understanding.

"One day, I hope I can see her again. I miss her so much," she says with a sad shake of her head. "I'm so thankful she took such good care of you."

"She really did," I say with a nod.

"And Henry?" she asks stiffly.

"For most of my life, he was indifferent. Christopher has been a little more...brutal."

My dad steps into the house, smiling.

"Does anyone need anything?"

When his eyes come to us, he can feel the heaviness of the moment he walked in on and he begins to back pedal.

"It's okay," I say. "You can stay. I uh, was telling mom how good to me Steph was."

"And how bad Christopher has been," my mom says, forcing my dad's jaw to clench tightly.

"What has he done to you?" he asks stiffly.

"Mostly psychological mind games, but there was one day... he was punishing Asher, forcing me to watch, and I...protected him."

Both of their brows furrow as I turn around, pulling down the shoulders of my sweater with a crisscrossed back, revealing my scars. They're healing well, but they'll always be there. My mother gasps, and I hear my father exhale savagely as I turn around, fixing the sweater into place.

"I'm so sorry, baby girl," she says with her hand over her mouth, tears in her eyes as she shakes her head.

"He will get what has been owed to him and his family. One day," my dad promises.

"The whole family isn't bad," I defend as my eyes come to Asher and Ronan who are carrying bags in from the car.

"We can see that," he agrees. "So many wrongs demand to be righted, though, and he will be at the forefront of the list."

My dad closes his eyes like it's physically painful for him to look at me for a moment before he blinks away the anger and smiles.

"We'll let you all get some sleep and see you in the morning."

My mom wraps her arms around me, holding me tight.

"I love you," she whispers.

"I love you too."

Pulling away, she rubs her hand against my arm gently as my dad lingers awkwardly. So, I make the first move, pulling him in for a hug. He wraps his arms around me, plastering me to his wide chest as he rocks us back and forth, placing a kiss to the top of my head before pulling away.

"Good night, Sky."

"Night," I smile as they step out of the house, shutting the door behind them.

A pair of arms wrap around me, resting their chin on my shoulder.

"You okay, baby?" Ronan grumbles into my ear.

"I'm better than okay. I'm so happy," I say as I look up at him.

He smiles down at me and nods.

"Good, that's just the way I like you."

His lips meet mine as I look up at him, his hand sliding up my front before wrapping around my throat to keep me in place. The kiss is so tender, not rushed or hurried. We just enjoy the comfort of one another when I hear some murmuring before the scraping sounds of furniture being moved.

I try to pull away to see, but Ronan doesn't let me, keeping me in place for several more seconds before he releases me. When my eyes come back to the room, the fireplace is lit and roaring, all furniture moved away from the living room, only leaving a large comforter on the carpet. The guys all watch me with contentment as Wesley is the first to approach. His hands cup my face, holding me tenderly as he brings his lips to mine.

The sound of kissing forces my eyes open, and I find Liam and Asher making out, similarly to how Wesley and I are, before Vincent walks up to me, stealing me from him as he captures my mouth. His tongue wraps around mine, his hand coming to the back of my head to deepen the kiss as he lifts me up into his arms, holding me in the air as my legs wrap around his waist.

Slowly, Vincent lowers me down to the ground, kissing his way down my body as he begins stripping me naked. Article after article of clothing flutters in the air before landing on the ground in a heap as Vincent sits back in appreciation of the work he's done. I'm laying down, bare naked, and suddenly, I have five sets of hungry eyes on me. Then, all as one, they swarm me. It's like a feverish need, hands everywhere, mouths everywhere. I can hear kissing between the guys, but I'm so lost in the stimulation of it all I can hardly see straight.

I moan when a tongue licks my pussy, followed by another right beside it. The tongues tangle together as they work me over, and I look down to see Ronan and Wesley, so lost in each other, in me, as they press themselves together, grinding against one another as they continue feasting on me.

Demise

Vincent's mouth is currently wrapped around my left nipple, his teeth nipping at it before licking away the pain. I smile down at him, running my fingers through his hair and he lets out a deep moan when I do. Like my touch alone brings him an insurmountable level of pleasure.

Liam's lips come to mine while Asher's move down my neck to my right nipple. Asher's hand cups my breast as he sucks on me, flicking his tongue against me in a way that has me shuddering.

My first orgasm hits me out of nowhere as I squirm and wiggle against my men. When I settle, I know without a doubt it won't be my last of the night.

"Flip over," Vincent commands, laying down and pulling me to him.

I straddle him happily as he pulls off his shirt, tossing it across the room before he makes quick work of discarding his pants. I lift up a little to let him kick them off before he pulls me back down, forcing me to sink onto his cock.

We both groan at that and I can't help but rock myself against him.

"Fuck, siren. You're already soaked."

"Thanks to all of you," I moan.

"Looks like you don't have the fanciest cock anymore, baby," Asher says to Liam as he stares at Vincent's tattoo.

Liam's head whips over in outrage as his mouth parts.

"When the fuck did that happen? Vinny you got your cock tattooed?"

"What?" Ronan scoffs as Vincent grunts in response.

"Fuck, color me jealous," Liam grouches. "Why haven't you got your cock tatted for me, Ash?"

"I definitely don't love you that much," Asher snaps back.

Liam makes a face like he's deeply hurt but there is a playful look to his eyes.

"You wound me," Liam says as he reaches for Asher's shirt, ripping it over his head while Asher does the same. Their hands are everywhere, mouths everywhere, and Liam whispers something into Asher's ear. He looks at him in shock for a moment before his eyes trace over Liam's face and he nods.

Asher sinks down to his knees, turning my head to the side and forcing his cock into my mouth. I swirl my tongue around his head, bobbing him up and down my throat before gagging and doing it all over again.

"Fuck yes," Asher groans. "Choke on my cock, princess."

I do as he says, forcing him further and further down, when I hear a bottle of lube open. I only assume it's a bottle of lube because, honestly, with five boyfriends, you get used to the sound really quick.

To my surprise, when I flutter my eyes open, I see Liam lining up behind Asher. I try not to make a big deal out of it, but I can feel my eyes practically bulging as Liam attempts to top Asher. I say attempt because this is a really hard angle with Asher basically straight up and down on his knees to accommodate me.

Lowering myself against Vincent more, it allows Asher the room he needs to sink down a little further, arching his back and letting Liam in.

"Shit," Asher winces as Liam pushes in slowly.

"Oh fuck," Liam whimpers.

I keep my eyes on them, not wanting to miss a moment of it as Liam runs his hand up and down Asher's back in a soothing way.

"Goddamnit, Ash!" Liam groans when he's fully seated inside him. "Your virgin ass is so fucking tight."

"Your cock is practically splitting me in half," Asher complains.

Demise

I pull my mouth away from him, lifting an eyebrow in amusement.

"Yeah, welcome to the fucking club," I scoff.

Everyone chuckles at that, and even Asher nods his agreement before I suck him back down my throat.

Slowly, Liam begins thrusting, forcing Asher to buck once.

"FUCK! What was that?" he moans.

"That's your prostate, baby," Liam smirks as he angles himself again and again.

Asher's moans fill up the room as Liam says to the other guys.

"Catch."

Someone does, popping open the bottle of lube and covering my asshole in it. It's cold at first but when his finger slides in me easily, I relax around it.

"Oh, she's already so fucking ready for me," Wesley smirks.

"Good, because I'm fucking ready for you," Ronan says as he steals the bottle, covering his cock with lube and forcing Wesley to bend over.

Wesley withdraws his finger, lining the tip of his head up to my ass before pushing in. I tense at the intrusion, the feeling of Vincent inside my pussy, Asher in my mouth and Wesley in my ass is almost too much. I don't want them to stop, though. Not for anything in the world.

Whimpering, everyone pauses their movements, allowing me to adjust before Wesley finishes pushing inside me. The burning aches for several seconds and it doesn't ease until Vincent begins playing with my clit. I moan around Asher's cock at that, and slowly, everyone begins moving once more.

Wesley pushes deep in me once and it forces Vincent to grit his teeth and bow his back. Pulling my mouth away from Asher, I frown at Vincent.

"Are you okay?"

"Oh, he's fine. He can just feel Wesley's cock rubbing against his and he's trying not to love it," Liam grins as he thrusts into Asher, pulling a moan out of him.

"Fuck you, Walcott," Vincent snarls.

"Once I'm done with Asher, bend over and I'll blow your fucking mind," Liam says with a wink as Vincent shakes his head and looks at me.

I lower my voice as I lean down to whisper into his ear.

"Do you like it?"

He doesn't say anything for a moment and then Wesley, being almost as big of a shit as Liam, pushes deep once more, forcing Vincent's eyes to roll into the back of his head. He begrudgingly gives me a terse nod of the head, and I can't help but smile at him, pressing my lips to his as Wesley begins fucking me hard. Vincent's thrusts are staggered and uneven as he attempts to control himself.

Moving my mouth from his, I whisper into his ear.

"It's okay to enjoy yourself, no one is going to judge you, baby. I promise."

He looks at me, those slate grey eyes practically shining as he drags my mouth back down to him and moans. Wesley seems to make it his life's mission to make Vincent fall apart as he angles his cock, rubbing against him through me. I feel Vincent's hips mimic the motion as he groans and gasps into my mouth.

"You enjoying that cock, Vinny?" Wesley jeers, using Liam's nickname for him.

Vincent tears his mouth from me, ready to tell him to fuck off or something when Wesley leans over me, inching his face across from him as he goads him.

"C'mon. Just one kiss, for our girl. You know how soaked she gets when we play together."

Vincent glares at him but he shoots me a quick look. I try to keep my face impassive, but I'm honestly just surprised he hasn't tried to stab Wesley for suggesting such a thing. Yet.

Wesley lifts his eyebrows in a daring move, that Vincent rolls his eyes at, ignoring him completely.

Pity.

Vincent instead focuses all of his efforts into making me come, and a quick slap against my clit is all it seems to take. I moan and wiggle, smashed between Wesley and Vincent as I fall apart. Wesley thrusts inside me hard, forcing Vincent's jaw to clench.

I look behind me to see Ronan line up to Wesley, slapping his ass hard as he grumbles into his ear. It's faint but I can just hear him.

"You trying to make me jealous? Trying to turn me into a savage?" he asks before he slams into Wesley's ass.

Wes shouts out a pained screech as Ronan does it again and again, fucking him like it's a punishment. Ronan is essentially setting the pace for all of us now. Especially when Asher drags my mouth back to his cock.

"C'mere. Give me that pretty little cock hole."

He pushes inside me, and for some odd reason, I've never felt more complete. All of us being connected in some way makes everything just feel right. It's a little difficult with six people, but eventually, we are able to find a rhythm. Dirty talk is spilling from so many mouths I don't even know what is coming from who.

"Such a good boy for me. Give me that ass."

"Fuck, you're choking the life out of my cock. You want that cum?"

"Shit, siren. You're leaking all over my lap."

Alright, well obviously that last one was Vincent, and he's not wrong. I've never been this wet in my life. I'm like a fucking fire hydrant that can't be turned off. I don't want to be either.

"Fuck, princess," Asher grits. "You and Liam are gonna make me come," he moans.

"Hell yes, we are. Be a good girl and cup his balls, babygirl," Liam says.

Somehow, I'm able to maintain my balance as I do, cradling Asher's balls as Liam litters his skin with kisses and picks up his pace. Asher moans once, twice, and by the third one, I feel his warm salty cum running down my throat. I drink him down quickly as he fucks my face and Liam follows right alongside.

"Ash! Fuck, fuck! Yes," he moans as he fills Asher.

I watch as Asher thrusts his ass back into him like he's trying to milk every last drop out of Liam, and it's so hot. Turning my head away from Asher, I look behind to see Ronan and Wesley making out, or trying to. Wesley has his head turned at an awkward angle as Ronan tries to close their distance. I see their tongues touching midair more than anything, but seeing someone like Ronan, who I never could have imagined like this, is just...perfection.

Ronan smacks Wesley's ass as he fucks him, harder and harder, until Wesley is bucking into me, moaning and groaning in Ronan's mouth. Turning my head, I face Vincent as he opens his arms to me.

"Come here, siren. Come lay with me."

I do as he says, laying my chest against his and poking my ass up as much as I can for Wesley as Vincent and I lose each other in our kiss. I feel the moment he loses it. It's the same moment that Wesley does that same wiggling motion again. Vincent's cock twitches inside me before Wesley's does the same.

Like the filling inside a very delicious and erotic sandwich, both men fall apart, Vincent's hand reaching between us as he begins slapping at my clit. I buck at the feeling, almost pushing

Wesley out of me as Vincent does it again and again, sending me falling apart on the fourth smack.

This orgasm, for some reason, is far more violent than the ones before. I practically shake the walls with my screaming. No doubt someone is going to assume I'm being murdered in here. Which will be an awkward conversation if it comes up, seeing as my mom and dad's cottage is less than five hundred feet away.

Ronan's release comes seconds after mine, his vicious groans rivaling the loudness of my own as he fucks Wesley's ass hard and deep before slumping over his back, riding out the pleasure.

When we all still, only heavy breathing can be heard for several seconds before Liam speaks up.

"I'm being serious, Vinny. I'm jealous. I'm getting a kiss one day."

We all laugh at that, except for Vincent, who flips Liam off. The rest of the night is spent with an insane amount of aftercare, cuddles all around, and the best sleep of my entire life.

Chapter Forty-Eight

Ronan

The next morning, we all sleep in, and when I mean all, I mean Skyla and Liam. Vincent, Wesley, Asher and myself agreed that just to be safe, we'd take watches. As much as I want to believe that Skyla's parents have nothing but the best intentions for her, I'm not willing to take that chance.

My eyes are burning from lack of sleep, but when I see that sleepy smile of hers, it makes it worth it to know she got a good night's rest. The only reason Liam got out of it is because Sky practically fell asleep on top of him and none of us wanted to wake her.

Fucker.

I'm still trying to process everything that we learned yesterday. The fact that Henry is not Skyla's dad....and knows about it is a wild concept. As is the fact that my brother has known the same. Though, it paints a clearer picture as to everything that occurred between them all and why Christopher went off the deep end for months after her 'death.' However sadistic and delusional he is and was, he clearly loved her, probably still does in his own way. And he had a hand in her planned murder.

There is fresh snow on the ground, we all bundle up, and we make our way over to Skyla's parents' house. Inside, we all freeze when we notice we are not alone. Jonathan and Giselle are here, as well as Rachel, but there are also three other women and one man sitting at the dining room table that has expanded to take up the entire living area. There are six empty spaces left, assumingly for us, and Skyla is the first to approach the table.

Conversation stops as they see us, and Giselle gets out of her seat, holding her close. Every hug they've shared since the shop has been like this, like two souls desperate to be near once again. I won't pretend to understand the impossible situation Giselle was put into, but I will say if it had been my daughter... I'd have fought a hell of a lot harder. I'd have taken on the whole goddamn Brethren barehanded if that's what it took. Skyla seems to have accepted it though, so I'll let it go. For now, at least.

Her father is next, giving her an equally heartfelt hug before shaking our hands. It's strange to be in a room full of witches, people we've been told are the worst kind to walk the earth. Even more strange is that there is no hostility. Well, I shouldn't say that. One of the women is watching us with a guarded sneer, along with Rachel who watches only myself, Asher, and Vincent closely. Not sure what makes Liam and Wesley so fucking special that they get a free pass.

"Skyla, this is Astrid and her wife Sariah," she says as she gestures towards the two women with smiles on their faces. Their arms are covered in tattoos, snaking up and across their chests. Astrid has both a septum piercing and a nose ring, while Sariah has gauges and long blonde hair that nearly touches the seat of her chair.

"It's so good to finally meet you." Astrid smiles.

Skyla nods with a smile of her own. "You too."

"And this is Jillie and her partner Ezra," Giselle introduces.

Jillie nods her head to Skyla but graces the rest of us with a disgusted look like she's revolted to be in the same room as us. Ezra attempts to greet us, but the sincerity doesn't make it to his eyes, and it puts us all on edge.

"Please, sit." Giselle encourages, gesturing to the sprawling display of food at the table.

Skyla takes a seat beside her mom as Liam sits beside her. Asher takes the head of the table before Wesley, me and Vincent take our seats. Vincent takes the seat beside Jillie, which is apparently over the line for her. She huffs, shaking her head as she stands.

"I'm sorry, G. I can't be here," she says as she hurries out of the house, Ezra right behind her as he shuts the door behind them.

Awkward silence descends on us for several seconds before Giselle smiles sadly.

"I'm sorry. Jillie has a gift with energies and—"

"Yours is suffocating," Rachel inserts. "Like I've said before," she says to Vincent.

He gives her a deadpanned stare that she meets before grabbing what looks like a cinnamon roll and some bacon. Jonathan shoots her a look that she conveniently ignores before he shakes his head.

"Apologies for my sister as well, I'd like to say she's normally better behaved, but—"

"I'm not," she says simply. "Especially not around Puritans," Rachel says with a wrinkle of her nose.

"Funny, we could say the same about witches," Asher throws back.

"What do you even know about us anyways?" Rachel says,

resting her elbows on the table. "You think we are a bunch of crackpots who dance around fires on full moons, brewing potions and sucking the lives out of people or something?" she mocks, shaking her head as she takes a bite of her food. "You know nothing."

"I'd like to learn," Skyla says, redirecting the conversation. "If that's alright."

Rachel softens to her like butter as she nods and smiles.

"Of course it is. What do you want to know?"

Giselle begins dishing up a plate, handing it to Skyla as she takes it gratefully. Wesley is the next to dish up, of course, followed by Liam. The rest of us wisely don't bother trying the food, a fact Giselle notices with a purse of her lips but shrugs it off.

"We talked about the jars and crystals in the shop a little. Is that all you can do? I mean, you guys don't have like...powers, do you? Is that offensive?" she asks, turning to her mom.

Giselle shakes her head softly as Jonathan speaks.

"Not at all, sweetheart. Everyone is different, some feel more drawn to one thing than another. Some are born with gifts, and others enjoy basking in the energy and positivity that can come from it all. Rachel was born with a gift of clairvoyance, like we explained last night. Occasionally, she will get visions, see things before they happen."

"Very rarely," Rachel intervenes.

"But it's happened," Jonathan defends. "It's what saved my Giselle," he says as he wraps his arm around his wife.

"Astrid here is gifted with tarot and palm readings."

Astrid nods with a smile as Skyla faces her.

"Like pulling your future and stuff? That's really cool."

"I rely heavily upon my ancestors when doing readings, but it brings me a lot of joy," Astrid says.

Jonathan nods as he faces Skyla again.

"Others like me or your mother were not born with a specific gift or proclivity towards anything, but we positively believe in the power of intention, manifestation and karma."

Liam frowns. "That doesn't sound like the witchcraft we've been taught."

"That's because you all have been taught by murderous neanderthals with their heads in the sand," Sariah says as Astrid shoves her shoulder softly.

"I'm going to guess you had family in the trials?" I ask

"My family's surname is Corey," Sariah says.

"And mine is Good," Astrid adds.

My eyebrows raise at that. Sarah Good is mentioned several times in Thomas Putnam's journal, even before the trials began. Her family was extremely impoverished and known mostly as beggars. He always seemed to have sympathy for her, though. Or at least that's how he wrote about her. Which is strange, seeing as he didn't have a sympathetic bone in his body when he had a hand in leading the largest witch hunt this country has ever seen.

"It's not just about gifts or no gifts either," Giselle says. "That's what I believed when I first met Jonathan and Rachel. As children, we were taught that witches have a great evil in them and will turn it against anyone and everyone. That's just not the case."

"No," Rachel agrees. "There are many kinds of witches that practice many kinds of practices. You can put it simplistically like light witches and dark witches. Our Coven all prefers to practice in the light, though. Myself, for example, I'm a moon witch. I'm very guided by the moon and its phases link with mine. Even my body's natural cycle syncs with the full moon, every month, without fail."

"Jillie, who left, is a nature witch, meaning she feels very closely connected to nature and all of its elements and energies," Sariah adds.

"And I identify as an eclectic witch," Astrid says. "I don't feel a draw to one certain thing. I enjoy practicing with all different elements, energies and practices. Though I prefer tarot, whereas my wife is a crystal whore," she teases.

Sariah's eyes widen comically. "They are incredible, there is literally a crystal for anything you could ever need!"

"Yes, but that doesn't mean we need two of each in our house, babe," Astrid laughs.

Shaking her head, Sariah mumbles under her breath.

"Agree to disagree."

Something plucks at my mind, a memory from a time that seems like forever ago when it was really just a few months back.

"Is that why Asher and Skyla's ceremony was rushed?" I ask.

Everyone gives me a quizzical look as I explain.

"My brother mentioned to me that there were rumors the witches were going to try something. That we needed to link Asher and Skyla on the thirty first of October because it is a sacred day for you all."

"It's not," Rachel corrects. "That's dark witches, so, disrespectfully, your brother doesn't know what the fuck he was talking about."

"Rach," Jonathan chastises, and she lifts her hands in surrender as she busies herself with her plate once more.

"It was a full moon the following day, though. I think I remember that because everyone was fucking feral at the university," I scoff, shaking my head. "Did you all have something planned? Or was that his own paranoia?"

They all share uneasy looks as Rachel speaks.

"We had heard of Skyla's return to Salem. We heard she

was engaged to a Putnam," Rachel sneers with a shake of her head. "We'd...discussed the idea of a rescue mission of sorts."

"And you were going to harness the full moon to do so?" Vincent guesses.

She nods. "Very good. We have a few other moon witches in our coven, and together, we were going to utilize it to create a protection spell, similar to the one we did for Giselle. You can't go into the lion's den without being properly guarded."

"What stopped you?" Asher asks. "Us being married...or married under the Brethren's standard," he says, causing Giselle to grimace, no doubt remembering her own ceremony. "Why did that keep you away?"

"It wasn't so much keeping us away as it was letting us know that we had a traitor among us. Someone leaked our plan to Christopher in exchange for asylum. She was young and scared, and unfortunately, we are told that she was taken captive," Giselle says.

Liam pales at her words and Asher and I share a look with him.

"What did she look like?" he rasps.

All eyes move to him, frowning as Astrid speaks.

"Long curly black hair, very petite. Soft eyes and—"

"Excuse me," Liam says, standing to his feet and stepping out the door.

Everyone stares after him in concern and I feel I have no choice but to give a brief explanation.

"We've seen her. She unfortunately did not survive."

Astrid's face falls as she nods. "We assumed not. She had so much potential, but she allowed fear to rule her."

A heavy silence falls over the room for several seconds before the door opens again, Liam stepping through, his face looking pale and clammy. Skyla gives him a concerned look, squeezing his hand as he tries to muster up a smile.

Demise

"I don't understand. Why was Christopher so hell bent on me as Asher's wife? Especially if he knew that I wasn't Henry's daughter," Skyla says.

A good point.

"You were Henry's daughter, though," Giselle says, causing a thunderous look to pass over Jonathan's face. "At least in the public eye. Don't forget, image is everything for those people. To them, you were not only his bond brother's daughter, but a miracle. You were the first daughter to be born of an elder since the trials ended."

"Why is that?" Wesley chimes in.

The witches share an uneasy look before they speak.

"We can't know for sure," Sariah says. "All we have to go off is the stories told to us from our ancestors, much like you all. One story in particular was that shortly after the Brethren was formed, the surviving families gathered, terrified for their safety and the future of those left behind in Salem. They wanted to prevent history from repeating itself."

I nod as Astrid continues.

"They couldn't focus on every single family of the townsfolk in Salem. That kind of magic would have required a Coven much larger than what they had. And at this point, they weren't even an official Coven. Just a group of people that had all survived the same horrors. A few of them weren't even witches, just unfortunate souls that got caught in the crossfire."

"To prevent history from repeating itself," Rachel says. "They needed to stop the birth of daughters, as much as they could, since men inherently believed women were more prone to witchcraft," she says with an exaggerated eye roll.

"And so, they selected the families that were to be affected. Nine of them," Giselle says.

"The Elder families," I say.

"Exactly," she nods, looking at Skyla. "You were able to be

born because you are not of Parris descent. You are half Thompson, half Proctor."

"So, witches can cast spells," Asher says. "I mean, that's what they did, right? Cast some kind of infertility spell on the Elder families and their bloodlines?"

"It's more complicated than that," Sariah says with a shake of her head. "This was hundreds of thousands of years ago. It's very possible there could be a misinterpretation in our stories."

"Or not," Rachel adds on.

"Or not," Sariah agrees with a nod of her head.

We all mull over this information for a few moments before Skyla turns to Astrid.

"Would you be able to do a tarot reading for me? If it's not too much trouble."

She smiles. "Sure. Let me go grab my cards," she says as she stands up, slipping out the door.

We all begin cleaning up breakfast when Astrid comes back in, sitting across the table from Skyla.

"Okay, I will pull six cards for you. Three cards on the top row and three cards on the bottom row. The bottom row will clarify the top row," Astrid says to Skyla as she lines up her cards on the table.

Wesley, Asher, and Vincent watch on curiously as Liam and I help clean up. I can't help but pause in my work for a moment as I watch.

Astrid flips over the first card on the top row and the first on the bottom. Her face flinches slightly but she masks it quickly as she looks at Skyla.

"The 5 of wands and the 3 of swords. Violence is in the air. A deathly battle that leads to suffering and heartbreak."

I look to Liam who gives me a look of concern before looking back to the table. Astrid flips the second top card and then the second bottom.

"The 9 of swords and the 7 of swords. You will be in a constant state of paranoia and anxiety. You will not know who to trust, and you will not know what to believe."

Fear flashes in Skyla's eyes, but she tries to smile and shrug her shoulders.

"Welcome to my life," she laughs bitterly.

A few sympathetic chuckles sound from around the room, and I can see, based on the looks being exchanged, that this reading is not going well. Though I don't know how much I buy all this...stuff, it's concerning, nonetheless.

Astrid flips over the remaining cards, inhaling deeply before making eye contact with Sky.

"Last, you have the tower card. I see destruction and ruin in your future. Your foundation will crack and fall apart. Paired with the ten of swords, I see painful final endings in your future."

"What do you mean by final endings?" Skyla whispers softly, her brows knitted together.

Astrid holds up the deck and flips it over to show the card at the back of the deck. The card is simple, one word and one image.

Death.

A heaviness settles in the room as Giselle's breath uptakes and she grips Jonathan's hand tightly. He wraps his arm around her with assurance, but nothing about his expression looks assured.

"So, I'm gonna die?" Skyla asks hollowly.

"No!" Giselle rushes. "Astrid's readings, all readings...they are subjective. The future is always changing. This is just—"

"Her future as of now," Vincent says bitterly.

No one responds as Astrid quietly begins gathering up her cards.

"I'm sorry," she whispers.

Skyla gives her a weak smile and shrugs her shoulder.

"Maybe the future will change. Or maybe it's not my death that will be coming."

Astrid gives her a smile and a nod that is in no way convincing.

"Maybe."

Jonathan moves to the living room to talk with Astrid, quietly, and I take the opportunity to speak to Giselle.

"Did you ever have feelings for my brother?" I ask, mostly out of curiosity.

She looks at me for a second, before shaking her head.

"Never. There was a time where I thought he might have been a better choice than Henry, a time where he adored me. I was quickly shown what a blessing it was that I was given to the other bond brother."

I nod.

"Have you ever had love in your heart for him?" she asks.

I open my mouth to ask her what she means when she gives me a look.

"Don't pretend to act like you're a faithful servant to the Brethren. We'd all be hanging by our necks by now if you were."

Fair point.

"I want him gone," I admit. "He's caused more hurt than one person should be allowed. The pain he has caused Skyla... the things he allowed to happen to her," I say with my eyes closed tightly. "They are unforgivable."

Giselle frowns. "Like what?"

"Has Skyla mentioned Corwin?"

"Nicholas Corwin?" she asks with her nose scrunched.

I nod. Giselle shakes her head, and I lower my voice from prying ears, i.e. Rachel, who is cocking her head just so as she not so subtly eavesdrops.

"He stalked Skyla for months. Slowly lost his mind. Her resemblance to you was so similar for him that he began to confuse the two. It started off innocent enough at first, adoring notes and gifts. He soon turned violent, almost killed Liam," I say as I gesture my head to him as he washes the dishes. "And then he took her."

"He took her?" she asks. "What do you mean?"

"He snuck into her house, spiked her favorite drink and took her in the middle of the night. Drove her up to a warehouse he'd converted into a house in Vermont. Dressed her in your clothes and..."

Her hand covers her mouth as she shakes her head. I don't feel like it's my place to discuss the details of what happened, so I don't continue.

"Where is he now?" she asks, a hardened edge to her voice.

"Dead," Vincent says as he steps into the kitchen with the remaining dish. "I made sure of it."

For the first time, the kind, soft woman I've come to know vanishes, a lethal anger to her as she tightens her jaw and nods stiffly.

"Good. What does this have to do with Christopher, though?"

I shake my head as I look up at her. "He knew. The whole time. He knew from the beginning and he didn't do a goddamn thing. We almost lost her. We almost—"

I stop myself, letting out a rough breath as fresh anger runs through my veins.

"I want him gone, and I think I have a plan."

Giselle cocks her head to the side in intrigue.

"I'm all ears."

Chapter Forty-Nine

Vincent

Skyla took over two hours to say goodbye when we had to leave the commune. Or Coven, whatever the fuck you want to call it. There were a lot of tears from her and her parents, with promises that she'd come back to visit the next weekend. They didn't exchange phone numbers for fear of it getting back to the Brethren someway or somehow, and I held Skyla as she cried the entire way home.

I don't think it was all tears from sadness. I think she feels relief. Relief that Henry isn't actually her father, that her real father is a kind man. But the biggest relief is that she got to actually meet her mother. She got the chance to hug her, memorize her scent, her face. She basically got her back from the dead. I'd do anything to have that feeling for Nate so I can recognize how special it is.

When we got home, Liam went to dinner with Maryia's parents while the rest of us ordered in and promptly passed the fuck out. Well, they all did. I was asleep for two hours when my phone went off.

The message was a little odd but simple.

Demise

Unknown: 58012 Barclay AVE New York City, New York
Stand by for target info.

I don't think I've ever been sent on a job where I wasn't given all the details ahead of time, but it's not like I can ignore it, and I sure as shit can't text back for clarification. So, I made my way to New York and am currently standing in the shadows of some abandoned warehouse.

The message didn't even tell me what the preferred outcome is, so I brought a few of my favorite toys for torture and for eliminating, just in case. The soft snick of a door from the second level catches my attention, my head whipping to the side as it does. I look around in the darkness, waiting for the next sound or movement, but nothing comes.

That is, until a throwing star is sailing across the room, embedding itself right beside my head. I duck quickly, rolling out of the way before I'm on my feet again when another star comes, and another, all missing by centimeters. I'm armed and at the ready, but my assailant is playing hide and seek in the darkness, and I know better than to walk into his established territory.

I hear the faint click of a safety and sprint in another direction as a bullet whizzes through the room before another. The gun clearly has a silencer on it, but it's still loud enough in this echoing warehouse.

A deranged giggle comes from the other side of the room as someone makes their way into the light.

"Graves?" I ask.

Zayden Graves nods his head, his face covered in his signature skeleton mask, but I can hear the smile in his voice.

"You aren't too bad, Griggs. Better than your parents were, I'd say."

"Thanks," I spit. "Any particular reason you're trying to kill me?" I ask as he steps up closer, swinging a knife at my gut.

I jump backwards, landing a hit across his face before he delivers one to mine. If he wanted me dead, he could just shoot me or plunge his knife into my neck or some shit. He's toying with me, playing a game. I enjoy the hunt as well from time to time, but to this sick fuck, it's the most exciting game he's ever played. Every target, every time. Fuck, am I the target? Or are we just after the same one again?

His knife comes swinging through the air, catching my arm and slicing it open. I grit my teeth, grunting through the pain as he swings another, getting the opposite arm. Dropping to the floor, I kick out my leg and sweep him to the ground. He goes down hard and begins laughing like a kid at the carnival before touching his head and finding blood on his hand.

"Nice one! You're a tough little fucker. Want a job?" he laughs.

I huff at him as he jumps to his feet, blood running down the side of his face as he swipes me with his knife again. This time, he catches me in the stomach, stabbing all the way into me. All the breath is sucked from my lungs as I gasp and stumble, falling to the ground. He tsks, as he circles me like a shark, the pool of blood beneath me growing by the second.

"Vincent Griggs," he sighs with a shake of his head. "Don't you remember the first rule of mercenary work? Don't hesitate. Strike fast and strike first. I was down, you almost had me!" he gushes like we're recapping a video game.

"I'm not gonna lie, I was kinda bummed when I heard you were my target. You've been fun to fuck with over the years, and you've got a lot of raw talent. A little coaching up and you could be a fucking animal."

My head begins to feel dizzy as my vision fades. I force myself to stay alert, latching onto a piece of his words.

Demise

"I'm your target?" I rasp. "Who took the hit out?"

He shrugs. "You know as well as I, we just take orders."

"And you know as well as I that you're a nosy fuck," I throw back.

Zayden laughs hysterically, throwing his head up to the ceiling before looking back at me, that creepy as fuck mask staring down at me.

"It was your boss," he says, his smirk creeping into his voice. "Must have done something to piss him off. Then again, mine gets pissy if I don't answer on the first ring. Maybe you don't deserve it, but business is business." He shrugs.

I attempt to lift myself, to run, defend, attack. Anything. I can't, though. My body is getting weaker by the second from the two gashes on my arms and the gaping one I'm trying to hold in my stomach, I don't have long, and we both know it.

"Nice knowing you, Griggs," he says as he stands over me, lifting his knife as I throw up my hands.

"Please, Zayden," I beg. I can't even believe I'm begging. I never thought I'd go out begging, but I have to try. I have something worth begging to live for now. "I got a girl," I wheeze. "She's everything. Please. I can't leave, not when she'll be alone in this world."

Because I don't give a fuck about the other guys. My siren will never be as protected as she is with me.

Something in my words seems to stir at Zayden, at least for a second. Then, any sympathy or window I was planning to play off disappears as he raises his arm once more and plunges his knife into me. My mouth opens, a squelching noise escaping me as Zayden twists the knife deeper and lowers his head to mine.

"Say hi to your mom and dad for me, kid."

With that, he rips the knife out of me and stares as a rush of blood escapes my upper abdomen. Pain like I've never felt lances through me until I don't feel anything at all. A biting cold sets in, and I feel my body begin to convulse in shock before I go completely still. All I can see is Skyla's face. She's smiling at me, holding her hand out for me.

    I try to take it, but I can't lift my hand, and she frowns before walking away. I try to call out to her, to beg her to wait for me, but she doesn't. She vanishes into thin air as she walks away. A numbness settles over my body before I slip away.

    I love you, Siren. I always will. Even in death.

Chapter Fifty

Skyla

The next morning, I woke up to find my left side empty. I fell asleep with Asher and Vincent, but woke up with only Asher. Looking to the bedside table, I see a quick hand scribbled note.

Got a job. Be back soon. Love you, Siren.

I smile at that, setting it back down as I snuggle onto Asher's chest, pressing kisses up and down his neck. He hums in his sleep before waking up fully, his eyes landing on me as they flutter open.

"Good morning, princess." He smiles as he runs his fingers through my hair.

"Hi." I grin.

"What do you want? You're looking at me like you want something." Asher laughs, his morning voice unbelievably sexy.

"Pancakes?" I ask.

"Pancakes?" he gruffs. "Ronan is the cook, have him make them."

"But it's so much better when you make them because you hate cooking. Pleaseee," I beg with a pouty lip.

Asher groans, capturing my lip between his teeth before biting hard. I yelp and he smirks before pulling himself out of bed. He's just in his boxers as he steps out of the room and I slip on a baggy shirt before following after him.

When we get down there, Wesley and Ronan are already drinking their morning coffee, both of them lighting up when I step into the room. I give them each a kiss and perch myself into Ronan's lap.

"Asher is making us pancakes."

"Since when?" Wesley laughs.

"Since the princess asked for them," Asher grumbles as he gets out the pancake mix and a bowl.

Liam sleepily makes his way down the stairs, wearing nothing but a pair of grey sweatpants that are doing wonderful things for him. He makes his way to me first, cupping my jaw as he brings his lips to mine before moving to Asher. Liam wraps his arms around his waist, resting his head on Asher's back.

"Whatcha making me?" Liam asks.

"Nothing. I'm making the princess pancakes. You all are on your own."

Liam frowns. "What if I give you an extra-long blow job in the shower?"

Asher perks up at that, looking back at him before the rest of us.

"Alright, Liam and the princess are getting pancakes, but the rest of you are on your own."

"Shit, I'll suck your cock for some pancakes." Wesley laughs.

"Don't lie," I say. "You'd do it for free."

He throws his head back laughing, shooting me a wink as Ronan grumbles.

"Can we not talk about sucking my nephew's cock? I'm still trying to wake up."

Demise

"Don't be upset, daddy," Liam teases. "How about I suck you off while Wesley sucks Asher. We'll trade boyfriends!"

"Wesley and I are NOT together," Ronan fires back.

"No, but Liam does have a hell of a mouth on him. Might want to take him up on this deal, Ro," Wesley says, giving Liam a quick wink.

God, we are all so horny and disgusting, and I love every second of it.

Ronan is literally saved by the bell as his phone rings. He doesn't even look at the screen before he's standing, moving me off his lap as he walks out of the room to take it. Wesley, though, doesn't seem to be done with this joke. Or maybe he's not joking.

As Asher begins pouring the pancake mix, Wesley saunters across the kitchen, leaning his hip against the counter beside Asher.

"What?" Asher asks as he looks at him.

"Just admiring," Wesley says as his eyes run over Asher's bare torso.

"Yeah, well, keep your admiring to yourself. I'm set on partners."

Wesley glances to me and Liam before back to Asher, scooting in a few inches.

"I'm gonna take a page out of Skyla's book and say, why choose?"

"Hey! That makes me sound like a whore," I throw out.

"You're not, little one. You just know what you like, and you go for it."

I shrug. That I can live with.

"Come on, Ash. You can't tell me you don't think about that night in that shack?" Wesley goads as he leans in closer and closer.

Asher watches him, his gaze bouncing from Wesley's mouth to his eyes. But he doesn't pull away.

"You can't tell me you didn't love my lips on yours, my tongue down your throat. You melted into me like putty."

"It was a heat of the moment thing," Asher says tightly.

Surprising me, Wesley reaches down, slipping his hand inside Asher's boxers and gripping his cock. My mouth drops as Wesley pushes his boxers down, revealing Asher's hard cock. Wesley drags his hand up and down it slowly as Asher's eyes shutter close. I can tell he's trying everything he can to fight it but when Wesley chuckles, his eyes flutter open.

"You remember how good I sucked your cock? Liam's too? Both of your cocks in my mouth, grinding together."

"Oh, I remember," Liam practically moans.

Asher still stays strong in his resolve, but when Wesley's mouth brushes against his, he loses it. Asher really is the one to initiate the kiss, his hips thrusting, forcing Wesley to stroke him as Wesley stays still, smiling against him like he's tasting victory. I'm not sure what game he's playing but I'm all for watching the prize go down right here and now. Screw the pancakes.

"Fuck," Asher moans into Wesley's mouth as he reaches for his pants, his hand slipping inside when Ronan steps back into the room.

He looks at Wesley and Asher and freezes. I expect him to be mad. He's been very clear that he's quite protective of Wesley, especially with Asher, but I don't see anger in his eyes.

"Knock it off," he says in a tone that grabs everyone's attention.

Wesley and Asher break apart, releasing each other as they tuck themselves away while Ronan's eyes come to me. They are hardened but also full of sadness. Coming to stand beside me, he crouches down until he's eye level with me before taking my hands in his.

"Baby..." he lets out a strangled breath as he shakes his head. "There was an incident."

Instantly, my stomach turns. Worst case scenarios running through my head. Did someone discover my parents? Steph? Oh my God. Is Maggie okay?

"I just got a call. A body was found at one of the Walcott's old storage warehouses in New York."

I stare at him, doing my best to hold my anxiety at bay as he fumbles with his words.

"Who?" Asher asks.

Ronan winces, staring at the floor.

"Who was it?" Wesley asks.

Still, Ronan just shakes his head.

"Who Ronan?" I urge, my entire body beginning to shake.

His eyes come to me, so much sympathy, so much pain in them as he delivers five of the most horrible words I have ever, and will ever hear in my life.

"It was Vincent...he's gone."

My body goes numb as I stare at him, my brain struggling to make sense of what my ears just heard. He's gone? Gone where?

"Christ," Liam chokes as Asher wraps his arm around him and Wesley runs his fingers through his hair with a sigh.

"Where did he go?" I ask, because I must be misunderstanding.

Ronan's lips flatten as he speaks.

"He's gone, baby. He died."

I shake my head, pulling away from Ronan.

"No. No," I say as I stand up and begin pacing. Ronan raises to his feet as he slowly approaches me.

I hold out my hand, keeping him back as I continue furiously shaking my head.

"No! NO! No, no, no," I scream before my shouts turn to sobs.

Ronan wraps his arms around me, and I fight against him. Beating on his chest, I attempt to push him away, but he only holds me closer.

"NO! You don't say that to me! You don't tell me this kind of shit! No!" I sob, my gut wrenching as I scream.

"I'm so sorry, baby. I'm so sorry," Ronan says, his voice breaking as he speaks into my ear.

"NOO! No, not Vincent. No. He can't be gone. He can't. He—" my voice breaks off into wails of despair as my fight gives out along with my legs.

I collapse to the floor, curling myself into a ball and Ronan follows me, dragging me into his lap as I feel my heart physically breaking. Pain like this, so deep, so visceral...it's consuming me whole.

"No," I whisper.

I stand there numbly. The rain is pouring down on us, almost turning to snow, but I don't feel it. I don't feel anything as I stand in the cemetery on campus, staring at the gravestone beside his parents.

Vincent Griggs
March 26th, 2003 – February 1st, 2025
A faithful servant to a holy cause

Demise

. . .

Yeah, a real holy cause. He went out on a job for the Brethren and ended up losing his life instead. For what? The Brethren is fucking nothing but a group of murderers. A group of bullies. A group of vindictive self-serving piece of shits.

I've seen Christopher smirk seven times now, I've counted. I know he was behind it. I can feel it in my bones. I don't know what I can do about it, but I know that I want him gone. Decimated. Buried beneath the dirt like my Vincent.

My heart breaks at just that thought. There is no way this is actually real. No way he's buried beneath my feet right now. There is no way I'll never see those silver eyes again. That I'll never hear him call me siren. That I'll never...

A sob rips through me as Asher holds me closer, hushing me softly.

"I know you're hurting, princess, but people are staring. We have to keep it together. Can you be my brave girl?" he whispers.

"What's the point?" I choke out, attempting to keep my voice soft. "He's gone. Nothing more can happen to him!"

"But it can to you. He lived and breathed you. If he knew that his death caused yours, he'd never forgive himself."

I want to tell him it doesn't matter. That he'd never know because he's not here, he's not anywhere. Ashes to ashes, dust to dust. I obviously grew up religious, but I don't feel so religious right now. I begged God to bring him back to me. For five days, I've begged and pleaded and bartered, yet here we are, standing over the grave of one of the loves of my life. A piece of me is forever gone, my heart forever shattered.

Once the priest is done talking about the afterlife and a whole bunch of other shit that doesn't matter, everyone disperses as Andrew Hutchinson approaches me. He gives me a sympathetic look.

"I'm sorry for your loss. I know you were close to him."

I don't respond and Andrew gives a quick sideways look before pulling me in for a hug. Asher goes to rip him away as he hastily whispers into my ear.

"Sweep your house. They planted more bugs."

"Get the fuck off my wife!" Asher snaps, and I push him off Andrew as I lean in closer.

"What do you mean?" I ask.

He shakes his head, making eye contact with his dad as he begins walking away.

"Sweep the place," he says before he's gone with the rest of the crowd.

"What did he say?" Ronan asks.

"He said to sweep the house. That they planted more bugs."

Wesley screws up his face. "Impossible. If anyone were going to do it, it would have been me."

"Unless Christopher doesn't trust you anymore," Asher points out.

Wesley frowns at that as Ronan nods.

"Let's go check."

Sure enough. Five new cameras and thirteen more listening devices were scattered around the house. Wesley and Ronan found and destroyed each of them as Asher began raging while I sat in Liam's arms numbly on the couch.

"WHO THE FUCK DOES HE THINK HE IS?" Asher

fumes. "He thinks that he can just bug my goddamn house whenever he feels like it? What the fuck is he hoping to find?"

"Anything he can use against you and Skyla. Just like he does with everyone."

"I don't give a fuck! I'm done. Maybe you had it right in the first place, Ronan. Let's just go in there, guns blazing. His security can't stop us all. One of us is bound to shoot the son of a bitch."

"So that Skyla can lose two boyfriends in one week? Maybe all of them? Use your fucking head, Ash," Liam scolds.

He flips around to face Liam, ready to give him hell when he looks at me. I feel my face frozen in place, a blank look, but I also feel silent streams of tears pouring down my face. It's an odd thing, to feel so much pain yet be so numb to it all.

Silently, I stand up and make my way to my room. No one asks me where I'm going, no one tries to follow me. I just climb the stairs, push inside my room and collapse on the bed.

God, if you're there, if you're listening. please wake me up from this nightmare.

Chapter Fifty-One

Skyla

I wake to the feeling of a body curling around me. Clearly, one of the guys decided I didn't need to be alone tonight. Sorry to inform you, you're wrong.

"Please leave me alone," I murmur as I turn away from him.

He holds me closer, running his fingers through my hair.

"You know I could never leave you alone, siren."

My eyes fly open at that nickname, and I scramble for the light, my eyes landing on Vincent. I can't tell if I'm dreaming, if this is all some weird fantasy realism dream or if he's actually here. I don't care what it is, I throw myself into him, wrapping my arms around him and swearing that I'll never let him go.

"Is it you?" I sob. "Are you really here?"

"I'm here, siren. I'll always be here."

I cry out, screaming for the guys.

"ASHER! RONAN! LIAM! WES! GET IN HERE!"

Feet begin thundering through the house as they burst into the room one by one. Each of them blanch with shock, their eyes round as Liam speaks.

"What the fuck? Vinny?"

Liam practically jumps onto the bed, hugging Vincent tight. He allows it for a second or two before shoving Liam to the ground. He lands with a hard thunk but pops up to his feet like nothing ever happened.

"What the fuck is going on?" Ronan asks.

I nod, wanting to know myself, as Vincent looks down at me before up to them.

"I made a deal with the devil."

We all frown at that, but I bury myself into Vincent. I don't care what he had to do. I can't believe he's here, in the flesh, with me. Nuzzling my head into his chest, his arms tighten around me as he speaks.

"I was sent on a job in New York."

"We know," Wesley says.

"And when I got there, I was met with another mercenary. One of the best in the world," Vincent says with a shake of his head.

"Him and his brother are legends. My parents would run into him from time to time, he's lethal, and apparently, his target was me."

My heart seizes at that as he lifts up his sleeves, showing two angry red scars that look like they are trying to heal, but have a long road of recovery. Then he lifts his shirt, showing two stab wounds on his stomach that look to be about the same in the healing process.

"I was bleeding out, fading in and out between life and death and he changed his mind."

"What do you mean he changed his mind?" Asher asks with a disbelieving face.

Vincent's eyes bore into mine as he speaks.

"I begged. I told him I had a girl I needed to be with, needed to protect. When I was fading, I told him I'd do anything. He took me up on it. Now, I officially owe him one."

"One what?" Ronan asks.

"One anything," Vincent says ominously, though to be honest, I don't care. I'm just relieved he's here with me.

"He called a mob doc he knew, had him patch me up, and I laid low in New York for a few days until I was healed enough to leave."

"What about the body that was found?" Ronan asks.

Vincent flicks his gaze to him and shrugs.

"Zayden apparently grabbed a security guard and set him on fire, charred the shit out of the body so they wouldn't know it wasn't me, and left it at that. Everyone knows he's unhinged for the fun of it, no one bothered to question it."

"Who ordered this hit on you?" Wesley asks.

A thunderous look passes over Vincent's face.

"Christopher Putnam."

I fucking knew it.

Angered looks pass in the room before Vincent speaks again.

"I don't give a flying fuck what it takes, I'm killing him. I'm killing all of them. They almost took me away from my siren. They all have to burn."

The room is tense with silence for several seconds before Ronan speaks.

"Agreed."

The drive to New Hampshire feels faster this time. Maybe because I'm just eager to see my mom, anxious of what Ronan has planned, or so fucking grateful that I'm currently in

Vincent's arms. He presses a kiss to the side of my head, and I plaster myself against him.

I've hardly let him out of my sight. He's lucky if I allow him to go to the bathroom alone. I'm terrified that if I leave him alone for too long, he'll disappear again. There was a debate about if we should leave him at the house while we go. I mean, everyone except for us believes him to be dead. With all the cameras in and around the house disabled, loading up in the garage, and the tinted out windows on the car, we decided it was safe enough. Oh, and I refused to leave without him.

When we turn off the highway and drive down the dirt road to the witches' houses, nerves begin churning inside me. Ronan hasn't shared all the details of the plan with me, and maybe it's for a good reason. I'm not sure knowing would put me at ease. At the end of the day, we can't go on like this. Because of this world, because of this society, I almost lost Liam, I almost lost Vincent. Who am I going to lose next? What if it isn't an almost next time? What if it's forever?

As soon as we park, my mom and dad begin making their way towards us, smiles on their faces. Because we don't have each other's phone numbers, it's not like I could tell them I absolutely was not planning on coming today like originally discussed. I was grieving, dying on the inside and had no plans to leave my depressive hole for an undetermined amount of time. Things change, this time for the better.

"There she is." My mom smiles warmly, wrapping her arms around me as she holds me tight.

That familiar scent of vanilla and coconut fill my senses, and I smile against her hold when she releases me, placing a loving kiss to my cheek while my dad stands there.

"We've missed you, Sky," he says, almost nervously.

I wonder if he feels uncomfortable because, although he was

there for the first three years of my life, I was never told about him. My memories don't really start coming in until four, almost five, so the only thing I really know about this man is what they have told me. Same could be said about my mom, though, just from Steph.

Regardless, that isn't the way it feels. From the moment I saw him I knew in my gut that there was something tethering us together. So, I close the distance and wrap my arms around him. He holds me, rocking us from side to side as he smiles.

"I've missed you guys too."

When we pull apart, I see my mom hugging each of the guys. Even prickly Vincent gives her a hug that melts my heart.

"Thank you all for making the drive, I really appreciate it." She smiles.

"Of course, Mrs..." Ronan trails off like he's unsure. Should he use Parris, Thompson or Proctor?

She smiles warmly, no offense taken as she nods. "Just call me Giselle, or G."

Ronan nods and Liam shoots her a dorky finger gun.

"You got it, G!"

Asher scoffs, shaking his head as Liam giggles and I can't help but laugh along. He is so ridiculous.

"Come on, we just made lunch," my dad says as he ushers us into the house.

We all file in, everyone taking a seat around the room. I make sure to practically plaster myself to Vincent and it doesn't escape the notice of my mom. She turns to us, smiling as she speaks.

"So, what's new?"

We're all silent for several seconds before Ronan begins.

"Giselle, do you remember what you and I discussed last time we were here?"

Her smile slips, a seriousness taking over her face as she nods.

Demise

"It's time," Ronan says with a stiff nod.

A conflicted look plays across her face as she glances up to my dad. Their hands intertwine as they both nod.

"We're in," my dad says.

Within thirty minutes, my parents' house is practically bursting at the seams. Every single witch part of their Coven is inside, all circling around me. I catch Astrid's eye as she smiles at me, Sariah giving me an encouraging nod. My gaze swings around, attempting to find my guys as they begin.

"Wait—" I say.

My mom looks at me in concern as I speak.

"Them too. I want them protected. Please. I can't risk losing them."

Rachel gets a conflicted look before she speaks for everyone.

"We can make that work."

I hear some grumblings of disapproval as my guys slowly slip inside the formed circle.

"You know this is all a load of shit, right?" Asher whispers into my ear.

"Hey!" Rachel says as she takes a cup, pouring it over his head.

"What the fuck!" Asher snaps while the room erupts into laughter. "What the fuck was that for?"

"To cleanse you and that nasty energy."

Rachel grabs another cup and dips her fingers inside it, running it along each of the guy's foreheads before my own. She draws patterns against our chests with the water, or maybe

I should say liquid since I'm not exactly sure what's in it, before she sets the cup down and nods.

Someone hands her a bundle of what I've come to know as sage before she lights it and begins running it over us and the rest of the room. I see Jillie line up over thirty white pillar candles, encasing us in the circle as she begins lighting each one.

She steps back into her position, and one by one, every person surrounding us lifts their palms to the sky by their sides before turning their right down. One by one, they all stack their hands together, flat palms pressed against the person beside them as they close their eyes and speak as one.

"Powers of the night, powers of the day, I summon thee. To cast your protection upon thee. By the light that surrounds me, be safe, be free. For powers of north, south, east and west, may they be ever blessed."

Suddenly, the flames of the candles flicker for a moment before burning brighter. It startles me, and Vincent tightens his hold on me instinctually. I look to Asher on my other side, as they both furrow their brows, and look around curiously as the witches continue.

"In shadows that linger, stand strong and bright. Protected and guided, I embrace the light. Negative forces, you cannot draw near. With this shield of protection, we cast out all fear."

With their final word, the candles dim, the flame back to their original height and brightness.

"What the fuck?" Liam whispers as Rachel steps forward with a handful of necklaces with protection jars on the bottom.

Each guy bows his head to her, a form of respect and acceptance as she places the protection necklace around each of them before coming to me. Mine looks a little different than theirs, with a large chunk of what I'm assuming is obsidian.

"Why is mine different?" I ask as she places my necklace around me.

"Because you're my niece and I love you more," she smiles.

"Like you love any of us," Asher scoffs.

Rachel casts him a look.

"I was warming up to you, Putnam, but then you go and do something stupid like speak."

Chuckles echo through the room as Asher rolls his eyes. My mom steps forward, holding my hands in hers. I don't have to be an expert on reading people like the witches are to know that she's scared.

"Are you sure this is the right thing to do? The right move?" she asks me before her eyes come to Ronan.

He nods and so do I. "We can't live like this anymore, we just...can't," I say.

My mom hesitantly nods before looking around the room. Several people begin leaving but not everyone. As I look around the room, I count the remaining people without counting my parents or Rachel. Eight.

As one, including Rachel, they all pick up something wrapped in cloth as they come to stand in front of us.

Everyone gets two cloths except for Liam, who gets one, and me who gets none. I frown as Asher unwraps one of his before Rachel's hand comes out, stopping him.

"Don't touch them yet. Wait until that night."

He holds it by the cloth and peeks inside.

"It's a dagger," he says as all the guys look down at their hands.

"We have anointed them with moon water. With tomorrow being a full moon, it will help," Rachel says.

"Help?" Wesley clarifies.

Rachel glances at the rest of the witches, all nodding in agreement.

"A wrong demands to be righted," Astrid says, her eyes on me. "A debt must be repaid. The evil that consumed those families must be cleansed from this world. Then and only then, do I see peace."

I nod stiffly, understanding what they are saying.

One by one, each witch in the room steps forward, resting her hand on their dagger that they gave the guys. They close their eyes, muttering something to themselves before opening their eyes and speaking.

"Bishop," one woman says as she touches the dagger in Ronan's left hand as Astrid touches the right.

"Good."

One by one, they all make it down the line in order.

"Corey."

"Nurse."

"Howe."

"Martin."

"Wildes."

Finally, Rachel is the last to speak, her eyes on Asher's, something heavy in her eyes as she speaks.

"Proctor."

I physically feel a shift in the room, though I don't know how to explain it other than just that. Pulling away from the guys, the witches nod their heads, almost in respect before leaving the house. Even Rachel leaves until it's just us and my parents.

"Do you think this will work? You will be able to convince the others?" my dad asks.

They all nod.

"We will make them see reason," Asher says stiffly.

My mother makes a concerned look as she addresses Asher.

"Don't underestimate them, especially him. You...you have no idea what he's capable of."

Demise

"With all due respect, Giselle, I've been under the man's thumb since birth. I know exactly what he's capable of."

She gives him a sympathetic frown and nods, cupping his cheek softly.

"Keep my girl safe."

"On my life," Asher swears.

"And mine," Liam adds on.

"And mine," Vincent says.

"Mine," Wesley agrees.

Ronan is the last to speak, all eyes on him as he gives a strong nod.

"Mine."

Chapter Fifty-Two

Asher

We went straight home last night despite how much Giselle and Jonathan wanted us to stay the night. I think they just wanted one more night with Skyla, should the worst happen. We weren't going to let that happen, though, not for anything.

Tonight is Hutchinson's initiation, and it gives us the perfect opening to do what needs to be done. First, we have to convince the others.

I'm standing in my kitchen, Skyla and Liam snuggling on the couch, when a knock comes from the door. They move apart an appropriate distance when Andrew Hutchinson steps inside, followed by Dane Lewis and Jeremy Stroughton. Lewis limps, braces holding his legs straight as he does his best to stand tall. Shit. Vincent really did fuck his life up. Good. Piece of shit should have died, in my opinion. Maybe he will by the end of this conversation.

"What the fuck is this?" Stroughton snarls.

"A discussion, welcome. The most important part is you shut the fuck up," I say before looking to the others.

Demise

My eyes roam over them in a calculated way. It's a move I've seen my father make a million times. It puts your opponent on edge, forces them to pay attention, and it seems to work for me now.

"The Brethren must fall. The Elders must be eliminated."

Concerned looks move through the room as Hutchinson, Stroughton and Lewis all glance at each other, while we all stare at them with a hardened certainty.

"What the fuck are you talking about?" Stroughton demands as I hold eye contact with him.

"I'm talking about starting over. Burning this society to the ground and building a new one in its ashes. I think we are all brainwashed enough to actually believe that there are advantages and benefits to being a part of the Brethren," I say as the three stooges nod.

"I think we can also all agree, our ancestors were evil, our heads of the family are evil, and in order to truly rebuild, we have to start from scratch."

"Meaning?" Hutchinson asks nervously.

"Meaning we are going to kill them all, tonight," Vincent says sharply.

Hutchinson's eyes bulge at that and I watch as he takes a nervous step backwards. I make eye contact with Wesley, who nods and stands behind Hutchinson, keeping him in place as I continue.

"Andrew, let's not pretend that your dad doesn't embezzle millions from the Brethren a year. It's only a matter of time before my father finds out and slaughters your whole family."

His face blanches as he looks to the ground.

Wesley found out that piece of information a few weeks ago, and we've been sitting on it for the opportune moment. Guess what, it's here.

"Stroughton, your father beats your entire family black and

blue and has been assaulting your half-sister since her seventh birthday, has he not?" I ask.

Jeremy has the decency to wince, throwing his eyes to the ground as he gives me a terse nod.

"Lewis," I say, his eyes filled with far too much hate. He's going to be our wild card for sure.

"Your uncle, the one who took over when your father passed away," I say, sharing a brief look with Vincent and Ronan. "Tell me you wouldn't love to gut him like a pig."

We didn't actually have anything on the Lewis family, but they are hotheads. They feel their emotions in sharp peaks, and I can tell by one look at Dane, that I hit the nail on the head.

"Then what?" Dane asks. "We become the new Elders? You rule us like your father?" he scoffs.

"I'm nothing like my father," I say, "But yes. We will rebuild, not with a centered focus on our past but our future. We will stop the abusive fucking rituals, the degrading hierarchy, and we will treat this as it always should have been. A brotherhood."

Dane seems surprisingly pleased with that, though none of them speak.

"If we say no, you're going to kill us, aren't you?" Andrew asks.

I lift a brow to him. "Is that an actual question, or hypothetical, Hutchinson?"

He looks ready to shit his fucking pants as his eyes drop to the ground.

"Hypothetical."

Shit, maybe he's the wild card.

"Andrew," Liam says, appealing to him the way only Liam could. "You haven't been inducted yet, none of you have," he says as he runs his eyes over the other two. "You don't know what it's like...what they make you do." Liam winces with a

Demise

shake of his head. "If we don't stop them tonight, you will, and you'll never be the same. Trust me."

My heart twinges at his words. I hate that his induction has affected him so much. He tries not to let anyone see it, but his spark has dimmed. His joy, muffled. He's not the same Liam, and I'm terrified he never will be again. That is why we have to stop them, that is why we have to take a stand.

"I'm in," Lewis says.

"Me too," Stroughton agrees.

All eyes come to Andrew, a fearful look in his eyes as he glances around the room. His gaze falls on Skyla, and she gives him a compassionate yet earnest nod that has him nodding his agreement.

"Me too."

After the last three legacies agreed, we weren't stupid enough to just let them go. The temptation to burn us all and save their own asses would be too great. So, each got an escort to the tunnels.

Ronan went with Andrew, like he would have anyways for his induction night. Wesley went with Stroughton and Liam went with Lewis. I'm double checking that I have everything when Skyla steps into the room, Vincent right behind her.

"I'm scared," she admits.

I stop what I'm doing and hold her in my arms. I don't want to tell her that I am too. That I can feel that we are on the verge of...something. I just can't tell if it's our demise or our salvation.

"Don't be," I say. "We will be fine. Vincent will be with you the entire time, and if you've changed your mind, you don't have to come. Fuck, I'd rather you didn't," I say with a rough chuckle that is not at all humorous.

She frowns. "I have to be there, Asher. This is my life, too. The Brethren took everything from me, they'll continue to. My fathe— Henry," she corrects. "He needs to suffer, and I won't miss it for the world."

I sigh, knowing we've already been round and round with this decision before. I was on the losing end of the argument, unfortunately. Nodding, I grip the back of her neck, pressing my lips to hers as I do.

"I'll see you soon, and this will be all over, okay?" I say.

She nods her head. "Promise me we will all make it out of this. That when we do, we'll go back to the cabin in New Hampshire. That we'll stay there for two weeks at least just the six of us?"

It's a promise I'm not sure I'll be able to keep, but I make it anyways, because how fucking perfect would it be if I could?

"I promise," I say.

Her shoulders seem to lighten at that, a true smile spreading across her face.

"I love you," she says.

"I love you more, princess." My eyes move to Vincent. "Keep her safe."

"Always."

I pause on my words for a moment before I drop our eye contact.

"Uhm, keep yourself safe too. Don't go dying again."

Vincent lifts a single eyebrow, almost in amusement, if I thought the guy was ever capable of the emotion.

"Will do."

Nodding to myself, I grab the bag I packed and head for my car, throwing it into the passenger seat before taking off for the university. When I get there, I park as usual, slip on my robe as usual, and walk in as usual. What isn't usual is the dagger I have strapped to my leg. The one that's been specially selected for my father. Maybe I should be feeling regret or something akin to sadness, but I don't. All I feel is anger, vengeance and a need to set things right. For everyone.

Because Lewis and Stroughton still technically aren't inducted, they won't be expected to be at the ceremony. And Vincent is considered dead to the Brethren, they definitely won't be expecting him.

The plan is to have Wesley wait with them outside the tunnels until Vincent and Skyla arrive, which should be, if we timed it right, only minutes after me. We didn't want us all to arrive at once, should anyone see and ask questions.

So, I move through the church, opening the secret door and making my way through the tunnels like everything is normal. Like it's any other induction night. Except it isn't.

I check in, smearing my bloodied fingerprint for the last time. Once I'm let through, I step into the room where the table is in the center of the room. Odd seeing as mine and Liam's ceremony was an empty room. Maybe they don't have something as...physical planned for Andrew.

I know tonight will be a struggle for him. I know he loves his father despite the shitty things he does. We can't go forth like this any longer, though. The Brethren has to be completely gutted. It's the only way to ensure old practices and old ideals don't continue.

My father meets my eyes, and I give him a respectful nod as I take my place behind him. It's the last goddamn time I'll be giving him a respectful anything. I can guarantee that. Carefully, I assess all who are in attendance tonight.

Wesley told us that Christopher did not expect his attendance for these matters. I'm unsure why, though, seeing as all Elders are required to attend despite whether or not they are the seat holder for the family. His father is currently on his phone, texting rapidly before tucking it away discreetly. Not sure my dad would like to know he snuck a phone in here. I don't know much about Matthew Preston, I don't need to know his background to know he is just like the rest of them.

The Ingersoll family seat holder is staring up at the ceiling, a bored look on his face. Vincent told me the other day he thinks he had a part to play in Nathan's father's death. He's already double claimed him tonight, and I had no problem agreeing to that.

The only extra Elder besides Ronan, me, and any of the guys is Charles Stroughton. He's Will's younger brother and completely uninterested in the Brethren. Kinda feel bad to kill him, he could be as disgusted with the Brethren as we are. But he's been alive for twenty years longer than us. He had so many chances to do what we are tonight, and he didn't, which makes him as guilty as the rest of them.

Liam slips in at the last minute, keeping his eyes on the ground as he slips behind his father. He gives me an encouraging nod and I do the same.

The door opens again and the man at the door allows Ronan and Andrew to walk in. Andrew is physically shaking as my father stands from his seat at the table. Glancing down at my watch, I notice that we are exactly on time. My eyes meet Ronan's, and he gives me the slightest of nods, confirming that Wesley, Sky, Vincent and the others are all inside the tunnels.

Perfect.

"Welcome, brother," my dad smiles at Andrew. "Tonight, you will be graduating from Legacy to Elder. Are you prepared?"

Andrew stutters, his shaking becoming more intense.

"Y-yes," he says.

Demise

I can see my father's smile fall for a moment before he nods.

"Andrew Hutchinson, do you swear your allegiance to the Brethren? Do you swear to honor our ways, fulfill our practices and protect our secrets?"

"I-I sw-wear," he stutters.

"Do you swear to slay our enemy when given the chance and keep our people safe?" my father continues.

"I swear," Andrew says, blowing out a ragged breath.

"Do you swear to enforce all law whenever deemed necessary, no matter the task?"

"I sw—"

A commotion sounds from outside the room, my eyes meeting Ronan's and Liam's before I nod. Pulling the dagger from under my robe, I jab it into my father's back.

"Sit down!" I snarl.

Members all around look at us in shock as Liam does the same, holding his dagger to his father's back.

"What is the meaning of this?" William Walcott fumes.

"Shut the fuck up!" Liam snaps.

Andrew moves, taking his position behind his father as Ronan stands behind Henry Parris. We all know that if someone was going to try something, it would be that slimy bastard.

"What the hell do you think you're doing, hm?" my father taunts like he doesn't have a care in the world.

The door opens in the next moment and Stroughton, Lewis, Wesley, and Vincent file in. Skyla is noticeably missing, but that's okay. She'll be here soon. Each person takes up residence behind their family, Vincent standing behind Ingersoll with a smile that makes even my skin crawl.

Charles Stroughton predictably looks ready to piss himself. Good. Let's hope he stays that way.

"You all have just made the biggest mistake of your lives," my father says, meeting the eyes of every one of us around the long table.

"Yeah?" I goad as another figure steps in through the doorway.

Wait, not one figure. Three.

I literally hear all the air sucked out of my father's lungs as he sets his eyes on our newcomers.

"N-no. It can't...how?"

Chapter Fifty-Three

Skyla

You could hear a piece of hair hit the ground as we step inside the room. It's that silent. I was so nervous to be back here. In these tunnels, in this room. I never wanted to step foot in here again. Something about it just seems right, though. Like something coming full circle, and the look on Christopher's face is priceless.

Together, we move further into the room, my father's arm looped on my right, my mother's on my left. Shock and fear shoot around the room as everyone takes in my seemingly risen from the dead mother. I can't help but relish in the panic and then anger that crosses Henry's face when he sees me holding onto my *real* dad.

"G-giselle?" Christopher asks, attempting to stand before Asher shoves him back down.

He doesn't seem upset about it, too awestruck by the woman before him. "How? How is this possible?" he asks.

My mother gives him a demure smile that is absolutely dripping vengeance.

"Well, despite your best efforts to kill me, I prevailed. I'm afraid the same won't be able to be said for you."

Like a deranged lovesick fool, he ignores the bold threat as he shakes his head in awe.

"I can't believe it. You're back. Baby, I—"

"I'd appreciate it if you would no longer address my wife," my father bites out, earning a thunderous look from Christopher.

"You! You...you Proctor scum! Giselle, my love, please tell me you have not...consorted with the descendants of a witch!"

"Of course not," she says. "I fell in love, married and had a baby with one. You've met my daughter, your daughter-in-law." She smiles.

Christopher gives me a disgusted look but shakes his head as Henry speaks.

"How the fuck did you survive?"

My mother lifts her hand, wiggling her fingers in a way that makes every Elder ease back into their seats. Like those few inches will grant them safety.

"Magic, Henry."

I try to hold in my laugh as I now fully understand that is not at all how magic or practiced witchcraft actually works. Though, it is entertaining to see how terrified every person in the room is currently.

My mom squeezes my arm, signaling me to take my place and I nod as I make my way through the room. All eyes track me carefully, and I hold eye contact with each of my boys, giving them loving smiles before taking up my position behind my father. Ronan steps to the side, pressing a kiss to the side of my head that has Christopher sneering.

Ronan ignores him as he stands behind Charles Stroughton, pressing his dagger against his back as I grab my own and do the same to Henry.

"Ronan?" Christopher snaps.

"I know you had your assumptions, Christopher, but let the record show. Yes, I am with all of them. I'm married to Asher, and dating Ronan, Liam, Vincent, and Wesley."

"Fucking whore," Henry hisses, to which Asher promptly reaches over, jabbing the butt of the dagger into the back of his head.

I smirk down at the sight, before looking to Asher.

"Thank you, baby."

"No problem, princess," he grunts before his dagger is aimed back on his father.

"Are you proud of yourself, Skyla?" Christopher asks me. "Tell me, what is your grand plan now? You're going to kill us all?" he laughs like it's impossible. "Then what?"

"Then...we live happily ever after, I guess? Sound good with everyone?" I ask all the guys, even Dane, Jeremy, and Andrew. They all nod their agreement, and I shrug as I look down at Christopher.

"The Brethren is finished, disbanded, decimated. Whatever word you would like to use."

"You can kill us all, but you will never erase our legacy! Erase our truths!"

"Like the truths in Thomas Putnam's journal?" I ask.

Christopher's eyes go wide and he doesn't even try to hide his fear.

"Like the truths behind those missing pages inside that journal. You know, funny thing about that. The Proctors, that's my biological father's surname for anyone who is slow," I say, addressing the room, "they also keep detailed records of their family history. Elizabeth Proctor was a bit of a hoarder in her later years. Even kept the journal entries that Thomas ripped out and gave to her."

I shake my head. The details don't matter. This idea of

hierarchy and superiority is all built up, in all of their own heads. It sure is satisfying to see it all crumble before Christopher's eyes, though.

"The foundation you were all built on. The man who led the cause to eradicate witches, not just during the trials, but after, as well? The one responsible for creating the Brethren was in love with a witch."

Several noises of surprise echo around the room at that, and Christopher seethes as he stares at me.

"In the end, he seems to have betrayed her, turned his back on the one he loved out of pressure to become some great leader. Kind of like you did to my mother," I say as I look between Christopher and my mom. "It's okay, though. Everything always comes full circle."

With that final word, more people begin spilling into the room. One by one, lining the room. Feared gasps and looks of terror splash across every Elder's face as every person from my parents' coven line the room. Rachel takes up her spot beside my father, staring straight at Christopher. Clearly, she knows who he is, and he knows her.

"I swear to Christ, I will make it my afterlife's mission to haunt and terrorize you for the rest of your days," Henry snarls at me.

I shake my head. "Where you're going, you won't be doing anything but swimming laps in a lake of fire."

Rachel speaks first, calling the entire attention of the room.

"See the cruelty and the pain that you have spread, our ancestors slain."

The entire room joins in, their tones steady and hardened.

"The fear you spread from a self-appointed throne, now under the light of the Snow Moon you shall atone. We bring light to your actions, we will be free. Together, we end the persecution of thee. When the moonlight fades, and the sun

Demise

comes through, our ancestors will come for you. We say this spell of karma tonight, we are witches. We will fight."

As one, we all lift our knives to our family's throats and Asher takes the last opportunity to speak into his father's ear.

"Burn in fucking hell."

With a fluid motion, throats are slit around the room. One by one, bodies slump forward onto the table, blood seeping out of their wounds and creating a collective pool in the center. A few gargle and choke on their blood, the sounds echoing throughout the room. I'm the last person to slice, making sure to go extra shallow so Henry suffers for as long as possible. He deserves it, and more.

My gaze moves to Liam, a vengeful look in his eyes that matches Wesley's and Vincent's. Dane seems to feel no sorrow, nor does Jeremy. Andrew is shaking, tears sliding down his face, but when he meets my eyes, he nods shakily. Like he knows he did the right thing.

Looking over my shoulder, I see Ronan watching me with an assured nod. I can't help but let the dagger slip from my hands, the iron clattering against the blood soaked table.

It's done. They're gone.

A wrong from over three hundred years ago has been righted and repaid.

We're free.

Epilogue
Skyla

The Brethren was not wiped from existence. How could it be? The society far outreached Salem. It was just a... managerial shift. Each of the guys took position as an Elder, but that means something very different now. Instead of all submitting to one power hungry leader, it's more like a board of directors in a sense.

The businesses are still underway, at least, the ethical ones that everyone deemed were worth salvaging, everyone is still wealthy and well connected as ever. Instead of leading out of fear and violence, it is led with loyalty.

For a minute, I thought Ronan was going to step into place and take charge. That's never been what he's wanted, though. It was always supposed to be Asher's destiny. He's come into his own well. He's harsh, but fair, and with the cooperation of the other Elders, they've all doubled their net worth in a matter of months. Sure, some of that comes from inheritance most of them earned when their family members were....so regretfully taken from this world. Still, it's impressive.

As for the rest of the members, at least the ones in Salem,

the Elders are doing a good job to keep an eye on everyone. Asher didn't want things turning into an all-out war, instead giving people the choice. Adapt to this much more fair and morally true way of operating, or leave.

A few people have expressed their upsets on the matter, Bridgette's father being the loudest of them all, and Vincent is ready if and when he's needed. He's still an eliminator for the Brethren, just for the right reasons, and he only goes after people who deserve it. He's still waiting for the day that Zayden Graves will call on his favor for sparing his life...after he almost took it. Can't say I'm exactly thrilled of what all that will take when the day comes.

Liam has taken over the Walcott family business in pharmaceuticals. He isn't passionate about it by any means, but all he has to do is occasionally sign some papers, go to board meetings and build more drift cars in his spare time. He's definitely not complaining.

Wesley has teamed up with Andrew, running his family's tech company together. Andrew still has a lot to learn about it all, and Wesley has been amazing at teaching him. Andrew has made more than a few obvious hints of having feelings for me, to which the guys swiftly reminded me no more spots were available in our little harem. I couldn't help but laugh at them because although he's sweet, I just don't feel that way about Andrew.

Ronan is focusing on what he loves, swimming. He's still a swim coach at the university, and I was able to even talk him into adding a women's team. To which I made the team, of course. He said it was a close one, to which I punished him for the remark by not allowing him to touch himself or us as Wesley and I fucked on his desk. That's the last time he will tease me, I'll bet.

As soon as we left the tunnels that night, I was on the

phone, demanding that Steph got on a plane immediately. I felt bad because she was terrified the entire time, but she did it, and when she showed up to my house and saw my mother in the living room, she fell to her knees, sobbing hysterically as they held each other. My dad wrapped his arm around me in comfort as he watched his wife finally get her sister back. There wasn't a single dry eye in the room that day.

Steph has since moved back to Salem, along with her now fiancé. He's incredible and treats her like the queen she is. He's also very accepting and understanding given our family's... unique situation. I mean, how often do you marry into a family where your sister-in-law is a practicing witch who lives in a commune with her Coven and your niece-in-law has a husband and four boyfriends? Wouldn't blame the guy for needing a moment to adjust. He didn't, though. He fit perfectly into our weird, unorthodox family.

We go visit my parents almost weekly, or they come and visit us. Now that witches are no longer forced into hiding, a lot of them actually moved back to Salem. Astrid and Sariah bought a house just down the road from us, and we get together for dinners often.

When the Brethren...gained new leadership, everything promised under it had been voided. Or at least we made it so, meaning Liam and Maryia were no longer engaged. Everyone was pleased with it, except for Liam's mom and Maryia's parents of course. Liam's mom was actually heartbroken to hear that her husband had died, despite how abusive he was to her. It didn't take away the love she thought they had, and no matter how awful she's been to me in the past, my heart hurt for her.

Maryia and Maggie are now together, out in the open for the world to see, and they are fairly happy. They fight a little bit more than I'd like for my best friend, but I'm by her side for whatever she thinks is best. Bridgette has all but disappeared

Demise

from society. Gone is the cliquey, mean girl who thinks she rules this town. She's meek, quiet, and I can't help but wonder what her story is. What changed?

I banish all the thoughts currently rattling around in my brain because today is my wedding day. Technically, Asher and I are married under the Brethren's old ways, as well as the forged document that made our marriage very legally binding. We never got a wedding, though, and the guys wanted to give me one. To all of them.

Like the sweet, gooey hearted loves they are, they all drove us up to the cabin in New Hampshire for two weeks after everything was done, just like Asher promised. Our first night there, they lit hundreds of candles and spread thousands of rose petals before all getting down on one knee. It was corny and cliché and absolutely perfect.

The only thing that made it better was that Ronan informed us all that he had bought the cabin, and it was now officially ours. We are planning to spend every Christmas there along with any other free time we can manage.

I look down at my ring. It's giant, as it goes almost all the way up to my knuckle. That's what happens when you have five rings soldered together. Asher's original ring, Liam's family ring, Wesley and Vincent's mother's rings, and a brand new one from Ronan. My finger is literally dripping with diamonds, sapphires and emeralds, and although it's gorgeous in an eclectic way, it's not as perfect as the sight of my five grooms standing at the end of the aisle.

No matter how powerful the Brethren may be, we can't change the laws and allow me to legally marry them all. So, legally, I'll only be married to Asher, but this wedding isn't for anyone but ourselves.

My father's arm is hooked around my own as my mother takes my other. They both smile down at me proudly as I move down the aisle. Nearly every Brethren member is here today, though I wouldn't have cared if Maggie and Steph were the only ones to show up. Maggie, Steph, Rachel, and Maryia are standing up at the altar as my bridesmaids, and they are all giving me proud smiles. I don't miss Maggie's eyes as they move from mine to the crowd. Curiously, I find Bridgette staring at her, so much pain and regret in her eyes. I'll never understand those two.

Turning away, I see my guys staring at me, all adoring smiles, as my parents kiss my cheeks and hand me to them. We glance at our officiant, Astrid of course, as she greets the entire room.

"Thank you for coming on this blessed day to join the beautiful union of these six souls for all eternity."

She goes off onto a long, drawn out speech about eternal love, balance, and harmony, but I'm practically shaking in my shoes with anticipation. When she announces us as joined together forever, Ronan grabs my face first, pulling me in for a kiss before Liam, Vincent, Asher, and finally Wesley.

When we turn to the audience, everyone cheers and hollers in celebration, a feeling of happiness like I never dreamed of sweeping through me.

Liam leans into my ear, whispering to me.

"Alright, babygirl. We have twenty minutes until photos. Race you to the bridal suite," he says with a waggle of his brows.

I look over my shoulder and grin as Asher scoffs but smirks. Vincent shrugs as Ronan and Wesley nod.

"Better run, siren."

Extended Epilogue
Ronan

We're lying in bed, Skyla nuzzled into my arms as everyone watches the movie playing on the TV in our room. I say our room, though technically it is Skyla's. Our rooms aren't even touched anymore. Not since we came back from our honeymoon in Bora Bora and found the custom bed Asher had built and delivered.

The thing literally takes up Skyla's entire wall and is over ten feet long. It takes up almost all the walking space in the room, but none of us complain too much. After all, the only things we do in this room are sleep and…

Wesley is on the other side of Skyla, his lips running up and down her neck as he gives me a wicked look. Skyla melts into him as their mouths tangle together. Fuck. We fuck a lot.

"You ready to give me that baby?" Wesley asks against Skyla's skin as he moves down to her cleavage.

"Wes," she laughs, gaining the attention of Liam, Asher, and Vincent.

Plastering myself against Skyla, I push her until she's wedged between us, my mouth going to her ear.

"He's got a point, baby. We can only wait so long."

"Is that all I'm good for? A baby maker?" she quips.

"No," Liam interjects. "You're also pretty to look at."

Vincent smacks him in the back of the head at the same time Asher does.

"Ow!" he scoffs, rubbing the back of his head as he glares at the two.

My eyes are solely focused on my girl, though. Slipping my hand around her throat, I force her eyes up to mine.

"Daddy wants to give you a baby, and you're gonna let him, okay?"

Her eyes practically sparkle as they look up to me, a million thoughts racing through them before a soft smile crosses her face. Slowly, her head nods as she speaks.

"Okay."

A shocked look spreads across Wesley's face. We've all been bugging her about starting a family for months now, I thought it was going to take a lot more convincing. She just had her twenty-first birthday, and her junior year at Gallows Hill is well underway, but I was sure we'd have to wait until she graduated at least. Then again, she has been softening to the idea lately. Maybe it's because Steph just had her baby boy, Nial. That's what got this conversation started in the first place.

When Steph had announced she was pregnant, it planted an idea in all of our heads, one that we haven't been able to shake. At least not one Wesley or I have been able to shake. Then again, we are older than the other guys, we're ready. Based on the hungry looks on the other three faces, though, I'd say they are more than ready as well.

Taking advantage of the situation, I roll Skyla onto me, forcing her to straddle me as Wesley stands on the bed. He pulls his cock out of his pants, stroking it several times before pushing it into Skyla's mouth. She takes his happily, and it's a sight that has my cock fucking leaking precum in my pants. I love watching her suck him off. His thick cock sliding in and out of her mouth is enough to make me come in my pants with no effort at all.

Pushing down my sweats, I lift Skyla up before settling her down on me. Her pussy is already soaked, and she slides down on me easily, sighing once she's fully seated. She grinds her hips into me and my cock jerks inside her as she begins bouncing.

"Fuck, yes, baby. Bounce on daddy's cock. You like getting fucked by daddy?"

"Yes," she whimpers around Wesley's cock.

"Good girl," he praises, cupping her face as he begins fucking her throat deeper.

"Always such a good little cock whore for us. Are you gonna let our daddy come in you, little one?"

Her eyes flick to me before she nods, forcing a pleasured chuckle out of Wesley.

"That's a good fucking girl," he says through clenched teeth. "Let daddy come in that sweet cunt, it's been too long."

I love it when he calls me daddy too. Sometimes I think Wesley loves the daddy kink more than I do, or at least, he loves being my good little boy.

He's right, though, it's been too fucking long. Skyla has been off her birth control ever since Steph had Nial, which I suppose should have been our indicator that she was toying with the idea. Since then, we've had to use condoms every time we are together and I have to say, feeling her raw for the first time in months is the closest to heaven that I'll fucking reach.

Skyla's hips gyrate against me, practically pulling the cum out of me as she does. I feel a hand come down to my balls, gently massaging them. My eyes connect with Wesley's as he continues fucking Skyla's throat, somehow still able to reach me as he pushes me closer and closer to the edge.

"Come on, daddy. Come for us," he goads, that fucking smile in place that I've become weak for.

I fuck Skyla deeper and deeper, forcing her body to shake and bounce against me as I pound into her. Just thinking about me being the first to come inside her, that I could potentially get her pregnant with my baby in her belly? It's enough to rob me of my vision, forcing it to blur as my release grabs a hold of me and drags me under.

Wesley

Ronan loses it. Just a few grazes of my fingers has him bucking like an animal into Skyla, falling apart inside her. His moans and groans have cum practically leaking out of me and down Skyla's throat. I feel the build of my own orgasm come and I know I have no choice.

Ripping Skyla away from Ronan, I bend her over, slipping into her from behind as I begin fucking her with the same vigor that Ronan was. She moans as I slide inside her, her hands fisting the pillows as my hands move to her hips.

"C'mon, little one. Play with that clit. I want to hear you come all over my cock."

I slide in and out of her so easily, Ronan's cum acting as the perfect lubricant. Just knowing that it's covering my cock, that I'm fucking it deeper and deeper into our girl? Goddamn, it has me ready to fucking lose it.

Glancing over, I see Ronan watching us with a lazy grin, his hand languidly stroking his already hardening cock. I pulse inside her and before I can stop myself, I'm leaning over Skyla sucking Ronan's cock into my mouth. It's a hard angle for a moment but when Ronan sits up, cupping my face into his hands as he fucks my face. Being buried inside my wife while sucking down my best friend's cock is something that I'll never

Extended Epilogue

tire of. He's so gorgeous and sexy, and the man fucks me until I see stars every goddamn day. Glancing up at him, he gives me an adoring smile that makes my heart clench. Fuck I love these two, I love all of them. One big happy fucking family. One that's about to get a lot bigger if I have anything to say about it.

My balls begin to draw up as Ronan continues fucking my face and I know I don't have long. Glancing to the other side of the bed, I see Asher and Liam are already hot and heavy. Their clothes are discarded, their cocks grinding against one another as they make out.

Reaching out to them, my hand wraps around Liam's cock and I stroke it several times, forcing him to groan in pleasure. He loves it when I play with him while Asher and him fuck around. Asher has gotten better about sharing him, though he still has his possessive streaks.

Asher practically gnashes at me, so I do the only thing I can and release Liam's cock to grab his. He tries to fight it, but when I twist my hand around the tip of his cock, stroking all the way down, his eyes roll into the back of his head. He tries to fight it but he loves my touch. Loves my mouth even more. And last night, while Skyla and Vincent had some one on one time, Asher, Liam and I enjoyed some threesome time. Let me just tell you, Asher may act like he hates me some days, but last night he fucked me like I was the love of his goddamn life. Or at least like my ass was.

Ronan never participates in boyfriend swapping, as I like to call it, except with me and the occasional blow job from Liam, which is a fucking sight to witness. Vincent has no interest in anyone but Skyla, which we all respect, even I'm still fucking dying for a taste of him. I think he's like the forbidden fruit of the group. He won't give in to anyone, won't let down his guard no matter how tempted he may be. It only makes me want him more.

Extended Epilogue

My eyes are on Vincent's as I continue stroking Asher and when he looks at me, I give him a wicked smirk and a wink. He rolls his eyes before focusing his gaze back on Skyla. Can't hate a man for trying, right?

Skyla moans beneath me and I look to see that Ronan has maneuvered himself beneath her, sucking on her tits while rubbing her clit for her. Such a good daddy.

"Yeah, suck on her tits, daddy. Make our girl come," I encourage as I release Asher's cock and focus all my energy into Skyla.

Ronan moans around her breast, and with a sharp thrust of my hips into hers, it sends us both falling over the edge.

Liam

One brutal thrust of Wesley's hips has him and Skyla screaming out their orgasms. Ronan sucks on Skyla's nipples, pulling every ounce of pleasure out of her as he can before they all collapse. They don't stay like that for long, since Ash and I decide it's our turn.

"Lay down, baby," Asher says to me, dragging my back to rest against his chest.

I smirk at him as I know what he's setting us up for. I reach a hand out for Skyla, pushing Wesley off her as I drag her to us. Her body is practically a noodle, her breathing ragged as she gives me a dazed smile.

"How you doing, babygirl?"

"Good," she pants.

"About to be a lot better," Ash promises as we drag her onto my lap.

I slip into her first. Holy fucking shit. It's been a hot minute since I've been able to fuck her bare, and goddamn did I miss it. Her pussy is a slippery fucking mess as cum begins leaking out of her. Two full loads in her and three more to go, there is no way in fuck my babygirl is leaving this room not pregnant tonight.

At first, I was all in for the teasing of getting her pregnant. Breeding kinks are hot as fuck normally, but now that it's real, that she has agreed and we are in this moment actively trying to get her pregnant, it has the excitement and allure rising to a dizzying level.

"Fuck," I groan. "You two really filled her up," I laugh as I look over at Ronan and Wesley, their chests together as Ronan kisses the side of Wesley's head and chuckles.

"Yeah, they did," Skyla laughs.

"So will we," Asher says as he lines his cock against mine, pushing inside her with the next thrust.

Skyla tenses, her breath sucking in sharply as her face pinches.

"Good girl," I praise. "Deep breaths. Relax around us, babygirl."

She nods, doing her best to relax, and honestly, so am I because having Asher's cock rub against mine as he pushes in deeper, making her that much tighter. Goddamn, I'm in heaven. My head rolls back against his shoulder, and he kisses my neck, teeth nibbling on my earlobe as he does.

"You like that, baby?" Asher rasps.

Just the sound of his voice is sexy and sends my cock throbbing. Nodding my head frantically, he chuckles, slowly lifting his hips and pulling a groan out of me and a cry out of Skyla.

"You okay, princess?" Asher grits out.

"I'm so full," she whimpers.

"I know, and you feel so fucking good," I moan as Asher begins controlling the pace of our thrusts.

"This is fair, princess. Liam and I will fill you up at the

same time. That way, we have equal chances of being the father," Asher says.

"As you fuck mine and Ro's cum deeper?" Wesley challenges.

"You guys have old man sperm. You probably couldn't father a kid even if you tried," Asher scoffs and I chuckle.

I love his and Wesley's relationship. Ash always acts like he can't stand Wesley, but he sure fucked the shit out of him last night. It wasn't the first night that we invited Wesley into bed with us, but it was by far the best time. The first few times, Asher just sat back and watched as Wesley and I played with each other. Then he'd watch Wesley fuck me while I sucked him off. Last night, as soon as the door shut, Asher's mouth was on Wesley's, and he was bending Wes over before he could even protest. Not that he would, look at Asher, he's like a fucking Greek God.

Asher isn't fooling anyone because after last night, I went and took a shower and found them snuggling in bed when I got out. I'm not jealous like Asher or Ronan. I love that we can all pleasure each other, besides Vincent, and care on a deeper level. It only makes our marriage to Sky stronger and the relationships among us better.

Wesley crawls over to us, his eyes on Asher's as he bends down and presses his lips to his. Asher groans against his mouth as Wesley's tongue tangles with Ash's. I find myself arching my head back further, attempting to get closer.

I really don't like being left out of playtime.

A chuckle shakes Wesley's chest as he cups my cheek.

"You feeling left out, babyboy?"

I give him a fake pout and nod, and he grins before making out with me.

"Oh, fuck," Skyla moans as she watches us.

I feel Asher sit up, his tongue tracing against mine and

Extended Epilogue

Wesley's mouth. We both adjust our positions until Asher, Wesley and I share a sloppy, hot as fuck, make out session. My eyes pop open, glancing to see Ronan watching us with a hint of contempt. I know he doesn't love sharing Wesley and I love being the little toy he plays with from time to time when he's jealous.

I don't even have to say anything before Ronan is moving across the bed, coming over to me. He pulls my head away from Wesley's before crushing his lips to mine. My eyes widen in surprise before they close altogether. Ronan isn't huge on kissing, only with Wesley and Skyla. So, this is definitely a new development. Fuck me, I'm not mad about it, though.

Wesley and Asher make out while Ronan devours my mouth, and when I peek my eyes open, I see that Vincent has consumed Skyla's. Her pussy throbs around Asher and me, forcing us both to moan in pleasure.

Ronan's strong tongue twirls around mine, sucking it into his mouth further and pulling another moan out of me before he pulls away. His hand is wrapped around my throat, his nose pressed to mine as he exhales deeply.

"I love when you take your jealousy out on me," I smirk against him.

"I know you do," he chuckles, burying his head into my neck as he inhales roughly.

"Fuck," I groan. "Don't do shit like that, daddy. Gonna make me think that you actually like me," I tease with a smile.

His head pulls away from my neck, deep blue eyes on me.

"Maybe I do."

My eyes spark with surprise before his lips are back on mine. Holy fuck. I didn't see that coming. Ronan has used me to get off a few times. A blow job here and there over the years, but all of it has been very detached, very pleasure centered.

Extended Epilogue

This kiss feels a hell of a lot more emotional, though, and fuck me, I'm here for it.

Ronan's mouth moves to my neck, sucking on the sensitive skin as I turn to see Wesley doing the same to Asher. Ash smiles down at me, his eyes squinting shut and hips bucking when Wesley bites his shoulder.

Skyla and I moan, and I feel my orgasm hit me as Ronan's hand traces down my stomach, pausing at the base of my cock. I throb as cum shoots out of me, forcing Asher to follow my lead. Both of our cocks jerk and spasm against one another, forcing the pleasure to last a lot longer than it normally would.

Vincent

When I hear Asher and Liam finish, I don't even let them fully come down from their high before I'm pulling Skyla away from them. I do it slowly for her benefit before I lay her on her back, covering my body with hers. They all love to share her, get off on it, but I get off on our time together. Just us.

Skyla is right on the edge of another orgasm, and when I push into her, I can hardly feel anything but all the fucking cum inside her. Her body tenses for a moment until she fully relaxes around me, letting me slowly work myself deeper and deeper inside.

"Vincent," she moans.

"I'm right here, siren. I'm here."

She nods her head, her bright blue eyes coming to me. Fuck. I get drunk just off one peek of them, addicted and ready for my next hit. She is the ruler of all the seas and the entirety of my goddamn heart. I'd happily follow her to the highest heights of heaven or the furthest depths of hell. Wherever she decides to go is okay with me.

"Are you sure you want this, siren? You want a baby?" I ask.

Extended Epilogue

The fuckers have been pressuring her for months, and as much as I'd love to have that piece of her, I won't let them push her into something she doesn't want.

She gives me a smile that fucking melts me as she nods.

"I've thought about it a lot. I want it, with all of you."

What my siren wants, she gets.

"Whatever you want, siren," I say as I begin snapping my hips harder, pumping in and out of her as my cock throbs.

A baby. My baby. Inside the love of my life. There are worse things to happen to a man. To be able to hold something so precious, so untouched from the evils of the world. A perfect little bundle of me and her, something to hold and care for and protect with my dying breath. Fuck, that doesn't sound too bad at all.

I don't even pretend that the others have a chance. My siren won't be getting pregnant by anyone but me, at least not the first time, that's a fucking promise. My hand comes to her clit as I begin rubbing her quickly. Her body shudders and shakes as she begins crying out my name.

"Vincent, Vincent, Vincent!"

"Siren," I grunt as I see stars.

It's by far the hardest orgasm I've ever experienced, and my body practically detonates as I come inside her. My cock throbs as I fuck my cum deeper and deeper into her, intent to make sure that my cum is the first to reach her eggs. I want her nice and pregnant with my baby, they can all try again the next time, if or when she allows it. This pregnancy, this one, is all mine.

Skyla's screams practically shake the house as her pussy spasms around me. I fuck her through her orgasm, only stopping when her body literally collapses. Then, I waste no time, pulling out of her before pushing my fingers inside. I gather up the leaking cum, pushing it deeper and deeper into her. My fingers are absolutely drenched and no matter how hard I push,

Extended Epilogue

more comes out. I'm determined to make her take every last fucking drop, though.

Once I'm satisfied, I pull my fingers out of her, pressing a soft kiss against her forehead as I whisper to her.

"Thank you, siren."

"For what?" she smiles.

"For carrying my baby. You're gonna take such good care of it."

She opens her mouth to say something when someone grabs my cum coated fingers, sucking them into their mouth. Turning to look over my shoulder, I see Liam happily sucking on my fingers, giving me a devilish smirk before winking.

"Couldn't let it go to waste," he teases.

I scoff and roll my eyes, turning back to my perfect wife. A heathen like myself has never deserved even a sliver of happiness, let alone the amount Skyla gives me, no doubt the same amount a baby shared with her will give me. I pray I never die because I'm already in heaven, right here, with her...and the band of idiots, too, I guess.

Skyla

Five Months Later

I wiggle as I try to find a comfortable position. The paper beneath me crinkles as I do, and five pairs of eyes move to me in concern. Ever since I peed on that positive test, I can hardly sneeze without having every free hand in the house rushing to wipe my nose. It's sweet how attentive they've become, and I'm sure it will be so amazing when I get into the harder stages of pregnancy but for now, I'm fine, and they are ridiculous.

I've been one of those people who hasn't suffered from too

much morning sickness, thank God. Just a little bit of food aversions like chili fries. Asher was eating some last week and one whiff of them had me puking my guts out. Which was super disheartening because they were one of my favorite foods. Hopefully, it won't be a forever thing.

My mom made me promise her that I'd facetime her after our appointment today, to which I happily agreed. I wanted to invite her, but the hospital has a strict limit of how many people can be in the room at a time. A rule they are already breaking for us and our...unique situation. One time, a nurse opened her mouth about it, and Ronan closed that conversation so fast it made my head spin. Since then, no one says a word or even attempts to give a dirty look. They greet us warmly for all our appointments, and honestly, it makes me laugh how afraid of my husbands they seem to be.

Then again, maybe there is a good reason. When the ultrasound tech walks in, she smiles nervously, to which Wesley and Liam are the only ones to smile back. Ronan, Asher, and Vincent watch her with a sharp look as she takes a seat, reaching for some jelly and the ultrasound device.

I lift my shirt up as she squirts some jelly onto my stomach and begins moving the wand around. It takes a few seconds before the baby is visible. Five sharp inhales, as well as my own, take up all the sound in the room as we stare at our little bundle with excitement and awe.

We have all decided we don't want to know who the father is. Well, I've decided that. The guys desperately want to know, but I put my foot down. Even though they would all love the baby, I know that each of them would be predisposed to love their 'biological' child more, and I don't want that for my baby, or babies, if the guys have anything to say about it.

We are very split on what sex we are hoping for. I have been hoping for a girl while the guys are all convinced it will be a boy. After all, there hasn't been a girl born to an Elder family in over three hundred years, since I clearly don't count.

"Are you wanting to know the sex?" the ultrasound tech asked, and we all practically shout, "Yes!"

She smiles as she nods before adjusting the wand, then looking back to us.

"It's a girl."

My mouth drops open, tears springing to my eyes as I look at my guys. Each holds a varying look of excitement and awe, as one by one, they press their lips to mine. Vincent is the last to before he places a quick kiss to my stomach just below the jelly.

"We love you, little siren," he murmurs against my skin, forcing my heart to flutter with happiness.

How could someone get so lucky in life?

Thank You

Thank you for reading the Gallows Hill series! It's bittersweet for it to come to a conclusion but don't worry, there is an extended epilogue with your name on it!

Claim yours here! bit.ly/4gWehZh

Want to read more about Maggie, Bridgette and what is in store for them? Start reading Deliverance on Amazon, kindle unlimited and Audible!

If you liked the Gallows Hill Series, check out some of my other work!

Stand Alones –
   Graves – An MFM stalker romance
   Gratify – Forbidden age gap romance
   Jagged Harts – Enemies to lovers MMA romance.

The Alphaletes Series –
   The Loyalties We Break – Ex-boyfriend's best friend sports romance

Thank You

The Walls We Break – Single mom sports romance
The Hearts We Break – Friends to lovers sports romance
The Rules We Break – Enemies to lovers sports romance

Acknowledgments

This series was something else. It was my first time writing a connected trilogy and my god, it was hard! Attempting to intertwine the entire story line, historical facts and six main characters was a difficult task I didn't know I was undertaking until I was already in the thick of it. That being said, it is hands down the collection of books this far that I am most proud of. There are so many people that helped not only make this book possible, but give it the amount of love, attention to detail and realism that it needed to become what it is today.

To my alpha, Sara, we did it! How many times did I ask you if this was actually going to come to fruition? If I had what it took, if the story was worth being told? I know without a doubt that I couldn't have even started this series, let alone finish it without you by my side. I'm so grateful for every second and every ounce of support you have given me through this entire process. I love you forever.

To my betas, Kreature, Elena and Sheyla, thank you so much for all of your help! This was a tight turn around and I definitely had to keep you guys on your toes. I'm so grateful for all of your dedication and hard work on not only this project but all projects you work on with me. I'm the luckiest author in the world to have amazing people like you in my corner.

To my editors, Brittany and Slasher, thank you for helping me not sounds like a total dumbass! Lol Your work is truly the noblest of them all and I'm forever grateful for all the time and attention to detail you put into making sure my story remains unchanged, just a little more grammatically correct. I love you both deeply.

To my experts, Rachel, Jillie and Jodie, thank you all so much! Each of you brought something unique and special to this book and I'm so grateful. All the time each of you took, educating me on what it means to be a witch in this day and age, or a tarot reader helped bring such a level of realism to this book that I'm eternally grateful for!

To my street and ARC team, I'm so grateful for all of you! All of your posts, hype and love for me and these books means the world to me. I could truly never select a better group of people to have by my side. I'm never letting go of each and every one of you.

Finally, to my readers. Thank you all for all of the love and support from book one to this one. The support I've felt with this series is indescribable and I'm so grateful to have such an incredible reader base! I hope you all enjoyed this series as much as I did and I hope you stick around for all that is to come!

Made in the USA
Coppell, TX
16 June 2025

50820116R00288